P9-DBM-208

# "SPECTACULAR . . . [A] PULSE-POUNDING THRILLER . . . Kellerman [is] the master of psychological suspense."
## —*Detroit Free Press*

"A brisk suspense thriller . . . Jonathan Kellerman's singular touch with wounded children pays off royally. . . . Despite having been used and abused most of his life, Billy has developed a sharp intellect and a keen code of ethics, along with the survival skills that are keeping him one short step ahead of the press, the murderer, and the other creeps on his trail. The kid is irresistible."
—*The New York Times Book Review*

"[Kellerman] takes us inside the minds of his characters, virtuous or wicked. . . . For all the depravity on display, *Billy Straight* affirms a moral order in which decency prevails. The title character is a notable creation: a kind of urban Huckleberry Finn, a heroically resourceful boy whose life is in perpetual jeopardy in the streets and parks of Los Angeles."
—*People*

"What gives the book its depth is Billy's heroic effort to survive while being pursued by bounty hunters, police, and the killer."
—*Los Angeles Times*

*Please turn the page for more reviews. . . .*

## "A MESMERIZING COMBINATION OF VIOLENCE, PATHOS, MISERY, AND HOPE . . .

The plot hurtles along at breakneck speed toward a cliffhanger of a climax that's guaranteed to surprise even seasoned mystery fans. Kellerman, already an icon in the genre, will further cement his status as a mystery master with this diabolically clever thriller."

*—Booklist*

"A broad cast of well-defined characters, a fast-moving plot, and themes sponged from the daily news yet turned fresh . . . Kellerman does a fine job revealing how memories of the Simpson case shadow the [Lisa] Ramsey investigation, affecting the ways Petra and Stu are allowed to go about their work. . . . By the dramatic climax, Kellerman has pushed a number of familiar buttons—but with enough panache and surprises to satisfy his most demanding fans."

*—Publishers Weekly* (starred review)

"This is very satisfying to read, with compelling people in interesting situations, and crisply—even absorbingly—drawn plot lines."

*—The New York Post*

# "AN ENGROSSING TALE . . . HIS BEST WORK YET."
### —*Kirkus Reviews*

"Taut . . . Riveting . . . Kellerman isn't just an Edgar Award–winning thriller writer, he's a prominent child psychologist, and it shows in *Billy Straight*. . . . Kellerman's main strength is his vivid invention of secondary characters and his skill at juggling subplots."
—Amazon.com

"Rich in tension and terror and deep in characterization . . . Kellerman breaks new ground for himself in the psychological thriller field . . . [with] a perceptive and honest street kid, Billy Straight, as the lead character. . . . A powerful finish."
—*San Antonio Express-News*

"As suspenseful as anything Kellerman has written . . . Billy Straight is a carefully drawn, highly sympathetic character."
—*The Register-Herald* (WV)

By Jonathan Kellerman:

Fiction
WHEN THE BOUGH BREAKS
BLOOD TEST
OVER THE EDGE
THE BUTCHER'S THEATER**
SILENT PARTNER**
TIME BOMB**
PRIVATE EYES**
DEVIL'S WALTZ**
BAD LOVE**
SELF-DEFENSE**
THE WEB**
THE CLINIC**
SURVIVAL OF THE FITTEST**
BILLY STRAIGHT*

Nonfiction
PSYCHOLOGICAL ASPECTS OF CHILDHOOD CANCER
HELPING THE FEARFUL CHILD

For children, written and illustrated
DADDY, DADDY, CAN YOU TOUCH THE SKY?
JONATHAN KELLERMAN'S ABC OF WEIRD
   CREATURES


*Published by Ballantine Books
**Published by Bantam Books

Books published by The Ballantine Publishing Group
are available at quantity discounts on bulk purchases
for premium, educational, fund-raising, and special
sales use. For details, please call 1-800-733-3000.

# BILLY
# STRAIGHT

A   N O V E L

# JONATHAN
# KELLERMAN

BALLANTINE BOOKS • NEW YORK

Sale of this book without a front cover may be unauthorized. If this book is coverless, it may have been reported to the publisher as "unsold or destroyed" and neither the author nor the publisher may have received payment for it.

A Ballantine Book
Published by The Ballantine Publishing Group
Copyright © 1998 by Jonathan Kellerman
Excerpt from *Monster* copyright © 1999 by Jonathan Kellerman

All rights reserved under International and Pan-American Copyright Conventions. Published in the United States by The Ballantine Publishing Group, a division of Random House, Inc., New York, and simultaneously in Canada by Random House of Canada Limited, Toronto.

This is a work of fiction. The characters and events in it are inventions of the author and do not depict any real persons or events.

Ballantine and colophon are registered trademarks of Random House, Inc.

www.randomhouse.com/BB/

Library of Congress Catalog Card Number: 99-65079

ISBN 0-345-41386-5

This edition published by arrangement with Random House, Inc.

Manufactured in the United States of America

First Ballantine Books International Edition: May 1999
First Ballantine Books Domestic Edition: October 1999

10  9  8  7  6  5  4  3  2  1

*To Faye. For Faye. At the core, it's always Faye.*

*"Unique is she, my constant dove, my perfect one."*

Song of Songs, 6:9

# CHAPTER 1

IN THE PARK YOU SEE THINGS.

But not what I saw tonight.

God, God . . .

I wanted to be dreaming but I was awake, smelling chili meat and onions and the pine trees.

First, the car drove up to the edge of the parking lot. They got out and talked and he grabbed her, like in a hug. I thought maybe they were going to kiss and I'd watch that.

Then all of a sudden, she made a weird sound—surprised, squeaky, like a cat or dog that gets stepped on.

He let go of her and she fell. Then he bent down next to her and his arm started moving up and down really fast. I thought he was punching her, and that was bad enough, and I kept thinking should I do something. But then I heard another sound, fast, wet, like the butcher at Stater Brothers back in Watson chopping meat—*chuck chuck chuck*.

He kept *doing* it, moving his arm up and down.

I wasn't breathing. My heart was on fire. My legs were cold. Then they turned hot-wet.

Pissing my pants like a stupid baby!

The *chuck chuck* stopped. He stood up, big and wide, wiped his hands on his pants. Something was in his hand and he held it far from his body.

He looked all around. Then in my direction.

Could he see me, hear me—*smell* me?

He kept looking. I wanted to run but knew he'd hear me. But staying here could trap me—how could he see anything behind the rocks? They're like a cave with no roof, just cracks you can look through, which is the reason I picked them as one of my places.

1

My stomach started to churn around, and I wanted to run so badly my leg muscles were jumping under my skin.

A breeze came through the trees, blowing up pine smell and piss stink.

Would it blow against the chili-burger's wrapping paper and make noise? Would he smell me?

He looked around some more. My stomach hurt so bad.

All of a sudden he jumped ran back to the car, got in, drove away.

I didn't want to see when he passed under the lamp at the corner of the parking lot, didn't want to read the license plate.

PLYR 1.

The letters burned into my mind.

Why did I look?

*Why?*

※

I'm still sitting here. My Casio says 1:12 A.M.

I need to get out of here, but what if he's just driving around and comes back—no, that would be stupid, why would he do that?

I can't stand it. She's down there, and I smell like piss and meat and onions and chili. Real dinner from the Oki-Rama on the Boulevard, that Chinese guy who never smiles or looks at your face. I paid $2.38 and now I want to throw it up.

My jeans are starting to get sticky and itchy. Going over to the public bathroom at the other end of the lot is too dangerous . . . that arm going up and down. Like he was just doing a job. He wasn't as big as Moron, but he was big enough. She trusted him, let him hug her . . . what did she do to make him so mad . . . could she still be *alive*?

No way. Impossible.

I listen carefully to see if she's making any sounds. Nothing but the freeway noise from across the east side of the park and traffic from the Boulevard. Not much traffic tonight. Sometimes, when the wind blows north, you hear ambulance sirens, motorcycles, car honks. The city's all around. The park looks like the country, but I know the difference.

Who is she?—forget that, I don't want to know.

What I *want* is to put tonight on rewind.

That squeaky sound—like he took the air right out of her. For sure she's . . . gone. But what if she *isn't*?

Even if she isn't, she will be soon, all that *chucking.* And what could I do for her, anyway? Breathe into her mouth, put my face in her blood?

What if he comes back while I'm doing it?

*Would* he come back? That would be stupid, but there are always surprises. She sure found that out.

I can't help her. I have to put this all out of my mind.

I'll sit here for ten more minutes—no, fifteen. Twenty. Then I'll get my Place Two stuff together and move.

Where to? Place One, up near the observatory, is too far, and so are Three and Four, even though Three would be good 'cause it has a stream for washing. That leaves Five, in the fern tangle behind the zoo, all those trees. A little closer, but still a long walk in the dark.

But it's also the hardest one to find.

Okay, I'll go to Five. Me and the animals. The way they cry and roar and smash against their cages makes it hard to sleep, but tonight I probably won't sleep anyway.

Meantime, I sit here and wait.

Pray.

Our Father in heaven, how about no more surprises?

Not that praying ever got me anything, and sometimes I wonder if there's anyone up there to pray to or just stars— humongous balls of gas in an empty black universe.

Then I get worried that I'm blaspheming.

Maybe some kind of God *is* up there; maybe He's saved me lots of times and I'm just too dumb to know it. Or not a good enough person to appreciate Him.

Maybe God saved me *tonight,* putting me behind the rocks, instead of out in the open.

But if he had seen me when he drove up, he probably would've changed his mind and not done anything to her.

So did God *want* her to . . .

No, he just would've gone somewhere else to do it . . . whatever.

In case You saved me, thank You, God.

In case You're up there, do You have a plan for me?

# CHAPTER 2

MONDAY, 5 A.M.

When the call came into Hollywood Division, Petra Connor was well into overtime but up for more action.

Sunday, she'd enjoyed unusually peaceful sleep from 8 A.M. to 4 P.M., no gnawing dreams, thoughts of ravaged brain tissue, empty wombs, things that would never be. Waking to a nice, warm afternoon, she took advantage of the light and spent an hour at her easel. Then, half a pastrami sandwich and a Coke, a hot shower, and off to the station to finalize the stakeout.

She and Stu Bishop rolled out just after dark, cruising alleys and ignoring minor felonies; they had more important things on their minds. Selecting a spot, they sat watching the apartment building on Cherokee, not talking.

Usually they chatted, managed to turn the boredom into semi-fun. But Stu had been acting weird lately. Remote, tight-lipped, as if the job no longer interested him.

Maybe it was five days on graveyard.

Petra was bugged, but what could she do—he was the senior partner. She put it aside, thought about Flemish pictures at the Getty. Amazing pigments, superb use of light.

Two hours of butt-numbing stasis. Their patience paid off just after 2 A.M. and another imbecilic but elusive killer hooked up.

Now she sat at a scabrous metal desk opposite Stu, completing the paperwork, thinking about going back to her apartment, maybe doing some sketching. The five days had energized her. Stu looked half-dead as he talked to his wife.

It was a warm June, well before daybreak, and the fact that the two of them were still there at the tail end of a severely understaffed graveyard shift was a fluke.

Petra had been a detective for exactly three years, the first twenty-eight months in Auto Theft, the remaining eight in daytime Homicide with Stu.

Her partner was a nine-year vet and a family man. Day shift suited his lifestyle and his biorhythms. Petra had been a nighthawk from childhood, before the deep blue midnights of her artist days, when lying awake at night had been inspirational.

Well before her marriage, when listening to Nick's breathing had lulled her to sleep.

She lived alone now, loved the black of night more than ever. Black was her favorite color; as a teenager she'd worn nothing but. So wasn't it odd that she'd never asked for nighttime assignments since graduating the academy?

It was adherence to duty that brought about the temporary switch.

Wayne Carlos Freshwater crawled out at night, scoring weed and crack and pills on Hollywood side streets, killing prostitutes. No way was he going to be found when the sun shone.

Over a six-month period, he'd strangled four streetgirls that Petra and Stu knew about, the last one a sixteen-year-old runaway from Idaho who he'd tossed in an alley Dumpster near Selma and Franklin. No cutting, but a pocketknife found at the scene yielded prints and led to a search for Freshwater.

Incredibly stupid, dropping the blade, but no big surprise. Freshwater's file said his IQ had been tested twice by the state: 83 and 91. Not that it had stopped him from eluding them.

Male black, thirty-six years old, five-foot-seven, 140, multiple arrests and convictions over the last twenty years, the last for an ag assault/attempted rape that sent him to Soledad for ten years—cut down, of course, to four.

The usual sullen mug shot; bored with the process.

Even when they caught him, he looked bored. No sudden moves, no attempt at escape, just standing there in a rancid hallway, pupils dilated, faking cool. But after the cuffs went on, he switched to wide-eyed surprise.

*Whud I do, Officer?*

The funny thing was, he *looked* innocent. Knowing his size, Petra had expected some Napoleon full of testosterone, but here was this dainty little twerp with a dainty little Michael Jackson voice. Neatly dressed, too. Preppy, brand-new Gap stuff, probably boosted. Later, the jailer told her Freshwater'd been wearing women's underwear under the pressed khakis.

The ten-year Soledad invitation had been for choking a sixty-year-old grandmother in Watts. Freshwater was released angrier than ever and took a week to get going again, ratcheting up the violence level.

Great system. Petra used the memory of Freshwater's moronic surprise to get herself smiling as she completed the report.

*Whud I do?*

*You were a bad, bad boy.*

Stu was still on the phone with Kathy: Home soon, honey; kiss the kids for me.

Six kids, lots of kissing. Petra had watched them line up for Stu before dinner, platinum heads, sparkling hands and nails.

It had taken her a long time to be able to look at other people's kids without thinking of her own useless ovaries.

Stu loosened his tie. She caught his eye, but he looked away. Going back on days would be good for him.

He was thirty-seven, eight years Petra's senior, looked closer to thirty, a slim, nice-looking man with wavy blond hair and gold-hazel eyes. The two of them had been quickly labeled Ken and Barbie, even though Petra had the dark tresses. Stu had a taste for expensive traditional suits, white French-cuffed shirts, braided leather suspenders, and striped silk ties, carried the most frequently oiled 9mm in the department, and a Screen Actors Guild card from doing bit parts in TV cop shows. Last year he'd made Detective-III.

Smart, ambitious, a devout Mormon; he and pretty Kathy and the half-dozen tykettes lived on a one-acre spread in La Crescenta. He'd been a great teacher for Petra—no sexism or personal garbage, a good listener. Like Petra, a work fiend, driven to achieve maximal arrests. Match made in heaven. Till a week ago. What was wrong?

Something political? The first day they partnered he informed her he was thinking about shifting to the paper track eventually, going for lieutenant.

Preparing her for good-bye, but he hadn't mentioned it since.

Petra wondered if he was aiming even higher. His father

was a successful ophthalmologist, and Stu had grown up in a huge house in Flintridge, surfed in Hawaii, skied in Utah; was used to good things.

Captain Bishop. Deputy Chief Bishop. She could imagine him in a few years with graying temples, Cary Grant crinkles, charming the press, playing the game. But doing a solid job, because he was substance as well as style.

Freshwater was a major bust. So why didn't it matter to him?

Especially because he was the one who'd really solved it. The old-fashioned way. Despite the Joe Clean demeanor, nine years had made him an expert on streetlife, and he'd collected a stable of low-life confidential informants.

Two separate C.I.'s had come through on Freshwater, each reporting that the hooker killer had a heavy crack habit, was selling stolen goods on the Boulevard at night and scoring rock at a flop apartment on Cherokee. Two gift-wraps: precise address, down to the apartment number, and exactly where the dealers' lookouts hung out.

Stu and Petra staked out for three nights. On the third, they grabbed Freshwater as he entered the building from the back, and Petra got to clamp the cuffs.

Delicate wrists. *Whud I do, Officer?* She chuckled out loud and filled the arrest form's inadequate spaces with her elegant draftsman's hand.

Just as Stu hung up his phone, Petra's jangled. She picked up and the sergeant downstairs said, "Guess what, Barbie? Got a call from the park rangers over at Griffith. Woman down in a parking lot, probable 187. Tag, you're it."

"Which lot in Griffith?"

"East end, back behind one of the picnic areas. It's supposed to be chained off, but you know how that goes. Take Los Feliz like you're going to the zoo; instead of continuing on to the freeway, turn off. The blues'll be there along with a ranger car. Do it Code 2."

"Sure, but why us?"

"Why you?" The sergeant laughed. "Look around. See anyone else but you and Kenny? Blame the city council."

She hung up.

"What?" said Stu. His Carroll & Company foulard was tightly

knotted and his hair was perfectly combed. But tired, definitely tired. Petra told him.

He stood and buttoned his jacket. "Let's go."

No gripe. Stu never complained.

# CHAPTER 3

I PACK UP MY PLACE TWO STUFF IN THREE LAYERS of dry cleaner's plastic and begin walking up the hill behind the rocks, into the trees. I trip and fall a lot because I'm afraid to use the penlight until I get deep inside, but I don't care—just get me out of here.

The zoo's miles away; it will take a long time.

I walk like a machine that can't be hurt, thinking what he did to her. No good. I have to put it out of my mind.

Back in Watson, after trouble with Moron or any kind of difficult day, I used lists to keep my mind busy. Sometimes it worked.

Here goes: presidents, in order of election—Washington, Adams, Jefferson, Madison, Monroe, Quincy Adams, Jackson, Martin Van Buren . . . the shortest president.

Oh shit, here I go again, down on my knees. I get up. Keep going.

Back in Watson, I had a book on the presidents, published by the Library of Congress, with heavy paper and excellent photographs and the official presidential seal on the cover. I got it in fourth grade for winning the President Bee, read it about five hundred times, trying to put myself back in time, imagine what it was like to be George Washington, running a brand-new country, or Thomas Jefferson, an amazing genius, inventing things, writing with five pens at one time.

Even being Martin Van Buren, short but still boss over everyone.

Books became a problem when Moron moved in. He hated when I read, especially when his chopper was busted or Mom had no money for him.

*Little fuck with his fuckin' books, thinks he's smartern everyone.*

After he moved in I had to sit in the kitchen while he and Mom took up my sleeper couch watching TV. One day he came in the trailer totally blasted while I was trying to do homework. I could tell because of his eyes and the way he just kept walking around in circles, making fists and opening them, making that growling noise. The homework was pre-algebra, easy stuff. Mrs. Annison didn't believe me the one time I told her I already knew it, and she kept assigning me the same work as the rest of the class. I was speeding through the problems, almost finished, when Moron got a container of bean dip out of the fridge, started eating it with his hands. I looked at him, but just for a second. He reached over and pulled my hair and slammed the math book on my fingers. Then he grabbed up a bunch of notebooks and other textbooks and ripped them in half, including the math book, *Thinking with Numbers.*

He said, "Fuck this shit!" and tossed it in the trash. "Get off your fuckin' ass, you little faggot, do something useful around here . . ."

My hair smelled of beans, and the next day my hand was so swollen I couldn't move the fingers and I kept it in my pocket when I told Mrs. Annison I'd lost the book. She was eating Corn Nuts at her desk and grading papers and didn't bother to look up, just said, "Well, Billy, I guess you'll have to buy another one."

I couldn't ask Mom for money, so I never got another book, couldn't do homework anymore, and my math grades started going down. I kept thinking Mrs. Annison or someone would get curious, but no one did.

Another time Moron ripped up this magazine collection I'd put together from other people's trash and most of my personal books, including the presidents book. One of the first things I looked for when I finally located the library on Hillhurst Avenue was another presidents book. I found one, but it was different. Not as heavy paper, only black-and-white photographs. Still interesting, though. I learned that William Henry Harrison caught a cold right after his election and died.

Bad luck for the first William president.

This is working; my head's clear. But my heart and stomach feel like they're burning up. More: Taylor, Fillmore, Pierce . . . James Buchanan, the only president who never got married— must have been lonely for him in the White House, though I guess he was busy enough. Maybe he liked being alone. I can understand that.

Lincoln, Johnson, Grant, McKinley.

Another *William* president. Did anyone ever call him Billy? From his picture, bald and squinty and angry-looking, I don't think so.

No one ever called me William except teachers on the first day of school, and soon then they switched to Billy, too, because all the kids laughed at *William*.

Billy Goat, Billy the Goat.

William Bradley Straight.

It's a plain name, nothing special about it, but better than some of the other things I've been called.

*Chuck chuck . . .*

Oops—I stumble but don't fall. Place Five is still far. It's a warm night. I wish I could take off my piss-stink clothes and run through the trees naked, a wild, strong animal who knows where he's going . . . I'll breathe ten times to cool down my heart.

. . . better. More lists: tropical fish: platys, swordtails, neon tetras, guppies, angelfish, oscars, catfish, tinfoil barbs, arowanas. Never had an aquarium, but in my magazine collection were old copies of *Tropical Fish Hobbyist* and the pictures filled my head with color.

One point the fish articles kept making was you have to be careful setting up an aquarium, know who you're dealing with. Oscars and arowanas will eat all the others if they're big enough, and if the arowanas get really big, they'll try to eat the oscars. Goldfish are the most peaceful, but they're also the slowest and get eaten all the time.

My stomach still burns, like someone's in there, chewing at me . . . breathe . . . animals you see in the park: birds, lizards, squirrels, snakes once in a while. I ignore them.

Same for people.

At night you sometimes see homeless crazy guys with carts full of garbage, but they never stay long. Also, Mexicans in low cars, playing loud music. When they stop, it's over by the trains. Junkies, of course, because it's Hollywood. I've seen them drive up, sit at one of the picnic tables like they're ready to have a meal, tie up their arms, jab in needles, and stare out at nothing.

After the dope really gets into their blood, they sigh and nod and fall asleep and they just look like anyone napping.

Sometimes couples park at the edge of the lot, including gay guys. Talking, making out, smoking—you can see cigarettes in the distance like little orange stars.

Everyone having a good time.

That's what I thought *they* were going to do, tonight.

Someone's always cutting the chain, and the rangers take weeks to fix it. The cops don't patrol much, because it's park ranger territory. The park's huge. In the library I found a book that said it had 4,100 acres. It also said the park got started in a weird way: A crazy guy named Colonel Griffith tried to kill his wife, and he had to give the land to the city in return for not going to jail.

So maybe there's something about the place that's unlucky for women . . .

Six hundred forty acres is a square mile, so with 4,100 we're talking major humongous. I know, because I've walked most of it.

Sometimes the rangers stop and smoke and talk, too. A few weeks ago, a man and a woman ranger pulled over to the picnic area just after midnight, got out, sat down on their car's hood, and started talking and laughing. Then they were kissing. I could hear their breathing get faster, heard her go, "Mmm," and figured they'd be getting it on pretty soon. Then the woman pulled her head away and said, "Come on, Burt. All we need is for someone to see us."

Burt didn't say anything at first. Then: "Aw, spoilsport." But he was laughing, and she started laughing, too; they kissed some more and felt each other up a little before they got back in their car and drove away. My guess is they didn't forget about having some sex, probably waited until work was over and then went somewhere else to do it. Maybe to one of their homes or one of those motels on the Boulevard where you pay for rooms by the hour and the prosties wait out in front.

Now I stay away from those motels, but when I first got

here a prostie—a fat black one wearing bright shorts and a black lace top with nothing underneath—tried to sell herself to me.

She kept saying, "C'mere, boy-child." It sounded like *"Me bocha, me bocha, me bocha."* Then she pulled up her blouse and showed me a gigantic black tit. Her nipple was lumpy, big and purple like a fresh plum. I ran away, and her laughter followed me the way a dog follows a chicken.

In a strange way she made me feel good, that she thought I could do it. Even though I knew she was probably kidding. I remember that nipple, the way she stuck it out at me, like, Here, take it, suck on it. Her mouth was wide open and her teeth were huge and white.

She was probably joking on me or just needed money bad and was ready to do it with anybody. Most of the prosties are junkies or crackheads.

The way those two rangers laughed was a little like the way the prostie laughed.

Is there such a thing as a *sex laugh*?

Being treated like a kid can be good or bad. When you go into a store with money, even if you're in line ahead of adults, the adults get served first. A bigger problem is the Boulevard, and all the smaller streets full of weirdos and perverts out to rape kids. Once I found a magazine in an alley and it showed pictures of perverts doing it with kids—putting dicks up their butts or in their mouths. Some kids were crying; others looked sleepy. You don't see the perverts' faces, just their hairy legs and their dicks. For a long time, it gave me nightmares, those kids, the way their eyes looked. But it also made me careful.

I've had guys pull up in cars when I'm walking, even in bright sunlight, waving money or candy bars or even their dicks. I ignore them, and if they don't butt out, I run. Used to be when I was in a bad mood because of no dinner or a night full of bad dreams, I'd flip them off before I'd run. But a month ago one of them tried to run me down with his car. I got away from him, but now I keep my finger to myself.

There's no telling what'll cause problems. A week ago, two guys got into a car accident on Gower, just a small dent in the front car, but the guy got out with a baseball bat and smashed the other guy's windshield. Then he went for the other guy, who ran away.

You've got maniacs yelling and screaming at everyone and no one, gunshots all the time at night. I've even seen guys walking around during the day with bulges in their pockets that could be guns.

The only dead person I saw was one of the old shopping cart guys lying in an alley, his mouth open like he was sleeping, but his skin had turned gray and flies went in and out between his lips. Nearby was the Dumpster I was going to dive, but I just got out of there, no more appetite. That night, I woke up really hungry, thinking I was stupid to let it get to me. He was old anyway.

When I get enough food, I'm full of energy. Super-fast. When I run, I feel jet-propelled—no gravity, no limits.

Sometimes I get into a running rhythm and it's like a music beat in my head, ba-boom, ba-boom, like nothing can stop me. When that happens I *force* myself to slow down, because it's dangerous to forget who you are.

I also slow down anytime I'm about to go into the park. Way in advance. I always look around to make sure no one's watching me, then I head in, relaxed, like I live in one of the huge houses at the foot of the park.

One of the books Moron ripped up was by a French scientist named Jacques Cousteau, on octopus and squid. One chapter talked about how octopi can match their colors to their backgrounds. I'm no octopus, but I know how to blend in.

▓

I take things, but that doesn't make me a thief.

I found the same octopus book in the library, borrowed it, brought it back.

I took the presidents book and kept it.

But no one had checked it out for nine months; that's what the card in back said.

Back in Watson the library was pathetic, just a store next to the VFW hall that nobody used, and it was mostly closed. The lady behind the desk always looked at me like I was going to take something, and the funny thing was I never was.

At the Hillhurst library, there's also an old one, but she mostly stays in her office and the one who actually checks books out is young, pretty, and Mexican, with really long hair. She smiled at me once, but I ignored her and the smile dropped from her face like I'd torn it off.

I can't get a library card because I have no address. My technique is I go in there looking like a kid from King Middle School with homework to do, sit down by myself at a table, and read and write for a while, usually math problems. Then I go back to the shelves.

I'll return the presidents book one day.

Even if I kept it forever, no one would miss it. Probably.

※

An *advantage* of looking like a harmless little kid is sometimes you can go into a store and take stuff without being noticed. I know it's a sin, but without food, you die, and suicide's a sin too.

Also—people aren't scared of kids, at least not white kids, so if you ask someone for spare change, the worst they usually do is shine you on. I mean, what are they going to say to me? Get a job, junior?

One thing I learned back in Watson: Make people nervous and you're the one who gets hurt.

So maybe God helped me by making me small for my age. I would like to grow eventually, though.

Mom, before she got sadder, would sometimes hold me under the chin and say, "Look at this. Like an angel. A damn *cherub*."

I *hated* that; it sounded so *gay*.

Some of those kids being raped in the magazine looked like angels.

There's no way to know what's safe. I avoid all people, and the park's perfect for that—4,100 acres of mostly peace and quiet.

Thank you, crazy Mr. Griffith.

The way he tried to kill his wife was by shooting her in the eye.

# CHAPTER 4

IN EIGHT MONTHS, PETRA HAD WORKED TWENTY-one other homicides, some fairly sloppy. But nothing like this. Not even the Hernandez wedding.

This woman looked shredded. Washed in blood. *Dipped* in it, like fruit in chocolate. The front of her dress was a mass of gore, glossy gray tubes of entrail popping out from slashes in the fabric. Silky fabric, not great in terms of latents. The blood would be a good cover, too—try lifting anything from skin. Maybe the jewelry, if the killer had touched it.

She and Stu arrived in darkness, encountering grim faces, radio static, a blinking symphony of red lights. They took reports from the rangers who'd found the body, waited for sunrise to have a careful look at the victim.

The blood had dried red-brown, streaking the skin and the surrounding asphalt, running down the parking lot in rivulets, some of the spatters still tacky.

Petra stood by the corpse, sketching the surrounding terrain and the body, tabulating the wounds she could see. At least seventeen cuts, and that was only the front.

Bending and getting as close as she could without messing anything up, she examined torn flesh; the lower lip almost completely severed, the left eye reduced to ruby pulp. All the damage on the left side.

*If you could see your squeamish kid now, Dad.*

Twenty-one previous bodies notwithstanding, viewing this one in sunlight jolted her with nausea. Then something worse hit her: the pain of sympathy.

*Poor thing.* Poor, poor thing, what led you to this?

Outwardly, she maintained. No one watching would have seen anything but trim efficiency. She'd been told she looked efficient. An accusation thrown at her by Nick, implying competence wasn't sexy. Along with all the other garbage he'd dumped on her. Why hadn't she realized what was going on?

She liked being thought of as businesslike. Had found a business she liked.

A month ago she'd gone to a Melrose salon, ordered the reluctant stylist to lop off six inches of black hair, and ended up with a short ebony minimal-care wedge cut.

Stu had noticed right away. "Very becoming."

She thought it framed her lean, pale face pretty well.

Her clothes were picked for nothing but practicality now. Good pantsuits bought on sale at Loehmann's and Robinsons-May that she took home and tailored herself so that they fit her long frame perfectly. Mostly black, like today. A couple of navys, one chocolate-brown, one charcoal.

She wore MAC lipstick, deep red with a brown tint, a little eye shadow, and mascara. No foundation; her skin was white and smooth as notepaper. No jewelry. Nothing a suspect could yank.

The victim wore foundation.

Petra could see it clearly where the crimson hadn't settled. Traces of blush, powder, mascara, applied a little heavier than Petra's, to the eye that remained intact.

The damaged eye was a sightless black-cherry hole, the eyeball collapsed to folded cellophane, some of the jellylike humor leaking out and specking the nose.

Nice nose, where it hadn't been slashed.

The right eye was wide, blue, filmed over. That dull *dead* look. You couldn't fake it—there was nothing like it.

Flight of the soul? Leaving behind what? A casing, no more alive than a snake's molt?

She continued studying the corpse with an artist's precision, noticed a small but deep cut on the left cheek that she'd missed. Eighteen. She couldn't flip the body till the crime-scene photographer was finished and the coroner gave the okay. The definitive wound count would be the pathologist's, once he had the corpse stretched out on his steel table.

She added the cheek wound to her drawing. Might as well be careful—the coroner's office was a zoo; doctors made mistakes.

Stu was over with the coroner—an older man named Leavitt—both of them serious but relaxed. None of that tasteless joke stuff you saw on cop movies. The real detectives she'd met were mostly regular guys, relatively bright, patient, tenacious, very little in common with cinema sleuths.

She tried to look past the blood, get a sense of the person beneath the carnage.

The woman appeared young, and Petra was pretty sure she'd been good-looking. Even savaged like that, dumped in the parking lot like refuse, you could see the fineness of her features. Not tall, but her legs were long and shapely, exposed to mid-thigh, her waist narrow in the short black silk dress. Big bust—maybe silicone. Nowadays when Petra saw a slender woman with a healthy chest, she assumed surgery.

No sign of any bizarre leakage in the torso, though with all that blood, who knew. What would happen to silicone breasts when slashed? What did silicone look like, anyway? Eight months in Homicide, the issue had never come up.

Panty hose ripped, but it looked like asphalt wear. No obvious sign of sexual assault or posing, no visible semen around the ruined mouth or the legs.

Big hair. Honey-blond, good dye job, a few dark roots starting to show, but nice, expertly done. The dress was a jacquard with hand stitching, and the way it was pulled up and bunched around the shoulders, Petra could read the label. Armani Exchange.

The shiny things Petra hoped would yield prints were a diamond tennis bracelet on the left wrist with nice-size cut stones, a sapphire-and-diamond cocktail ring, a gold Lady Rolex, small diamond studs in the ears.

No wedding band.

No purse, either, so forget instant identification on this one. How'd she end up here? Out on a date? Big hair, minidress— a callgirl lured onto the streets by an extra bonus?

The purse gone, but the jewelry hadn't been taken. The watch alone had to be three grand. So not a mugging. Unless the mugger was an even-stupider-than-usual street fool who'd taken the purse and panicked.

No, that made no sense. All these wounds didn't spell panic or robbery. This piece of dirt had taken his time.

Snatching the purse to fake robbery, not thinking about the jewelry?

She pictured someone ripping away out of rage. Deep

wounds, no defense cuts, but defense cuts were rarer than most people thought, and a decent-size man wouldn't have had much trouble subduing a woman this slender.

Still, it might indicate someone she knew.

The wound overkill sure did.

Had the blond woman been caught off guard?

Petra's brain flooded with fast-motion images. She quelled them. It was too soon to theorize.

God, it looked ferocious. A predator's attack. The massive frontal disemboweling wound was her guess for the fatal one, but most of the punishment had been concentrated on the face.

Gutting the woman, then trying to wipe away her beauty? Such intense hatred; an *explosion* of hatred.

Something *personal*. The more Petra thought about it, the more that made sense. What kind of relationship had led to *this*? Husband? Boyfriend? Some reasonable facsimile of a *lover*?

A beast let loose.

Petra unclenched her hands, jammed them into the pockets of her pantsuit. DKNY, Saks overstock, lightweight crêpe, true black. Comfortable, so she'd worn it to the Freshwater stakeout.

The blond woman's dress had just a touch of blue in it. Blue-black rinsed in rusty water.

Two women in black; the mourning had begun.

❈

Stu continued to confer with Leavitt, and Petra stayed by the corpse, a self-appointed guardian.

Protecting a molt?

As a little girl in Arizona, on summer digs with her father and her brother Dick, she'd found plenty of shedded skins, the lacy donations of snakes and lizards, collected them, tried to braid them, fashion lanyards. They'd turned to dust in her hands, and she'd started to think of reptiles as fragile, too, and somehow less frightening.

But they continued to poison her dreams for years. As did scorpions, wildcats, owls, horned toads, flying beetles, black widows, the seemingly endless stream of creatures that came in off the interstate.

Poor Dad, sentenced to hour-long nightly routines—stories and dumb jokes and obsessive-compulsive checking rituals, all so his youngest child would sleep and allow him some single-parent quiet time.

When he finally got some solitude, what did he do with it?

Knowing Dad, any spare time was spent grading papers or working on the textbook that never got finished. A tall glass of Chivas for fortification. She knew he kept a bottle in his night-stand and that it was emptied often, though she never saw him really drunk.

Professor Kenneth Connor, physical anthropologist of medium repute, now fossilized by Alzheimer's, dead prematurely, twenty months ago. She remembered the day; had been chasing a stolen Mercedes all the way down to Mexico when the station patched through the hospital call. Cerebral accident. Fancy name for stroke. The neurologist suggesting Dad's brain had been weakened by placque.

Dad had specialized in invertebrate genetics but collected shells, skins, skulls, shards, and other bits of organic antiquity, their tiny, highway-bordering house outside of Phoenix crammed with detritus and relics, smelling like a neglected museum. A kind man, a caring father. Petra's mother had died birthing her, but never once had Dad showed any resentment, though she was certain he must have felt something. She'd certainly punished herself, turning into a wild, angry teenager, setting up confrontations till Dad had been forced to send her to boarding school and she could luxuriate as a victim.

His will specified cremation, and she and her brothers had complied, tossing his ashes over a mesa in the dead of night.

Each one of them waiting for the other to say something.

Finally, Bruce broke the silence. "It's over, he's at peace. Let's get the fuck out of here."

Dad, the tissue collector, reduced to gray particles. Maybe one day, millions of years in the future, some archaeologist would find a Kenneth Connor molecule and hypothesize about what life had been like back in the twentieth century.

Now here was *this* lump of dead flesh, right next to her, fresh and pathetic.

Petra guessed the woman's age at twenty-five to thirty. The tight jawline said not too much older; no tuck scars behind the ears that she could see.

Good cheekbones, judging by the right side. The entire left side was crimson mush. Probably a right-handed killer, the head rolling to the right as he cut her.

Except for Freshwater, her twenty-one previous cases were the typical stuff: bar shootings, one-jab knifings, beatings. Stupid men killing other stupid men.

The ugliest had been the Hernandez wedding, a Saturday affair in a VFW hall near the border of Rampart Division, the groom killing the bride's father at the reception, using a brand-new pearloid-handled cake knife to slit the older man from sternum to groin, just *filleting* him as his new eighteen-year-old wife and a hundred other people watched in horror.

Some honeymoon.

Petra and Stu found the groom hiding out in Baldwin Park, served the warrant, brought him in. A nineteen-year-old gardener's assistant, the knife hidden in a fertilizer sack in the back of his boss's truck, the idiot.

*Look, Dad, I solved it, no heebie-jeebies.*

She imagined her father's surprised smile at the trajectory of his shuddering, phobic baby.

*Efficient.*

She swallowed morning air. Sweet; you could smell the pines. Suddenly, she was tired of waiting around, itching to do something, learn something.

Finally Stu walked away from Dr. Leavitt and passed behind the tape into the outer region of the parking lot, where the police and coroner vehicles had grouped. Being his usual methodical self, telling the techs what to do, what not to do, what to take back for analysis. The coroner drove away, and the morgue attendants stayed behind, listening to rap music in their van, the bass thumping.

Everyone waiting for the photographer and K-9 units to arrive so the body could be taken away and the dogs could check out the wooded area above the parking lot.

Stu talked to a uniform, barely moving his lips, profile noble, framed by sunlight.

Chief Bishop. If he didn't get a big movie role first.

Two weeks into their partnership, he'd taken out his wallet to pay for lunch at Musso and Frank and she'd seen the SAG card, next to a frequent-flyer Visa.

"You're an actor?"

His Celtic skin reddened and he closed the wallet. "Purely by accident. They came to the station a few years ago, filming a *Murder Street* on the Boulevard, wanting real cops as extras. They bugged me till I finally agreed."

Petra couldn't resist. "So when do your hands and feet go in the cement?"

Stu's swimming-pool-aqua eyes softened. "It's an unbelievably stupid business, Petra. Incredibly self-centered. Do you know how they refer to themselves? The *industry*. As if they're manufacturing steel." He shook his head.

"What kind of roles have you had?"

"Minor walk-ons. It doesn't even cut into my routine. A lot of the filming goes on at night, and if I'm still in town, leaving later makes the freeway ride shorter. So I don't really lose any time."

He grinned. It was protest-too-much time and they both knew it.

Petra smiled back wickedly. "Got an agent?"

Stu turned scarlet.

"You do?"

"If you're going to work, you need one, Petra. They're sharks, it's worth the ten percent to have someone else deal with it."

"Ever get any speaking parts?" Petra was genuinely interested, but also fighting back laughter.

"If you call 'Freeze, scumbag, or I'll shoot' speaking."

Petra finished her coffee, and Stu worked on his mineral water.

She said, "So when do you write your screenplay?"

"Come on, give me a break," he said, opening the wallet again and taking out cash.

But the next week he took a part as an extra out in Pacoima. Everyone in L.A., even a straight guy like Stu, wanted to be something else.

Except her. She'd come to California, after a year of state college in Tucson, to attend the Pacific Art Institute, got a fine arts degree with a specialty in painting, and entered the workplace with a husband sharing her bed. Nick had a great job designing cars at the new GM future lab. She earned chump change illustrating newspaper ads, sold a few of her paintings out of a co-op gallery in Santa Monica for the price of supplies.

One day it hit her: This was it; things were unlikely to change in any big way. But at least she had Nick.

Then her body failed her, Nick showed his real soul, or lack of, leaving her baffled, broken, alone. A week after he walked out, someone broke into her apartment and stole the few valuable things she owned, including her easel and her brushes.

She sank into a two-month depression, then finally dragged herself out of bed one November night and drove around the city, limp, deadened, defenseless, thinking she should eat. Her skin looked terrible and her hair was starting to fall out, but she wasn't really hungry; the thought of food made her sick. Finding herself on Wilshire, she turned around, headed for home, spied an LAPD recruitment billboard near Crescent Heights, and amazed herself by copying down the 800 number.

It took her another two weeks to call. The police commission said the department had to actively recruit women. She got a nice warm welcome.

Entering the academy on whim, thinking it a stupid, incomprehensible *mistake*, she'd surprised herself by liking it, then loving it. Even the physical-fitness challenges, learning to use her flexibility rather than brute strength getting over the Wall. Avoiding the turtle squad and learning she had good reflexes, a natural talent for using leverage to floor hand-to-hand opponents.

Even the uniform.

Not the wimpy powder-blue top and navy pants of the cadet, the real one, all navy, all business.

She, who'd bucked so many boarding school fascists over issues of rank conformity, ended up attached to her uniform.

Lots of the guys in her academy class were buffed jocks and they had their blues tapered to second-skin tautness, emphasizing biceps, deltoids, latissimi.

Boys' version of a push-up bra.

One night, impulsively, she'd customized her own uniform, using the old chipped Singer sewing machine she'd brought with her from Tucson, one of the few things the burglars had left behind.

She was five-seven, 132 pounds, with slim legs, boyish hips, big square shoulders, a butt she thought too flat, and a small but *natural* bust that she'd finally come to appreciate. Growing up with a father and four brothers, she'd found it valuable to learn how to sew.

She worked mostly with the shirt, because it bagged around her waist, and with those hips she needed *some* shape. The result had flattered her figure without flaunting it.

After graduation, she was even happier, though she didn't invite anyone to the ceremony, still nervous about what Dad and her brothers would think.

A month into her probationary year, she told them, and they were all surprised, but no one put her down. By then, she was in the groove.

Everything about police work felt right. Keeping fit, cruising, roll call, shooting on the range. Even the paperwork, because one thing boarding school had taught her was good study habits and proper English, and that put her ahead of most of the buff-jocks with their pencil-chewing agony over syntax and punctuation.

Within eighteen months, she made Detective-I.

Earning the right to guard a molt.

※

A new car joined the others in the parking lot. Subcompact with a department emblem on the door. A woman police photographer came out lugging a professional Polaroid camera. Young, around the victim's age, in sloppy clothes and long, too-black hair. Four pierces in one ear, two in the other, just holes, no earrings. Plain face, sunken cheeks, a spot of acne on each. Combative Generation-X eyes.

As she approached the body, Petra constructed a hypothetical identity for her: like Petra, an artistic type gone practical. At night she probably put on black duds, smoked dope, and drank stingers at Sunset Strip clubs, hanging out with failed rock musicians who took her for granted.

She opened her camera, looked down, and said, "My God, I know who this is!"

Petra said, "Who?" as she waved Stu over.

"I don't know her name, but I know who she is. Cart Ramsey's wife. Or maybe it's ex-wife by now. I saw her on TV around a year ago. He hit her. It was one of those tabloid shows, showbiz exposé. She made Ramsey out to be a real asshole."

"You're sure this is her?"

"Hundred percent," said the woman, peeved. Her photo badge ID'd her as Susan Rose, Photog.-I. "This is her, believe me. They said she was a beauty queen and Ramsey met her at a pageant—God, look at her, what a sick *fuck*!" The hand holding the camera tightened and the black box swayed.

Stu came over, and Petra repeated what Susan Rose had said.

"You're sure," he said.

"Jesus. Yeah, very." Susan began to shoot pictures rapidly, thrusting the camera forward as if it were a weapon. "On the show she had a black eye and bruises. Fucking *bastard*!"

"Who?" said Petra.

"Ramsey. He's probably the one who did this, right?"

"Cart Ramsey," Stu said without inflection, and Petra found herself wondering if Stu had ever worked on Ramsey's show. What was it called? *The Adjustor,* some private-eye hero who solved the problems of the downtrodden.

Wouldn't that be cute?

Susan Rose removed a cartridge and dropped it into her case. Petra told her, "Thanks, we'll get verification. Meanwhile, do your thing."

"It's her, believe me," said Susan Rose, irritably. "Can I turn her over? I already got all of the front."

# CHAPTER 5

■

TWO HOURS OF WALKING. I'M NOT TRIPPING as much.

The way he stabbed her.

PLYR 1. There's a bar on the Boulevard called Players where pimps hang out. Maybe they call themselves that because they fool around, don't do real work.

What he did to her makes me think of something I saw in Watson, out in one of the dry fields behind the orange groves.

These two dogs were passing each other. One was white with brown spots, full of muscles, kind of like a pit bull but not exactly. The other was a big black mutt that didn't walk well. The white dog looked calm, happy with life, had almost a smiley face. Maybe that's why at first the black dog didn't seem afraid of him. Then the white dog just turned without barking, jumped on the black dog, got his jaws around the black dog's neck, twisted a couple of times, and the black dog was dead. That fast. The white dog didn't eat the black dog or lick the blood or anything, he just kicked the dirt with his hind legs and walked away, like he'd done his job.

He *knew* he had the power.

I was wrong. I'm not close yet. My feet weigh a ton, and I start to feel stupid for living in the park, tell myself I'm not it's a smart decision.

What's the choice, something like the Melodie Anne? That's a building on Selma, just off the Boulevard, burnt-out from a fire, with the windows boarded up. Lots of kids crash there, and late at night you can see them bringing older guys in there. Sometimes you actually see them giving the old guys blow jobs right outside in the alley, boys and girls.

I would rather kill myself than do that. Suicide is a sin, but so is living the wrong life.

I check the Casio: 4:04. I must be close. No matter how many lists I try, my head is filled with terrible pictures. Men hurting women, dogs killing dogs, planes blowing up, kids snatched from their bedrooms, drive-by shootings, blood everywhere.

I think about Mom but see Moron instead and now I'm thinking about the way he called Mom a whore all the time and she took it, just sat there.

On bad days he hit her. I used to close my eyes, grind my teeth, try to beam myself somewhere else. For a long time, I couldn't understand why she took him in. Then I figured out she thinks she's not worth much 'cause she's got no education and he's what she deserves.

She met him at the Sunnyside, which is where she finds all the losers she brings home. She wasn't working there any- more, but she was still going there to drink and watch TV and joke with the guys shooting pool.

The other losers never stayed long and they ignored me. The first night she brought Moron home he stank up the trailer with body odor and motorcycle grease. The two of them got stoned. I was out on the sleeper couch, could smell the joints they lit up, hear them laughing, then the bed squeaking. I put my fingers in my ears and got totally under the blankets.

The next morning he came out into the front room naked, holding his shorts in one hand, flaps and folds of tattooed fat all over his body. I pretended to still be sleeping. He opened the door, grunted, put his shorts on, and went outside to pee. When he finished he said, "*Yeah,*" and cleared his throat and spit.

On the way back to Mom's bed, he tripped and his knee came down on my back. It felt like an elephant crushing me; I couldn't breathe. He came back, went into the kitchen, got a box of Cap'n Crunch, and scooped cereal into his mouth, spilling it all over.

I pretended to wake up. He said, "Oh man, a rug rat. Hell, Sharla, you didn't say you had onea *them.*"

Mom laughed from the bedroom. "We wasn't *talking* much, was we, cowboy?"

Moron laughed too, then he held out a hand for a high five. His nails were black around the edges and his fingers were the size and color of hot dogs.

"Motor Moran, bro. Who're you?" For such a big guy he had a high voice.

"Billy."

"Billy what?"

"Billy Straight."

"Ha, same as her—so you got no daddy. Little fuckin' accident, huh?" I lowered my hand, but he grabbed it, shook it hard, hurting me, looking to see if I'd show it. I ignored him.

"This your cereal, bro?"

"Kind of."

"Well, too fuckin' bad." That made him really laugh.

Mom came in and she giggled along with him. But her eyes had that sad look I've seen so many times before.

*Sorry, honey, what can I do?*

I don't protect her, either, so I guess we're even.

He punched my arm hard. "Motor Moran, little bro. Don't fuckin' use it up." Tossing me the cereal box, he went to the fridge and got beer and salsa.

"Got any chips, woman?"

"Sure, cowboy."

"Then move your ass and fix me some dip."

"You got it, cowboy."

She calls all the losers she brings home "cowboy."

Moran thought it was all for him. "Back in the saddle, baby, we goin' gallop!"

Motor Moron. His real name is Buell Erville Moran, so you can see why he'd want a nickname, even a stupid one. I saw it on his driver's license, which was expired and full of lies. Like his height being six-four when it's maybe six-one. And his weight being two hundred when it's at least two-eighty. In the picture he was wearing a huge red beard. By the time Mom brought him home, he'd shaved off the chin hairs and the mustache and left humongous sideburns that stick out, really stupid.

He wears the same thing every day: greasy jeans, smelly black Harley T-shirts, and boots. Trying to make like he's a Hell's Angel or some big outlaw biker, but he has no gang and his chopper is a rusty hunk of junk, usually broken. All he does is fool with it alongside the trailer, get blasted, watch talk shows, and eat, eat, eat.

And spend the AFDC and the disability checks. The AFDC's are basically mine. Aid to families with *dependent children*. My money.

At least I'm not dependent anymore.

※

Mom changed when I turned around five. She was never educated, but she used to be happier. More interested in how she looked, using a hot comb and makeup and wearing different outfits. Now it's all T-shirts and shorts, and even though she's not really fat, she kind of droops and her skin's pale and rough.

She used to work the Sunnyside weeks and only drink and toke on weekends. I don't want to blame her—she's had a hard life. Started picking in the fields when she was fourteen; had me when she was sixteen. Now she's twenty-eight and some of her teeth are gone, because she has no money to take care of them.

She never had much schooling, because her parents picked fruit, too, traveling up and down with the crops, and they were alcoholic and didn't believe in education. She can barely read and write and she doesn't use good grammar, but I never said anything to her about that; it really didn't bother me.

She had me nine months after her parents died in a car crash. Her dad was drunk, coming back to Watson from seeing a movie in Bolsa Chica, and he drove off Route 5 straight into a power pole.

Mom and I passed by the exact spot lots of times on the bus. Every time we did, she'd say, "There it is, that damn pole," and start rubbing her eyes.

She didn't die, because she was out partying with some grove workers instead of being with her parents at the movies.

She used to tell me the whole story, over and over, especially when she was drunk or stoned. Then she started adding stuff to it: The party was at some fancy restaurant, with big shots from the farm workers' union. Then it turned from a party into a date, her and some rich union guy, and she was all dressed up, "looking hot." Then she really got going, saying the rich guy was handsome and smart, a lawyer who was a genius.

One night she got totally blasted and made this big confession: The rich guy was supposed to be my father.

Her version of Cinderella, only she never got to live in the palace.

Having a rich, smart, handsome father would be a cool thing, but I know it's bull. If he had money, why wouldn't she go after it?

When she got that way, she sometimes pulled out old pictures of herself, showing me when she was slender and pretty and had thick, dark hair that hung down past her waist.

She has no pictures of the amazing rich guy. Big surprise.

When she told Moron the story, he said, "Cut that bullshit, Sharla. You fucked a million assholes, can't remember nonea them."

Mom didn't answer and Moron's face got dark and he looked over at me and for a minute I thought he was going to come after me, too. Instead, he just laughed and said, "How you ever gonna know which gleam in the eye produced this little piecea shit?"

Mom smiled and twisted her hair. "I just know, Buell. A woman *knows*."

That's when he backhanded her. She fell back against the fridge, and her head snapped back like it was going to come off.

I was sitting at the table, eating the little he'd left me of a jumbo can of Hormel chili, and all of a sudden fear and anger were burning through me and I looked for something to grab, but the knives were across the kitchen, too far away, and his gun was under his bed with him right in the way.

Mom sat up and started crying.

"Cut the bullshit," he said. "Shut the fuck up." He raised his hand again. This time I did stand up, and he saw me and his eyes got really small. He turned red as ketchup, started breathing hard, made a move toward me. Maybe Mom was trying to help me or maybe she was just helping herself, but all of a sudden she was in his lap, wrapping her arms around him, saying, "Yeah, you're right, baby, it is bullshit, total bullshit. I don't know jack. Sorry. I'll never lay that bullshit on you again, cowboy."

He started to shake her off, but changed his mind, said, "You gotta cool it with that bullshit."

Mom said, "I ain't arguin'. C'mon, baby, let's scoot into town and party."

He didn't answer. Finally he said, "Fucking A." Looking over at me, he licked her cheek and slipped his hand under her tank top.

Moving his hand in slow, slow circles.

"Let's party right *here,* baby," he said, starting to pull the tank top off of her.

I ran out of the trailer, hearing him laughing, saying, "Looks like the rich guy's kid got all *hot.*"

❖

He started off with more hand squeezes, tripping me, pinching my arm. When he saw he could get away with that, he started slapping me for stupid reasons, like when I didn't get him a pickled egg fast enough. It made my head buzz and I couldn't hear right for hours.

The worst time of the day was when I came home from school. He'd be outside the trailer working on his bike. "Hey you, rich guy's jizz! Get the fuck over here."

There was only one door to the trailer and he was in front of it, so I had to do it.

Sometimes he bugged me, sometimes he didn't, and that was almost worse, 'cause I kept waiting for it to happen.

*Rich man's kid, fuckin' rug rat snotty-little-asshole think-you're-smartern everyone.*

Then he started with the tools. Putting a chisel under my chin, sticking my thumb in a lug wrench and tightening it on the bone, watching my eyes to see what I would do.

I worked hard at not moving my eyes or any other part of me. The wrench felt like when you catch your hand in a drawer, but at least that's over fast—this kept throbbing and throbbing. I could imagine my bones cracking and breaking and never healing again.

Going through life with broken hands and being called Claw Boy.

Next time was a screwdriver. He tickled my ear with it, pretended to jam it in with the heel of his hand, laughing and saying, "Shit, I missed."

A few days later, his hacksaw blade went up against my neck and I could feel its teeth, like an animal biting me.

After that, I couldn't sleep well, would wake up a bunch of times a night, and in the morning I'd have a sore face from clenching my teeth.

Why didn't I just sneak over to their bed and get his gun and shoot him?

Part of it was being scared he'd wake up, get to the gun first. And even if I did shoot him, who'd believe I had a good reason? I'd end up in jail, ruined forever; even when I got out I'd be an ex-con, with no right to vote.

I started thinking about running away. The thing that decided it for me happened on a Sunday. Sundays were the worst because he sat around all day drinking and smoking weed and popping pills and watching Rambo videos and soon he'd feel like being Rambo.

Mom was in town getting groceries and I was trying to read.

He said, "Get the fuck over here," and when I did, he laughed and pulled out a pair of wire cutters, then yanked down my jeans and my shorts and put my dick between the blades. The sac, too.

Billy No-Balls.

I almost peed, but forced myself to hold it in because if I wet him I was sure he'd cut it off.

"Rich guy's kid got a *little* one, don't he?"

I stood there trying not to feel, wishing I could be somewhere else. Lists, lists; nothing was working.

He said, "Snip, snip, go sing in the fuckin' pope's choir."

He licked his lips. Then he let me go.

Two days later, when they were both at the Sunnyside, I went through the trailer looking for money. All I found at first was eighty cents in change under the couch cushions, and I was getting discouraged and wondering if I could leave without money. Then I came across the Bathroom Miracle—some money Mom had been hiding in a Tampax box under the sink. I guess she never really trusted Moron, figured he wouldn't look there. Maybe she felt trapped, too, wanted to get out one day. If I messed up her plans, I'm sorry, but she still has the AFDC and it was my balls between the blades of that cutter and if I stayed longer he would've killed me. Which would make her feel terrible and probably get her in trouble for child neglect or something.

So by leaving I was doing her a favor.

The money in the Tampax box came out to $126.

I wrapped it in two Ziploc bags, put *them* in a paper bag tied with four rubber bands, and stuffed it all in my shorts. I couldn't take books or too many clothes, so I just put my most comfortable stuff in another paper bag, buckled my Casio on my arm, and walked out into the night.

There are no street lamps in the trailer park, just lights from inside the trailers, and at that hour most people were in bed, so it was nice and dark. It's not really a park, just a dirt field next to a grove of old twisted orange trees cut low by the wind that don't fruit anymore and one long, curvy, open road that leads to the highway.

I walked the highway all night, staying on the grass, far as I could from the road so cars and trucks couldn't see me. It was mostly trucks, big ones, and they just zoomed by, creating their own storms. I must have walked twelve miles, because the sign at Bolsa Chica said it's that far to Watson. But my feet weren't hurting that bad and I felt free.

The station was closed because the first bus to L.A. was at 6 A.M. I waited around till some old Mexican went behind the counter, and he took forty of my Tampax dollars without even looking up. I bought a sweet roll and milk at the station and a *Mad* magazine from the news rack, was first on the bus, sitting in the last row.

Everyone else was Mexican, mostly workers and a few women, one of them pregnant and moving around in her seat a lot. The bus was old and hot but pretty clean.

The driver was an old white guy with a crushed face and a hat too big for him. He chewed gum and spit out the window; started off slowly, but once he got going, we were rolling along and some of the Mexicans took out food.

We drove by some used-car lots on the outskirts of Bolsa Chica, all these windshields reflecting white light like mirrors, then some strawberry fields covered with strips of plastic. When I'd passed them with Mom, she'd always say, "Strawberry fields, just like the song." I thought about her, then made myself stop. After the fields came nothing but road and mountains.

A little while later we passed the place where Mom's parents drove off the road. I stared at it, watched it disappear through the back window. Then I fell asleep.

## CHAPTER 6

STU DREW PETRA ASIDE. "CART RAMSEY. IF IT'S true."

"She seemed sure."

He glanced at Susan Rose, loading her tripod back in her car. "She looks like a stoner, but she does have a certain conviction."

"My first thought seeing all that overkill was someone the vic knew."

Stu frowned. "I'm calling Schoelkopf right now, get some guidelines. Any idea where Ramsey lives?"

"Nope. Thought you might."

"Me? Why—oh." His smile was thin. "No, never did his show. Have you ever seen it?"

"Never. He plays a P.I., right?"

"More like a one-man vigilante squad. Fixing stuff the cops can't."

"Charming."

"Bad even for TV. It started out on network, got dropped, went indie, managed to pull some syndication. I think Ramsey owns the show." He shook his head. "Thank God I never got called for it. Can't you just see the fun some F. Lee Bombast would have with that?" His lips twisted, and he looked ready to spit as he turned his back on Petra.

"What's especially bad about the show?" she said.

He faced her. "Wooden dialogue, weak story lines, no character development, Ramsey can't act. Need more? It fills space in a late-Sunday time slot, so the station probably picks it up at budget price."

"Meaning Ramsey's only a minor gazillionaire."

Stu thumbed a suspender and looked over at the body, now covered. "Ramsey's ex means media carrion. While I call Schoelkopf, would you please go over to Ms. Rose and ask her to keep her mouth zipped till the bosses have weighed in?"

Before she could reply, he started for their car. A uniform began waving frantically from the far end of the parking lot and they both hurried over.

"Found this right over there." The cop pointed to some brush near the entry gate. "Didn't touch it."

A black ostrich purse.

A tall young tech named Alan Lau gloved up and went through it. Compact, lipstick—also MAC; that made Petra's stomach flutter. Loose change, a black ostrich wallet. Inside the wallet were credit cards, some made out to Lisa Ramsey, others to Lisa Boehlinger. California driver's license with a picture of a gorgeous blonde. Lisa Lee Ramsey. The birthdate made her twenty-seven years old. Five-five, 115; matched the corpse. Address on Doheny Drive—an apartment, Beverly Hills. No paper money.

"Emptied and tossed," said Petra. "A robbery, or wanting to make it look like one."

Stu didn't comment, just headed for the car again as Lau began bagging the contents. Petra returned to the body. Susan Rose was near the feet, capping her camera lens.

"Finished," she said. "Want me to shoot something else?"

"Maybe the hills up there," said Petra. "We're waiting for the K-9's; depends on what they find."

Susan shrugged. "I get paid either way." She reached under her grubby sweatshirt, drew out a necklace, and began playing with it.

Guitar picks on a steel chain. Bingo for Detective Connor's intuition!

"Play music?" said Petra.

Susan looked puzzled. "Oh, this. No. My boyfriend's in a band."

"What kind of music?"

"Alternative. You into it?"

Petra kept her smile within bounds and shook her head. "Tone-deaf."

Susan nodded. "I can carry a tune, but that's about it."

"Listen," said Petra. "Thanks again for the ID. You were right."

" 'Course I was. But no big deal—you would've found out soon enough." The photographer turned to leave.

"One other thing, Susan. Who she is complicates things. So we'd appreciate it if you don't talk to anyone about this until we work out a plan for handling the press."

Susan fingered the necklace. "Sure, but someone like this, everyone'll know before you can say *senseless murder.*"

"Exactly. We've got a narrow window of opportunity. Detective Bishop's calling the brass right now, trying to get a plan. We're also going to need to inform Cart Ramsey. Any idea where he lives?"

"Calabasas," said Susan.

Petra stared at her.

The photographer shrugged. "It was on that tabloid show. Like *Lifestyles of the Rich and Famous.* Sitting in the Jacuzzi, drinking champagne, a little putting green. Her in some beauty pageant bathing suit competition or something, then, after he beat her up, with a black eye, split lip. You know, before and after."

"A beauty queen," said Petra.

"Miss Something. They showed her playing the saxophone. Look where her talent got her—hey, here're the dogs."

❊

Two K-9 officers, one with a German shepherd, the other with a chocolate Labrador, took instructions from Stu and started up the slope above the parking lot.

Captain Schoelkopf was in a meeting at Parker Center, but Stu managed to get patched through. When Schoelkopf found out who the victim was, he let out a stream of profanity, ending with a warning not to "F-up" (Stu's cleansed translation). Doheny Drive was a jurisdictional mess, cutting through L.A., Beverly Hills, West Hollywood. A lucky break: Lisa's apartment was LAPD territory and uniforms were dispatched. A maid was working there and she was detained. With no knowledge of other relatives, Stu and Petra's immediate assignment was to notify the ex-husband.

Now they watched as the dogs circled and sniffed and made their way upward methodically, toward a wooded area, thick with cedar and sycamore and pine, fronted by outcroppings of boulders. A stone ridge, midway up the slope, some of the rocks graffitied, most worn smooth and shiny. The Labrador was ahead, but both dogs were moving fast, closing in on a particular formation.

Something up there? thought Petra. No big deal; this was Griffith Park—there had to be tons of human scent all over the place. Pulling tire marks from the parking lot was useless for the same reason. The asphalt was one giant mural of black rubber.

Soon they'd be heading out to Calabasas. Sheriff territory. That edged the whole thing up another notch on the complication scale.

Cart Ramsey. What a name—had to be a fake. His real one was probably something like Ernie Glutz, which would play havoc with the Mr. Rockjaw image.

She rarely watched TV, but she was vaguely aware Ramsey had knocked around on the tube for years. Never achieved major stardom, but the guy did seem to work pretty steadily.

A bland type, she'd always thought. Was he capable of this kind of brutality? Were all men, given the proper circumstances?

Her dad had once told her it was a lie that only people murdered. Chimpanzees and other primates did, sometimes just to dominate, sometimes for no apparent reason. So was bloody homicide aberrant behavior or just basic primate impulse taken to an extreme?

Pointless, time-filling conjecture. Head-game horseshit, her brother Bruce used to call it. Though not the oldest of the Connor boys, he was the biggest, the strongest, the most aggressive. Now an electronics engineer for NASA in Florida, he thought anything that couldn't be measured with a machine was voodoo.

When she'd finally confessed her new police status to the family, Dick, Eric, and Glenn had been stunned, muttering congratulations and telling her to be careful. Bruce had said, "Cool. Go out and kill some bad guys for me."

The cop with the shepherd came out in front of a boulder pile and said, "You'd better take a look at this."

Nature had arranged the rocks in a tight U, like a backless cave. The boulders were high—seven or eight feet tall—and there were cracks where the rocks pressed up against each other, invisible from below, but Petra could look between them and see the parking lot clearly.

Perfect vantage point for an observer.

And there'd been someone there observing. Recently.

The floor of the U was a soft bed of leaves. Petra was no forest ranger, but even she could see the body-shaped compression. Nearby was a piece of wrinkled yellow paper, darkening to brown translucence where grease had saturated it.

Food wrapper. Specks of something that looked like ground beef.

The shepherd had sniffed out bits of shredded lettuce, barely wilted, amid some dry leaves a few inches from the paper.

Petra sniffed the wrapper. Chili sauce. Last night's taco dinner?

Then the dog began nosing frantically at one corner of the U, and Stu summoned a tech over to check it out.

"Probably body fluid," said the shepherd's handler. "He acts that way when he smells body fluid."

Alan Lau came over. Petra noticed he had nervous hands.

A few minutes later, the field kit results: "Urine. On these leaves."

"Human?"

"Human or ape," said Lau.

"Well," said Stu, "unless some chimp got loose from the zoo and bought himself dinner, it's probably safe to say Homo sapiens."

Lau frowned. "Probably. Anything else?"

"Any other fluids?"

"Like blood?"

"Like anything, Alan."

Lau flinched. "Not so far."

"Check it out. Please."

Lau returned to swabbing, dusting, probing. Susan Rose was summoned back to take pictures of the rocks. Petra sketched them anyway, then drifted away.

All that scientific work going on, but it was she who had the next find.

Twenty feet above the rocks, where she'd gone to explore because there was nothing for her to do and the dogs had moved on.

But they'd missed something, half concealed by leaves and pine needles. Flash of color beneath the green and brown.

Red. At first she thought: More blood, uh-oh. Then she bent and saw what it was; looked around for Stu.

He was back at the car, talking on his cell phone—the minuscule one his father the retired eye surgeon had given him for Christmas. Petra beckoned Lau. He sifted and found nothing around the red object, and Susan snapped away. They left, and Petra gloved up and picked it up.

A book. Thick, heavy hardcover; rebound in red leatherette. Library call number on the spine.

*Our Presidents: The March of American History.*

She flipped it open. L.A. Public Library, Hillhurst branch, the Los Feliz district.

Checkout card still in the pocket. Not much action on this one. Seven stamps in four years, the most recent nine months ago.

Stolen? Deacquisitioned? She knew the library got rid of stock all the time, because back in her starving artist days she'd filled her bookshelves with some great rejects.

She flipped pages. No deacquisition stamp, but that didn't prove anything.

Petra's mental camera began snapping. Had some homeless guy with an interest in U.S. history found himself a nice little natural lean-to where he could read and eat a taco and take a leak in the great wide open, only to witness a murder?

But no grease on the book, so maybe it had no connection to the person who sacked out behind the U-shaped rocks.

Or maybe Mr. Taco was a neat eater.

Even if the book *was* his, no big deal. There was nothing to say he'd been around precisely when Lisa Ramsey was being butchered.

Except for the fact that the urine *was* fresh. Within twelve hours, according to Lau, and Dr. Leavitt had estimated the murder at between midnight and 4 A.M.

A witness, or the murderer himself? The Fiend from the Hills hiding behind the rocks, waiting for the perfect victim.

Susan Rose had made the logical assumption that wife-beater Ramsey was the prime suspect, but other theories had to be considered.

But what would have brought Lisa Boehlinger-Ramsey to Griffith Park at night? And where was her car? Jacked? Was robbery the motive, after all?

Would someone this vicious *need* a motive?

A nut crime? Then why had the money been taken? Why not the jewelry?

Something didn't mesh. She just couldn't see a woman like Lisa coming alone to the park at that hour, all made up, wearing jewelry, that little black dress.

It spelled date. Out for the evening and she'd detoured. Or had been detoured. Why? By whom? Something hush-hush?

Buying drugs? There were lots of easier ways to score dope in L.A.

A date with the murderer? Had he driven her here with intent?

If Lisa had gone out on the town with a man, maybe someone had seen the two of them together.

One thing was sure: If it was a date, the lucky guy hadn't

been some loner who read old library books and ate tacos and peed behind rocks.

Crashing in the park, no indoor plumbing, spelled homeless.

Modern-day caveman staking out his spot behind the rocks and marking it?

A spot from which he had a vantage view of the murder scene.

Or maybe he'd wet himself out of *fear*.

Seeing it.

Looking between those rocks and *seeing* it.

## CHAPTER 7

ALMOST THERE FOR SURE NOW. THE SUN IS OUT and I feel uncovered—like a target on a video game, something small that gets eaten.

I can walk forever if I have to. All I've done in L.A. is walk.

The bus let me off in a station full of people and echoes. Outside, the sky was a strange brownish gray and the air smelled bitter. I had no idea which way to go. In one direction were what looked like factories, power poles, trucks going back and forth. People seemed to be going the other way, so I followed them.

So much noise, everyone staring straight ahead. Between each block were alleys full of garbage cans with weird-looking guys sitting against the wall. Some of them watched me pass with cold eyes. I walked three blocks before I realized I was being followed by one of them, a real crazy-looking guy with rags around his head.

He saw me spot him and came at me faster. I ran and slid into the crowd, feeling the money in my shorts bouncing around but making sure not to touch it or look at it. Everyone was taller than me and I couldn't see too far in front of me. I kept pushing through, saying, "Excuse me," and finally, two blocks later, he gave up and turned around.

My heart was going really fast and my mouth was dry. People kept piling onto the sidewalk, mostly Mexicans and a few Chinese. Some of the signs on restaurants were in Spanish and one huge movie theater with gold scrolls over the sign was playing something called *Mi Vida, Mi Amor*. A bunch of guys were selling fruit ices and churros and hot dogs from carts and now my mouth filled with spit. I started to wonder if I was dreaming or in some foreign country.

I walked till I found a street where the buildings were cleaner and newer. The nicest-looking building was something called the College Club, with U.S. and California flags out in front and a pink-faced guy in a gray uniform and hat with his arms folded across his chest. As I walked by he looked down his nose, as if I'd farted or done something rude. Then a long black car pulled up to the curb and all of a sudden he was just a servant, hurrying to open the door and saying, "How are *you* today, sir?" to a white-haired guy in a blue suit.

I made it to a little park that looked nice, with a fountain and some colorful statues, but when I got closer I saw that the benches were full of more weird guys. Right next door was a place called the Children's Museum, but no kids were going in. I was tired and hungry and thirsty, didn't want to spend any more of the Tampax money till I had a plan.

I sat down on a corner of grass and tried to figure it out.

I came to L.A. because it was the closest real city I knew, but the only neighborhoods I'd heard about were Anaheim, where Disneyland is, Beverly Hills, Hollywood, and Malibu. Anaheim was probably far, and what else was there besides Disneyland? I'd seen a TV show about Hollywood that said kids still came there looking for movie stars and got into trouble. Beverly Hills was full of rich people, and the way the guy in the gray uniform had looked at me told that wouldn't be safe.

That left Malibu, but that was the beach—nowhere to hide.

Maybe something *near* Hollywood would be okay. I wasn't like those other kids, thinking life was a movie. All I wanted was to be left alone, no one putting my dick in a wire cutter.

I sat there for a long time, thinking I'd been crazy to leave. Where would I live? What would I eat; where would I sleep?

The weather was good now, but what would happen in the winter?

But too late to go back now. Mom would find out about the money and think of me as a thief. And Moron . . . My stomach started to hurt really bad. I started to think people were looking at me, but when I checked, no one was. My lips felt like sandpaper again. Even my eyes felt dry. It hurt to blink.

I stood up, figuring I'd just walk. Then I saw two people coming through the park holding hands, a guy and a girl, maybe twenty or twenty-five, wearing jeans and long hair and looking pretty relaxed.

I said, "Excuse me," and smiled, asked them where Hollywood was—and Malibu, just to play it safe.

"Malibu, huh," said the guy. He had a fuzzy little beard and his hair was longer than the girl's.

"My parents are in there," I said, pointing to the museum. "They took my little brother in, but I figured it was boring. They promised to take me to the beach and Hollywood if we can find it."

"Where're you from?" said the girl.

"Kinderhook, New York." The first thing that spilled out.

"Oh. Well, Hollyweird's about five, six miles that way— west—and the beach is the same direction, another fifteen miles after that. Kinderhook, huh? That a small town?"

"Uh-huh." I had no idea. All I knew was it was Martin Van Buren's birthplace.

"You a farm boy?"

"Not really, we live in a house."

"Oh." She smiled again, even wider, and looked at the guy. He seemed bored. "Well, tell your parents Hollyweird *is* weird; all kinds of freaks. Be careful, you know? During the day if you're with your parents it should be okay, but not at night. Right, Chuck?"

"Yeah," said Chuck, touching his little beard. "If you go, check out the Wax Museum on Hollywood Boulevard, little dude. It's pretty cool. And the Chinese Theater, ever hear of that?"

"Sure," I said. "Where the movie stars put their hands and feet in the cement."

"Yeah," said the guy, laughing. "And their minds in the gutter."

They laughed and walked on.

The first bus I got on the driver said I needed exact change, so I had to get off and buy a lime snow-cone and get change. Which was fine, because it took care of my thirst and put a sweet taste in my mouth. Half an hour later, another bus came along and I was ready with the right coins, like someone who belonged.

The bus made a lot of stops and there was so much traffic I could see the sky turning grayish-pink through the tinted bus windows by the time the driver called out, "Hollywood Boulevard."

It didn't look that much different from where'd I'd just been: old buildings with cheap-looking stores and theaters. Same noise, too. Waves of noise that never stopped. Watson has its sounds—dogs barking, trucks rumbling over the highway, people yelling when they're mad. But each noise is separate; you can make sense of things. Here in L.A., everything's one big soup.

At the trailer park, I could walk around at night, look in windows. I've even seen people doing sex—not just young people, old ones, too, with white hair and flabby skin, moving around under a blanket with their eyes closed and their mouths open, holding on to each other like they're drowning. I knew places in the groves where it was always quiet.

Hollywood didn't look like a place where I could find quiet, but here I was.

I walked up Hollywood Boulevard, looking out for the freaks Chuck had warned me about, not sure who they really were. I saw a big tall woman with huge hands that I realized was a man, and that sure qualified; teenagers with rooster hair and black lipstick; more drunks, some of them pushing shopping carts; black people, brown people, Chinese, whatever. The restaurants sold stuff I'd never heard of, like gyros and shwarma and oki-dogs. The stores sold clothing, costumes and masks, souvenirs, boomboxes, fancy underwear for girls.

Lots of bars. One of them, called the Cave, had a row of Harleys parked in front and guys coming in and out, big and ugly, dressed like Moron. Seeing them made my stomach burn. I went past there really fast.

I saw a hamburger stand that looked normal, but the guy inside was Chinese and he didn't look up when I stood there.

One hand kept frying meat, and his face was half hidden by smoke and steam.

Two dollars forty-two cents for a burger. I couldn't spend anything till I had a plan, but I did manage to take some ketchup packets lying out on the counter. I ducked behind a building, opened them, and sucked out the ketchup, then I kept walking to a street called Western Avenue and turned right, because I saw some mountains in the distance.

To get to them I had to pass a porno theater with XXXXX's all over the front and posters of blond women with big, open mouths, then some really dirty buildings with wood over the windows. I saw women in short shorts talking on pay phones and giving each other cigarettes and guys hanging nearby smoking. The mountains were pretty and by now the sun was behind them, with a yellow-orange glow shooting up and spreading on top, like a hat made of melted copper.

A block later I had to cross the street because teenagers were laughing and pointing at me. I passed another alley. No weird drunks here, just lots of garbage Dumpsters and the back doors of stores and restaurants. A sweating fat guy wearing a stained white apron came out of a place called La Fiesta holding armfuls of bread wrapped in plastic. He threw them in a Dumpster and went back inside.

I waited for him to come back, but he didn't. Looked around to make sure still no one was watching and went over to the Dumpster. To get a look inside, I had to stand on a cardboard box that didn't feel too strong and keep hitting flies away. Once I got up there, the smell was terrible. The bread sat on top of rotten-looking vegetables with brown edges, wet paper, scraps of meat and bones and hunks of uncooked white fat. Little white worms crawled all over the meat, which smelled worse than a dead dog. But the bread looked clean.

Hot dog buns, still totally wrapped. Probably stale. When people go to restaurants they want everything superfresh. One time—the only time—Mom and Moron and I went to a restaurant, it was a Denny's in Bolsa Chica and Moron sent his fried chicken back because he said it tasted like "warmed-over shit." The waitress called the manager, who told Moron not to use that language. Moron stood up to show he was taller than the manager, with Mom holding on to his arm, saying, "Cowboy, c'mon, c'mon." Finally, the manager agreed to give us our food to go for free if we left.

I reached in and grabbed two packages of buns, almost falling into the Dumpster and getting some crud on my T-shirt.

But I had the buns, and they were clean. After looking around some more, I walked a ways into the alley, found a dark spot between two other Dumpsters, tore open the first package, bit into a bun.

Stale, all right, but my chewing mushed it up and by the third mouthful it started to taste sweet. Then the smell of the Dumpster came back to me and I started to gag.

I got up, walked around, took deep breaths, and told myself it was my imagination; pretend these were homemade buns right out of the oven, baked by some TV commercial mom with a wide-awake smile and a strong interest in nutrition.

It worked a little. The rest of the bun didn't taste great, but I got it down. Back to the mountains.

As I climbed, the road got steeper and I started to pass houses. Mowed lawns, and all sorts of trees and plants and flowers, but no people I could see, not a one. Now, after four months in L.A., I'm used to that. People here like to stay inside, especially at night, and anyone out there after dark is probably prowling for something.

At the top, Western curved and turned into another street called Los Feliz and these houses were *huge*, behind high walls with fancy metal gates and surrounded by pine trees and palms. This must have been what Hollywood was like when the movie stars lived here.

The mountains were still far away, but in front of them was a big stretch of clean green grass, a few people lying on blankets, some of them sleeping, even with all the traffic noise. Behind the grass, tons of trees.

A park.

I waited for traffic to slow down and ran across the street.

GRIFFITH PARK, the sign said.

The only park in Watson is a dry little square in the center of town with one bench, an old cannon, and a brass sign saying it's dedicated to men who've died in wars. This was different. Humongous. You could get lost in here.

# CHAPTER 8

"INTERESTING," SAID STU, HEARING ABOUT THE library book, but he sounded distracted.

He'd been on the phone and now it went back in his pocket. "West L.A. uniforms are with Lisa Ramsey's maid, it's not Beverly Hills, a few blocks away. Sunday was the maid's day off, she just got back, Lisa hadn't slept in her bed. Lisa's Porsche isn't in the garage, so it looks like she drove herself somewhere, either hooked up with the killer and switched to his vehicle or got jacked. We've got to hustle over to Ramsey's place in Calabasas to do the notification, then return to interview the maid. He wasn't at his studio office, and protocol says we make every attempt to notify in person. He lives in one of those gated-estate deals; I've got the address."

They walked to their white Ford. It was Stu's day to drive and he got behind the wheel.

"Calabasas is tan-shirt territory," said Petra as he started the engine. He drove slowly. As usual. More slowly than any cop she'd known.

"Tan as an anchorman," he said. "Schoelkopf called the boss sheriff out at the Malibu station to define some ground rules, but seeing as it's a 187, they punted to their downtown Homicide boys. The jurisdiction's ours, but they want to be there when we notify, 'cause Ramsey's house is their turf— they don't want to be perceived as out of the loop. A couple of their downtown Homicide investigators will meet us outside the gates."

"Big drive from downtown to Calabasas," said Petra. "So on some level they *do* think they're investigating it?"

"Who knows. Maybe they can help us."

"As in getting hold of Ramsey's domestic-violence history?"

"That. Anything."

45

As they got on the stretch of road that ran between the park and the 5 freeway, Stu said, "Schoelkopf gave me the kind of lecture I haven't heard since I rookied: Don't go in without permission, don't climb any walls, treat him a hundred percent like a grieving ex, not a suspect. No searching of any kind, don't go to the *john* if it can be construed as a search. No asking questions that might incriminate anyone, because then you'd have to Mirandize the guy and I don't want even a hint that he's a suspect."

"What about getting hold of that TV tape?"

"Not even that yet, because it would show clear signs of suspicion."

"Come on. It's public domain," said Petra.

Stu shrugged.

Petra said, "When do we get to detect?"

"When we know more."

"But we're not allowed to look for more."

Stu gave a tight smile.

Petra said, "All this smoke because Ramsey's VIP?"

"Welcome to Locustland. I love my job."

Till recently he had. What was going on?

He entered the freeway heading north. A mile later, Petra said, "What about the book and that food wrapper? Potential witness?"

"If whoever was eating and/or reading just happened to be there when Lisa was killed. My religion tells me to believe in miracles, but . . ."

"And/or?"

"Could be two separate guys. Even if it's one, the scene spells homeless guy, or woman. Lau said the body impression was small."

"A bag lady," said Petra.

"Whoever it was didn't call 911, so if he/she was there, it shows a certain lack of civic responsibility. Don't hold your breath waiting for someone to come forward."

"So many bag ladies are schizophrenic," said Petra. "Witnessing a murder would be terrifying to anyone, but someone already over the edge . . ."

Stu didn't answer. Petra let him drive awhile before she said, "I was also thinking—I know it's remote—what if whoever was behind the rock killed Lisa?"

He thought about that, then rattled off the same objections Petra had come up with.

"Plus," he added, "I agree with your first impression: All that facial damage, the overkill, implies passion, someone she knew. If what Susie Shutterbug said about Ramsey beating up Lisa is true, he sure fits that bill."

"But we can't treat him like a suspect."

"But we *can* psych him out while playing sympathetic public servant during the notification. Which is why I'm glad you're here. He's an actor—a bad one, but even bad ones are better at hiding their feelings than the average person."

"What does that have to do with me?" said Petra.

"You're good at reading people."

Not at reading you, she thought.

※

Soon after they got on the 134 West, they got stuck in traffic.

Common enough situation, and whenever Petra found herself in a jam she fantasized about flying cars of the future—those VW-with-propeller gizmos predicted in Dad's old *Popular Mechanics.*

Just sitting there drove her crazy and both of them knew it. Stu was a calm driver, sometimes maddeningly so.

"We could take the shoulder," she said.

He'd heard it a hundred times before and smiled wearily.

"We could at least put on the lights and the howler," she added.

"Sure," he said, shifting the car into park and gunning the engine. "Let's use our guns, too, shoot our way out . . . so what approach should we take with Ramsey?"

"Sympathetic, like you said. Be there with tissues for his crocodile tears."

"Crocodile," he said. "So you've decided hedunit."

"If Mormons gambled, where would you put your money?"

He nodded, turned his head in order to suppress a yawn, and they crawled a quarter mile, then stopped again. Rubbing her eyelids, Petra created twin kaleidoscopes behind the thin flesh. A headache was coming on. She had to learn to deal better with frustration.

"All these years working Hollywood," Stu said, "and I

never had a celebrity murder. Closest I came was this old guy, Alphonse Dortmund. German émigré character actor, used to play nazis in World War II movies. Got strangled in his apartment on Gower. Real dump. He hadn't worked in years, drank, let himself go. Uniforms responding to a bad odor call found him all tied up in his bed—hog-tied with the rope around his neck, complicated knots."

"Sexual asphyxia?"

"That was my first impression, but I was wrong. He didn't do it to himself. Turns out he picked up a fifteen-year-old on the Boulevard, showed the kid how to truss him, then the kid decided to take it further, choked him out, ransacked the apartment."

"How'd you catch the kid?"

"What do you think?"

"He bragged."

"To anyone he could find. My partner at the time—Chick Reilly—and I went to all the usual places, talked to all the usual people, and *everyone* knew what had happened. It made us feel like rubes just off the farm." He laughed. "Thank God most of them are idiots."

"Wonder how smart Ramsey is," said Petra. "Any particular reason he wouldn't be in his office?"

"You're thinking he rabbited already? No, we can't assume that. He's not filming. All this year's shows are already in the can."

"His show specifically, or all of the shows?"

"All the main ones," said Stu. "He could be playing tennis, soaking in the Jacuzzi. Or on a chartered jet to the south of France."

"Wouldn't that be inopportune."

"Indeed. Hey, maybe we *should* shoot our way out of this."

Forty-five minutes later, they got off the freeway at Calabasas Road and took a curving road north, into the Santa Susanna Mountains. Smooth, rolling slopes sported groves of live oaks that had survived progress. The trees were acutely sensitive to overwatering, and irrigation had killed hundreds of them before someone had caught on and designated them protected.

Fires had fun out here, too, Petra knew, racing through dry brush and chaparral, devouring the big vanilla retro-Spanish houses that seemed to be the thing in upscale, West Valley neighborhoods. No matter how much money went into them, they never looked anything *but* retro.

They passed several tracts of vanilla now, some behind gates. Twin-paddock horse setups, small corrals alongside tennis courts, and stone-and-waterfall swimming pools. The air was good, the lots were generous, and once you got away from the freeway, it was quiet. But Petra knew it wasn't for her. Too far from bookstores, theaters, museums, L.A.'s meager cultural mix. Too calm, also. Cut off from the *pulse*.

Not to mention the commute—two hours of your life each day spent studying the white lines on the 134, wondering if this was success.

Calabasas was popular with what Petra, secretly a snob, thought of as the nonthinking rich: athletes, rock stars, overnight entrepreneurs, actors like Ramsey. People with long blocks of leisure and a melanoma-be-damned view of sunshine.

Petra suspected the free time caused problems. A recent Parker Center memo had warned of white Valley teenagers starting to emulate the inner-city gangbangers. What did kids *do* out here except get into trouble?

Back in her artist days, she'd sometimes fantasized about what her life would be if she ever made it big—twenty thousand a canvas, no need for commercial jobs. Half the year in L.A., half in London. It had never come to that, of course. She'd sketched and T-squared twelve hours a day just to pretend she was contributing financially to the marriage, telling Nick what he earned was his. How noble. How stupid.

"Here we are," said Stu.

RanchHaven sat atop a knoll planted with golden poppies. High, scrolled gates on pink columns. Behind the wrought iron were the biggest haciendas they'd seen so far, scattered thinly on multiacre lots. An unmarked Dodge was parked on the side of the road, twenty yards before the gates. No-frills wheels and multiple antennae made it every bit as obtrusive as Stu and Petra's Ford.

They pulled up behind it and two men got out. One was Hispanic, forty-five, five-ten, heavy-set, with a gigantic swooping black mustache and a tie full of birds and flowers. His partner was white, much younger, same height, thirty pounds lighter, also with lip hair, but his 'stache was clipped and yellow-gray. Both wore gray sport coats. Black and navy slacks, respectively. The white deputy's tie was narrow and maroon, and he had a pleasant boyish face just short of handsome.

They introduced themselves as De la Torre and Banks. Greetings all around; nice and friendly so far.

"What exactly happened?" said De la Torre.

Stu filled them in.

"Ugly," said Banks.

Petra said, "Your boss never told you?"

Banks shook his head. "We were told Ramsey's wife had been killed, but not how. The order was to get here, wait for you. We were also told it wasn't our case; we should just be here so later no one could say we weren't. Where'd it go down?"

"Griffith Park."

"Just took my kids to the zoo there last Sunday," said Banks, shaking his head. He looked bothered, and Petra wondered how long he'd been in Homicide.

"Think he did it?" said De la Torre.

Stu said, "Our info is he beat her up last year and they got divorced soon after."

"There's a couple of high riskers for you."

"One thing for sure," said Stu. "It was no street-idiot mugging. Mega-wounds, mega-fury. Someone took cash out of the purse but left credit cards and her jewelry. We figure someone she knew or, less probably, a sex fiend. Whoever it was either drove off in her car or took her there in his."

"What did she drive?" said Banks.

"Porsche 911 Targa, four years old, black. We put a want out for it."

"To some people, that's worth killing for."

"Maybe," said Stu, "but stabbing her two dozen times for wheels? Why bother?"

Silence for a few seconds.

"Cash, no jewels," said De la Torre. "Attempted fake-out? Ever watch Ramsey's show? I did. Once. Stinks."

Petra said, "It would be good to know if he ever caused problems around here."

"We can check with the locals for you," said Banks, offering her a brief, puzzling smile.

"That would be great."

"So exactly how do you want to proceed?" said De la Torre. "I mean, seeing as we're just here for the chorus line, we don't want to screw up your solo."

"Appreciate it," said Stu.

"So what's the plan?"

Stu looked at Petra.

"Low profile," she said. "No treating him like a suspect, no biasing the case prematurely."

"Ramsey's an actor, so everyone's got to put on a performance—don't you just love this town?" said Banks. "Okay, we'll just hang behind, be discreet. Think you can do that, Hector?"

De la Torre shrugged and said, "Me no know," in a cartoon Mexican voice.

"Hector's an intellectual," said Banks. "Earned a master's degree last summer, so now he thinks he's entitled to have opinions."

"Master's in what?" said Petra.

"Communications."

"Thinks he's going to do sports on TV one day," said Banks. "Or the weather. Do the weather for them, Hector."

De la Torre smiled good-naturedly and looked up at the sky. "High pressure hitting a low pressure coming down and encountering a medium pressure. Possibly leading to precipitation. Also, actors beating on their wives, possibly leading to murder."

※

Both unmarkeds pulled up to the pink column. The gates had a green pseudo-patina. On the left column was a talk-box and a sign that said DELIVERIES. Twenty feet up the drive on the other side of the gate was a guardhouse.

Stu leaned out, pushed the button on the box and said, "Police for Mr. Cart Ramsey."

The uniformed guard stuck his head out and came forward. Stu's badge was out, and by the time the gates slid open, Petra could see from the guard's body language that he was ready to cooperate.

"Help you?" he said. Older guy, round gut, deep tan, lots of wrinkles, hair dyed beige. Walkie-talkie and baton, but no gun.

"We need to talk to Mr. Ramsey," said Stu. "Privately. I guess you understand how highly Mr. Ramsey and his neighbors value privacy."

The guard's eyes widened. "Oh, sure."

"So we can count on you, Officer . . . Dilbeck, to be discreet?"

"Sure, sure—should I call ahead to tell him you're coming? Usually, that's what we do."

"No thanks," said Stu. "As a matter of fact, please don't. Tell me, Officer, has Mr. Ramsey entered or exited Ranch-Haven today?"

"Not during my shift—that's from eleven o'clock on."

The normal thing would be to ask who'd been on night shift. Instead, Stu said, "Thanks. How do we get up there?"

"Keep going to the top and take the first left, which is Rambla Bonita. Go up again, straight to the top, and that's his place. Big pink place, just like these columns."

"Pink," Petra repeated.

"Pink as it gets. When he bought it it was white, but he and the wife repainted."

"Ramsey have any problem with that?"

"Not that he told me. But he don't say much at all. Like that character he plays—Dack whatever his name is."

"Strong and silent?" said Petra.

"You might say that." Dilbeck stepped aside.

As they reached the top of the first rise, Petra said, "Well, that clinches it, doesn't it? It's always the quiet ones."

# CHAPTER 9

THE PARK TOOK ME IN LIKE A FRIEND. I LEARNED.

Things like what times the rangers patrolled and how to avoid them. Which restaurants threw out the freshest food and how, if you worked in the dark, you didn't get bothered while Dumpster-diving.

Who people were.

The guys on Western were drug dealers and all they wanted was to do their business without being annoyed, so I stayed on the other side of the street. After about a month, one of them crossed over and said, "Smart boy," and gave me five dollars.

I learned how to get stuff.

If you go far enough east on Los Feliz, the fancy houses stop and there are apartments. On Sunday, the people who live in the apartments sell stuff out on their front lawns, and if you wait till the end of the day, you can pick up things extra-cheap because they don't want to bother packing it up.

I bought a green blanket that smelled of wet dog for one dollar and a sleeping bag for three, and I got the guy who was selling the sleeping bag to throw in a pocketknife with three blades, one of them a screwdriver, for free.

Sometimes the people selling looked at me strangely—like, What's a kid doing buying underwear?—but they never turned down my money.

I bought a flashlight, two packets of AA batteries, some old T-shirts, a sweater, and a round couch pillow that was hard as rock and rotted, a total waste.

I spent thirty-four more Tampax dollars the first month. Adding the five I got from the dope dealer, that left fifty-four dollars. I found the Five Places and spread my stuff around them.

I learned when to smile, when not to, who to look at, who to ignore. Found out money is a language.

I made mistakes. Ate bad food and got sick, one time really bad, throwing up for three days straight, with fever and chills, and sure I was going to die. That time I was in a cave in Three, living with bugs and spiders and not caring. On the third day, I crept out before sunrise and washed my clothes in the brook. My legs were so weak it felt like someone was kicking me in back of my knees. I got better, but since then my stomach hurts a lot.

I learned about prosties and pimps and saw people doing sex in alleys, mostly women down on their knees sucking on guys who didn't move, just groaned.

I realized that to get enough money so no one would use me, I'd have to be educated, but how was I going to do that living in the park?

The answer I came up with was: teach yourself—meaning schoolbooks, meaning a school. A junior high, because back in Watson, I was in seventh grade, even though a counselor visiting from Bakersfield once showed me some puzzles and told me I could skip to eighth if Mom signed some forms. She said she would, but she never did, and then she lost the forms and the counselor never asked, so I stayed in seventh, and unless I let my imagination race around I was so bored my mind felt like wood.

I found a Yellow Pages in a phone booth, took it back to the park, and looked up SCHOOLS. There were no junior highs listed and that confused me, so the next day, I called the school board, making my voice as low as possible and saying I'd just moved to Hollywood with my twelve-year-old son and he needed a junior high.

The woman on the other end said, "One second, ma'am," and put me on hold for a long time. Then she came back, saying, "Thomas Starr King Middle School on Fountain Avenue," and she gave me the address.

I walked over at noon. It turned out to be around two miles away from Place Three, in a grungy-looking neighborhood and gigantic—all these pink buildings with bright blue doors, a humongous yard surrounded by high fences. I watched from across the street and learned that school ended at 1 P.M., with tons of kids flooding out of the yard laughing and punching each other. That gave me a pain in my throat.

One P.M. dismissal meant I could walk around in the afternoon and not get busted.

I made a schedule: Mornings would be for washing up, eating whatever I'd put away the night before for breakfast, reading and studying, checking out the Places to make sure no one had found the stuff I hid. Afternoons would be for getting new food and whatever else I needed.

I went back to King Middle School again, during ten o'clock recess. Kids were out in the yard, and the teachers I saw were talking to each other. I slipped in through one of the gates and walked around like I belonged. There were two separate supply rooms where the books were stored.

It took eight visits to get what I needed.

It was easy. Who'd suspect a kid would take books?

I got myself textbooks for seventh, eighth, and ninth grade, some pens and pencils and pads of lined paper. English, history, science, math all the way up to algebra.

Without rowdy kids or Moron distracting me, I could concentrate; it only took two months to get through all the books. Even algebra, which I'd never had before and looked hard—all those letter symbols that didn't make any sense at first—but the beginning was all review, and I just moved ahead page by page.

I liked the idea of variables, something meaning nothing by itself but taking on any identity you wanted.

The all-powerful X. I thought of myself as X-boy—nothing, but also everything.

I took all the books back to King Middle School one night and left them at the fence. Except the algebra text, because I wanted to practice equations. I knew I had to keep my mind busy or it would get weak, but I was tired of schoolbooks, wanted some vacation. Different types of knowledge—encyclopedias, biographies of people who'd succeeded. I missed my presidents book.

No storybooks, no science fiction; I don't care about things that aren't true.

I found a library right off Los Feliz, just a few blocks down on Hillhurst, a strange-looking place with no windows, stuck in the middle of a shopping center. Inside was one big room with colorful posters of foreign cities trying to imitate windows and just a few old people reading newspapers.

I was dressed neat and had the algebra book, pencil and paper, and a backpack. Sitting at a table in a far corner, I pretended to be doing equations and checked the place out.

The woman who seemed to be the boss was old and sourlooking, like the librarian back in Watson, but she stayed up front talking on the phone. The young Mexican with the really long hair was in charge of checking out books and she did notice me, came over smiling to ask if I needed help.

I shook my head and kept doing equations.

"Ah," she said, in a very soft voice. "Math homework, huh?"

I shrugged, just ignored her completely, and she stopped smiling and walked away.

The next time I came in, she tried to catch my eye, but I kept shining her on and after that she ignored me, too.

I started to show up once or twice a week, always after 1 P.M., starting with phony homework, then examining the shelves till I found something, and reading for two hours.

Sometimes I could finish a whole book in that time. On the third week, I came across the *exact* Jacques Cousteau book I'd had back in Watson and thought: I am definitely in the right place.

I found the other presidents book soon after. It was the first one I took. It's the only one I kept and I'm still not sure why. I took excellent care of it, wrapping it in dry cleaner's plastic. So there was no real crime.

Still, I felt bad about it. Kept telling myself that one day, when I was an adult and had money, I'd give books *to* the library. Sometimes I wondered if I'd last long enough to be an adult.

Now, after what I've seen, everything seems shaky. Maybe it's time to leave the park. But where would I go?

My foot catches on a rock, but I keep my balance—finally, here's Five, the smell of the zoo blowing through the fern tangle. Time to hide, get some rest, do some thinking.

I've got to do some *serious* thinking.

# CHAPTER 10

SEEING RAMSEY'S HOUSE, PETRA THOUGHT BACK to her architectural history course and tried to come up with a label. Confused Spanish pseudo-Palladian? Postmodern Mediterranean Eclectic? Hotshot Hacienda?

One big heap of stucco.

The structure sat atop a peak so steep Petra had to crane to see the top. Pink, as the guard had promised, a rosy hue darker than the columns behind another set of columns and gates—cage within a cage. The driveway up to the house was stamped to look like adobe bricks, lined with Mexican fan palms. Through the posts she saw a shiny black Lexus parked in front.

They drove up to the gates, and now Petra could see at least an acre of sloping front lawn. The house was two and a half stories tall, the half being a bell tower above limed-oak double entrance doors. A real-life bell looked to be a knockoff of the one in Philadelphia. Wings flared at oblique angles, like those of a turkey that had cooked too long and loosened. Lots of odd-shaped windows, some leaded and stained. Verandas and balconies were fronted by verdigrised iron railings and the roof tiles had been artificially antiqued rust-gold. To the right of the limed doors was a five-door, extra-deep garage. Room for Ramsey's studio-supplied limo, she supposed.

No other houses nearby. King of the mountain.

More palms rose behind the house, their fringed tops extending above the roofline like some kind of New Age buzz cut. Petra could smell horses, but she couldn't see any. The Santa Susannas were chalky blue in the distance. No live oaks here. Too many sprinklers.

Stu nosed the Ford close to the box. "Ready, O ye messenger of doom?"

"Oh yeah."

He pushed the button. Nothing for a second, then a woman's voice said, "Ya?"

"Mr. Ramsey, please."

"Who this?"

"Police."

Silence. "Hold on."

A long minute passed, during which Petra looked back at the sheriff's car. Hector De la Torre was at the wheel, saying something she couldn't read. Banks was listening, but he saw her and gave a small wave just as a short, stout Hispanic woman in a pink-and-white uniform came out through the double doors. She walked halfway down the driveway, stared at them. Fifty to sixty years old and conspicuously bowlegged, she wore her hair tied back tight and had a face as dark and static as a bronze casting. She pressed the remote.

The gates opened and the cars drove onto the property. All four detectives got out. The air was a good ten degrees warmer than in Hollywood, and now Petra spotted a section of posts and stakes to the left of the house—a corral. Brown patches of equine flesh moved in and out of view.

Dry heat; her eyes felt gritty. Off to the north, a small plane hovered over the mountains. A cloud of crows burst out of a thicket of sycamore, then dispersed, squawking, as if in fear.

"Ma'am," said Stu, showing his badge to the maid.

She stared at him.

"I'm Detective Bishop and this is Detective Connor."

No answer.

"And you are, ma'am?"

"Estrella."

"Last name, please, ma'am."

"Flores."

"Do you work for Mr. Ramsey, Ms. Flores?"

"Yes."

"Is Mr. Ramsey here, Ms. Flores?"

"Playing de golf."

She looks scared, thought Petra. Immigration anxiety? Unless Ramsey planned on running for office, he didn't need to worry about checking papers, so she could easily be illegal.

Or something else. Did she know something? Problems in the Ramsey household? Ramsey's comings and goings last night? Petra wrote down the woman's name and then an asterisk: Be sure to recontact.

Closing her pad, she smiled. Estrella Flores didn't notice.

"Mr. Ramsey's not here?" said Stu.

If so, it was a contradiction of what the guard had said.

"No. Here."

"He is here?"

"Yes." The woman frowned.

"He's playing golf, here?"

"De golf in back."

"He's got his own putting green," said Petra, remembering Susan Rose's recollection of the TV show.

"May we speak to him, please, Ms. Flores?"

The woman glanced at the two sheriffs a few feet away, then back at the wide-open doors to the house. Inside, Petra saw cream walls and floors.

"Wan' come in?" said Estrella Flores.

"Only with Mr. Ramsey's permission, ma'am."

Puzzlement.

"Why don't you go tell Mr. Ramsey we're here, Ms. Flores."

Petra smiled at her again. Lot of good it did. Estrella Flores bowlegged herself back to the house.

Not long after, Cart Ramsey came running out, followed by a blond man.

The TV sleuth wore a bright green polo shirt, jeans, and running shoes. Good shape for a guy his age, which Petra figured to be forty-five, fifty. Six-two, 200, with big shoulders, narrow hips, flat gut, tight waist, no love handles. Black curly hair, TV tan.

The jaw.

The mustache. What was his character's name? Dack Price.

His companion was about the same age, just as big, the same kind of halfback shoulders, but wider hips. More of the typical middle-aged setup here: significant swell of belly above the belt, looseness at the jowls, jiggling of the breasts as he ran. The fair hair was thinning, longish at the back, pink skin showing at the crown. He wore little round sunglasses with black lenses. His bright blue silk shirt was long-sleeved and oversized, and his pleated black cotton pants were tight around the waist. Ramsey outpaced him easily and reached the car breathing normally.

"Police? What is it?" Deep TV voice.

Stu showed his badge. "I'm sorry, sir, but we've got some troubling news."

Ramsey's blue eyes startled, blinked, froze. Very pale blue, dramatic against the ruddy-tan skin, though up close Petra could see that the hair was too sable to be real and the skin was grainy, with open pores in the cheeks and veins spidering the nose. Too many dressing-room vodkas? Or all those years of pancake makeup?

"What kind of news? What are you talking about?" Ramsey's voice had started to thicken with panic.

"Your ex-wife—"

"Lisa? What happened?"

"I'm afraid she's dead, sir."

*"What!"* Bug-eyed. Ramsey's big hands tightened into huge fists and his biceps swelled. Petra put on a sympathetic look as she looked for cuts and bruises up and down his arms. Nothing. De la Torre and Banks were doing the same thing, but the actor didn't realize it. He was bent over and covering his face with one hand.

The big blond man in the blue shirt arrived huffing, shades askew. His hair was too blond, another probable tint job. "What's going on, Cart?" Ramsey didn't answer.

"Cart?"

Ramsey spoke from behind his hand. "They . . . Lisa." His voice choked up between the two words.

"Lisa?" said the blond man. "What happened to her?"

The hand dropped, and Ramsey turned on him. "She's *dead*, Greg! They're telling me she's *dead*!"

"Oh my God—what—how—" Greg's mouth gaped as he looked at the detectives.

"She's dead, Greg! This is *real*!" Ramsey roared, and for a moment it looked as if he'd haul off and hit the blond man.

Instead, he turned back suddenly and stared at them. At Petra. "You're sure it's her?"

"I'm afraid so, Mr. Ramsey."

"How can you—I can't—she—how? This is crazy—where? What happened? What the hell happened? Did she total her car or something?"

"She was murdered, Mr. Ramsey," said Petra. "Found this morning in Griffith Park."

*"Murdered?"* Ramsey sagged and covered the bottom of his face, this time with both hands. "Jesus God—Griffith Par— what the *hell* was she doing *there*?"

"We don't know, sir."

It was an opening for Ramsey to fill, but the actor just said, "This morning? Oh God, I can't believe this!"

"Early this morning, sir."

Ramsey shook his head over and over. "Griffith Park? I don't get it. Why would she be there early in the morning? Was she—how was she . . ."

Blond Greg came closer and patted Ramsey's shoulder. Ramsey shook him off, but the other man didn't react—used to it?

"Let's go inside, Cart," he said. "They can give us the details inside."

"No, no, I need to know—was she shot?" said Ramsey.

"No, sir," said Stu. "Stabbed."

"Oh Christ." Ramsey sank an inch. "Do you know who *did* it?"

"Not yet, sir."

Ramsey rubbed his head with one hand. Liver spots, Petra noticed. But a big, strong-looking hand, fingers as thick as hour cigars, with sturdy squared-off nails.

"Oh shit! *Lisa!* I can't believe it! Oh, Lisa, what the hell did you *do?*" Ramsey turned his back on the detectives, walked a few steps, doubled over as if about to vomit, but just remained in that position. Petra saw a shudder course along his broad back.

The blond man let his hands drop limply. "I'm Greg Balch, Mr. Ramsey's business manager—"

Ramsey wheeled around suddenly. "Did it have anything to do with drugs?"

A second of silence, then Stu said, "Did Mrs. Ramsey have a drug problem?"

"No, no, just a while back—actually she's not—wasn't Mrs. Ramsey anymore. We got divorced six months ago and she took back her maiden name. It was friendly but . . . we didn't see each other." He shielded his face again and began to cry. Big wracking baritone sobs. Petra couldn't see if there were any tears.

Balch put his arm around Ramsey, and the actor let himself be guided into the house. The detectives followed. A moment later, when Ramsey made eye contact, it was with Petra, and she saw that his eyes were dry, steady, the whites unblemished, the sky-colored irises clear.

※

The house smelled of bacon. The first thing Petra noticed once she got past the fifteen-foot ceilings and the junk art and all that endless cream furniture—like being dropped into a vat of buttermilk—was the five-door garage.

Because a wall of plate glass offered a view from inside the house. This was a garage like da Vinci was a cartoonist.

Fifty by twenty, with true-white walls, mega-buffed black granite floor, black track lighting. Five spaces, but only four were filled. And no limo. These were all collectibles: tomato-red Ferrari roadster with a predatory nose; charcoal-gray Porsche speedster with racing numbers on the door; black-and-maroon Rolls-Royce sedan with wonderful swooping fenders, a gigantic, ostentatious chrome grille, and a crystal hood mascot, probably Lalique; bright blue early Corvette ragtop, probably 1950s—the same blue as business manager Greg Balch's silk shirt.

In the fifth space, only a gravel-filled drip tray.

On the walls were framed racing posters and airbrushed depictions of penile cars.

Stu and the sheriffs had stopped to look. Men and cars. Petra was one woman who actually understood that syndrome. Maybe it was four brothers, maybe her sense of aesthetics, an appreciation of functional art. One of the reasons she'd hit it off with Nick was because she was able to stroke his ego and mean it. No stretch; the bastard had no soul, but he could carve masterpieces. His favorite was the '67 Stingray, the apex of design, he called it. When Petra told him she was pregnant, he looked at her as if she were an Edsel . . .

Greg Balch was a few feet ahead, squiring Ramsey into the next room, as the detectives pulled themselves away from the glass wall. Balch sat Ramsey down on an overstuffed cream silk loveseat and the actor remained hunched as if praying, head down, hands laced together on his right knee, bulky neck muscles tight.

The four detectives took places on a facing nine-foot-long sofa, moving around pastel throw pillows to find space. One cushion ended up in De la Torre's wide lap, and his stumpy brown fingers drummed the glossy fabric. Banks sat calmly, not moving. A coffee table composed of a granite boulder with a slab of glass on top marked the space between Ramsey and the cops. Balch took a side chair.

Petra scanned the room. Grotesquely big. She supposed it was a den. It looked into three equally cavernous spaces, each with the same pale overscale furniture, bleached wood accents, huge, terrible pastel abstractions on the walls. Through glass doors she saw grass and palms, a rock pool with waterfall, a four-hole putting course, the grass mown to the skin, nearly gray.

*De golf.* Two chrome irons lay on the nubby grass; behind the green was the corral and a cute little pink barn.

Where was vehicle number five? Hidden so it could be cleaned, scrubbed of blood?

And they couldn't even ask about it. She'd seen how long it took the techs to go over a vehicle carefully. If the investigation ever got to the point where they had a search warrant, just doing all the Ramsey wheels would require a major crew for days.

Her eyes drifted back to the corral. Bales of hay, piled up neatly. Two horses lolling, one brown, one white. She imagined Lisa on the white one, wearing a tailored jacket and custom jodhpurs, honey hair streaming.

Had the woman been a rider? She knew nothing about her.

Two horses. Five cars. And a partridge in a—what belonged in the *empty* spot?

Ramsey remained bowed and silent. De la Torre, Banks, and Stu were studying him without being obvious. Balch looked uncomfortable, the helping hand not knowing how to help. De la Torre looked back at the cars again. Grim-faced, all business, but managing to take in the chrome, the lacquer paint, the oiled leather, licorice-black tires. Banks saw him, smiled. Made eye contact with Petra and smiled a little wider.

Stu just sat there. The blank-tablet look, he called it. Let the interviewee fill in the spaces. Maybe he found it easy with Ramsey because he had no car lust—not that he'd shown to

Petra, anyway. His civilian ride was a white Chevy Suburban with two child safety seats and toys all over. Petra had been a passenger a few times, the Bishops' dinner guest, if you could call transporting six children to Chuck E. Cheese dinner. The video games were fun, though. She liked kid stuff . . .

She found herself touching her flat belly, stopped, and directed her attention back to Ramsey.

Black curls bounced as the actor kept shaking his head, as if telling himself no. Petra had seen that so many times. Denying. Or pretending to. The guy was a TV private eye. Actors did research; he had to know the drill.

Greg Balch patted Ramsey on the back again. The business manager still wore that helpless-lackey look.

Petra watched Ramsey some more. Thought, What if he's clean? What if this is the worst kind of whodunit?

Then she reminded herself that he'd beaten Lisa up. Played parts for a living.

She gazed at the huge, formless rooms. Den 1, den 2, den 3—how many dens did a wolf need?

Finally, Ramsey straightened and said, "Thanks for coming over . . . guess I'd better call her folks . . . oh Jesus . . ." He threw up his hands.

"Where do her folks live?" said Stu.

"Cleveland. A suburb, Chagrin Falls. Her father's a doctor. Dr. John Boehlinger. I haven't talked to them since the divorce."

"I can call them," said Stu.

"No, no, it should be someone who . . . do you usually do that? I mean as a normal part of procedure?"

"Yes, sir."

"Oh." Ramsey breathed in and let the air out, wiped his eye with a pinkie. "No, it should still be me . . . although . . . the problem is we're not exactly—Lisa's folks and me. Since the divorce. You know how it is."

"Tension?" said Stu.

"I don't know if my calling will make it worse—I mean, I really don't know what my place is in all this." Ramsey looked miserable. "Officially, I mean. We're not married anymore, so do I have an official role?"

"In terms of?" said Stu.

"Identifying her, arrangements—you know . . . Lisa and I . . . we loved and respected each other but we were . . . apart." Up went the hands again. "I'm rambling, must sound like an idiot. And who gives a *fuck* about arrangements!" Ramsey's hand slammed into a palm. He turned to the right and flashed a profile.

What a chin, thought Petra. In his world, love and respect meant a black eye, split lip. His lower lip began to shake and he bit down on it. *Could* he be posing?

She said, "If there's anything you could tell us about Lisa, it would be helpful, sir."

Ramsey swiveled slowly and stared at her, and Petra thought she saw something new in his pale eyes—analysis, cold thought, a hardening. Then, a second later, it vanished and he looked grief-stricken again and she wondered if she'd imagined it.

In the interim, Ramsey's eyes had moistened. He said, "She was a great girl; we were married for nearly two years."

"What about the drug situation, sir?" said Petra.

Ramsey looked at Balch, and the blond man shrugged.

"No big deal," said Ramsey. "I shouldn't have said anything. The last thing I want is for the media to get hold of that and smear her as—Jesus, they *will*, won't they? Oh *shit*! It's ridiculous, she was no big-time addict, just . . ."

He looked down at his lap.

"You're right, sir," said Petra. "Sooner or later it'll be out, so we might as well know the facts. With drugs there's always the possibility of violence, so if you could tell us . . ."

Again, his eyes changed and Petra was certain he was appraising her. Were the other D's noticing? Not overtly: De la Torre was ogling the cars again, and both Stu and Banks just sat there, noncommittal.

Petra touched her hair and crossed her legs. Ramsey kept his eyes at face level, but he blinked as the black crêpe rustled. She let her ankle dangle.

"There's nothing to tell," he said.

"It really wasn't any big deal," said Greg Balch. His eyes were blue, too, but an insipid, cloudy shade, suffering by proximity to Ramsey's. "Lisa had a little coke problem, that's all."

Ramsey glared at him. "Goddamnit, Greg!"

"They might as well know, Cart."

Holding on to the glare, Ramsey took a deep breath. "All right, all right. Coke was basically what finished our marriage. Though, to be honest, the age difference was an issue, too. I'm from another generation, when 'party' still meant you went to a party and talked and danced. I drink socially, but that's it. Lisa liked to sniff—Jesus, I can't believe she's *gone!*"

He started to hide his face again, and Petra spoke a little louder to stop him.

"How old was Lisa, Mr. Ramsey?"

His eyes rose, dropped to her knees, then back to her face. "*Was*," he said. "*Was* . . . I can't believe from now on it's always going to be *was* . . . she was twenty-seven, Detective . . ."

"Connor."

"Twenty-seven, Detective Connor. I met her four years ago at the Miss Entertainment pageant. I was MC'ing and she was Miss Ohio. She played sax and had a great voice. We dated for a while, lived together for a year, got married. Got divorced. First time for both of us . . . guess we needed practice . . . is there anything else? 'Cause this is . . ." He touched his neck. "I'm feeling lousy, I really need to be *alone*."

"Guys," said Balch. "Can we let Mr. Ramsey have some privacy?"

Ramsey continued to stroke his own neck. His color had faded, and his face had taken on a shell-shocked numbness.

Petra softened her voice. "I'm sorry, sir, I know this is stressful. But sometimes things that come up during periods of stress are really valuable, and I know you want us to find your wife's killer."

Saying wife, not ex-wife, to see if Ramsey would correct her.

He didn't, just nodded feebly.

Balch started to speak, but Petra broke in: "Any idea who she got her drugs from, Mr. Ramsey?"

"No. I don't want to make it sound like she was some kind of addict. She sniffed for fun, that's all. For all I know, she never bought, just borrowed."

"From who?"

"No idea. It wasn't my world." Ramsey sat up straight. "Getting dope in the industry is no big challenge. I'm sure I don't have to tell you folks that. Was there something about . . . what happened . . . that makes you suspect drugs?"

"No, sir. We're really starting from scratch."

Ramsey frowned and stood up suddenly. Balch did a Pete-Repeat, edging right next to the boss.

"Sorry, I've *really* got to rest. Just got back from a location trip to Tahoe, not much rest for two days, read scripts on the plane, then Greg had me signing papers, we both collapsed pretty early. Now this. Jesus."

Offering a detailed alibi without being asked, thought Petra. Fatigued but bright and bushy-tailed the next morning, playing *de golf.*

All four D's were listening actively. No one spoke. No one was allowed to probe too deeply.

Balch filled the silence. "It was a long couplea days. We both crashed like test dummies."

"You stayed here for the night, Mr. Balch?" said Petra, knowing she was treading on dangerous ground. She glanced at Stu. He gave her a tiny nod.

"Yup. I do it from time to time. Live in Rolling Hills Estates, don't like making the drive when I'm wiped out."

Ramsey's eyes were glazed. He stared at the floor.

Stu nodded again at Petra, and all four detectives stood up. Stu held out his card and Ramsey pocketed it without reading. Everyone headed toward the front door. Petra found Ramsey next to her. "So you'll call Lisa's folks, Detective?"

"Yes, sir." Even though Stu had made the offer.

"Dr. John Everett Boehlinger. Her mother's name is Vivian." He recited the number and waited as Petra stopped to copy it down. Balch and the other D's were several feet ahead, approaching the glass garage wall.

"Chagrin Falls, Ohio," she said.

"Funny name, isn't it? As if everyone regretted living there. Lisa sure did; she loved L.A."

Petra smiled. Ramsey smiled back.

Measuring her. But not as a cop. As a woman. The grieving ex-husband was giving her the once-over.

It wasn't a judgment she jumped to easily. She didn't view herself as God's gift to men, but she knew when she was being evaluated.

"L.A. was for Lisa," said Ramsey as they resumed walking. "She loved the energy level."

They made it to the glass. Petra extended her hand. "Thanks, sir. Sorry you have to go through this."

Ramsey took it, held it, squeezed. Dry and warm. "I still don't believe it happened. It's unreal—like a script." He bit his lip, shook his head, let go of her fingers. "I probably won't be able to sleep, but I guess I should try before the vultures swoop in."

"The media?"

"It's just a matter of time—you won't give out my address or number, will you?"

Before Petra could answer, he called out to Balch. "Tell the gatehouse no one gets close. Call them now."

"You bet." Balch hurried off.

Petra touched the glass, raised her eyebrows, made a show of staring at the cars.

Ramsey shrugged. For a middle-aged man, he did boyish pretty well. "You collect toys, then realize they don't mean much."

"Still," said Petra, "nothing wrong with having nice things."

Ramsey's blue eyes flickered. "Guess not."

"What year's the Ferrari?"

" 'Seventy-three," said Ramsey. "Daytona Spider. Used to be owned by an oil sheikh; I picked it up at auction. It needs to be tuned every week and an hour behind the wheel kills your back, but it's a work of art."

His voice had picked up enthusiasm. As if realizing it, he grimaced, shook his head again.

Trying to keep her voice light, Petra said, "What goes over there, in the empty slot?"

"My everyday wheels."

"The Lexus?"

He looked over at the entry hall where the three other D's had congregated. "No, that's Greg's car. Mine's a Mercedes—thanks for your kindness, Detective. And for calling Lisa's folks. Let me see you out."

＊

Both cop cars left the development and cruised down a quiet side road. Stu drove until houses gave way to fields, then motioned the sheriffs over to the side. When they got out, De la Torre was smoking.

"Gave himself an alibi," he said. "Here all night with old *Greg*. And all that shit about not knowing where he fit in."

"That," said Banks, "could have been trying to dissociate himself from it. Both for our sake and in his own mind."

Stu said, "Coulda been," and looked at Petra.

She said, "All that's interesting, and so is the way he brought up the subject of drugs, first thing. Then he gets all prissy and reluctant, protecting her reputation when *we* want to discuss it."

"I think he's dirty as hell," said De la Torre. "The alibi especially bugs the hell out of me. I mean your old lady gets sliced up, you're clean, cops show up to notify, do you feel a need to tell them you went to bed early the night of the murder?"

"I agree," said Petra. "Except here we've got a domestic-violence thing that's gone public in the post–O.J. era. He knows he'll come under scrutiny, has a reason to protect himself."

"Still," said De la Torre, "too damn cute. The guy does a crime show, probably thinks he knows all the angles." He grunted and smoked.

Petra thought of the way Ramsey had checked her out. Then sidled next to her. None of them had mentioned it. Should she? No point.

"I hate cop shows," said De la Torre. "Bastards catch all the bad guys by the third commercial and damage my self-esteem."

"He's not a cop on the show," said Banks. "He's a P.I., this macho do-gooder who protects people when the police can't."

"Even worse." De la Torre pulled his mustache.

"Lots of tears, but he turned pretty businesslike when he ordered Balch to call the guardhouse," Banks said. "The wife's not even cold and he's covering his rear with the media."

"Hey," said De la Torre, "he's a big fucking *star*." He blew smoke at the ground. "So . . . what can we do for you guys?"

"Check out local files, see if there've been any other domestic-violence calls—or anything else on him," said Stu. "But quietly, at this point. We can't afford even a hint that he's being investigated."

"So what was that, a condolence call with four D's?"

"You bet."

"He'll buy that?"

"Maybe. He's used to special treatment."

"Okay," said Banks. "We flip paper quietly. Anything else?"

"Not that I can think of," said Stu. "Open to suggestions, though."

"My *suggestion*," said De la Torre, "is we keep the hell outta your hair, go to church, and pray for you. Because this ain't gonna be any slam dunk."

Petra said, "Pray away. We'll take any help we can get."

Banks smiled at her. "I noticed you talking by the glass. He say what the fifth car was?"

Petra studied his eyes for a moment. "His daily wheels. A Mercedes."

"Think it's sponge-and-solvent time?"

"Could be," said Petra. "With all that blood, there'd be a good chance of transfer."

"What about shoe prints at the scene?"

"Nothing," said Stu. "He managed to avoid *stepping* in the blood."

"Meaning he stepped back. Or pushed her away. Either would mean he was prepared."

Stu thought about that, his lips compressed. "I'd like to warrant that Mercedes, all right, but we're not even close to that without evidence."

"What if the guy learned something from his show?" said De la Torre. "Some ultra-high-tech way to really zap something clean. These celebrities, there's always someone to clean up after them. Some walking-around guy, manager, agent, guesthouse bum, whatever—but hey, what am I moanin' about? It's your case. Good luck."

Handshakes all around, and the sheriffs were gone.

"They seem decent," said Petra.

They returned to the Ford. As Stu started it up, she said, "Did I go too far in terms of leaning on Ramsey?"

"Hope not."

"What'd you think about all those other hot rods?"

"Predictable. People in the industry are in an eternal quest for the Best."

He sounded angry.

"Think he's it?"

"Probably. I'll notify the family when we get back."

"I can do it," said Petra, suddenly craving contact with Lisa's family. Contact with *Lisa*.

"No, I don't mind." He began driving. His starched collar was tinged with grime and his blond beard was coming in like new straw. Neither of them had slept for over twenty-four hours. Petra felt fine.

"No sweat for me either, Stu. I'll call."

She expected an argument, but he sagged and said, "You're sure?"

"Absolutely."

"You did notification on Gonzales and Chouinard, and Chouinard was no party."

Dale Chouinard was a construction worker beaten to death outside a Cahuenga Boulevard tavern. Petra had informed his twenty-four-year-old widow that her four kids under six were orphans. Had thought she'd done okay, comforting the woman, holding her, letting her sob it out. Then, in the kitchen, Mrs. Chouinard went berserk, striking out at Petra, nearly clawing out an eye.

She said, "At least no one can slug me over the phone."

"I really don't mind doing it, Petra," he said.

But she knew he did. He'd told her, early in their partnership, that it was the part of the job he hated most. Maybe if she'd go the extra mile, he'd see her for the perfect partner she was and open up about what was bugging him.

"I'm doing it, pard. If it's okay with you, I'll talk to the maid, too."

"Lisa's?"

"I meant Ramsey's, if I can get her out of the house without being obvious about making Ramsey a suspect. But I can do Lisa's, too."

"Wait on Ramsey's," said Stu. "Too tricky." He pulled out his notebook and flipped pages. "Lisa's maid is Patricia . . . Kasempitakpong." He enunciated the unmanageable name very slowly. "Probably Thai. The blues are holding her, but if she asks to leave, they can't stop her from flying back to Bangkok. Or calling the *National Enquirer*."

"I'll go right after I call the family."

He gave her the Doheny Drive address.

She said, "Cooperative of the sheriffs, letting us lead with Ramsey."

"All the bad press both departments have been getting, maybe someone's finally getting smart."

"Maybe." Last month the sheriffs had been exposed for releasing several murderers through clerical error, giving county-jail prisoners gourmet food at taxpayer expense, and losing track of millions of dollars. Half a year before that, some deputies had been busted for off-duty armed robbery and a rookie had been found naked and dazed, roaming the hills near the Malibu substation.

Stu said, "The address reminds me—just a few blocks from Chasen's. Which they're tearing down in order to build a shopping center."

"Aw gee," said Petra. "No more celebrity dinners for us, pard."

"I actually got to go there once," he said. "Handled security for a wedding reception, big entertainment lawyer's daughter, major stars all over the place."

"I didn't know you did that kind of thing." *Also.*

"Years ago. Mostly it was a drag. That time, though, at Chasen's, was okay. They fed me. Chili, ribs, steak. Great place, class atmosphere. Reagan's favorite restaurant . . . all right, you'll take the Thai maid and notify the parents, I'll try to figure out a way of discreetly asking some industry types about Ramsey, run DMV on the Mercedes, check back with the coroner and the techs before I go home. If they come up with any good forensics, I'll let you know. So far so good?"

"I'll also call the phone company, pull Lisa's records."

"Good idea."

Basic procedure.

"Stu, if Ramsey is the guy, how can we touch him?"

No answer.

Petra said, "I guess what I'm saying is what's the chance of something like this improving the quality of our lives? And how do we do our best by Lisa?"

He fooled with his hair, straightened his rep tie.

"Just take it step by step," he finally said. "Do the best we can. Just like what I tell my kids about school."

"We're just kids on this one?"

"In a way."

# CHAPTER 11

THE MONKEYS ARE THE WORST SCREAMERS. IT'S only 6 A.M. and they're already complaining.

In four hours the zoo will open. I've been up here when it's full of people, heard mostly noise, but sometimes I catch words, like little kids, whining for something. *"Ice scream!"* *"Lions!"*

When people are in the zoo, the animals get quiet, but at night they really go at it—listen to those monkeys screech—and here's another one, deep, something heavy and tired, maybe a rhino. Like, *Let me out of here! We're stuck here 'cause of people; don't people suck?*

If they did ever get out, the carnivores would go straight for the herbivores, the slow ones, the weak ones, killing and eating them and picking at the bones.

About a month ago, I explored the barbed wire fence around the zoo, found a gate up on top, above Africa. A sign said ZOO PERSONNEL ONLY—GATE TO BE LOCKED AT ALL TIMES, and there was a lock on it but it was left open. I took it off, walked through, put it back, found myself in this parking lot full of little tan dune-buggy things the zoo people drive around in. Across the lot were some buildings that smelled like animal shit, with cement floors that had just been hosed down. On the other side were more thick plants and a pathway with another sign: AUTHORIZED ACCESS ONLY.

I made like I belonged and walked right into the zoo, climbed into the big walk-in birdcage with all the people, saw the little kids whining. Then I checked out the whole zoo. I had a pretty good time that day, studying and reading the signs that teach about their natural habitats and diets and endangered species. I saw a two-headed king snake in the reptile house. No one looked at me weird. For the first time in a long time I felt relaxed and normal.

I'd brought some of my money roll with me and bought a frozen banana and caramel corn and a Coke. I ate too fast and got a stomachache, but it didn't matter; it was like a clear patch of blue sky had opened up in my brain.

Maybe I'll try to get in today.

Maybe I shouldn't. I need to make sure I'm not an endangered species.

※

I can't stop thinking of that woman, what the guy did to her.

Horrible, horrible, the way he hugged her, *chuck chuck.* Why would anyone want to do that?

Why would God *allow* it?

My stomach starts to kill and I take five deep breaths to quiet it down.

Walking all night my feet didn't hurt too much, but now they do and my sneakers feel tight. I pull them off; also my socks. I must be growing; the shoes have been getting tighter for a while. They're old, the ones I came with, and the soles have thin spots, almost worn through.

I'll give my feet some air, wiggle my toes before I unroll my plastic.

Ahh . . . that feels good.

There's no water up in Five for bathing. Wouldn't it be cool to get into the zoo, jump in the sea lion tank and flip around? The sea lions, freaking out, not knowing what's going on—I have to control myself not to laugh out loud.

I stink from piss. I hate stinking, don't want to turn into one of those shopping-cart guys; you can smell them a block away.

I always loved to shower, but after Moron moved in, the hot water was always gone. Not because he used it. Mom wanted to smell good for him, so she started taking half an hour in the shower, then putting on perfume spray, the works.

Why would she want to impress him? Why would she want to be with *all* those losers?

I've spent a lot of time wondering about that and the only thing I keep coming back to is she doesn't like herself very much.

I *know* that's true, because when she breaks something or makes any kind of mistake, like cutting herself shaving her legs, she cusses herself out, calls herself names. I've heard her crying at night, drunk or stoned, calling herself names. Not so much since Moron moved in, because he threatens to smack her.

I used to go into the bedroom and sit next to her, touch her hair, say, "What's the matter, Mom?" But she always moved away from me and said, "Nothing, nothing," sounding angry, so I stopped trying.

Then one day I realized she was crying about *me*. About having me without planning to, trying to raise me, figuring she wasn't much good at it.

I was her sadness.

I thought about that for a long time, too, decided my best bet was to learn as much as possible so I could get a good career and be able to take care of myself and her. Also, maybe if she saw I was doing okay, she wouldn't feel like such a failure.

※

The sun is up all the way, hot and orange through the trees. I'm really tired, but there's no way I'm going to be able to sleep. Time to unroll the plastic.

I use plastic dry cleaning bags to wrap and carry things and to protect them from rain and dirt. Each sheet is printed with a warning that babies can suffocate in them and they're thin, easy to tear. But if you layer them three at a time, they're really strong and excellent for protection. Mostly I find them in the trash, keep them rolled up in all five Places, under rocks, my cave, wherever.

One good thing about Five is a tree: a huge eucalyptus tree with round, silver-blue leaves that smell like cough drops. I know it's a eucalyptus because that time in the zoo I went to the koala house and it was full of exactly the same species and they were labeled EUCALYPTUS POLYANTHEMUS: SILVER DOLLAR GUM. The sign said koalas ate eucalyptus polyanthemus, could live off them, and I wondered what it would be like if I got stuck up in Five with nothing to eat but trees. I asked a zoo girl, and she smiled and said she didn't know but she preferred hamburgers.

This particular tree has a trunk so thick I can barely reach around it, and branches droop down, touch the ground, keep going. Inside, it's like being in a silver-blue cloud, and hidden behind the branches, right next to the trunk is a big, flat gray rock. It looks heavier than it is and I can lift it and prop something underneath it to keep it partly open, the way you jack up a tire. It didn't take long to scoop out dirt and create a hiding hole. Once the rock's back down, it works like a trapdoor.

Lifting it now is a little harder, because my arms are sore from carrying my Place Two stuff all night, but I use one of my shoes to prop up the rock and pull out my Five stuff wrapped in plastic: two pairs of Calvin Klein underwear that I got last month at a Los Feliz yard sale, too big, with LARRY R. inked inside the waistband; after I soaked them in the Fern Dell stream, they came out gray but clean. A spare flashlight and two AA batteries; an unopened package of beef jerky that I took from a Pink Dot on Sunset. A half-gallon bottle of Coke and an unopened box of Honey Nut Cheerios that I bought the next day at the same market 'cause I felt bad about taking the jerky. Some old magazines I found behind someone's house on Argyle Street—*Westways, People, Reader's Digest*—and the old 1-percent-fat Knudsen milk carton that I use to keep pens and pencils, folders, rolled-up notebook paper, and other stuff in.

There's a boy's face on the carton, a black kid named Rudolfo Hawkins who was kidnapped five years ago. The picture is from when he was six years old, and it shows him wearing a white shirt and tie and smiling, like at a birthday party or some other special occasion.

It says he was kidnapped by his father in Compton, California, but could be in Scranton, Pennsylvania, or Detroit, Michigan. I used to look at the picture and wonder what happened to him. After five years he's probably okay . . . at least it was his father and not some pervert.

Maybe he's back in Compton with his mother.

I've thought about Mom looking for me, and can't get it straight in my head if she is.

When I was young—five, six—she used to tell me she loved me, we were some pair, just us against the fucking world. Then her drinking and doping got more intense and she paid less and less attention to me. Once Moron moved in, I became invisible.

So would she look for me?

Even if she wanted to, would she know how, not being educated?

Moron would be a problem. He'd say something like, "Fuck, the little prick split, Sharla. He didn't give a shit, fuck him— gimme those nachos."

But even without Moron, I can't get it straight how Mom would feel. Maybe she's sad I left, maybe angry.

Or maybe she's relieved. She never planned to have me. I guess she did the best with what she had.

I know she took good care of me in the beginning, because I've seen pictures of when I was a baby that she keeps in an envelope in a drawer in the kitchen and I look healthy and happy. We both do. They're from Christmas, there's a tree full of lights and she's holding me up like some trophy, with a great big smile on her face. Like, Hey, look what *I* got for Christmas.

My birthday's August tenth, so that would make me four and a half months old. I have a gross, fat face with pink cheeks and no hair. Mom is pale and skinny and she's got me dressed up in a stupid blue sailor suit. She's wearing the widest smile I've ever seen her wear, so some of her happiness must have been because of me, at least at the beginning.

Because her parents died in that car crash before I was born, what else would make her smile like that?

On the back of the photos are stickers that say GOOD SHEP-HERD SANCTUARY, MODESTO, CALIFORNIA. I asked her about it, and she said it was a Catholic place, and even though we're not Catholic, we lived there when I was a baby. When I tried to ask her more about it, she grabbed the pictures away and said it wasn't important.

That night she cried for a long time and I read my Jacques Cousteau book to block out the sound.

I must have made her happy back then.

Enough of this stupid stuff, time to unroll the Place Two plastic, here we go—toothbrush and Colgate gel, free samples I got out of someone's mailbox, no name on it, just RESIDENT, so it really didn't belong to anyone. Another pair of under-pants, out of a garbage can behind one of the huge houses at the foot of the park, a bunch of the ketchup and mustard and mayonnaise packets taken from restaurants. My books—

Only one book. Algebra.

Where's the presidents book from the library? Got to be somewhere inside the plastic; I used three layers . . . no, not here. Did it fall out when I unpacked?—no . . . did I drop it nearby?

I get up, look.

Nothing.

I backtrack for a while.

No presidents book.

I must have dropped it in the dark.

Oh no. Shit. I was planning to give it back one day.

Now I am a thief.

# CHAPTER 12

STU DROPPED PETRA OFF BEHIND THE STATION and drove off.

Back at her desk, she called Cleveland information for a backup work number for Dr. Boehlinger at Washington University Hospital. The home number was in the book, too. Maybe folks were more trusting in Chagrin Falls.

She dialed, got a woman's recorded voice.

The time difference made it afternoon in Ohio. Was Mrs. Boehlinger out shopping? Some surprise Petra would have for her. She visualized Lisa's mother shrieking, sobbing, maybe throwing up.

She remembered Ramsey's show of grief, the nearly dry eyes. Bad actor unable to produce copious tears?

The Boehlingers' tape machine beeped. Not the time to leave a message. She hung up and tried the hospital. Dr.

Boehlinger's office was closed, and a page produced no response.

Feeling no relief, only an ordeal postponed, she called the phone company and went through a couple of supervisors before finding a sympathetic voice. Lots of paperwork would be necessary for a full year's worth of Lisa's records, but the woman promised to fax over the latest bill when she found it. Petra thanked her, then she drove to Doheny Drive, ready for Lisa's maid, Patsy Whateverhernamewas.

Sunset was clogged and she took Cahuenga south to Beverly Boulevard and got a clearer sail. As she drove, she played one of her private games, composing a mental picture of the Thai maid: young, tiny, cute, barely able to speak English. Sitting in another cream-colored room, terrified of all the cops who were playing strong and silent, not telling her a thing.

The building on Doheny was ten stories tall and shaped like a boomerang. The lobby was small, four walls of gold-streaked mirror, some plants, and mock Louis XIV chairs guarded by a nervous-looking young Iranian in a blue blazer name-tagged A. RAMZISADEH, kept company by a uniform. Petra showed her badge and inspected the two closed-circuit TVs on the desk. Black-and-white long view of hallways, nothing moving, the picture shifting every few seconds.

The guard shook her hand limply. "Terrible. Poor Miss Boehlinger. It would never happen here."

Petra clucked sympathetically. "When's the last time you saw her, sir?"

"I think yesterday—she come home from work six P.M."

"Not today?"

"No, sorry."

"How'd she leave without your seeing her?"

"Each floor has two elevator. One to the front, one to the back. The back lead down to garage."

"Straight down to the garage?"

"Most people call down to have car brought around."

"But Ms. Boehlinger didn't."

"No, she always drive herself. Go straight to the garage."

Petra tapped one of the TV monitors. "Does the closed-circuit scan the garage?"

"Sure, look." Ramzisadeh indicated a slowly scanning black-

and-white view of parked cars. Murky spaces, glints of grille and bumper.

"There," he said.

"Do you keep tapes?"

"No, no tapes."

"So there'd be no way to know exactly when Ms. Boehlinger left?"

"No, Officer."

Petra walked to the elevator and the cop tagged along. "Big help, huh?" He pushed the button. "Up at the top. Ten-seventeen."

❊

The door to Lisa Ramsey's apartment was closed but unlocked, and when Petra walked in she saw the maid sitting on the edge of a couch. The physical similarity to Petra's mental image threw her so hard she almost lost her balance. Ten points on the ESP meter.

Patricia Kasempitakpong was five-one, tops, maybe a hundred pounds, with a pretty heart-shaped face under a thick mop of long, layered ebony hair. She wore a beige cotton knit top, blue jeans, and black flats. The sofa was as overstuffed as those in Cart Ramsey's house. But not cream—Petra's prophecy-fest ended there.

Lisa Ramsey's apartment was a study in color. Red and blue velvet couches with tasseled skirts, parquet floors stained black, a zebra-skin rug thrown across the wood. A real zebra rug; the animal's head pointed toward a black glass vase filled with yellow daffodils.

From what Petra could see, the apartment was small, the kitchen just a cubby of white lacquered wood and gray tile counters. The ceilings were low and flat. Basically the place was just another L.A. box. But the tenth-floor-corner location and sliding glass doors gave it fantastic views of the west side, all the way to the ocean. Beyond the door was a skimpy balcony. No furniture; no potted palms. A cigar of smog floated above the horizon.

Two uniforms were enjoying the view, and they turned to Petra just long enough to see her flash the badge. On the wall behind Patricia Kasemwhatever was a black metal shelving unit housing black stereo equipment and a twenty-five-inch TV.

No books.

Petra hadn't seen any in Ramsey's place, either. Nothing like common apathy as the basis for a relationship.

The hard-edged color scheme suggested that Lisa had tired of pastels. Or maybe she'd never liked them in the first place.

Had cream and pink been *Ramsey's* idea of tasteful? Interesting.

She smiled at Patricia, and Patricia just stared. Petra went over to her and sat down.

"Hi."

The maid was scared, but loosened up after a while. Fluent English; American-born. ("Don't even bother with my name; they call me Patsy K.") She'd only worked two months for Lisa, couldn't see how she could help.

A one-hour interview produced nothing juicy.

Lisa had never said why she'd left Ramsey, nor had the domestic-violence episode come up. She had mentioned once that he was too old for her, that marrying him had been a mistake. The maid slept in the spare bedroom, kept the place clean, ran errands. Lisa was a great boss, Lisa always paid on time, was neat and tidy herself. A "real neat person."

Patsy K. had no trouble crying.

On the subject of spousal support, the maid said Lisa received a monthly check from a firm called Player's Management.

"The card's there on the fridge." Petra retrieved it. Address on Ventura Boulevard in Studio City. Gregory Balch's name at the bottom: financial manager. Ramsey paying through his company.

"Any idea how much the checks were for?"

Patsy blushed, no doubt recalling an indiscreet peek.

"Anything you can tell us would be really helpful," said Petra.

"Seven thousand."

"A month?"

Nod.

Eighty-four thousand a year. Enough to pay the rent and some bills and have some fun, but not much of a dent in Ramsey's seven-figure income. Still, things like that chafed. Paying money to someone you resented, someone who'd humiliated you on national television.

It spelled tension, but was far from probable cause.

So Lisa had thought Ramsey too old for her. He'd alluded to a generational rift too. "Did Lisa and Mr. Ramsey talk on the phone?"

"Not that I ever saw."

"Is there anything else you can tell me, Patsy?"

The maid shook her head and began to cry again. The uniforms on the balcony were watching the sunset, didn't even bother to turn. "She was nice. Sometimes it was like we were more like friends—eating dinner together up here when she wasn't going out. I know how to cook Thai, and she liked it."

"Did Lisa go out a lot?"

"Sometimes two, three times a week, sometimes not for weeks."

"Where'd she go?"

"She never really said."

"No idea at all?"

"Movies, I guess. Screenings. She was a film editor."

"Who'd she work for?"

"Empty Nest Productions—they're over at Argent Studios in Culver City."

"When she went out, who was it with?"

"Guys, I guess, but since I've been here she never brought them up here."

"She went down to meet them?"

Patsy nodded, and Petra said, "But you assume they were guys."

"She was beautiful. Had been a beauty queen." Patsy eyed the officers out on the balcony.

"During the two months you worked here, none of her dates ever came up?"

"One guy came up, but I don't know if he was a date. She worked with him. I think his name was Darrell—a black guy."

"How many times did he come up?"

"Twice, I think. Maybe it was Darren."

"When was this?"

Patsy thought. "Maybe a month ago."

"Can you describe him?"

"Tall, light-skinned—for a black guy, I mean. Short hair, neat dresser."

"Facial hair?"

"No, I don't think so."

"How old?"

"I guess around forty."

Another older man. Patsy had a blank look in her eyes. The irony had eluded her.

Lisa searching for Dad?

"What was Lisa's work schedule?"

"She worked all hours," said Patsy. "Whenever they called her, she had to be ready."

"And Mr. Ramsey never showed up here."

"Not when I was here."

"And no phone calls."

"Lisa hardly spoke to anyone on the phone—she didn't like the phone, used to disconnect it so she could have peace and quiet."

"Okay," said Petra. "So your day off is Sunday?"

"Saturday night till Monday morning. When I got here at eight, Lisa was already gone. I thought maybe she got a night call. Then the officers showed up."

Patsy held herself tight and began to rock; coughed; gagged on her own saliva. Petra got her a Pellegrino water from the miniature white fridge. There were three more bottles in there, and fresh grapes, three cartons of nonfat raspberry yogurt, cottage cheese. Lean Cuisine in the freezer.

Patsy drank. When she put the bottle down, Petra said, "You've been very helpful. I appreciate it."

"Whatever . . . I still can't believe . . ." Patsy swiped at her eyes.

"Now I'm going to ask you something tough, but I have to. Was Lisa into drugs?"

"No—she—not that I saw." The Pellegrino bottle shook.

"Patsy, the first thing I'm going to do after we finish talking is search this apartment from top to bottom. If there's dope here, I'll find it. Personally, I don't care if Lisa used. I'm Homicide, not Narcotics. But drugs lead to violence, and Lisa was murdered very violently."

"It wasn't like that," said Patsy. "She wasn't a head. She used to sniff a little, but that was it."

"Any other drugs besides cocaine?"

"Just some grass." Downward glance. Meaning maybe Lisa had shared her cannabis with Patsy? Or the maid had pilfered?

"She hardly used anything," Patsy insisted. "It wasn't regular."

"How often?"

"I don't know—I never actually *saw* it, the coke."

"What about the grass?"

"Sometimes she'd smoke a joint while watching TV."

"Where'd she do the coke?"

"Always in her room. With the door closed."

"How often?"

"Not often—maybe once a week. Every two weeks. The only reason I know is I'd see powder on her dressing table. And sometimes she left a razor blade out and her nose was pink and she acted different."

"Different, how?"

"Up. Hyper. Nothing crazy, just a little hyper."

"Grumpy?"

Silence.

"Patsy?"

"Sometimes it made her a little moody." The tiny woman curled up. "But basically, she was great."

Petra softened her tone. "So once a week. In her room."

"She never did it in front of me. I'm not into *anything* like that." Patsy licked her lips.

"Any idea where she got her drugs from?"

"No way."

"She never said?"

"Never."

"And there were no drug transactions up here?"

"No way, never. I assumed at the studio."

"Why's that?"

"Because it's all over the industry. Everyone knows that."

"Did Lisa tell you that?"

"No," said Patsy. "You just hear about it. It's on TV all the time, right?"

"Okay," said Petra. "I'm going to look around now. Please wait a while longer."

She stood and looked toward the balcony. Beyond the railing, the sky was a strange, deep sapphire blue streaked with orange, and the two cops were transfixed. Suddenly, Petra heard traffic from Doheny. It had been there all along. She'd been wrapped up in work. Interview hypnosis.

She went into Patsy's bedroom first. A glorified closet, really, with a single bed, small oak dresser, and matching nightstand. Clothes from Target, the Gap, Old Navy. A portable TV sat on the dresser. Two books on cosmetology and an old copy of *People* in the nightstand drawer.

One bathroom, shared by both women, cramped, with black and white tiles, a black whirlpool tub. Petra learned from the medicine cabinet that Patsy K. had taken cortisone for a skin rash and that Lisa Ramsey suffered from periodic yeast infections, for which an antifungal had been prescribed. No birth control pills, though maybe they were in a drawer. The rest was all over-the-counter mundanity. She went into Lisa's bedroom.

Twice as big as Patsy's, but still far from generous. All in all, a tight little apartment. Maybe Lisa had wanted the refuge of simplicity after the pink hacienda.

The bed was queen-size, with a bright red satin throw and black linens. Black lacquer furniture, a black cross-country-ski machine tucked in the corner, perfume bottles—Gio and Poison—on the dresser. Bare walls. Very tidy, just as Patsy had said.

She found the dope in the bottom drawer of the bedroom dresser. White granules in a glassine envelope and another packet with three small, neatly rolled joints, tucked beneath ski sweaters and pants and other winter clothes. Still no birth control pills, no diaphragm. Maybe Lisa really had wanted peace and quiet.

She tagged and bagged the drugs, called over the cops from the balcony, showed them the cocaine, and asked them to get it over to Hollywood Evidence.

Atop the dresser was a jewelry box full of shiny things. Mostly costume pieces, along with two strings of cultured pearls. So Lisa had been wearing her best stuff last night. Hot date? Petra moved on to the lower drawers.

They bore Victoria's Secret lingerie—alluring but not trashy—a couple of sensible plaid flannel nightshirts, cotton and silk underwear, T-shirts and shorts, sweaters and vests, and three pairs of crisply laundered made-in-France blue jeans from Fred Segal on Melrose. The wall-length closet was full of Krizia and Versus and Armani Exchange pantsuits, dresses, and skirts and blouses, sizes 4 to 6.

Lots of black, some white, some red, a spot of beige, one

bright green jacquard wraparound that stood out like a parrot in a dead tree. Thirty pairs of shoes were lined up in three precise rows on the floor of the closet, toes out. The pumps were all Ferragamo, the casual stuff Kenneth Cole. Two pairs of white New Balance running shoes, one nearly brand-new.

In the nightstand drawer Petra found a Citibank checkbook, a Beverly Hills branch Home Savings passbook, and, tucked into the check register, the business card of a broker at Merrill Lynch in Westwood—Morad Ghadoomian—whose name and number she copied down.

Three thousand dollars in the checking account, twenty-three thou plus some change in the savings account, with two conspicuous monthly deposits: the seven thousand spousal support and another thirty-eight hundred—probably film-editing salary checks.

A pair of regular monthly withdrawals, too. Twenty-two hundred—that had to be rent—and twelve hundred, which Petra guessed was Patsy K.'s salary. Variable expenditures ranged from two to four thousand a month.

Over eleven thou in each month, five, six out, leaving a nice sum to play with for a single girl. Taxes on the salary were already withheld. Those on the spousal support would probably soak up some of the gravy, and coke and designer duds could consume a lot more. But given the fact that Lisa had managed to stash away twenty-three thousand, Petra was ready to believe her dope habit hadn't been monstrous.

Occasional hits at home. Maybe at work, too, supplied by pals from the industry.

In return for what?

Ramsey was the prime suspect, but there were plenty of blanks to fill.

※

She was finished by three-thirty; took down the name of a friend in Alhambra where Patsy K. would be staying, had the uniforms watch as the maid packed up her belongings.

The next two hours were spent going door to door on Lisa's floor and the two stories immediately above and below, and on the side streets that flanked the building. Of the few people home, no one had seen Lisa leave Sunday night or early Monday morning, nor had they spied the black Porsche.

Five-thirty; now she had to try the Boehlingers again.

Why hadn't she let Stu do it? Ms. Samaritan. He hadn't shown much gratitude.

The smartest thing to do was return to the Hollywood station and use a department phone for the notification call, but she just didn't feel like seeing the office again, and drove to her apartment on Detroit Avenue, just east of Park La Brea.

Once inside, she tossed her jacket on a chair and realized she craved a cool drink. But instead of indulging herself, she called the Boehlinger home. Evening in Cleveland now. Busy signal. She hoped someone else hadn't reached the family first.

Taking a can of root beer out of the fridge, she kicked off her shoes and sat drinking at the dinette table. Contemplating dinner, though she wasn't really hungry. Her father's voice, gently prodding, reverbed in her head. *Nutrition, Pet. Got to keep those amino acids nice and rich.*

He'd raised her since infancy, had a right to mother. When she thought about his cruel, rotting death, it hurt so bad. Quickly, she chased his picture from her mind, but the resulting blank space felt horrible, too.

Nutrition . . . force down a sandwich. Dry salami on stale ciabatta, mustard and mayo, something green—a kosher pickle, that qualified. There you go, Food Police.

Fixing a plate but not eating, she tried the Boehlingers a third time. Still busy. Could the story have hit the news that fast?

She switched on the TV, channel-surfed. Nothing. The radio, preset to KKGO, offered her someone's symphony while she nibbled the stiff sandwich.

Her own tight little apartment. Less than half the rent of Lisa's.

She and Nick had started out sharing a West L.A. flat, but right after the impulsive Vegas wedding, they'd leased a much bigger place. Up-and-down studio on Fountain near La Cienega, leaded windows, parquet floors, courtyard with fountain, gorgeous Spanish architecture. More than enough space for both their workspaces. Nick insisted he needed room to stretch, and claimed the master bedroom for his studio.

They'd never furnished—lived with boxes and crates, slept on a mattress in the smaller bedroom. Petra's easel and paints ended up downstairs in the breakfast room. Eastern exposure. She dealt with morning glare by drawing the blinds.

Now her easel was in the living room and she still had almost no furniture. Why bother; she was seldom here except to sleep, had no visitors.

The triplex she lived in was just south of Sixth Street, a charming old place with thick walls, high ceilings, crown moldings, waxed oak floors, moderate crime in the neighborhood. At eight hundred a month, a bargain, because the landlord, a Taiwanese immigrant named Mary Sun, was thrilled to have a cop tenant. Confided, "This city, all the blacks, very bad."

Museum Row was a short stroll, as were the galleries on La Brea, though Petra had yet to visit any of them.

When she had Sundays off, she scanned the papers for auctions, flea markets, antique shows, even garage sales, when they were in good neighborhoods.

Pickings were slim. Most people thought their garbage was treasure, and she was more of a browser than a buyer. But the few things she had bought were good.

Lovely iron headboard, probably French, with an impossible-to-fake patina. Two birch nightstands with floral stenciling and yellow marble tops. The old woman she'd bargained with had claimed they were English, but Petra knew they were Swedish.

A few old bottles on the ledge of the kitchen window; a bronze statue of a little boy with a small dog, also French.

And that was about it.

She got up and put her plate on the counter. The tile was clean but old and cracked in a few places. The kitchen at Fountain had featured a Euro range and blue granite counters.

Cold counters.

Nick had two ways of making love. Plan A was telling her how much he loved her, caressing her softly, sometimes too softly, but she never protested and eventually he got around to exerting the right pressure. Kissing her neck, her eyes, her fingertips as he kept up the romantic patter, how beautiful she was, how special, what a privilege it was to be inside her.

Plan B was hoisting her up on blue granite, hiking her skirt, sliding off her panties while managing to unzip himself, placing both hands on her shoulders, and plunging in like an enemy.

In the beginning, she'd been excited by both A and B.

Later, she lost her taste for B.

Later, all he wanted was B.

Suddenly, the remains of the salami and the bread and the mustard and the mayo looked like lab supplies. Pushing the plate away, she picked up the phone.

This time, a man with a cultured, middle-aged voice answered.

"Dr. Boehlinger."

Remote but calm. So they hadn't found out.

Petra's heart was racing; would telling the mother have been worse?

"Doctor, this is Detective Connor of the Los Angeles Police De—"

"Lisa."

"Sir?"

"It's Lisa, right?"

"I'm afraid so, Doctor. She—"

"Dead?"

"Unfortunately, Doc—"

"Dear God—goddamnit, *goddamnit,* that *bastard,* that goddamn bastard, that bastard!"

"Who, Doc—"

"Who else? *Him,* that piece of garbage she *married.* She *told* us if anything happened it would be him—oh God, my little girl! Oh *Jesus*! *No, no, no!*"

"I'm sorry—"

"I'll *kill* him. Oh Jesus, no, my little girl, my poor little girl!"

"Doctor," she said, but he kept on. Ranting and cursing and pledging vengeance in a voice that managed, eerily, to remain cultured.

Finally, he ran out of breath.

"Dr. Boeh—"

"My wife," he said, incredulously. "She's out tonight, goddamn Hospital Auxiliary meeting. Usually *I'm* the one who's out and *she's* in. I *knew* Lisa was worried about him, but how could it come to *this*!"

Then silence.

"Dr. Boehlinger."

No answer.

"Sir? Are you all right?"

More silence, then a very small, strangled *"What?"* and she knew he'd been crying, was trying to hide it.

"What?" he said.

"I know it's a horrible time, Doctor, but if we could talk for a—"

"Yes, yes, let's *talk.* At least until my wife comes home—then . . . Jesus . . . what time is it—ten-forty. Just got home myself. Saving fools' lives while my little—"

Petra nearly recoiled from the loud, terrible laugh on the other end. Needing to reel him in, she said, "Are you a surgeon, sir?"

"Emergency room surgeon. I run the ER at Washington U. Hospital. How did he do it?"

"Pardon?"

"How? *Method.* Did he strangle her? Usually husbands shoot or strangle their wives. Least that's what I've seen—*how the hell did he do it?*"

"She was stabbed, sir, but we don't know yet who—"

"Oh yes you do, Miss—I don't remember your name—you certainly do know, I'm *telling* you, so you know. It was him. Don't doubt it for a goddamn minute. Don't waste your time looking anywhere else, just haul in that piece of garbage and you'll have it solved."

"Sir—"

"Don't you *understand* what I'm telling you?" Boehlinger shouted. "He *beat* her—she called us and told us he beat her. A goddamn *actor.* One step above a *whore*! Too damn old for her, but when he *hit* her, that was the last straw!"

"What did Lisa tell you about the incident?"

*"The incident!"* he roared. "He went crazy over something and hauled off and hit her. She said it would be on TV, wanted us to know first. She said she was frightened of him—it's the same old story every week in the ER, but to have your own daughter—you said you were a detective, right? Miss . . ."

"Connor. Yes, sir, I am. And I know about domestic violence."

"Domestic violence," said Boehlinger. "More PC crap. All we do is rename things. It's wife beating! I've been married thirty-four years, never laid a finger on my wife! First he woos her like Prince Charming, then it all goes to hell in a hand-

basket and he's Mr. Hyde—she was *frightened* of him, Miss
Connor. Scared clean out of her mind. That's why she left him.
We begged her to come back to Ohio, not to stay in that psy-
chotic swamp of yours. But she didn't want to, loved the movies,
had her goddamn *career*! Now look where it got her—oh Jesus
God, my little baby girl, my baby my baby *my baby*!"


## CHAPTER 13


SHARLA STRAIGHT, QUEASY, STILL HALF STONED,
sat on the couch in the trailer's front room as Buell "Motor"
Moran ate cold beef stew out of the can and finished the last
beer. She was still sore. He'd been rough with her, doing her
from the back, clawing her buttocks. Her thoughts cleared partially and she pictured Billy's face.

Her sweet little— Motor grunted and destroyed her thoughts.

He liked doing it that way because he could stand, not put
weight on his hands or strain his back. The only benefit to her
was she didn't have to see his face.

Even from the back, he smelled. Like unwashed clothes.

Her whole *life* smelled like unwashed clothes.

Her head hurt; tequila wasn't good for her, specially the
cheap stuff Motor got at the Stop & Shop. Beer was better, beer
and weed the best of all because it made her feel far away from
things, but they were out of weed and he hogged all the beer.

He *was* a hog—one big mean, hairy pig, even bigger than
Daddy. Remembering his nails digging into her hips, knowing
they were black around the edges, she kept thinking: Dirty,
he's dirty, I'm dirty.

Did she have to end up like this, or was there some
other way?

She didn't know, she just didn't know.

The hot, dead haze that passed for air in the trailer felt smothering. The piece of cloth she'd nailed up to cover the small window over the bed had fallen half loose, but all she could see was a square of black. Everyone in the park was asleep, must be late—what time was it, anyway?

What time was it where Billy was? If he was somewhere and not—

Four months since that terrible day, and when she let it, the memory stuck her like a knife.

Worrying about him lying in some ditch.

Or cut up by some sicko.

Or run over by a truck on some lonely road. That small, skinny white body, so small, he'd always been so small, except when he was a baby and had that fat face . . . 'cause she nursed him, she didn't want to stop nursing him, even when nothing came out and her nipples bled, but the nuns made her stop, one of them, the tall one whose name she forgot ordering her, "Stop, girl. You'll have plenty of opportunity to sacrifice."

Billy gone. It had taken her almost two days to realize it was really true.

He wasn't there when she and Motor got home that night, but sometimes he took walks by himself, so she just fell asleep, not waking up till ten and then she figured he'd gone to school. When it got dark the next day, she knew something was wrong, but she was already stoned and couldn't move.

The next morning, no one to bring her instant coffee, she realized it had been *way* too long. Like a big knife, the panic cut through her and she started screaming silently to herself, Oh no, can't be—where, why, who, why?

She never said anything out loud, never showed the way she felt to Motor. To anyone.

That day, after Motor went out, she left the trailer for the first morning in maybe a month, the sun hurting her eyes, aware now that her dress was dirty and one of her shoes had a big hole in it.

Looking all around Watson; walking till her feet hurt.

A real hot day, plenty of birds out, people she never really looked at, cats and dogs and more people. She covered every field and grove, the stores, the Stop & Shop, the Sunnyside, even the school, because maybe he just spent the night somewhere and went to school by himself, even though that made no sense at all—why would he do that?

But lots of times things didn't make sense; she'd learned a long time ago not to wait for things to make sense.

So she kept walking, looking, checking it all out. Buying a Pepsi at the Stop along with a Payday bar, just to keep fueled; those peanuts were good energy.

Not asking anyone if they'd seen him, just looking, because she didn't want anyone to think she was that bad of a mother.

Not telling the sheriff, for sure, because he might get suspicious, go through the trailer, find the stash.

That night, she told Motor, and he said, Big deal. It was just a fucking runaway situation, happened all the time, hell, *he'd* run away when he was fifteen after beating the shit out of his old man, and hadn't she done it, too? Everyone ran. Finally the little shit had developed some balls.

But Billy, only twelve, looking younger, so small—that wasn't the same thing as her running or a big hog like Motor, no way.

The day she looked everywhere, no one asked what she was doing, where Billy was. Not the first day, the second, the third, never. Not once.

Four months now, still no questions. Not the school, the neighbors—for sure no friends, because Billy never had friends, probably her fault, because when he was little she was living all by herself out in that even worse trailer with some people she was still trying to forget about. Man, she'd been wasted; she didn't think anyone had hurt Billy.

He'd always been a quiet kid, even as a baby, so quiet, you'd never know he was even there . . .

Tears flowed from deep inside her head, flooding her closed eyelids, swelling them, and she had to open them a little to let the water out.

When she did, she was almost surprised to find herself back in the trailer, nothing changed, seeing the dim outlines of the kitchenette, Motor sitting there stuffing his face, dirty dishes, sour, more sour, everything sour.

*Where was her little man?*

The day after he disappeared, she had a nightmare of it being some dark, damp place, a torture chamber, some crazy person finding him walking in the groves, one of those guys you hear about, cruising near schools, other places, snatching kids, doing what they want with 'em, cutting 'em. She woke up shaking and sweating, her stomach burning like she'd swallowed fire.

Motor snored as she watched the sun lighten the cloth over the trailer window. Too afraid to move. Or think. Then thinking about the torture chamber and getting sick to her stomach.

Rushing to the john and throwing up, trying to do it quietly so as not to wake Motor.

Every night for a week she woke up sweating from the dreams, careful not to move or say anything to wake up Motor.

Sick with guilt and fear, the horrible person she was, the worst mother in the world, never shoulda been a mother, never shoulda been born *herself*, all she caused in the world was misery and sin, she deserved to be pronged from the back by a hog . . .

The nightmares went away when she found the Tampax money missing and knew what had happened.

Escape. A plan.

She'd saved that money for a long time, keeping it from Motor and all the others before him, her own stash.

For what?

Just in case.

In case what?

Nothing.

Better Billy should have it; let's face it, she'd never use it, didn't *deserve* to use it, the worst mother in the whole world.

Maybe not *the* worst—that crazy girl who drove those two babies into a lake, that was worse. And she'd seen on TV about some girl jumping off a building holding her baby. That was worse.

Some people burned their kids or beat 'em—she sure knew about that—but it didn't say much for her that the only worse thing she could compare herself to was stuff like that, did it?

The truth was, she was bad enough.

No wonder Billy'd had to escape.

No escape for her, she wasn't smart enough, good enough, just like Daddy had said: *Something missing,* tapping his head with one hand.

Trying to say she was stupid or crazy.

She wasn't, but . . .

She could think fine when she wasn't stoned.

Okay, reading was hard for her, so were numbers, but she could think, she knew she could think. She herself didn't understand the things she did sometimes, but she wasn't crazy. No way.

Better not to think . . . but where would Billy *escape* to?

So small and skinny.

No surprise there. Look where he'd come from.

Weird the way it had happened. Because she usually liked the big ones. Big like Daddy. Hogs, like Motor and others. Names and faces she'd forgotten—all those high school football players and wrestlers doing to her just what Daddy suspected they were doing, Daddy beating her ass even though he could never prove it.

She'd wanted to explain it to Daddy: *It ain't hotpants; it's the only chance to get close to people with goals.*

You didn't explain to Daddy.

Goals . . . it had been a long time since she'd thought about the future.

Too many years of sour notes.

Mixed in with one solitary sweet night, the prettiest little baby; those nuns had been grumpy but pretty good to her. She appreciated that, even though she knew they wanted her to give Billy up.

No way; what was hers, was hers.

She fed herself a little gumdrop memory of Billy's fat baby face—she deserved a little sugar, didn't she?

That night, the night of—

She'd been so much younger, prettier, skinnier, lying alone in the grove after midnight. Her choice to be alone—maybe that's where Billy got it from!

So maybe they were the same in at least *one* way!

She found herself smiling, remembering that night, how she'd actually *felt* something.

The warmth between her legs, all over her, the hard dirt didn't even hurt her back.

The orange trees green as bottle glass in the moonlight, snowy with flowers, because this was the blossom season, the whole grove smelling so creamy and sweet, a beautiful sky, dark with a halo of nice light overhead because the moon was big and fat and gold and dripping with light, like a butter-soaked pancake.

Lying there after he kissed her and said sorry, have to go, her skirt still up, floating.

Then a vibration—loud, close, as fast-moving clouds blocked out the moon.

Cicadas, millions of them, swarming through the grove.

She'd heard stories about them but had never seen them.

Never seen them since, either.

A onetime thing.

Maybe it had been a dream, that whole night a dream . . .

Huge bugs like that, should have been scary.

Twice as huge as the shiny black wood bees that freaked the hell out of her when they zoomed out of nowhere.

The cicadas were even noisier, so many of them, she should have been all froze up with fear.

But she wasn't. Just lay flat on her back, feeling sweet and female, one big package of pollen and honey, watching as the cicadas settled on row after row of orange tree, covering the entire grove, like bunches of gray-brown blanket.

What were they doing? Eating the flowers? Chewing away at the tiny green oranges, bitter and hard as wood?

But no, all at once they were all gone, zipping up into the sky and disappearing like some cartoon tornado, and the trees looked exactly the same.

Night of the cicadas.

Magic, almost like it had never happened.

But it had. She sure had the proof.

Where was *Billy*?

## CHAPTER 14

LISA, YOU COKE-SNORTING BITCH.

Dance with me and this is what happens.

Dance *around* me and this is what happens.

Oh, the joy.

Ode to joy—wasn't that Bach?

He hated Bach. In the hospital where they'd taken his mother when she had to wear a football helmet, they played Bach and other classical crap.

Trying to soothe the patients.

Patients. Inmates is what they really were.

Lisa had tried to drive him crazy.

Tried to lead.

Oh, the look on her face . . . dance with me, darling.

## CHAPTER 15

THE DOMESTIC-VIOLENCE TAPE PLAYED ON ALL the eleven o'clock news broadcasts: Lisa and Cart Ramsey, both smooth and tan, immersed in Jacuzzi bubbles, lining up putts on the home green, doing a Roy Rogers–Dale Evans number on sleek horses, smooching for the paparazzi. Lisa as a beauty queen and a gorgeous bride, cut frantically with close-ups of her post-beating face.

Then somber reporters intoning about the brutality of the dead woman's wounds, followed by the department spokesman, a photogenic Parker Center captain named Salmagundi, fielding questions without really answering them.

Petra watched it at her dinette table, hunched over another sandwich, feeling violated.

After getting off the phone with Dr. Boehlinger, she'd tried to paint: a desert landscape she'd been working on for months, swirls of sienna and umber highlighted with acra red, the faintest hints of lavender, nostalgic flashes of hikes with her dad. As she dabbed, she was certain it was working.

But when she stepped away from the canvas, she saw only mud, and when she tried to fix it, her strokes felt clumsy, as if her hands had suddenly seized up.

Washing her brushes, she turned off the TV and thought some more about Dr. Boehlinger, and the mother who had yet to come home.

What it was like to lose a child. A real child.

What it would be like to *have* a child. That opened up the gates of hell as she remembered what pregnancy felt like, the almost crushing sense of *importance*.

Suddenly she was crying, just gushing tears. Uncontrollably, except for one tiny corner of left hemisphere that watched and scolded: What the hell has gotten into you?

What, indeed?

She took several gasping breaths before she was able to stop, gave her eyes a brutal swipe with a paper napkin.

Lord, what a spectacle, disgustingly maudlin. Poor John Everett Boehlinger and his wife have lost a human being, and you go on like the thing you expelled from your womb was close to human.

A grape-size piece of pulp in bloody soup.

A mass of bloody *potential* floating in the toilet as she'd knelt and retched and cramped in agony, hating Nick enough to kill him for bringing it on.

Because he *had;* she was sure of it. The stress, the cold disapproval.

Walking out on her—exactly what he promised he'd never do. Because he'd been made to understand that she'd grown up without a mother, that her father was wasting away in a Tucson sanatorium, that being alone would be true hell. He must never, never walk out on her.

Maybe he'd been sincere when he promised.

A fertilized egg changed everything.

*I thought we agreed, Petra! We were using birth control, for God's sake!*

*Ninety percent effective isn't one hundred, honey.*

*So why didn't you use something more reliable?*

*I thought it was good enough—* Apologizing? Was she really apologizing?

*Great, Petra. Fuck around with our lives like that. You're an educated woman! How could you do anything so stupid?*

※

Bloody potential. Cramping so badly she felt she was being torn apart, she'd rested her cheek on the cold porcelain rim of the toilet, flushed, listened to it whirlpool away.

Alone, barely able to stand, she drove herself to the hospital. Tests, a D and C, more tests, three days in a semiprivate bed next to a woman who'd just birthed her fourth baby. Two boys, two girls, family members all around, cooing and ahing.

The postcard from Nick came two weeks later. Brilliant sunset over sand. Santa Fe. *Taking some time off to think.* She never saw him again.

The hole that opened in Petra's consciousness expanded, hollowing her, lowering her immunity. More cramps, fever, an infection, back to the hospital.

Outpatient follow-up. Feet in stirrups, too drained to feel demeaned.

Dr. Franklin's sad sympathy. *Let's talk in my office.* Charts and pictures.

Unable to focus any better than she had during all those mind-numbing boarding school health classes, she played dumb.

*What are you saying? I'm sterile?*

Franklin averted his eyes, dropped his glance to the floor. Just like suspects did when they were about to lie.

*No one can say that for sure, Petra. We have all sorts of procedures nowadays.*

She'd flushed away life, flushed her marriage.

Gravitated toward a career full of death. Using the grief of others as a constant reminder of how bad it could get, her situation was okay—right? In that sense, the more brutal the better. Bring on the bodies.

So why the hell was she *crying*? She hadn't cried in years.

This case? It had barely begun; she had no feel for the victim.

Then she heard Lisa's name and her aching eyes flew to the screen as the story flashed. Feeling stupid for being surprised—how could it be any other way? Now millions of people were viewing sixty seconds of tape that Stu and she hadn't been allowed to ask for.

Had Stu seen it? She knew he got to sleep as early as possible, especially when making up for lost nights. If he hadn't seen it, he'd want to know. She supposed.

She phoned his house in La Crescenta. Kathy Bishop answered, sounding subdued.

"Did I wake you? Sorry—"

"No, we're up, Petra. We just watched it, too. Here's Stu."

None of the usual small talk. Kathy usually liked to chat. Something different with both of them—a marital thing? No, couldn't be, the Bishops were poster children for marital solidity, don't disillusion me, Lord.

Stu came on. "Just got off the phone with Schoelkopf. Quote: 'We don't want another f-ing O.J. My office, eight A.M.' "

"Something to wake up for."

"Yeah. How'd the notification go?"

"Spoke to the father. He hates Ramsey's guts, is positive Ramsey did it."

"He back that up with anything?"

"The beating. And he says Lisa was scared of Ramsey."

"Scared of what?"

"He didn't say."

"Aha . . . okay, eight A.M."

"What do you think about the broadcast?"

Silence. "I guess it could help us. Make Ramsey a de facto suspect and get the brass worried about looking stupid if we *don't* press him a little."

"Good point," she said.

Silence.

"Okay, I won't keep you—just one more thing: Dr. Boeh-linger runs an ER, probably a take-charge kind of guy. I'm sure he and his wife will be coming out ASAP. He hates Ramsey. What if he decides to get proactive?"

"Hmm," he said, as if it were mildly interesting. Same way he'd reacted to the library book. Was she off her game? "Share it with the captain. He's such a sharing person."

※

Tuesday, 7:57 A.M.

Edmund Schoelkopf looked more Latin than Teutonic. A short, trim man in his early fifties, he had moist black eyes, thick, artificial-looking black hair combed back from a flat, shallow forehead, and delicate lips. His skin was the color of All-Bran. He wore knockoffs of Armani double-breasteds and aggressive ties; looked like a former cop who'd gone on to corporate security. But he'd spent every moment of his work life in LAPD and would probably never leave till mandatory retirement.

His office was unimpressive, the usual mix of city-issue and community donations. He let Stu and Petra right in.

"Coffee?" His bass voice was morning-thick, barely into the human register. On the walls behind him were the usual graphs and pin charts—tides of crime that could be surfed but never tamed.

The coffee smelled burnt. They were supposed to refuse it, and they did. Schoelkopf pushed back his desk chair and crossed his legs, tugging up knife-crease slacks.

"Tell me," he said, the basso corseted now.

Stu caught him up on the visit to Ramsey's house, and Petra summed up her talk with Patsy K., the search of the apartment and the door-to-door, the notification of Dr. Boehlinger. Presented that way, it sounded as if she'd done a lot more work than Stu. She had. He didn't seem to care; kept looking around. Schoelkopf seemed distracted, too, even when Petra talked about the discovery of Lisa's dope.

"The father blames it on Ramsey, sir," she said. "He really hates Ramsey's guts."

"Wouldn't you? So . . . you'll follow up with that black guy at the studio—Darrell."

"Right away. What if Dr. Boehlinger tries to get involved?"

Schoelkopf's black eyes fixed on the center of her forehead. "We'll deal with that if and when it occurs. Let's concentrate on getting some data. I know the lab's got all the stuff, but is there anything even remotely resembling physical evidence yet?"

Petra was about to shake her head when Stu said, "Petra found something interesting. A library book, hundred feet or so above the body. And there are some other indications someone could have been up there recently. There's a rock formation—"

"I've seen the crime-scene photos," said Schoelkopf. "What other indications?"

Petra's hands had tightened. She tried to catch Stu's eye, but he focused on the captain. *Something interesting?*

Schoelkopf said, "Tell me about the other indications, Barbie."

"Food wrappers," she said. "Like from a fast-food joint. Specks of ground beef, maybe tacos. And urine on one of the rocks—"

Schoelkopf said, "Someone eating and peeing and reading? What kind of library book?"

"Presidents of the United States."

That seemed to annoy him. "Checked out recently?"

"No, sir. Nine months ago."

"Oh, c'mon—that sounds like bullshit." He tossed coffee down his throat. The mug was steaming. It had to hurt. "What makes you think this person was up there recently?"

"The meat wasn't dried out, sir."

"A speck of meat?"

"A few specks. Ground beef."

"How long does it take for ground beef to dry out?"

"I don't know, sir."

"I don't either, but I'll bet it varies, depending on how much fat in the meat, temperature, humidity, who knows whatever the fuck else. What about the urine?"

"The crime techs thought it was—"

"It's a park," said Schoelkopf. "People come up there to eat and relax, maybe they take a leak when no one's watching— there are picnic tables not far from there, right?"

"Yes, but not right there, sir. These rocks—"

"Sometimes people don't bother going to the john—is there a john nearby?"

"Just past the picnic tables."

"People are lazy—okay, I can see you liking the food and

the pee, but the book tells me you're barking up the wrong tree. Because it was *dark*, Barbie. Why the hell would anyone be out there reading in the dark?"

"The person could have arrived earlier, stayed till after dark—"

"What, some intellectual with an interest in political science is reading about the presidents—God knows why, they're all scumbags—eats, takes a leak, and lays his head down on a rock and falls asleep and just happens to wake up to see the girl get sliced? Fine, so where is he, your witness?"

"We're not saying the book was even related to the food," she said. "It was found a ways up from the—"

"Hey," said Schoelkopf, "you want a gift from Santa Claus, fine. But for all we know it was *Ramsey* behind those rocks munching a burger and taking a leak—sitting in wait for her. She shows up, he jumps her."

"The way she was dressed, sir, she seemed to be out on a date."

"With who?"

"Maybe Ramsey. His everyday car, a Mercedes, was gone when we visited his house. If we're allowed to ask questions, maybe we can find out where it is."

Schoelkopf shot forward in his chair. "You don't think you're being *allowed*?"

Petra didn't answer.

Stu said, "We have been told to be careful."

"And what the fuck's wrong with that? Ever hear of Orenthal James Asshole? Remember what happens when people aren't careful?"

Silence.

Schoelkopf drank more coffee but remained slanted forward. "You'll proceed appropriately once the evidentiary basis has been established. Let's get back to your scenario, assume she was having some kind of date that ended in a meeting at the park. Ramsey, dope, or she's trysting with some married guy. Or cruising some fucking whips-and-chains club, who the hell knows. And let's say your *potential* witness *was* behind the rock. What kind of witness bunks out in the park at night and pees on rocks? Sees a brutal murder and doesn't call us. That sound like Joe Citizen?"

Petra said, "Maybe a homeless person—"

"Exactly," said Schoelkopf. "A lowlife, a mental case. No sane person—no *legit* person—would be out at night alone in Griffith Park. Meaning, we've got a bum or a wacko or even the bad guy himself. Hell, I'll go for a scumbag who reads about the presidents, but till you get me a lead, I'm not gonna authorize any media release for the info, because we are not going to look like idiots on this one."

"I wouldn't expect you to, sir," said Petra.

Schoelkopf stroked his upper lip. Had he ever worn a mustache? "Okay, so what you're telling me is we've got fuck-nothing. Run forensics on all of it—food, book, pee—but don't get sidetracked, because it's weak. And find the *vic's* goddamn car. Meanwhile, here's what I did for you in the real world: made sure the coroner assigned a *competent* pathologist and not one of those slicer-dicers. I asked Romanescu to personally supervise the post, and he agreed, but who the hell trusts him— he used to work for the Communists. Same for the crime techs: I've asked Yamada to oversee, we don't want mumblebums screwing everything up, another fucking travesty like you-know-who, and you better believe the media would love to turn it into one. They should have some prelims soon; keep in touch. What I'm saying is: Every bit of fiber and juice gets microanalyzed up the yin. Don't tell me ninety-nine percent of the time forensics is useless, I know it is, but we've got to cover all bases. Also, there were no defense wounds on the girl's hands, but that doesn't mean she offered no resistance at all, so let's pray for transfer, one damn molecule of body fluid with a story to tell."

He scratched a front tooth with a fingernail. "No cuts on Ramsey, huh?"

"Nothing visible," said Stu.

"Well," said Schoelkopf, "don't count on getting the guy to take his clothes off anytime soon." The black eyes dropped to the phone messages. "At least the race thing isn't an issue. So far."

"So far, sir?"

Picking up the empty mug, Schoelkopf looked into it, meditating. "This black guy, Darrell. Wouldn't that be lovely? What else do we know about him?"

"The maid said he worked with Lisa. And that he was older than her. Just like Ramsey."

"So she wants to fuck her dad. Write a Psych 101 essay." Schoelkopf put the mug down, stared at both of them, then avoided their eyes. "Next item: Ramsey called me last night at ten P.M.—himself, not some lawyer. The page operator wisely decided to put him through. First he pours on the grief, says anything he can do to help. Then he tells me about the domestic-violence thing. It's going to be on the news tonight—he wants to explain that it only happened once; he wasn't making excuses, but it was only once. He says the true story is she pushed him and he got pissed. He said it was the stupidest thing he ever did, he felt ashamed."

Schoelkopf waved a finger around and around. "Et-fucking-cetera."

"Covering his rear," said Stu. "He never mentioned the DV to us."

"He's a star," Petra half muttered. "Goes straight to the top."

Schoelkopf's color deepened. "Yeah, the bastard's obviously trying to finesse, calling with no legal shield. That tells me he thinks he's smarter than he is. So if we do get some physical evidence, maybe there'll be a way to wedge him open. Not that we'd be able to talk turkey without his getting a lawyer mouthpiece faster'n Michael Jackson gets new faces. But meanwhile we finesse, too. *That's* what I meant by context: no premature hassling; no getting accused of tunnel vision."

Petra said, "The news broadcast—"

"Gives you a good reason to talk to him about all sorts of things, but at the same time you need to do an exhaustive check of all similar homicides. I'm talking two years' worth—make it three. All city divisions. Keep *precise* written records."

Petra was stunned. This was scut work—hours . . . days of it. She looked at Stu.

He said, "How closely related are we talking about?"

"Start with girls cut up with multiple wounds," said Schoelkopf. "Girls killed in parks, blondes killed in parks, whatever, you're the D's. And make sure to check if any new slashers have been operating in noncity areas that border the park, like Burbank, Atwater. Maybe Glendale, Pasadena—yeah, definitely Glendale and Pasadena. La Canada, La Crescenta. Start with those."

Neither Stu nor Petra spoke.

"Don't give me that surly shit," said Schoelkopf. "This is

insurance for you. 'Yes, Mr. Pusswipe Defense Attorney, we looked into every goddamn nook and cranny before we busted Mr. Ramsey's ass.' *Think*—about your faces on *Court TV*, old Mark Fuhrman sitting around in Idaho. Because you're the ones on the line unless the case gets too big and we don't produce and they kick it over to downtown Robbery-fucking-Homicide."

"Which they could do anyway," said Stu.

Schoelkopf's grin was murderous. "Anything's possible, Ken. That's what makes this job so charming." He began thumbing through the phone messages.

"What's the procedure with Ramsey?" said Stu. "Do we wait to look into all those similars before approaching him, or are we allowed to start now?"

"*Allowed,* again? You two think this is being *imposed* on you?"

"Just trying to get the rules straight."

Schoelkopf looked up. "The only rule is be smart. Goddamn yes, you talk to Ramsey. If you *don't,* we'll be in a sling over *that.* Just do the other stuff, too. That's why God invented overtime."

He picked up a message slip and the phone, but Stu remained seated and Petra followed his cue.

Stu said, "In terms of Ramsey's background, I've got some sources at the studios—"

"I can see a problem there," said Schoelkopf, looking up. "Movie people are loose-lipped assholes. The fact that your sources blab to you means they're not real good at keeping their mouths shut, right?"

"That's true of any case—"

"This isn't any case."

"What's to stop them from talking to the press, anyway, Captain?" said Petra. "What if the tabloids start throwing around money and a real feeding frenzy develops? Do we keep bird-dogging the nightly news?"

Schoelkopf's top teeth gnashed his bottom lip. "Okay, pick one or two sources, Ken," he said, as if Petra hadn't spoken. "But know this: You *will* be graded. Talk to that black guy, see what he's all about. Sooner rather than later. Have a nice day."

# CHAPTER 16

◼

My eyes are closed, and I'm thinking when I feel it. Ants are crawling over me; they probably smelled the Honey Nuts. I jump to my feet and slap them off, stomp as many as I can. Someone watching me would think I'm crazy.

After what I saw, I don't feel great even being in the park, but what's my choice? For a second I imagine him finding me, chasing me, cornering me. He's got the knife, the same one, grabs me and stabs down. My heart jumps up to meet the blade.

Why would I think that?

It's 11:34 A.M., have to take my mind off it. I open the algebra book, do equations in my head. I'll try to eat—maybe a piece of beef jerky—and at 1:00 P.M., I'll go down to that place along the fence, see if the lock's still off.

◼

Made it. Super-quiet up in Africa. Five dollars in my pocket; the rest of my money's wrapped up and buried.

Hot—summer's coming early. Lots of sleepy animals, most of them hiding in their caves. Not a lot of people—some tourists, mostly Japanese, and young moms with babies in strollers. I've got a notebook with me and a pencil, to make it look like some kind of school assignment. My smell isn't too bad out in the open. No one's looking at me weird, and someone actually smiled—a couple of tourists—a man and a woman, Americans, old, kind of geeky, with lots of cameras and this zoo map they can't seem to figure out. I probably remind them of their grandson or something.

I keep going to the top of Africa. Most of the animals are sleeping, but I don't care, it feels good to walk without having

to. One rhino is out, but she just gives me a dirty look, so I head
for the gorillas.

When I get there, it's a scene.

Two of the young moms are there, freaking out; one of
them's brushing off her blouse and screaming, "Oh God, gross!"
and the other's wheeling her stroller backward fast. Then they
both race away toward North America.

I see why right away.

Shit. All over the ground near the fence that blocks off the
gorilla exhibit.

Five gorillas are out, four sitting around and scratching and
sleeping and one standing the way they do, bent over with his
hands almost reaching the ground. A girl. The males have
humongous heads and a silver stripe down their backs.

She starts walking around, stops to check out the other gorillas, scratches, walks some more. Then she bends and picks
up a giant piece of shit.

And throws it.

It misses my head, and lands on the ground right next to me,
exploding into nasty-smelling dust. Some of it gets on my
shoes. I try to kick it loose and another chunk flies by me. And
another.

"You idiot!" I hear myself scream. No one's around.

The gorilla folds her arms across her chest and just looks
at me and I swear she's smiling, like this is some terrific
gorilla joke.

Then she points at me. Then she picks up another hunk.

I get out of there. The whole world has gotten crazy.

※

I buy a lemonade from a vending machine and walk around
drinking, hoping all the shit dust comes off, because I'm really
tired of gross things.

Maybe I'll visit the reptile house; it's cool and shaded and
seeing another two-headed king snake would be cool.

On the way in, I meet those same two grandparent tourists
coming out and they smile again, still looking confused. I
cruise by the boas and the anaconda, adders and lizards, rattle-
snakes, vipers, and cobras. Spend some time looking at an
albino python, huge and fat, with pink-white scales and weird
red eyes.

Will its ugly pale face get into my dreams tonight?

That wouldn't be bad if I could get it to eat PLYR 1.

I stand there thinking of myself as the Snakemaster, communicating with reptiles through mental power. Calling the albino python to wrap itself around PLYR 1, crushing him, squeezing him like a juice orange.

Knowing what's happening to him. That's worse than just dying. Knowing.

A little while later, near the edge of the zoo, next to a playground that I guess they keep for little kids who get bored with the animals, is a vegetable patch with a rope around it.

Corn and beans and tomatoes and peppers. The sign says it's for the animals, so they'll have fresh food. I've seen chimps eating corn, so gorillas probably do, too, and that gets me thinking.

I also love corn, steamed sweet, but we never had it at home. Once, when I was in sixth grade, the school threw a Thanksgiving brunch out in the play yard—turkey and corn and sweet potatoes with marshmallows for anyone who paid. Everything piled high on long tables, moms in aprons spooning it out. I went into town to have a look, even though I had no money to buy anything. I hung around till the end, found a couple of loose quarters and played some ski-bowl, but lunch was out of the question—five dollars.

But one of the PTA ladies saw me looking at the corn and gave me a whole ear, daisy-yellow and shiny with butter, along with a turkey leg big enough for a family. I took it under a tree and ate, and that was the best Thanksgiving I ever had.

Now I move closer to the vegetable patch and look around. Clear.

Quickly, I hop over the rope, go straight to the corn, break off three ears, and stuff them in my pockets. They stick out, so I tuck them under my T-shirt, hop back over like nothing happened, and walk slowly till I find a bathroom.

I go into one of the stalls, close the door, sit on the toilet lid, and take out one of the corns, peeling off the leaves and that hairy stuff and wondering what it'll taste like raw.

It's pretty good. Hard, crunchy, not nearly as delicious as steamed corn with butter, but it does have a sweet corn taste. I eat two ears quickly, the third more slowly, chewing hard and getting every bit down while reading the cuss-word graffiti all over the walls. When I'm finished, I lick all the corn taste from the cobs, toss them into the corner of the stall, take a leak, and use the bathroom sink to wash my face and hands. Then I roll up my jeans and wash the sides of my legs, too.

My stomach hurts, but differently.

Too full. I pigged out.

Your lunch is now mine, gorilla.

Revenge is as sweet as corn!

# CHAPTER 17

WALKING BACK TO THE SQUAD ROOM, STU SAID, "He only beat her once. What a guy."

"Going over us, to Schoelkopf," said Petra. "Manipulative." Being collegial, then telling herself to hell with it. Say what was really on her mind.

She stopped and leaned against a locker. "Why'd you bring up the book?"

Stu leaned, too. "It was something tangible, and I didn't want one of his lectures on wishful thinking versus evidence."

"We got a lecture anyway."

He shrugged.

She said, "He thinks the book's bull. You agree with him, don't you?"

He straightened and, with one hand, pinched the knot of his tie. "Do I think it's thunder and lightning? No, but the lab will run prints on the book, and if it's a homeless guy, there's a chance he's got a file somewhere so maybe we can locate him. If it turns out to be nothing, we're no worse off."

She didn't answer.

He said, "What's the matter?"

"It threw me, your bringing it up like that."

"Hey, even I can be full of surprises." His eyes didn't yield. He walked away, not looking back to see if she'd followed.

Petra stood there, hands clenched. She recalled Kathy's curtness last night on the phone. If it was a marital thing, she couldn't expect him to let it ride. Okay, cool down, concentrate on the job. But she hated surprises.

❖

Of the twenty-five other Hollywood detectives on the morning roster, six were at their desks, sorting mug shots, typing at newly donated and still-baffling computers, muttering into phones, reading murder books. All looked up as Petra and Stu entered, and shot sympathetic looks.

Any detective who loved mysteries going into the job had a quick change of heart. The Ramsey case was the worse kind of whodunit. The room smelled exactly like what it was: a windowless space seasoned by mostly male frustration.

A black D-II named Wilson Fournier said, "Knew you were gonna have fun when the boss came in early chewing gum but with no gum in his mouth."

Petra smiled at him, and he resumed scanning gangbanger photos. Stu was at his desk facing hers, at the rear. She sat down and waited.

Stu said, "What do you want to do about looking for similars?"

"Not much."

He hooked his thumbs under his suspender straps. His 9mm was nestled in a high shoulder holster. Petra was wearing hers the same way. It hurt her arm, and she removed it.

"The way I see it," said Stu, "we've got two choices. Go over to Parker and pull microfiche all week, then we'd still have to get on the horn in order to check out Burbank and Atwater and Glendale or any county district. Or do it all telephonically with every homicide D we can find. Schoelkopf said two or three years; let's do two. We could get lucky and move through it within the week. Personally, I'd rather talk to real people than deal with the files downtown, but it's up to you."

"The realer the better," said Petra. "How do we prioritize? Do I call around first or try to reach this Darrell?"

"Let's devote mornings to the scut, do real work in the after-noon." He glanced at his watch. "You check out Darrell, and I'll start nosing around the studios."

Petra stared down the length of the room. "Speaking of real people, we can start with our colleagues here. It's a waste of time, but so's the rest of it."

"Charity begins at home. Go for it."

She stood up, pushed hair back from her face, cleared her throat dramatically. Three of the six detectives looked up.

"Gentlemen," she announced, and the remaining three stopped what they were doing.

"As you know, Detective Bishop and I have been assigned a fascinating case, one *so* fascinating that word has come from above to be extra thorough. In order to establish the proper *context*." Snickers. "Because we will—quote unquote—be graded."

Grim looks all around.

"Detective Bishop and I desire a good grade, and so we request your help in locating the unknown perpetrator of this nefarious crime—who, of course, is totally unknown and must be sought out with the utmost care so as not to prejudice the investigation."

Knowing smiles. She described the crime scene, Lisa's wounds, and said, "Any 187's within the last two years bear any resemblance?"

Head shakes.

A detective named Markus said, "Where was O.J. at the time?"

Laughter.

"Thank you, gentlemen." She sat down to light applause.

Stu was clapping, too. He looked fine now, the blue eyes warm again. Maybe he was just sleep-deprived.

"Six down," he said. "A few hundred to go—how about we divide up the districts on the vertical. I take east of here and you take west?"

There was lots more crime east of Hollywood—more detectives, more files. He was giving himself the lion's share of the scut. Feeling guilty? Petra said, "You've got all the studios; I've only got Darrell. I'll take east."

"No, it's okay," he said. "I told Kathy not to expect me

soon." He blinked rapidly, as if his eyes hurt, and picked up the phone.

A divorce after all this time? Petra wanted to reach out to him. She said, "Noon break before we go our separate ways? Musso and Frank?"

He hesitated. Then: "Sure, we deserve it." Starting to punch numbers, he stopped himself. "Someone should also call those sheriff's guys—De la Torre and Banks—find out if they learned anything about Lisa's DV complaint."

"The news broadcast said she never filed a formal complaint."

"There you go," said Stu. "The news broadcast always tells the truth."

※

She called Downtown Sheriff's Homicide and asked for Hector De la Torre or Detective Banks, not remembering—or knowing—the younger one's first name. Banks came on the line, greeting her with surprising warmth. "Thought you might call."

"Why's that?"

"Last night's news. Unfortunately, I've got nothing for you so far. Agoura substation has no previous complaints on file— not even the one she went public on—so it looks like she never called it in."

"Okay, thanks."

"My pleasure," he said, sounding nervous. "No messy interdepartmental competition here. Our guys beat your guys in boxing last month, so we're feeling secure . . . anyway, you have my sympathy. They replayed it on the news early this morning, too. Made the house look even fancier than it was. Nothing on his little car museum, though."

What a gabby guy.

"Just Jacuzzi bubbles and horses and golf."

"Interesting, isn't it?" said Banks. "People getting life handed to them on a platter and still manage to mess it up royal . . . anything else you need?"

"Actually," she said, suddenly inspired, "if you've got time, we've been directed to do a file search on similar homicides over a two-year period. Do you have easy access to county data?"

Banks laughed. "This is L.A.—nothing's easy. But sure, we've learned to walk without scraping our knuckles on the sidewalk. Similars? As in the unknown lurking perp? Why?"

"The brass is nervous."

"Oh. Sure, I'll check for you."

"Really appreciate it, Detective Banks."

"Ron."

"This is scut, Ron. Don't put your schedule out of joint."

"Do you have a direct number?"

She gave it to him, and he said, "By similar I'm assuming crime-scene layout, wound type and quantity, idiosyncrasies, victim characteristics. Anything unusual about the crime scene I should know about?"

"No," she said, feeling protective of her information. "Just your basic butchery."

"Okay, then. Get back to you if anything comes up. Either way."

"Thanks, Ron."

"Sure . . . um . . . listen, I know this kind of case there isn't going to give you much spare time, but if some does come up . . . I mean if you want to get together—maybe just for a cup of coffee . . . if I'm out of line, just say so."

Stumbling like a high school kid.

The warmth of his greeting made sense now.

He wasn't remotely her type—whatever that was. She could barely remember his face, had been concentrating on Ramsey's. Had he been wearing a wedding ring? He *had* mentioned taking his kids to the zoo.

At least he *had* kids. Didn't *hate* kids.

She must have taken too long, because he came back with "Listen, I'm sorry, didn't mean to—"

"No, no, that's fine," she heard herself saying. "Sure, when things ease up a bit. That would be fine."

God help her.

# CHAPTER 18

PARAGON STUDIOS TOOK UP THREE BLOCKS OF the north side of Melrose, east of Bronson, a confusion of faded tan towers and corrugated steel hangars, all surrounded by fifteen-foot walls, one of the last major film lots actually located in Hollywood.

The rococo front gates were open, and Stu Bishop, anxiety polluting his head, tried to look businesslike as he inched the unmarked Ford toward the guardhouse.

Two vans in front of him, one of them taking its time.

Petra had left the station before him, taking her personal car.

Petra trusted him a little less than she had yesterday.

Couldn't blame her, the way he'd tossed the library book thing at Schoelkopf without warning her. Impulsive. Had the noise in his life finally gotten too loud?

Truth was, he didn't think the book was worth a darn, had used Petra to fend off the captain. Schoelkopf had preached anyway.

All the preaching Stu had endured. Teachers, elders. *Father.* Easton Bishop, M.D., was never more at home than when declaring absolute truths to a mute audience of eight kids. Stu had avoided that kind of authoritarianism with his children, trusting them to learn by example, knowing Kathy was the main influence. Kathy . . . dear God.

Stu believed in a forgiving God, but he lived his own life as if the Lord were a harsh, unyielding perfectionist. It made him careful, a sin avoider. So why now, at this point in his life, was everything coming apart?

Stupid question.

The second van passed through and Stu drove right up. The guard, Ernie Robles, was someone he knew from his four weeks as a bit player ("nonspeaking squad room inhabitant, lots of typing and phoning") on *L.A. Cop*. Decent fellow, relaxed attitude, no police experience, just a rent-a-cop from way back.

He was scribbling on his clipboard as Stu stopped and let the Ford idle.

"Hey, how's it going, Detective Bishop! Beautiful day, huh?"

And it was. Warm and clear, the sky as blue as one of the matte-painting backdrops the film crews used to make L.A. look heavenly. Stu hadn't noticed.

He said, "Gorgeous, Ernie."

Robles picked up the clipboard. "Got a part? Where?"

"Where do you think?"

"The *Cop* lot? They're not filming."

"Nope, all wrapped for this year, but there's someone I've got to see—oh, by the way, here's something I picked up for you at the station."

He handed Robles what looked like a thin, glossy magazine. Bright yellow letters rimmed with red blared THE SEN-TINEL at the top. Below that was a high-quality photo of a nasty-looking black USP semiautomatic pistol with silencer and black-tipped brass bullets. Promo from Heckler & Koch; stacks of them left at each police station. Stu had thumbed through it at a red light. Features on Benelli shotguns, HK training, the PSG1—"a $10,000 rifle & worth it!" Stu appreciated what guns did but found them boring.

Robles was already thumbing through, looking at the pictures.

"Hot off the press, Ernie."

"Look at some of this stuff! Hey, man, thanks."

Stu drove through.

※

He parked and walked to the Element Productions complex, where he found Scott Wembley easily enough. The assistant director was stepping out of a low, unimpressive bungalow, long arms dangling, licking his lips.

Lunch hour. Wembley was alone, probably headed for the commissary.

Stu came up from behind him. "Hi, Scott."

Wembley turned and stopped and his long, pale face froze. "Stu. Hey."

Like most A.D.'s, Wembley was just a kid, a couple of years out of UC Berkeley with a fine arts degree, tolerating the low pay and long hours and abuse by those who mattered for the impressive-sounding title and the chance to make connections.

Like many kids, he lacked spine and judgment.

They shook hands. Wembley was wearing film-lot preppy: baggy Gap jeans and an oversized plaid button-down shirt that looked too warm for the weather and too expensive for his budget. A steel Rolex made Stu wonder even more.

The kid looked even thinner than last year, had a bony, somewhat androgynous face fit for a Calvin Klein ad. Pimples on his cheeks. That was new.

The palm Stu grasped was soft and cold and wet. Sweat beaded Wembley's unlined forehead. Too-warm shirt. Long-sleeved shirt, buttoned at the cuffs.

And, of course, the eyes. Those pupils. Poor Scotty hadn't learned a thing.

During Stu's month on the set, Wembley had tried to get next to him, asking questions incessantly, wanting to know what the streets were *really* like. Because he was doing a screenplay, like everyone else, even though his real dream was to be Scorsese—directors had all the control.

Stu had answered him patiently, finding the kid a touching combination of Gen-X bravado and utter ignorance.

Then, the last Friday of the shoot, after working hours, he'd stuck around to finish some paperwork, using an empty sound-stage as his office. Loud sighs brought him to a corner of the giant room, where he discovered Wembley huddled on the floor, half hidden by prop walls, a spike of heroin embedded in his arm.

The kid didn't hear him approach, had his eyes closed, veins popping like angel-hair pasta on his long, skinny arm. The needle was one of those cheap plastic disposable things.

Stu said, "Scott!" sharply, and the kid's eyes opened on a junkie's worst possible scenario. Yanking out the needle, Wembley tossed it to the ground, where it plunked and spotted the concrete with milky liquid.

"Oh man," said Stu.

Wembley burst into tears.

Moral conundrum.

In the end, Stu chose not to bust the kid, even though that was a clear violation of departmental regulations: "*Upon witnessing a felony . . .*"

Pretended to believe Wembley when the kid insisted it was his first time, he was just experimenting. Two other puncture marks on Wembley's arms proved otherwise, but both had the sooty look of old tracks, so at least the kid wasn't mainlining regularly—yet. Stu confiscated the dope kit he found in the pocket of Wembley's bomber jacket and tossed the works in a Dumpster on the lot—putting him in greater legal jeopardy than Wembley, but thank God the kid wasn't smart enough to know that.

He drove Wembley to Go-Ji's coffee shop on Hollywood Boulevard, plunked him down in a rear booth, and filled him full of strong, black coffee—technically, as much of a drug to Stu—then let the stupid kid glance around the putrid restaurant and see what advanced junkies looked like.

The load in the syringe must have been light, because Wembley was rattled and clear-eyed. Or maybe fear had out-adrenalized the opiate.

He ordered the kid a hamburger, forced him to eat while he delivered the requisite stern lecture. Soon, Wembley was mumbling sad biography—the horrors of growing up with affluent, multimarried Marin County parents who refused to set limits, post-college loneliness and alienation and fear of the future. Stu pretended to take it seriously, wondering if his own kids would be like that when they reached that age. By the end of an hour, Wembley was taking solemn vows of chastity, charity, and loyalty to the flag.

Stu drove him back to the studio. The kid looked ready to kiss him, almost girlishly grateful, and Stu wondered if he was gay, on top of everything else.

After that, Wembley avoided him on the set. It didn't matter. Wembley was in his debt big-time, and if the kid didn't drop out and move back home, he was someone Stu might be able to use one day.

And now the day had arrived. *Ta dum!*

"Good to see you, Scott."

"You too." The kid lied miserably. His mouth trembled and he sniffed. Red nose. Those eyes. Stupid little idiot.

"How've you been?"

"Great. What can I do for you, Detective?"

Stu put his arm around Wembley's bony shoulder. "Actually, quite a bit, Scott. Let's find somewhere to talk."

He ushered Wembley to a bench and said, "I need information on Cart Ramsey. Discreet information."

"All I know is what's been on the news."

"No rumors around the lot?"

"Why would there be?"

"Because no one gossips more than industry folk."

"Well, if there is gossip, I haven't heard it."

"You're telling me no one's said anything about Ramsey?"

Wembley chewed his cheeks. "Just . . . whatever everyone else is saying."

"Which is?"

"He did her."

"Why do they say that, Scott?"

"He beat her up, right? Maybe he wanted to get back together and she said no."

"That your theory or someone else's?"

"Everyone's. Isn't it yours?" said Wembley. "Otherwise, why would you be here?"

"Does Ramsey have any sort of reputation?"

Wembley snickered. "Not as an actor—no. I don't know shit about him. The whole thing doesn't interest me."

"Well," said Stu. "Now it does, Scott. It interests you a lot."

# CHAPTER 19

I HAD A PRETTY GOOD TIME TODAY, GETTING that corn and being left alone. I'll go back to Five, make some plans.

I head back toward the open fence, see someone waving.

The geeky grandparents. Standing right where the road curves off.

The old guy holds up his camera. They're both waving, and the woman calls out, "Young man? Could you help us for a second?"

I don't want to attract attention by running away or acting weird, so I go over to them.

"Hey, big fella," says the guy. What a dork. He's wearing a Dodgers T-shirt and shorts and socks and shoes and a light blue hat. His skin's pink and he has a big lumpy nose, like the guys at the Sunnyside.

His camera is huge, in a big black case full of buckles and snaps, and his wife's got one just like it.

"Sorry to bother you, my friend, but you seem like a nice guy," he says, giving me a smile full of yellow teeth.

"Thank you, sir."

"Polite," she says, smiling. "Not everyone we've met is polite. I'm sure he can do it, honey."

He clears his throat and taps his camera case. "This is a Nikon camera from Japan. My wife and I were wondering if you could do us a favor and take a picture of us, so we could have one together."

"Sure."

"Thanks a lot, son." He reaches into his shorts and takes out a dollar bill.

"You don't have to pay me," I say.

"No, dear, we insist," says the wife, and even though her

eyes are hidden behind sunglasses, something changes on her face—just for a second, her mouth turns down. Like she's sad. Full of pity. Like she knows I need the money.

I'm thinking, maybe if I look poor enough, she'll give me more, and I hunch over a little but all she does is pat my hand.

"Take it. Please."

I pocket the dollar.

"All righty," he says. "So now we've got a business deal." More teeth. "Okay, hon, where's the best spot?"

"Right where we were, the sun's perfect." She points and walks up the hill a bit, stamps her foot, and touches her own camera. Why they need two cameras is a good question, but I guess some people don't trust machines. Or their memory. They probably want to make sure they capture everything they see, maybe to show the grandkids.

She says, "Okay!" Kind of sings it out. She's short, skinny, wears a man's jacket over her Dodgers T-shirt and green pants.

He takes his camera out of his case and gives it to me and goes up next to her. It looks expensive, and I'm nervous holding it.

"Don't worry," she says. "It's simple, and you look like a smart young man."

I look at them through the viewfinder. They're too far away, so I come closer.

"It's preset, son," he says. "Just push the button."

I push. Nothing happens. I try again. Still nothing.

"What's the matter?" he says.

I shrug. "I pushed it."

She says, "Oh no, did it jam again?"

"Let me take a look," he says, coming down again. I give him the camera and he turns it around. "Uh-oh. Same problem."

"Oh, for Pete's sake," she says, stomping her foot. "I told you it was a good idea to bring mine along. When we get back home, first thing I'm doing is going straight back to that dealer and tell him to fix it right this time!"

He gives me an embarrassed smile, like he doesn't like her bossing him around.

She joins us, smelling of some kind of soap. He smells of onions.

"Sorry, sweetie, this will just take a minute," she says,

opening her camera case and taking out . . . something big and black but not a camera—it's a gun. I can't believe it, and all of a sudden she's jabbing it really hard into my belly button, and I can't breathe and she's pushing it there, like she's trying to force it right through me, and her other hand's around my neck squeezing hard. She didn't look that strong, but she's really strong, and he's holding me, too, pinning my arms to my sides.

They're on both sides of me, like they're my parents and the three of us are a family, only I can't breathe and they're hurting me and she's saying, "Now, just come with us, street trash, and don't make the wrong move or we'll kill you, we really will."

Smiling again. Not pity, something else—the same look that was all over Moron's face before he went for the tools.

They lead me toward the open fence. They know about it too—not a secret place! I'm so stupid!

Her face is like a mask, but he's breathing hard, excited, his mouth's open, his skin's pink as a pencil eraser, the onion smell's blowing on my face, and they're dragging me toward Five, and he's saying, "You're gonna get *done*, kid. Like you *never* been done."

## CHAPTER 20

PETRA STAYED AT HER DESK, CALLING HER PHONE company contact about Lisa's records and being assured they'd arrive today. She began the preliminary paperwork on the court order for the extended records, phoned the coroner and the criminalists. No medical findings yet, no prints retrieved from Lisa's clothes or body or jewelry. Maybe a glove, the tech opined. Fortified by vending-machine coffee, Petra checked all the approved police tow yards and consulted rosters of found autos. Lisa's Porsche wasn't listed.

Time to go back on Schoelkopf's scut line. She'd already talked to dozens of detectives, covering the day watch from Van Nuys to Devonshire, then West L.A. Now she started in on Pacific.

Each time the same reaction: *You've got to be kidding.*

Everyone knew who the bad guy was on this one. But they also understood brass-generated busywork, and after the laughter died down, she had their immediate sympathy.

The end result: no similars. Meanwhile, Cart Ramsey got to hit golf balls, soak in the hot tub, enjoy the chrome and polish of his little car museum while his ex-wife was laid out on the coroner's table getting her face peeled off.

The Mercedes was probably scrubbed and steamed and vacuumed cleaner than an operating room.

She thought about Lisa's body, that gaping blood-filled hole in the abdomen, protruding entrails, what had been done to the young woman's face, and wondered what it took to turn love to *that.*

Could it happen anytime passions ran high, or did the guy have to be twisted?

Domestic bliss, domestic blood. There'd been one moment—an eye-blink instant—when she'd been capable of murder.

Why was she thinking about the past?

Deal with it, kid.

She tortured herself with memories.

A twenty-five-year-old art student pretending cool but so blindly, dumbly in love she'd have been willing to shed her skin for Nick. That rush of feeling, passion like she'd never felt before. Lovemaking till she couldn't walk. Postcoital pillow talk, lying flank to flank, her vagina still humming.

Nick had seemed such a good listener. It was only later she figured out it was phony. He kept quiet because he refused to give her anything of himself.

She told him everything: growing up motherless, the irrational guilt she felt about causing her mother's death, driving her father crazy to the point where boarding schools were the only solution, half of her adolescence spent in musty shared rooms, the other girls giggling and smoking, talking about guys, sometimes masturbating, Petra could tell by the rustle of comforters.

Petra, the weird, silent girl from Arizona, just lying there, thinking about killing her mother.

She'd entrusted Nick with the secret because this was true love.

Then one night she told him a new secret: Guess what, honey? Patting her tummy.

She'd expected surprise, maybe some initial resentment, knew he'd melt eventually because he loved her.

His eyes froze and he turned white. The fury. Glaring at her across the dinner table with contempt she'd never imagined. The special meal she'd prepared just sitting there, his favorites—ostensibly to celebrate, but maybe deep down she'd known he wouldn't be pleased, maybe the veal and the gnocchi, the twenty-dollar Chianti classico, had been nothing more than bribes.

He just sat there, not moving, not talking, those thin lips she'd once thought aristocratic so bloodless, the hateful mouth of an old, nasty man.

*Nick—*

*How could you, Petra!*

*Nick, honey—*

*You, of all people! How could you be so stupid—you know what childbirth does!*

*Nick—*

*Fuck you!*

If she'd had a gun then . . .

She opened her eyes, realized for the first time that they'd been closed. Squad room noise blew back at her, the other detectives busy doing their jobs.

What she needed to do.

She got back on the phone, prepared to waste more time.

But four Pacific detectives later, something *did* come up.

A three-year-old unsolved cutting of a pretty blond girl on the southern tip of Venice, near the marina, handled by a D-II named Phil Sorensen, who said, "You know, when I heard about the Ramsey girl, it struck me, but ours was a German girl, Lufthansa stewardess on vacation, and our leads pointed to an Austrian boyfriend, baggage handler, returned to Europe before we could talk to him. We put wants out with the Austrian police, Interpol, all that good stuff, never found him."

"What made him a suspect?" said Petra.

"The girlfriend the vic was traveling with—another stew—said he showed up unannounced at their hotel all upset because the vic—Ilse Eggermann's her name—had left Vienna without telling him. Ilse told the friend they'd fought a lot, the boyfriend had a bad temper, roughed her up, she dumped him. The last straw was having to work in first class with a black eye. Still, when the boyfriend showed up in L.A., he was able to convince her to go out with him. They left at nine P.M. She was found at four A.M., body dumped in a parking lot near Ballona Creek. We traced the boyfriend's flight—he'd come in on Lufthansa the previous morning, employee discount. No checked-in luggage, and he never registered at any hotels or motels here in L.A."

"So he intended it to be a short trip," said Petra. "Accomplished what he wanted and split."

"That's what it looked like." Sorensen sounded like an older man. Gentle voice, slow talker, slightly hesitant. *Stew,* not flight attendant.

"How was Ilse dressed when you found her?" said Petra.

"A nice dress, dark—blue or black. Black, I think. Very pretty girl; she looked very nice. Considering." Sorensen coughed. "No sexual assault. We didn't need to sherlock to establish her being with the boyfriend—Karlheinz Lauch—that night. The waiter who served them dinner, Antoine's on the pier at Redondo Beach, he remembered them, because they didn't eat or talk much. Or tip. We figured Lauch was angling for reconciliation, it didn't work, he got upset, drove her somewhere, killed her, and dumped her. What he drove, I don't know, because we could never trace a rental car and he had no known associates in California."

Sorensen's voice had risen a bit. Lots of details at his fingertips for a three-year-old crime. This one had stayed with him.

"She was found at four," said Petra. "Any idea when she was killed?"

"The guesstimate was two, two-thirty."

Early morning, just like Lisa. Dumped in a parking lot. And the Ballona Creek marshlands were a county park, like Griffith. "Lots of stab wounds?"

"Twenty-nine—clear overkill, which would also fit the

boyfriend. Add the domestic-violence history, and it seemed pretty clear. Sound at all like yours?"

"There are definite points of similarity, Detective Sorensen," said Petra, keeping her voice steady. Looked at a certain way, it was a damn Xerox.

"Well, you know these guys," he said. "The woman-haters. Tend to fall into patterns."

"True," she said. "Where did this Lauch handle baggage?"

"Vienna airport, but he had family in Germany. After the crime, he didn't return to work or to his hometown. We checked with other airlines too, but no dice. He could have changed his name or just rabbited to some other country. Would have been nice to go over there and nose around personally, but you know the chance of prying a European trip out of the budget. So we had to rely on the Austrian police and the Germans, and they weren't all that interested, because the crime took place here."

"If Lauch is working baggage under another name, he's eligible for an employee discount," said Petra. "Maybe he's still flying back and forth."

"And ended up in L.A. again and did a repeat?"

"I sure hope not, Phil, but with what you've told me, it looks like we're going to have to check him out all over again. Could you please fax me his data?"

"Give me an hour," said Sorensen. "Wouldn't that be something, the guy having that kind of nerve. Of course, first you'd have to establish Lauch was here when the Ramsey girl was killed, then you'd have to connect him with her—meanwhile, you've got DV on the husband. Sounds like fun."

"Big fun. Thanks for your help, Phil."

"Hey," he said, "if by some miracle it ends up helping you, it'll help me, too. It always bothered me, not being able to close that one. She was a nice-looking girl, and he turned her into something horrible."

It was 1 P.M., time to start looking for Darrell/Darren the film editor, but now she wanted to wait around until Karlheinz Lauch's data came through the fax.

The Ilse Eggermann news was a surprise, but Sorensen was right: The points of similarity could be explained by domestic-violence patterns, the same old tragedies, all the way back to Othello.

Or statistical fluke—seek and ye shall find something. Over a three-year-period, L.A. saw well over three thousand homicides. One similar in all that time wasn't the stuff of the *Guinness Book*.

Meanwhile, she'd reach the rest of the Pacific detectives, do follow-up on some Valley D's she'd missed the first time around, maybe pay another telephonic condolence call to Lisa's family in Chagrin Falls, see if Mrs. Boehlinger was available, find out when the parents were coming out to see what was left of their daughter.

Did Mrs. B. feel as strongly about Ramsey as her husband?

Petra sorted out her own feelings about the guy: providing an alibi right off, letting them know about Lisa's drug problems, going over their heads to Schoelkopf. The subtle Don Juan stuff he'd thrown her way.

It smelled of ego, real narcissism. Did that make him someone who'd go berserk if a woman angered or rejected him?

Hard to say, but in her mind, Ramsey had done nothing to dispel suspicion. Despite Ilse Eggermann, the actor was clearly the main man.

She played out a scenario in her head: Lisa, like Ilse Eggermann—like so many battered women—had somehow allowed her ex to talk her into a date. Renewal of old passions, or maybe Ramsey'd tossed her the ultimate female bait: the chance to talk things out.

Because once upon a time there'd been chemistry between them, and chemicals didn't disappear, they just faded. Because memories could be selective, and women kept hoping men would change.

A date . . . where? Not at a restaurant—somewhere private. Romantic. Secluded.

Not the Calabasas house, too risky. Even if Greg Balch was lying for his boss, someone else could have taken note—the guard, a neighbor. The maid.

Petra remembered how squirrelly Estrella Flores had been. Definitely worth a recontact, but how to do it without alerting Ramsey? And something basic needed to be added to the list: talk to the night-shift guard at RanchHaven. A glaring omission. The hands-off policy was really mucking things up.

So many things to do . . . she returned to her last-date melo-drama. Where would Ramsey have taken Lisa?

Did he have another home, a weekend hideaway? Didn't actors always have weekend places?

The beach? The mountains? Arrowhead, Big Bear? Or up north—Santa Barbara, Santa Ynez. Lots of industry folks had gotten into the ranch thing . . .

The beach would probably be Malibu. Waves crashing, smooth sand, what could be more romantic?

She made a note to search records for every real estate parcel Ramsey owned.

Go with the beach, for the moment. She pictured it: Ramsey and Lisa on an overstuffed sofa in some wood-and-glass thing on the sand. The three c's: champagne, caviar, coke. Maybe a nicely hissing fireplace. Ramsey turning on the charm.

Lisa responding? That sexy little black dress riding up on her thighs? Chemistry . . . helped along by fish eggs, Moët & Chandon, and Medellín's finest? Or another kind of incentive: money. Lisa had a job, but Ramsey still provided the bulk of her income.

The purchase of love? Same old story? Petra felt sad, then reminded herself not to judge. If her own phone rang on a par-ticularly lonely and/or horny night and it was Nick on the other end, saying, "Hey, Pet," what would *she* do?

Hang up on the selfish fuck and wish she could make his ears bleed.

Back to Malibu. Tides crashing, tender reminiscence, the nudge toward intimacy.

Ramsey makes his move.

But Lisa changes her mind, resists, shuts him down.

Ramsey seethes, feels like slugging her. But remembering the way she went public, he keeps his rage to himself.

Stays cool, drives her home.

Malibu to Doheny Drive Hills would mean Pacific Coast Highway to Sunset or the freeway through the Valley, then down one of the canyons. But instead of hooking south, he continues east, maybe Laurel Canyon down Hollywood Boule-vard, up Western to Los Feliz, then over to Griffith Park.

That hour, not much traffic. He drives to the parking lot. Lisa knows something's wrong, tries to escape.

He holds out for one last embrace.

Then a steel kiss.

No sexual assault, because he'd had a blood orgasm.

It felt right to Petra.

It also depended on Gregory Balch lying straight-facedly about Ramsey's alibi.

She'd have to learn more about Balch, too. Eventually.

Along with Ilse Eggermann and Karlheinz Lauch. A similar—unbelievable. She imagined Schoelkopf's grin, the disgusted look on Stu's face. When she'd left, he hadn't looked up, just muttered a halfhearted good-bye.

The library-book thing, so out of the blue. Stu was compulsive, mega-organized. Maybe it wasn't his marriage; maybe it was career anxiety—the chance to apply for lieutenant suddenly coming up and he found himself stuck with a big-time loser whodunit? For Petra, just another case. For him, do or die?

Would he bail on her? Sacrifice her if he needed to?

For eight months, they'd ridden together, eaten together, worked side by side, Stu spending as much time with her as he did with Kathy, sometimes more, and he'd never laid a hand on her, never made a suggestive comment, not even the slightest hint of double entendre.

She'd thought she knew him, but eight months wasn't very long, was it?

She and Nick had been together over two years. About the same as Lisa and Ramsey.

Men and women . . .

Once, when she was fifteen, home for summer vacation, she'd woken up at 1 A.M. on a long night in Arizona, hearing imaginary things, finally realizing it was the hot desert wind scraping the side of the house. Itchy, jumpy, she'd walked out to the hallway, spied the familiar splinter of light under the door of her father's office, knocked, entered the tiny, dim, detritus-clogged room.

Dad was sitting low in his oak chair facing his Royal manual, blank sheet in the roller. He saw her, gave a slack smile, and when she came closer, she smelled the Scotch on his breath, saw the dullness in his eyes, and took advantage of it as only a teenager can. Getting him to talk about what he hated talking about—the woman who'd died birthing her.

Aware that it would cause him pain, but damnit, she had a right to know!

And talk he did, in a low, slurred voice.

Anecdotes, remembrances, how gawky Kenneth Connor and gorgeous Maureen McIlwaine had met on the Long Island Ferry and found true love. The same old stories, but she thirsted for them, could never get enough.

That night she sat at his feet on the warped hardwood floor, motionless, silent, afraid any distraction would cause him to stop.

Finally, he did grow quiet, staring down at her, then slapping his hands over his face and holding them there.

"Daddy—"

The hands dropped into his lap. He looked so sad. "That's all I remember, sweetheart. Mother was a wonderful woman, but . . ."

Then he began crying, and had to hide from her again.

Men hid when they cried.

Petra came over and hugged his broad, bony shoulders. "Oh, Daddy, I'm so—"

"She *was* wonderful, baby. One in a million, but it wasn't perfect, Pet. It was no storybook situation."

He opened a desk drawer and peered down at what had to be the bottle.

When he turned back to Petra, his eyes were dry and he was smiling, but it wasn't any of the smiles Petra knew—not the warm, protective one or the wry, sarcastic one or even the soft-around-the-edges drunk one that used to bother her but no longer did.

This was different—flat, hollow, frozen as statuary. In her tenth grade English class they had learned about tragedy, and she was sure this was it.

Defeated, that smile. As terrifying as a glimpse of eternity.

"Daddy . . ."

He scratched his scalp, shook his head, hiked a droopy sock up a pale ankle. "The thing is, Pet, no matter what . . . I guess what I'm saying, sweetheart, is men and women are really two separate species. Maybe that's the anthropology talking, but it's no less true. One little scrap of DNA separates us—here's something funny: The X chromosome's really the one that counts, Petra. The Y doesn't seem to do much but cause problems—aggression—understand what I'm getting at, sweetheart? We men aren't really worth that much."

"Oh, Daddy—"

"Mom and I had our problems. Most were my fault. You need to know that so you don't romanticize things, expect too much out of . . . demand too much from yourself. Understand, baby? Am I making sense here?"

Taking hold of her shoulders, the light in his eyes almost maniacal.

"You are, Daddy. Yes."

He let go. Now the smile was okay. Human.

"The point is, Petra, there are big questions out there, cosmic questions that have nothing to do with stars and galaxies."

Waited for her response. She didn't know what to say and he went on:

"Questions like, can men and women ever really know each other or is it always going to be one stupid, clumsy dance around the interpersonal ballroom?"

He flinched, suppressed a belch, sprang up, went into his bedroom, and closed the door, and she could hear the latch turn and knew he'd locked himself in.

The next morning her brother Glenn, the only one still living at home, got to the breakfast table first and said, "What's with Dad?"

"What do you mean?"

"He's gone, went out on a field trip, must have been before sunrise. Left me this." Waving a piece of notebook paper that said, *Out to the desert, kids.*

"Just one of his bone hunts," said Petra.

Glenn said, "Well, he took his camping stuff—that means a long one. Did he mention anything to you? 'Cause yesterday we were talking about going over to the Big Five and getting some hockey stuff."

"Actually, he did," she lied.

"Great," said Glenn. "That's just great. He tells *you* but never mentions it to me."

"I'm sure he meant to, Glenn."

"Yeah, right, great—fuck, I really need a new *stick.* Do you have any money I can borrow?"

※

She phoned seven more detectives, endured seven more you've-got-to-be-kiddings, no more similars.

From the far end of the room, the fax machine started humming and she jumped up and was there in a second, snatching papers out of the bin. Moving so quickly, a couple of the other D's looked up. But not for long; they were busy, too. This room, this city—the blood never stopped.

Karlheinz Lauch was big—six-foot-four—and ugly. Small, dark, squinty eyes popped like raisins in a pasty, misshapen crêpe of a face. The merest comma of a lopsided mouth, a mustache that looked like a grease squirt. Straight, fair hair—the stats called it brown, so probably dishwater—styled in that modified shag some Europeans still wore.

To Petra, he appeared a grubby loser.

The photo was from a four-year-old Vienna mug shot, lots of fifty-letter German words and umlauts. Sorensen's typed note said Lauch had been busted for assault in Austria the year before Ilse Eggermann's murder—barroom brawl, no time served.

In the photos, Lauch looked mean enough for anything. Wouldn't it be something if the bastard *had* come to L.A., cruising for good-looking blondes, somehow connected with Lisa?

Wouldn't it be amazing if Lauch stuck around so they could pick him up? A nice easy solve so Stu could get his promotion and she could add brownie points to her file.

Fantasies, kid.

She studied Lauch's face some more and wondered how someone like him could get Lisa to put on a little black dress and diamonds.

On the other hand, he *had* gotten close to Ilse Eggermann, who, by Phil Sorensen's account, was also a looker. But a stewardess wasn't the ex-wife of a TV star who'd experienced the good life.

Then again, Lisa had opted *out* of the good life. And some women, even beautiful women, liked to bottom-fish, turned on by whatever was crude and brutish, a man below them on the social ladder.

Beauty and the beastly? Lisa taking risks with rough trade and paying for it?

Petra kept staring at Lauch's photo. The thought of allowing his flesh to come into contact with hers turned her stomach.

She liked her men intelligent, considerate, conventionally handsome.

Probably because her father was an intelligent, nice-looking, gentle man. For the most part, a gentleman.

What was Ilse Eggermann's father like?

What was Dr. John Everett Boehlinger like when he wasn't crazed with grief?

Enough with the psychoanalysis. She'd taken it as far as she could for the moment.

She inserted the Eggermann-Lauch data in Lisa's murder book, crossed the room to the Nehi-orange lockers, opened hers, and took a Snickers bar from the bag she kept on the top shelf, above her gym shoes and sweats and the cheap black sweaters she kept handy for cold nights and messy corpses.

Death mops, she called them.

Acrylic that looked like acrylic. Attention, Kmart shoppers, our full-style cardigans now on sale for $13.95 in a wide range of colors. She bought five at a time, always black, threw them out the moment they got gory.

In eight months, she'd been through ten.

She hadn't worn one to Lisa's crime scene because the call had been an off-schedule surprise.

She hadn't been stained by Lisa's corpse.

Hadn't gotten close enough.

# CHAPTER 21

"MOVE, MOVE, MOVE—KEEP MOVING, YOU LITTLE bastard."

Hiss-whispering in my ear, they squeeze me, poke me, push me.

She's the angry one; he sounds afraid, nervous. He even trips a couple of times.

"Come on!" She sticks the gun in my ribs, and when I cry out she sticks me harder and says, "Shut up!" Not nervous at all.

She's in charge.

As we get closer to where all the buggies are parked, I start to pray for some zoo person to be there this time, but there's no one. Should I scream? No, the gun is up against me; it wouldn't take much for her to pull the trigger and blow up my insides— now we're at the fence. The lock is on—and it's clamped!

"Do it," she orders as she looks in all directions. She keeps the gun on me, and he takes a key out of his pocket and opens the lock.

*They know this place.*

They're prepared. They will rape me.

He comes back, grabs me, breathes into my ear, and suddenly my stomach starts turning over and over, hard, fast, painful, like I have to go to the bathroom.

They push me forward again. It's like I'm drifting along in some movie, playing a part, and now I realize the fear is gone and something else has taken over my mind—it's like being asleep and awake at the same time, like being in a dream but knowing you're in one, and you can control everything if you just concentrate, make it come out the way you want.

Maybe that's what it's like after you die.

We go through the gate and start climbing up, into the trees. He's making these low wet grunting noises.

"You," he says, squeezing my arm harder. Like I've done something wrong.

I keep my head down, seeing my shoes, his.

"Okay, come on, come on," she says, waving her hand as we walk into the fern tangle, through the same path I took down, what I used to think was my secret.

They keep pushing me, telling me to move faster, lead me toward a big tree, not my eucalyptus, another one, also with low branches.

We go past it. Walk a ways till we're in front of another tree and it's so quiet, no one's around, even if I scream no one will hear me.

She stands to one side, still aiming the gun, looks at her camera case. Holding on to my arm, he takes out her camera and gives it to her.

"Okay," she tells me.

I don't know what she wants, so I don't speak or move.

She walks up and slaps me hard across the face and my head spins around, but it still doesn't hurt as much as it should.

"Do it, you little shit!"

"What?" I say, but it sounds like another kid's voice. Like I'm out of my body, watching myself move around in some robot movie.

She raises her hand to hit me again, and I try to protect my face with my arm. He knees me in the back and *that* hurts.

"Off with the pants, Streetsmarts—let him pull 'em down, honey."

He lets go of me as she keeps the gun on me. I touch my pants but don't pull them down. He pulls his down, lets them fall around his legs. He's wearing baggy white boxers and now he reaches into the fly hole—I turn away.

"What?" She laughs. "Something you haven't seen before? Yank 'em down, show us your good side."

I don't move. She slaps me again. If she didn't have the gun, I'd stomp her face, twist her head off.

She laughs again. "Obey and it'll all be over before you can say ouch. A little owie, that's all."

She makes kissy noises, and he does too.

"Sure," that other kid's voice says. "Sure, I know what you mean. Only . . ."

"Only what?" She moves closer, puts the gun up against my nose. It feels cold and it smells like a gas station.

The corner of my eye sees that his boxers are all the way down, but still around his ankles, like he doesn't want to really take everything off. He's moving his arm back and forth—

"Only," the kid says. "I . . . it . . . like I—I can do it. Sure, okay, but you—it—like now—first I've got to . . ."

"Got to what?" The gun waves in front of my eyes.

"You know."

"I don't know! *What?*"

"Got to . . . shit."

Silence.

"Hear that?" she says to him.

"Yeah," he says, very quietly, and I'm thinking, Oh no, does he like that even better, did I just make a big mistake?

She turns and looks at him and for a second I think of running for it, but then her face is back right in front of mine and I don't know why I think this, but the way she looks, she could be a teacher, someone's mother or grandma, it's not my fault—

"So?" she asks him.

"Um . . . not today."

"Okay, trash," she tells me. "Go ahead and do your thing— use your shirt to wipe your ass, *then* you're gonna show us your good side."

I pull down my pants, and even though it's a warm day, a beautiful day, a lemonade and corn day, my legs feel like stone.

"So white," he says.

"C'mon, go, go." Her voice is thick, and I understand: His sickness is doing it to kids; hers is being in *charge*. Watching.

"Undies off, goddamn you—off, off, come on, finish up."

I pull down my shorts. Bending down, I manage to move a little farther away from her, but only inches. All around it's so quiet, so green, even the leaves don't move. It's like the three of us are part of one big photograph or maybe this is the last moment before God destroys the world, and why shouldn't He?

"Get going or I'll kill you!" The gun and the camera are aimed at me. She's going to take pictures of everything. I'm her souvenir.

The problem is, before I had to really badly but now I can't; it's like my organs are blocks of ice jammed up against each other.

"Do it or I'll *shoot* it out of you!"

The sound of her voice, the thought of being shot, gets my stomach going again and I do it.

Then I reach behind with one hand to catch it.

Gross, I hate doing it, but I tell myself it's just digested food, stuff that was already inside me—

"Look at that," she says. "You disgusting little animal."

"Disgusting," he says. But he means something else.

I look up at her and nod. And smile. She's surprised, wasn't expecting a smile, and for a second she looks away.

I reach back, and even though I was never good at sports, I aim and throw.

Bam! Right in her face and all over her camera, over her blouse.

She's screaming and stumbling back and slapping at herself and he's tripping over his shorts, confused. He straightens up and charges me, but she's the one to watch, because she's got the gun. She's still screaming and slapping. I yank up my shorts and pants, and even before they're completely in place, I'm runrunrunning, through branches that scratch my face, through space, through green, green that never stops, time that never stops, running, tripping, flying.

Floating.

I hear a loud hand clap, don't stop, nothing hurts, I'm okay or maybe I'm not I don't feel it, can't feel anymore, that wouldn't be bad, that wouldn't be bad at all.

I throw myself through green.

Thank you, gorilla. If I could breathe, I'd laugh.

# CHAPTER 22

■

J<small>UST AS</small> P<small>ETRA WAS ABOUT TO CALL</small> E<small>MPTY</small> N<small>EST</small> Productions for Darrell/Darren, another fax came through: Lisa's last phone bill.

Patsy K. was right—the woman really had hated the instrument. Fifteen calls the whole month, one long-distance, on the first, to Chagrin Falls, three minutes long. Brief chat with Mom? Just once a month. Not a close relationship?

Three toll calls, all to Alhambra. The number matched one in Petra's notes: one of Patsy K.'s friends. The rest were all locals: three to Jacopo's in Beverly Hills for takeout pizza; two to the Shanghai Garden, same city, for Chinese; one each to Neiman-Marcus and Saks.

The last four calls were to a Culver City exchange that turned out to be Empty Nest. Petra phoned it and asked for Darrell in editing. The receptionist said, "Darrell Breshear?"

"Yes."

"One moment, I'll connect you."

Breshear had no receptionist, just a machine. His voice was pleasant. Patsy K. had said he was forty, but he sounded like a young man. Rather than leave a message, Petra decided to call back later and ran Breshear through a superficial NCIC check. Clean. Laughing to herself, because they hadn't run Ramsey.

She phoned the county assessor and, after hassling with a snotty clerk, managed to learn that H. Carter Ramsey owned more than a dozen pieces of property in L.A., all in the Valley: the house in Calabasas, commercial buildings on Ventura Boulevard and on busy Encino, Sherman Oaks, North Hollywood, and Studio City cross streets. One in Studio City matched the address she had for Greg Balch's office at Player's Management.

Nothing in Malibu or Santa Monica, nothing that sounded

like a romantic hideaway, but maybe when Ramsey got away, he really wanted distance. Go north, young woman, and if that didn't work, the eastern mountain resorts.

At the Ventura assessor's, she got a more cooperative clerk but nothing. Next came Santa Barbara—even more hassles than L.A., but bingo: H. Carter Ramsey—what did the H. stand for anyway?—was the deed holder on a house in Montecito.

Copying down the address, she ran his name through DMV. Full name, here: *Herbert.*

Herb. Herbie C. Ramsey—that just wouldn't do for *The Adjustor.*

Tracing vehicle ownerships, she came across all the vintage cars she'd seen in the little museum, plus a Mercedes 500, personalized license plate PLYR 1.

*Plus* a two-year-old Jeep Wrangler: PLYR 0. That one was registered to the Montecito address.

Player's Management: PLYR. The fact that Ramsey used vanity plates was interesting. Most celebrities craved anonymity. Maybe he sensed his fame was fading, felt he needed to advertise.

PLYR . . . fancying himself quite the stud?

Something else: He'd mentioned the Mercedes but not the Jeep. Because the Jeep was stashed in Montecito, or was the omission deliberate?

Was the four-wheel-drive the murder vehicle; the Mercedes, a red herring?

Could the guy be that devious? Devious but stupid, because that kind of ruse wouldn't work long. He'd have to know they'd run a DMV early on.

But if Petra's last-date scenario was correct, the crime had been impulsive up to a point—the instant where Ramsey packed a knife as he got into the car. So maybe he'd acted out overwhelming rage, was now scrambling to do what he could.

Montecito . . . The neighborhood was ultra-tony; multiacre estates like Calabasas, older, classier. No cozy little pied-à-terre for Ramsey; he craved space. Lord of two manors.

Greedy guy in more ways than one? If I can't have her, no one can?

It brought to mind a Thomas Hart Benton in an art book she'd pored over as a child. *The Ballad of the Jealous Lover of*

*Lone Green Valley.* A rawboned, Stetsoned hick with psycho-path eyes stabbing a woman in the breast, country musicians playing a sad score in the foreground, verdant earth dipping and swooping, evoking the victim's vertigo. It had scared the hell out of her, for all she knew had colored her view of men and romance, maybe even her career choice.

The jealous lover of Calabasas/Montecito.

For all the Hollywood angles, this one would probably play out as the same old story, and she realized that if she stayed in Homicide, she'd be spending her life inhaling the worst of clichés.

※

The lunch plan had been to meet Stu at Musso and Frank, but at 1:45 he phoned in and said, "Sorry, I'm getting hung up, do you mind?"

Relieved, she said, "No problem. Anything earth-shattering?"

"All I'm getting so far is no one respects Ramsey as an actor. How about you?"

She told him about the Montecito place and the Jeep, then said, "Guess what, a similar," and gave him the details of the Ilse Eggermann murder.

"Wonderful," he said. "Phil Sorensen's good. If he didn't solve it, it was probably unsolvable. Maybe we *should* let Robbery-Homicide take it."

Now she *knew* something was wrong. Stu had little use for the downtown hotshot elite, considered them arrogant, not nearly as good as they thought they were. Losing a big case was always a sore point for all but the laziest divisional detec-tives, and Stu had never occupied the same continent as lazy. Now he was willing to let R-H roll over him? And her.

If it was a career thing, pending promotion, that didn't make sense—unless he was certain this one was bound to end badly, figured early damage control was better than being the global-village idiot.

"You're kidding," she said sharply.

"Yeah, I guess I am," he said, wearily. "I just didn't want to hear about a valid similar, but no big deal, we'll ride with it." She heard him inhale. "Okay, beep me if you need something. No news yet of Lisa's car?"

"Nope. I'd like to check out Ramsey's Montecito place."

Silence. "Before we get that assertive, we should clear it with Schoelkopf."

"I don't see why we need to," said Petra. "What I got from the meeting this morning was once we do the scut, we're free to be real-life detectives. He admitted if we don't talk to Ramsey soon we'll look like boobs. I think we need to arrange another face-to-face, soon. No lackey to run interference. If Ramsey refuses to speak to us without a lawyer, that tells us something. If he doesn't, we come on friendly but try to pry him."

"I think you misunderstood Schoelkopf, Petra. For him it's not about getting things done, it's about self-protection. And we need to think that way, too—"

"Stu—"

"Hear me out. Who got burned on O.J.? D's, not the brass. The moment we ask to get a close look at Ramsey's houses and his cars, even just an informal request, no warrants, Ramsey becomes the prime suspect and it's a whole other game. If someone finds out you *DMV'd* him, it'll be a whole other game."

"I don't believe this."

"Believe."

"Fine," she said. "You know better."

"I don't, Petra," he said, in the most mournful tone she'd ever heard him use. "I just know we have to be careful."

※

She left the station fuming, was three blocks away when she realized she was driving to see Darrell Breshear without setting up the appointment. Using a pay phone, she called again. This time she talked to the taped message, giving her name and title and asking Breshear to call her at the soonest opportuni—

"This is Darrell."

"Mr. Breshear, thank you. I'm working Lisa Boehlinger-Ramsey's murder and would like to talk to you about her."

"Because we were friends?"

Odd response. "Exactly."

"Sure," he said, sounding anything but certain. "What would you like to know?"

"If you don't mind, I'd prefer a face-to-face meeting, Mr. Breshear."

"Oh . . . any particular reason?"

Because I want to study your facial expressions, evaluate your eye contact, see whether you're sweating or twitching or looking at your feet too frequently, because that's a clear sign of lying.

"Procedure," she said.

He didn't answer.

"Mr. Breshear?"

"Well," he said, "I guess so—could we not do it here, at the lot?"

"May I ask why?"

"It's—I'd prefer to keep a low profile at work, and the police stomping in is . . . bound to attract attention."

"I promise you I don't stomp, sir."

He didn't think that was funny. "You know what I mean."

"I understand, sir," she said. The guy was antsy. Why? "Where would you suggest?"

"Um . . . how about a coffee shop or something like that? There are plenty of places around here."

"Pick one."

"How about . . . the Pancake Palace on Venice near Overland, let's say tomorrow at ten A.M.?"

"The Pancake Palace is fine, Mr. Breshear, but I was thinking sooner. Like in half an hour."

"Oh. Well . . . the problem is, I'm elbow-deep in a big project. Final cut on a picture, there's a screening—"

"I understand, sir, but Lisa was murdered."

"Yes, yes, of course—okay, the Pancake Palace, half an hour. May I ask who told you I'd be worth talking to about Lisa?"

"Various people," said Petra. "See you there, sir, and thanks for your help."

She got back in the car and drove as fast as safety would allow down Western to Olympic. Hoping the guy would show and not complicate her life further.

# CHAPTER 23

■

BLUE WALLS, BROWN BOOTHS, THE TOO-SWEET fumes of fake maple syrup.

Darrell Breshear wasn't hard to spot. At this hour, the Pancake Palace was almost empty and he was the only black man in the place, sitting in a corner booth looking miserable.

Young voice, but indeed older. Patsy K. had said forty, but Petra pegged him at forty-five to fifty. He'd already started on a cup of coffee; for all his attempts to delay, he'd showed up early. Definitely antsy.

He was thin and sat tall, had close-cropped graying hair, skin nearly as pale as Petra's, African features. He wore a black polo shirt under a gray herringbone jacket.

Bags under his eyes made him look weary. When she got closer, she saw the eyes were amber. A few freckles dotted the bridge of his nose.

He saw her and stood. Six-one.

"Mr. Breshear."

"Detective."

They shook hands. His was dry.

"Coffee?" he said, indicating his half-full cup. More like half-empty, judging from his expression.

"Sure."

Breshear waved for service and ordered for Petra, saying please and thank you and getting the waitress to smile. "Sorry to play hard-to-get," he said. "Lisa's murder shocked me, and then to be part of an investigation." He shook his head.

"So far you're a very small part of the investigation, Mr. Breshear." She took her pad out, began writing, then sketching his face.

"Good." His eyes wandered to the left. "So . . ."

Rather than answer, Petra drank coffee. Breshear's eyes started bouncing around.

"Please tell me about your relationship with Lisa Ramsey, sir."

"We worked together."

"You're a film editor, too?"

"I'm a senior editor; Lisa worked on my team."

"Senior editor," said Petra. "So you've been doing it for a while."

"Twelve years. I did some acting before that."

"Really."

"Nothing big. Not film—musical theater, back east."

*"Guys and Dolls?"*

Breshear smiled. "Did that one. And others. It taught me one thing."

"What's that?"

"I wasn't as talented as I thought."

Petra smiled back. "Did you hire Lisa?"

"Empty Nest hired her and assigned her to me. She was good. Considering how new she was. She learned fast. Intelligent. What happened to her is unbelievable."

Breshear's shoulders dropped and now he maintained eye contact.

Petra said, "Did she have prior experience as a film editor?"

"She was a theater arts major in college, took some editing courses."

"How long did she work with you, sir?"

"About half a year." Up with the eyes. He sipped, kept his cup in front of his mouth, blocking it from view.

"Are editing jobs easy to come by?"

"Not at all."

"But Lisa got one because of her college training?"

"I—not exactly," said Breshear. The cup continued to shield his mouth. Petra shifted forward, and he lowered it. "She—I was told she got the job through connections."

"Told by who?"

"My boss—Steve Zamoutis. He's the producer."

"Connections with who?"

"Ramsey. He made a call, and she got hired."

"Six months ago," said Petra. "Right after the divorce."

Breshear nodded.

Doing favors for the ex. Did it confirm Ramsey's claim of a friendly parting? Or had he carried the torch for Lisa, tried to get back with her?

"Let me get something straight, sir. Was Lisa qualified for the job?"

"Yes," Breshear answered quickly. "Considering her inexperience, she was very competent."

Petra wrote. And sketched.

Breshear said, "That's not to say there weren't things she needed to learn."

It took a second for Petra to untangle the double negative. Was Breshear a complex thinker, or was he looking for something other than a coffee cup to hide behind?

"And you taught her."

"Tried my best."

"So you and she worked together on the same movies."

"Two pictures," he said, naming them. Petra had never heard of either.

Breshear added, "They haven't been put into release yet."

"What kind of pictures are they?"

"Comedies."

"No murder mysteries, huh?"

Breshear gave a snorting laugh that he seemed to regret, because he inhaled deeply, tried to compose himself. "Not hardly." He looked at his watch.

"What else can you tell me about Lisa?" she said.

"That's about it. She had no problems on the job. When I found out she was murdered, it made me sick."

"Any ideas about who might have killed her?"

"Everyone's saying it was Ramsey, because he beat her up, but I don't know."

"Did Lisa talk to you about that?"

"Never."

Petra put the finishing touches on his portrait. She'd drawn him nervous—with haunted eyes. "Not even once?"

"Not even once, Detective. His name never came up, period."

"Did you ever see Lisa use drugs?"

Breshear's mouth opened and shut. Out came another snort laugh. "I really don't—is it absolutely necessary to get into that?"

"Yes it is, sir." Petra moved closer again, sliding her hand across the table so it was only inches from his.

He pulled back. "Let me say this: Lisa wasn't a heavy doper, but in the industry people tend to—yes, I saw her snort a couple of times."

"A couple meaning two."

"Maybe more. Three or four. But that's it."

"And this was at work?"

"No, no." He was light enough to blush. Good. Down went the eyes. He said, "Not at work, strictly speaking. I mean, we weren't actually working—I'm her supervisor. Anything that happens on my shift is my responsibility."

"I understand, Mr. Breshear. You'd never have allowed cocaine to interfere with her work. But you saw her snorting three or four times on the lot after work. Where exactly?"

"In the editing room, but it was after hours. May I ask why you want to know this? Do you think what happened was related to dope? Because it's not some kind of crazy scene around here. We're all business, have to be. Without us, the picture doesn't get made."

Long speech. The heightened color remained, lessening the contrast between freckles and background skin.

"Where else, besides the editing room, did you see her snort?"

"At—in my car. *That* took me by surprise. I was driving and she just pulled out this little glass tube, waited till I stopped for a red light, and sucked it up through her nose."

"In your car," Petra wrote, watching as Breshear's eyes did a little ocular roller coaster. "Where were you going?"

"I don't remember." Breshear snatched up his cup and emptied it. The waitress came by and poured some more and he started drinking.

Petra declined the refill, and when she and Breshear were alone again, she sketched some more, inserting shadows and contours, making him look older. "So you don't recall where you were going. How long ago was this?"

Down went the cup. "I'd say one, maybe two months ago."

"Were you two dating, Mr. Breshear?"

"No, no—we were working together. Late. That's the way it is in editing. They call you, you cut."

*You cut.* The word choice sailed right by him.

"So you and Lisa were working late and . . ."

He didn't fill in the blank, and Petra said, "How'd you end up in your car?"

"I was probably taking her home, or maybe out for a bite—may I ask why you're questioning me?"

"We're questioning all the men Lisa knew, Mr. Breshear. Someone told us you'd dated Lisa and we're following up."

"That's wrong. We never dated."

"So I guess our source is mistaken." She smiled, guessing that the existence of a "source" would rattle him.

He colored again and his eyes bounced around. This guy was no smooth psychopath, but he was hiding something.

"Guess so," he said.

"Can you tell me where you were on the night Lisa was murdered?"

He stared at her. Touched his forehead, wiping it, though it was dry. Now his eyes were big and frightened—exactly the expression Petra had drawn on her pad. Look, Dad, I'm a prophetess, too!

"I was with another woman." Saying it just above a whisper.

"Could I have a name, please?"

Breshear smiled. A sick, guilty, dirt-eating, totally unattractive smile. "That's kind of a problem."

"Why's that, sir?"

"Because I'm married and the woman wasn't my wife."

"If she can be discreet, so can I, Mr. Breshear." Petra waved her pen.

"I'd rather not," he said. "Look—I'm going to be straight up with you, Detective Connor. Because I don't want you finding out somewhere else and thinking I was hiding anything. Lisa and I had a short-term thing, but it was no big deal."

"A thing."

"We slept together. Seven times."

He'd counted. A scorekeeper?

"Seven times," she said.

"A one-week thing."

She wanted to say: Now, tell me, Darrell, was it once a day for seven days, or did you double up a few days and take a break? "A one-week thing."

"That's it." The amber eyes bounced. "Actually, we really didn't even sleep together. Strictly speaking—God, this is embarrassing."

"What is?"

"Talking about the details—I guess if you were a man it would be easier."

She grinned. "Sorry about that."

He was staring into his coffee cup again and looked ready to slide under the table.

"So," said Petra, "how long into Lisa's employment did this thing occur?"

"A month ago, six weeks."

That matched Patsy K.'s recollection.

"So you were intimate," said Petra, softening her voice, trying to keep him on the edge but still willing to talk. "But you never slept together."

"Right," said Breshear. "I never stayed over at her place, and obviously, I couldn't take her to mine."

"Where'd you go?"

The blush was deeper than ever. A nice rusty mahogany. It gave him some depth, actually made him more appealing.

"Jesus—is this really necessary?"

"If it relates to your relationship with Lisa and to your whereabouts the night she was murdered, I'm afraid it is, sir."

"And you have to write this all down?"

"If what you tell me shows you had nothing to do with Lisa's death, there'd be no reason for anyone to find out." A crock, everything went into the file, but she closed the pad anyway.

He rubbed his temples and studied his coffee some more. "Man . . . okay, the night Lisa was murdered, I was with a woman named Kelly Sposito. Her place."

"Address, please?" said Petra, opening the pad.

He recited a number on Fourth Street, in Venice.

"Apartment number?"

That question seemed to bother him even more, as if specificity drove home her seriousness.

"No, it's a house—"

"And you were at Ms. Sposito's house from when to when?"

"All night. Ten P.M. to six A.M. Before that, from around five to six, we had dinner at a restaurant—a Mexican place near the studio. The Hacienda, right down the block, on Washington Boulevard."

"Ms. Sposito works with you?"

Nod. "She's an editor too."

Ah, the rub. Lots of rubbing on the job.

"So you never went home and your wife didn't suspect anything?"

"My wife was out of town—she's a salesperson, travels a lot."

Mr. Take-Charge-Politely Darrell was emerging as the editing room stud. Meaning there were probably plenty of other "things" he didn't want unearthed.

"Do you have to call Kelly?" he said.

"Yes, sir. Do you know where she is?"

"At work. Is that it?"

"Almost," said Petra. "Can you tell me who Lisa's coke source was?"

"No," he said. "Absolutely not."

"No one at the studio?"

"I have no idea. No one at Empty Nest, that's for sure."

"Because?"

"Because I know everyone and they don't deal drugs."

"Okay," said Petra. "But I imagine it probably wouldn't be any big deal finding someone at the studio to supply, would it?"

"Oh, come on," he said, angry now. "You think 'cause it's the industry we're just running around partying all day. It's a business, Detective. We work hard as hell. I've never seen anyone on the lot try to sell anyone else dope, and Lisa never talked about her source. In fact, the first time she snorted she offered me some and I told her, 'I don't want you doing that in my car.' "

"But she continued to snort anyway," said Petra. "In your car."

"Well, yes. She was an adult. I couldn't control her. But I didn't want any part of it—for me." He held the cup with both hands. "You want a confession? I'll give you one. I've had my share of problems with alcohol. Been sober for ten years and intend to stay that way."

The amber eyes were flashing. Righteous indignation that looked real. Or he should have been on film rather than splicing it. Or on *stage*—singing his heart out.

"All right," said Petra. "Thanks for your time."

"Sure," said Breshear. "Call Kelly, fine. Just not my wife, okay? Because she was out of town, couldn't help you. Lisa and I were friends, that's all. Why would I hurt her?"

"Just friends, except for that one week."

"That was nothing," he said. "A passing thing. She was lonely, kind of down, and it just so happened things weren't going so well between me and my wife. We worked late, one thing led to another."

He gave a you-know-how-it-is shrug.

One thing had led to seven others.

Seven things had led to another. Petra said, "But you never stayed together overnight. Unlike the situation with Kelly Sposito."

"That's because Lisa didn't want to. It was a point of pride with her—she was independent, doing her own thing."

"Where did the two of you go?"

"Nowhere. Just—we—oh, Jesus. All right, here's the complete picture: It all happened in my car. We went out for a bite and on the way back to the lot, Lisa asked me to take a little drive, toward the beach. We took PCH, ended up near the old Sand Dune Club. She asked me to park; I had no idea what was going on. Then she pulled out that tube and snorted."

"So it was powdered cocaine, not crack."

Breshear smiled. "Only black people use crack, right?"

Petra ignored that.

He said, "It was powder."

"She snorted, then what?"

"Then she got kind of . . . active. Physical."

"Then you had sex in your car," said Petra.

"That's the way it ended up," he said. New tone of voice. Amused?

"Seven times," said Petra. "You'd go out and she'd snort and you'd have sex in the car."

"Actually, five of the times were that way. Twice—the last two—I followed her home and waited till she got ready, then we went out for dinner. But we never dated, as in a real relationship. Both times she had to go home for something."

"Dope?"

"I don't know," said Breshear.

But he did. They both did. So far, his story meshed perfectly with Patsy K.'s.

Breshear sucked in breath. "I don't know why I'm telling you this, but you might as well know everything. We never really had intercourse. She just wanted to give to me."

Looking right at her now, sitting straighter, challenging her to press for details.

Because sex was his thing, and once he got over the initial shame, talking about it boosted his confidence.

Petra said, "Oral sex."

"Yes," said Breshear, closing his eyes for a second. "First she'd get high, then she'd do it. Seven nights, once a night, the same routine. The eighth time, she said, 'I like you, Darrell, but . . .' I didn't argue, because to tell the truth, I thought the whole thing was weird. She wasn't nasty about it. Very nice, just, like, time to move on. I got the feeling she'd done it before."

"Why's that?"

"Just a feeling. She seemed . . . practiced."

Petra didn't speak, and Breshear's eyes saucered again.

"What is it, sir?"

"It's hard to think of her . . . cut up like that. The news said it was brutal."

Petra gave him more silence, and he said, "She was a beautiful person. I hope to God you catch whoever did it."

"Hope so, too. Anything else you want to tell me, Mr. Breshear?"

"Nope, can't think of anything—please don't call my wife, okay? Everything's going real well between us now. I don't want to mess it up."

# CHAPTER 24

AFTER BRESHEAR LEFT, SHE CALLED EMPTY
Nest and asked for Kelly Sposito, the current flame. Things
going well with the wife meant only one on the side?

Sposito was in, had a high, unpleasant voice that got shrill
when Petra identified herself and explained the nature of
the call.

"Darrell? Are you for real?" But a moment later, she verified Breshear's alibi.

"So he was with you all night?"

"That's what I said—listen, you'd better not put this in the
paper or anything, I don't need the grief."

"I'm a detective, not a reporter, Ms. Sposito."

"I see my name in the paper, I sue."

Paper tigress. What was with her?

"Why are you hassling Darrell? Because he's black?"

"We're talking to people who knew Lisa, Ms. Sposito—"

"Everyone knows who did it."

"Who?"

"Right," said the woman. "Like you don't. And he'll get off
because he's rich."

Petra thanked her for her help, hung up, and drove the five
blocks to the studio, used her badge and a combination of firm-
ness and charm to get in. She got directions to Empty Nest
from a guy with long hair who looked like an actor but wore a
tool belt.

The production company occupied several white clapboard
green-shuttered bungalows scattered between whitewashed
soundstages and office buildings, the entire place spotless, with
that too-perfect Potemkin village look. Billboards for TV shows
and movies stood on metal towers. A field of satellite dishes
resembled a giant crockery collection.

A woman in Bungalow A told her Breshear worked in D. Petra walked into a small, empty reception area, brass and glass and black wood floors, three phones, no typewriter or computer. More movie posters, cheapie flicks she didn't recognize, the smell of fish. Through a door she heard voices, and she opened it after the merest knock.

Breshear and two women in their twenties were sitting at a long table mounted with several gray machines—products of a mating between a film projector and a microscope. In an open Styrofoam takeout box were three sushi rolls.

One woman wore an oversized black sweater over skintight black leggings, had a sharp pretty face, bronze skin probably from a bottle, and a mane of big black curls that trailed down her back. The other was arctic pale and had thin blond hair held in place by a pink sawtooth clip. Pleasant-looking but not the buxom looker Curly was. Breshear, sitting between them, started to shift his body backward, distancing himself.

"Detective Connor," he said. Steaming mug in his hand, Gary Larson cartoon silk-screened on the side. The guy claimed he didn't dope, but like many ex-alcoholics he had a caffeine jones.

"Hi," said Petra. "Ms. Sposito?"

Curly said, "What?" and stood. Tall, five-nine, terrific curvy body evident even under the baggy sweater. Her dark eyes were ten years older than the rest of her. She wore so much mascara her lashes resembled miniature wiper blades. Too hard-looking to be a model or an actress but definitely someone who'd turn heads. A lioness, with that mane.

"Just thought I'd drop by and talk to you in person."

Breshear's head swiveled fast as he looked at his girlfriend. Trying to figure out what she'd said over the phone that had complicated things.

Sposito glared as she walked toward Petra with big fluid steps.

The blond girl watched the whole thing, baffled.

When she was two steps away, Sposito said, "Let's talk outside." To the blonde: "We're gonna use your office, Cara."

"Oh, sure," said the blond girl. "Should I just stay here?"

"Yeah. It won't take long."

Out in the front room, Sposito put her hands on her hips. "Now what?"

Your fault, Jungle Girl, all that out-of-proportion anger.

"You had some pretty strong opinions about Mr. Ramsey," said Petra.

"Oh, for God's sake! Opinions is all they were—everyone's saying the same thing. Because Mr. *Ramsey* was abusive. It's nuts to even consider that Darrell had anything to do with Lisa just because the two of them dated a couple times. But okay, you asked where he was, I told you. And that's all there is. I take enough crap for being with Darrell, I don't need this."

"Crap from who?"

"Everyone. Society."

"Racism?"

Kelly laughed. "Just a few weeks ago, we were at the Rose Bowl swap meet and some idiot made a rude comment. You'd think it'd be different, L.A., the nineties. I mean, who's the richest woman in America—Oprah." She frowned and lines formed around her mouth. "What Darrell and I have is good and I don't want anything messing it up."

If you only knew, honey.

"I understand," said Petra. "Any other opinions you'd like to share? About Lisa's murder? Lisa, in general?"

"Nope. Now, can you please let me get back to work? We do work around here."

Why were movie people so defensive about doing honest labor?

"How long have you been working here, Kelly?" Kelly, not Ms. Sposito, because this one would always try to dominate.

The wiper blades opened and shut. "A year."

"So you worked with Lisa."

"Not with her, like on the same project. She needed training, so Darrell worked with her. I've always been on my own."

"Lisa was inexperienced?"

Kelly snickered. "She was a rookie. Darrell was always picking up her slack."

"The whole six months she worked here?"

"No, she learned, she was okay, but to tell the truth—no, forget it, I don't want to put her down."

Petra smiled, and Kelly bared her teeth. Petra supposed it was a return smile.

"Okay, I opened my big mouth. I was just going to say editing jobs are hard to come by, you pay dues. Lisa was totally green. I figured she had to have connections."

"What kind of connections?"

"Don't know."

Something else Darrell hadn't shared with the Lioness. Suddenly, Petra felt sorry for her. "What'd you think of her as a person, Kelly?"

"She did her job, I did mine, we didn't socialize."

Petra said, "Did you like her?"

Kelly blinked. "Honestly? She wasn't my favorite person, because I don't think she treated people well, but I really don't want to speak badly about her now."

"Didn't treat who well?"

The dark eyes narrowed. "I'm talking in general. She had a sharp mouth, that's probably what did her in."

"What do you mean?"

"She was sarcastic. Had a way of saying something without saying it, know what I mean? Looks, tone of voice, the whole body language thing." She rubbed her hips, bent one leg, ballerina-style, flexing, then straightening. "Lisa thought a lot of herself, okay? And if someone didn't measure up, she'd be sure to let them know one way or the other. You want my opinion? Maybe Ramsey was trying to get her back and she shut him down. Aren't those abusers always obsessed?"

Out of the mouths of hostile babes. "They can be," said Petra, looking as fascinated as she felt.

"So Ramsey could have still been into Lisa in a big way," said Kelly, "and let's say they got together and he tried to make it with her but couldn't get it up or whatever, and she let him know what she thought about that in that Lisa way of hers, and he freaked."

Petra hid her amazement. The woman had gone from hostile resistance to criminological theory in five minutes— offering a theory that buttressed Petra's final-date scenario.

"What makes you think Ramsey was impotent?"

"Because Lisa said so—at least she hinted at it. It was about three, four months ago. We were eating lunch—all of us, Darrell, Cara, me, Lisa, and another editor who works here, Laurette Benson, she's gay. And the topic came up about actors, how they get all the glory and how so many of them have totally warped personalities, are totally screwed up, but the public never knows it because everything they hear is bullshit created by the media and publicists. Anyway, we started talking about how actors become sex icons, bigger than human—like Madonna having that baby and everyone's treating it like she was the other madonna and this was some kind of sacred birth, right? Like all those idiots still looking for Elvis or thinking Michael Jackson's gonna stay married. We editors look at these people day after day, scene after scene, through the window of a Moviola. You see enough rough cuts, see how many takes you need to get them to look good and sound smart, you realize how few of them are even talented in the first place. Anyway, we were talking about that and we got into all the sexual fantasies that the public develops about people who probably half the time can't even cut it in bed. Then Laurette started in about how many actors were gay, even the ones who the public thinks are hetero sex gods, how sexuality and reality are like two completely different planets. And Lisa rolled her eyes and said, 'You have no idea, guys. You have no fucking clue.' So we all stare at her and she cracks up and says, 'Take it from me. You go in thinking you're eating at the Hard Rock Cafe and it turns out to be the Leaning Tower of Overcooked Pasta.' Then she laughs even harder, then her face takes on this whole different expression—really bummed, angry—and she just stomps out and goes to the bathroom and stays there for a while. Laurette says, 'Boy, someone's shorts got yanked.' Then Lisa comes back and her nose is red and she's in a too-good mood, know what I mean?"

"She got high."

Kelly pointed a finger gun. "You must be a detective."

"Did she do that a lot?"

"Enough. Not that I paid attention."

"So the topic of impotence upset her."

"Wouldn't it upset you?" said Kelly Sposito. "Life's tough enough, all the crap you get from men when they're at their best. Who has time for limp spaghetti?"

It was after five when Petra left the lot, and she wouldn't have minded a long, hot bath and a good meal prepared by someone else, maybe some torture at the easel. But she still needed to trade notes with Stu, and if he suggested they make their move on Ramsey tonight, she wouldn't argue.

She called the station. Stu wasn't back, but Lillian, the civilian receptionist, said, "Some stuff came for you from the coroner, Barbie."

"Big envelope?"

"Medium big. I put it on your desk."

"Thanks."

She ate a tuna sandwich at the Apple Pan, washed it down with a Coke, scanned the paper—nothing on Lisa—drove back to Hollywood as quickly as the traffic would allow. By the time she arrived, the night shift had come on, but most of the D's were already out serving warrants and looking for bad guys and her desk was clear. Stu still hadn't checked in.

Inside the brown envelope were preliminary postmortem findings signed by a Dr. Wendell Kobayashi—countersigned as Schoelkopf had promised, by the head coroner, Dr. Ilie Romanescu.

Quick turnaround; usually even preliminaries took a week.

She sat down and read the two typed sheets. Traces of cocaine and alcohol had been found in Lisa Ramsey's body, enough to intoxicate but not cause stupor. Meaning she'd been easier to take by surprise. No final autopsy report yet, but the docs were able to provide a wound count and cause of death. Twenty-three cuts—close enough to Ilse Eggermann's twenty-nine. So far, the coroner was guessing that the fatal one had been the very deep abdominal slash Petra had tagged. Point of insertion just above the pubic bone, continuing eight inches upward—a vertical wound that had sliced through intestines and stomach and liver, bisecting the diaphragm, cutting off respiration.

A gutting. Street fighter's move.

As she drops, he hits her twenty-two more times.

Frenzy or fun. Or both.

Dr. Kobayashi guessed that he'd been standing close to her for that first, lethal lunge. Meaning blood on him, too, and if they lucked out and got an exchange, something *he'd* left on *her.* But fiber and fluid analysis would take several days. No footprints, as Alan Lau had noted. Either he'd taken off his shoes or gotten lucky.

She thought about what Darrell had told her about Lisa's sexual proclivities: oral sex in the car. Like a throwback to high school. Had Lisa been fixated at the cheerleader stage? Cheerleaders and older men?

Kelly had described Lisa as full of herself, but she'd ended up ministering to Darrell, wanting nothing for herself.

Sex in a car. The killer *taking* Lisa somewhere in a car.

Mr. Macho Ramsey, unable to function?

A chronic problem? The date Ramsey's last-ditch attempt to prove himself?

*In the car? Because he and Lisa had done it before in cars?*

That damn car museum! Had it been more than just a millionaire's trophy thing? Ramsey's *marital aid*? All that chrome and steel, big engines, reminding him he was rich, handsome, semifamous—a gazillion dollars' worth of toys all so the blood would remain in his penis?

Breshear had said Lisa seemed practiced. With Ramsey? Others? After the divorce—before?

But the phone records showed no contact with other men, no apparent social life. Maybe she'd used her work phone for personal contact. Getting those records would be a major hassle; she was sure the production company was the legal owner. She'd start the paperwork tomorrow morning.

Back to the murder night. Lisa dolling herself up.

*The car, in the car, let's do it in the car.*

And Ramsey couldn't cut it—

*Cut.* There it was again.

Unable to cut it, so Lisa unleashes the sarcasm and he cuts *her.*

After he'd been such a nice guy, forgiving the way she'd blabbed to the tabloid show, getting her the job at the studio, and still sending her seven grand a month.

Twenty-three in cash, a brokerage account at Merrill Lynch—she'd speak to the broker, Ghadoomian, something else for tomorrow.

Sex, money, failure.

Failure in the car, so he'd *used* the car to kill her?

*Driving* her to her final destination.

Doing her in a *parking lot*.

How L.A.

She needed access to PLYR 0 and PLYR 1 and every other vehicle in Ramsey's collection. For all she knew, the death car had been one of the others—that phallic Ferrari, sitting right there in front of them, Stu and the sheriff's guys gawking, unaware they were looking at a slaughterhouse on wheels.

No, too conspicuous, even for L.A. One of the others . . . her phone rang, had to be Stu.

But it was Alan Lau calling from Parker Center, and the criminalist sounded exhausted. "Got some initial results on those food wrappers and the urine. The food was a mixture of ground beef and ground pork, peppers, onions, a tomato-based sauce, chili powder, garlic powder, some other spices we haven't identified yet. Bread crumbs, too. Not mixed in, separate. Probably the bun. White bread."

"Chili-burger."

"Quite possibly. The urine was definitely human, but I hope you don't want any fancy DNA on it, 'cause we barely had enough to do a presumptive type. Even if we did, it would cost a fortune and take a long time."

"What else did you get?" said Petra.

"Prints off the wrapping paper and also off that book you found. The book was full of them. Fulls, partials, nice ridge impressions. I'm no expert, but it looked like some matches between the wrapper and book. We sent it all to ID and so far no matches to any files. So looks like your reader isn't a big-time criminal or a government employee. Also, from the size of the finger pads, it probably is a woman."

Bag Lady squatting on a rock, thought Petra. Eating furtively, reading some old library book that probably fed some schizo fantasy—who knew what the presidents meant to her.

Sad. If nothing turned up, it might be worth checking with the park rangers and some Hollywood patrol officers, see if one particular street woman frequented that section of Griffith.

"Thanks, Alan. Anything show up in the vacuum?"

"Just a pile of dirt, so far. For all the blood, this was a pretty clean one."

Stu came into the squad room at 6:34 P.M., looking like prey. Petra was snacking on her second Snickers bar and wondering where Ramsey was at this very moment, what thoughts were going through his head, did he regret what he'd done or was he exulting in the memory of butchering Lisa?

She asked Stu how he was. He said fine and reported on his day with the dutiful tone of a child giving an oral report. Visits to three studios, three wells dug, wait and see. It didn't sound like enough to turn his normally clear irises rosy pink.

He removed his suit jacket and draped it neatly over the back of his chair. "No one had anything personal to say about him; he doesn't seem to hang with any particular industry crowd. The fact that he beat Lisa up makes them assume he killed her."

"I've got something personal." Petra told him about her talks with Breshear and Sposito, Lisa's hints about impotence.

He said, "Interesting." As if all men went through it. Did they?

"It's a motive," she said.

"Definitely. Too bad it's tough to verify—you trust Sposito on Breshear's alibi?"

"I called her before Breshear got to her and she wasn't the least bit hinky about it, just p.o.'d at being questioned. You don't want to keep working Breshear, do you?"

"No, I just want to make sure we eliminate him cleanly. Let's keep a nice, neat flow chart on this one."

He put his palms down on his desk and leaned, stretching his fingers. "Now, about that German girl—"

Petra gave him the fax on Karlheinz Lauch. He read it and put it down.

She said, "So where do we go with it?"

"The Austrian police, again. Other countries where they speak German and have airports, which I guess would be Switzerland. Also Interpol, U.S. Immigration, though with a three-year window, good luck finding anything at passport control."

"Sorensen already did all that."

"Three years' time lapse means we do it again. Now that we've found one similar, we need to widen the net, make sure we don't miss others. That means Orange County, Ventura,

Santa Barbara, even San Francisco. If we find nothing, I'd feel comfortable putting any notion of a local serial killer to rest. But you never know. There was a guy a few years ago, Jack Unterhoffer—an Austrian, as it turned out—moved between Europe and the U.S., strangling women. Took a long time to see the pattern. If we don't turn up other leads on Lisa and Schoelkopf gets really paranoid, he'll want us to go national, so let's preempt him, run Lauch through NCIC, whatever else the feds have to offer."

Almost as if he *wanted* to do scut. That didn't fit her chance-for-promotion theory. Or did it?

"Fine," she said, surprised at the impatience in her voice. "But Ramsey's still clearly our main guy, and now we've learned something that adds to his motive. I know the impotence thing is hearsay—"

"Less than hearsay. Lisa hinted in general terms."

"But if we don't follow up on it, it's beyond malfeasance."

"No argument," he said, sitting back and playing with his suspenders. "We're not arguing here, Petra, we're prioritizing. There are only two of us, so either we ask for reinforcement, which will mean Robbery-Homicide boots us out, or we split the job. How about I take the whole Eggermann/Lauch thing and you talk to Ramsey? The phone work we continue to divide."

Petra couldn't believe what he was saying. Giving her sirloin and keeping the gristle for himself. "You want me to do Ramsey alone?"

"It might work to our advantage, Petra."

"In what way?"

"If Ramsey does have woman problems, your presence could get him antsy, open some cracks."

*Woman problems.* Not potency problems. Not *man* problems. She said, "Okay, but I don't mind some scut."

"Don't worry about it, Petra. Tell the truth—" He started to say something, stopped. Falling into something he'd taught her about when they started working together: Watch out for suspects who say *truthfully* or *frankly* or *to be honest* or *tell the truth*. They're usually hiding something.

"I really think you're the best one to psych out Ramsey," he said. "Not just the gender thing. It'd be better not to overwhelm him, make it obvious that we're interrogating him. One person rather than two could help with that. Also, back at his house, he seemed to focus on you."

"What do you mean?"

"He wasn't exactly coming on, but there was interest. At least, I thought so. It tells us something about the way his mind works. His ex has just been murdered, he's putting on the grieving husband bit, and he's checking you out."

So he *had* seen it. What else had he kept to himself?

"I'm not talking bait, Petra. If you don't want to do it alone, I understand. But you've got the talent for this one."

"Thanks." Why didn't she feel complimented? Was she growing truly paranoid?

She nodded.

"Okay, then it's all set." He picked up his phone.


# CHAPTER 25

RUNNINGRUNNING RUNNING NOTBREATHING, No looking back.

Trees jumping in front of me, trying to grab me, change direction.

Tear through the branches, they tear back, my face, my arms, my legs, all on fire.

I want to close my eyes, hurl myself through space, a missile. I try and it's good, but then I fall and roll, hitting rocks and branches and sharp things, hurting my head, opening up a hot wet cut on my arm.

It keeps bleeding. I can feel it dripping down, but it doesn't hurt. Nothing hurts; am I made of clay? Of shit?

Don't know where I'm going, don't care, just out of there, the park was a traitor.

Now I can breathe.

I can hear it in my ears, fuzzy, big bursts of fuzz that fill up my head, in air, out air, fuzz air, my chest hurts.

No more Places. Nothing's safe . . . my heart's beating too hard, too fast, suddenly I have to throw up.

I stop, bend over, it shoots out of me like lava, all over the ground, burning my throat.

When will I have a clean life?

No more, empty now, have to be quiet, have to be quiet.

I am quiet.

Everything's quiet.

I taste and smell like something dead.

※

I run some more, fall get up, run, walk, start to feel better and stop to breathe, but then I start shaking and can't stop.

I'm in a part of the park that I've maybe seen before, but I'm not sure.

Lots of trees, leaves all over the ground, rocks and dirt, could be anywhere in the park. I lie down and hug myself. My throat is still on fire, my teeth start knocking against each other dadadadadadadada.

It stops. I want to sit up, but so tired. The ground is bumpy. I find a rock, a smooth, cold one, hold it in both hands, squeeze hard, then I throw it away and take a deep breath.

The bleeding cut has dried into this purple line with wet spots and gold-colored stuff leaking out. Probably plasma. It helps you clot.

I start to hurt all over and find all the other cuts and marks, on my arms, my face. I scratch, raise some bloody spots, watch them clot too.

My body's working.

A bird cry makes me jump and my heart shoots up into my throat and I feel like vomiting again.

Breathe, breathe, breathe . . . now I'm dizzy.

Breathe. Listen to the birds, they're just birds.

Okay. I'm okay.

Time to start moving again.

※

Finally, the night comes.

I'm on a high spot, almost a hill, nothing to see but trees and behind them the huge black shadows of real mountains.

Still in the park, but not for long. Traitor.

I've got nothing now, my books, my clothes, my plastic bags, my food, it's all back at Five.

All the Tampax money. Except what's left of the five dollars I took to the zoo. I reach down in my pocket and feel three bills and some change.

How did all this happen? How did they know to go for *me*? The park was their place, too.

My fault. Stupid thinking I could relax.

Nice and dark now. Darkness covers me, time to move, again.

I walk till I hear cars. Still can't see them, but I must be getting closer to Los Feliz Boulevard. I keep rubbing the hand that held the shit against rocks and dirt and tree trunks and after a while there's no more stink. The cars are really loud now and it *is* Los Feliz and I know where I am.

Hiding myself behind a thick tree, I think about what to do and *she* comes into my head.

The one who got *chucked*.

Why do I keep meeting evil, gross, sick people?

Is there some message I wear on my face like this kid is a loser; he should get messed up? Do I look weak, wimpy, something to be hunted down?

Am I giving off some kind of sign I can't see, the way you can't tickle yourself?

Do I need to be different?

One thing's for sure: I need to be clean.

And gone.

# CHAPTER 26

AT 7:15 P.M. PETRA CALLED RAMSEY'S HOUSE. The Spanish maid answered with "Wan min" and put her on hold.

Two minutes, three, five, six.

Was Ramsey figuring out a way to avoid her? Had he shot a call to his lawyer on another line? She prepared herself for a stonewall, would duly note it and try the Boehlingers again.

A voice came on. "Detective Connor." The man himself.

"Evening, Mr. Ramsey."

"Have you learned anything?"

"Afraid not, sir, but I thought we might talk again."

"Fine. When and where?"

"How about your house, as soon as possible?"

"How about right now?"

She caught the tail end of the evening rush back to the Valley. Some idiot had overturned a truckload of garden furniture near the Canoga Park exit, and thousands of misery voyeurs just had to slow and stare at mangled lounges and shattered faux-cement birdbaths. What's so fascinating about someone else's misfortune? Who was she to talk? She earned a living off it.

Use the time constructively. Psych out Ramsey.

But there was no sophisticated plan, no details to nail down, because planning too precisely when you had no facts could be worse than no preparation at all. One thing was clear: no confrontation. She'd go in friendly, and even if Ramsey gave her a hard time or renewed the Don Juan thing, she'd stay friendly.

That was her strength, anyway. She was able to elicit confessions gently, just as effectively as the bullies, sometimes more so. Stu had built her confidence by letting her take over some serious interrogations. "Use your inherent personality as a weapon, Petra. The way a therapist does."

She'd never thought of therapy as warfare, but she understood the message: It was all manipulation, and the best manipulators didn't overact.

Stu's interview persona was Kind But Strict Big Brother, a smart, pleasant, but essentially tough guy you were a little afraid of but admired and wanted to please.

Hers was Regular Gal, the kind guys liked to talk to.

*Not bait. Talent.* But Stu knew damn well bait was a significant part of it. Ramsey, a ladies' man—in his own mind—so dangle a lady.

A *player* packing limp spaghetti.

No lawyer's name had been mentioned yet, but Petra was sure there was one lurking in the background, feeding Ramsey lines. Just like they did when filming—what did they call those guys?—prompters. Machines did it now—TelePrompTers.

Ramsey had years of practice mouthing words and making them sound right.

Even a bad actor had it over the average suspect. The typical sad soul she interrogated was so full of anxiety, he gave you more than you needed even when he thought he was lying effectively, and the key was to Mirandize him right away, get every last drop legally. The exception was your basic stone-psychopath who had little or no anxiety, but those guys were so boringly self-destructive, they usually managed to trip themselves up being clever.

So where did Ramsey fit in? A calculated killer, or just some pathetic, impotent loser who'd freaked out?

Give him lots of rope, sit back, look, and listen. A self-hanging was too much to hope for, but maybe he'd at least knot himself up.

※

She reached RanchHaven at 8:40, got waved through by the guard. Before she drove through, she asked him if he'd been on night duty Sunday and he said no, that was someone else. Then he closed the guardhouse door.

She drove up the hill. Artificial lights bleached the pink house off-white, made it appear even bigger, but just as architecturally confused.

A young Hispanic woman, not Estrella Flores, answered her ring, opening the door halfway. What Petra could see of the house was dark.

"Hello," she said. "Detective Connor for Mr. Ramsey."

"Jes?" The woman was pretty, with a round face, wide eyes the color of concord grapes, and black hair tied in a bun. About twenty-five. Same pink-and-white uniform Estrella Flores had worn.

Petra repeated her name and showed the badge.

The maid stepped back. "Wan min." Same voice as over the phone. Where was the older woman?

"Is Estrella Flores here?"

Confusion. The young woman started to turn, and Petra tapped her shoulder. "Donde esta Estrella?"

Head shake.

"Estrella Flores? La . . . housekeeper?"

No answer, and Petra's attempt at a warm, sisterly smile failed to alter the maid's stolid expression.

"Como se llama usted, señorita?"

"Maria."

"Nombre de familia?"

"Guerrero."

"Maria Guerrero."

"Sí."

"Usted no sabe Estrella Flores?"

"No."

"Estrella no trabaja aqui?"

"No."

"Cuanto tiempo usted trabaja aqui?"

"Dos dias."

Two days on the job; Estrella gone. Knowing something she didn't want to know and rabbiting? Petra wished she'd gotten to her sooner.

As Maria Guerrero turned again to leave, a male voice said, "Detective," and Ramsey appeared out of the darkness, wearing a white, seriously wrinkled linen shirt, cream silk slacks, cream loafers, no socks.

A vision in pale tones? *I'm a good guy.*

He held the door open for Petra and she walked in. The house smelled stale, and only a table lamp at the rear of the big sitting room was lit. The car museum was dark, too, the glass wall a sheet of black.

He walked two feet ahead of her, to the lamp, switched on another and winced, as if the wattage hurt his eyes. Had he been sitting in the darkness till now? His sleeves were rolled carelessly to his elbows and his curly hair looked lumpy and uneven.

"Please, have a seat." Waiting till she'd settled on one of the overstuffeds, he picked his own spot at a right angle to hers, their knees two feet apart.

Placing his hands at his sides, he sat there. His face looked drawn, older. More gray hairs among the curls, but maybe it was just the lighting. Or some dye wearing off.

"Thanks for meeting with me, sir."

"Of course," he said, inhaling and rubbing one corner of his mouth.

Petra took out her pad, letting her jacket fall open so he could see the badge on her shirt pocket. Showing him the side of the pad with the blue LAPD stamp. Trying to study his reaction to those small bits of official presence.

He was looking somewhere else. At the big stone fireplace, cold and dark.

"Would you like something to drink, Detective?"

"No thanks, sir."

"If you change your mind, let me know."

"Will do, Mr. Ramsey." She opened the pad. "How's everything?"

"Rough. Very rough."

Petra gave her best understanding smile. "I noticed you have a different maid than when I was here the first time."

"The other one walked out on me."

"Estrella Flores?"

He stared at her. "Yes."

"How long had she been working for you?"

"Two years, I guess. Give or take. She said she wanted to go back to El Salvador, but I know it was the . . . what happened to Lisa. She liked Lisa. I guess all the . . . when you people were here it must have upset her, because that night she was busy packing." He shrugged. "Then all the media calls. It's been hard keeping my head clear."

"Have there been many calls?"

"Tons, all on the business line. The number I gave you was my private line. I had everything forwarded to Greg's office. He's not talking to anyone, so hopefully it'll taper off." He rubbed his eyes, shook his head.

"So you got a new maid immediately," said Petra.

"Greg got her."

She sat there, not writing. Giving Ramsey some silence to fill, but he lowered his head. Wide shoulders rounding as he slumped, your classic grieving posture. Chin in hand now. The Thinker.

"Estrella Flores liked Lisa," she finally said, "but she didn't go with Lisa when Lisa moved out."

"Nope," said Ramsey, looking up. "Why's Estrella so important?"

"She probably isn't, sir. I'm trying to get a feel for Lisa's personality—was there something about her that would have stopped Estrella from going with her? Was she hard to work for?"

"Doubt it," said Ramsey. "It was probably the money. I paid her more than Lisa would've wanted to. Social Security, withholding, everything legal. Lisa had a small place; she wouldn't need someone that expensive."

So Flores's nervousness that first day hadn't been immigration worries. And now she was gone . . .

Ramsey widened his legs a bit. "No, Lisa wasn't hard to work for. She was bright, full of energy, had a great sense of humor. Sometimes she could get a little . . . sharp with people, but no, I wouldn't call her hard to live with."

"Sharp?"

"Sarcastic."

Exactly what Kelly Sposito had said.

"Not in a mean way," said Ramsey. "Just a bit of an . . . edge. Part of it was her sense of humor. She told a joke better than any woman I've ever—"

He stopped himself, pressed his legs close together. "Guess that sounds sexist, but I haven't really known that many women who enjoyed telling jokes. I don't mean your Phyllis Dillers or your Carol Burnetts. Women who aren't pros."

"And Lisa liked telling jokes."

"When she was in the mood . . . you have no idea who killed her?"

"Not yet, sir. We're open to ideas."

"It just doesn't make sense, Lisa hooking up with some maniac and going to Griffith Park. For the most part, she went for older guys—conservative types, not the type to get . . . wild."

"She went for older guys after your divorce?"

"I wouldn't know about that," said Ramsey. "But I do know that before we started dating, she'd had two older boyfriends back in Cleveland. A dentist and a high school principal."

"How much older?"

"Ancient. Older than me," he said, smiling. "She made a crack about going out with me even though I was too young for her. At the time she was twenty-four and I was forty-seven."

Making him fifty.

"What were the names of these other men?"

"I honestly can't recall—the principal was Pete something, I think the dentist was Hal. Or maybe Hank. She'd been dating Pete right before she met me, broke up with him the day of the pageant—that's where I met her, Miss Ohio Entertainment—I told you that, didn't I?"

Petra nodded.

"Going senile." He tapped his head. "One good thing about Alzheimer's—you get to meet new people every day."

Thinking of her father, wasting away, Petra forced a smile. Onset at sixty, one of the earliest the doctors had seen. One of the quickest progressions, too. Kenneth Connor, dust at sixty-three . . .

"Are you okay?" said Ramsey.

"Pardon?"

"For a second you looked upset—was it the Alzheimer's joke? That was one of Lisa's—if it was too sick for your taste, I'm—"

"No, not at all, Mr. Ramsey," she said, appalled. What had he seen on her face? "So Lisa liked jokes."

"Yes—do you have any idea when there might be a funeral?"

"That would depend on the coroner, Mr. Ramsey. And Lisa's family's wishes."

"Are they coming out to L.A.?"

"I don't know, sir."

"By the way, I ended up calling them myself, thought it

should be me, not some . . . not a stranger. But all I got was a machine."

"I got through to Dr. Boehlinger."

He frowned. "Jack. He hates my guts, always did. Probably told you I was a terrible husband, you should be investigating me."

Rope.

She waited.

"He's a tough guy, but not a bad sort," said Ramsey. "Lisa marrying me really blew his mind." He touched his mustache, tracing a vertical line through the center, stroking the left side, then the right, bisecting again.

"He didn't approve," said Petra.

"He went crazy. Didn't come to the wedding—it was just a small civil thing at their country club—Jack's and Vivian's. Vivian came. And Lisa's brother, John—Jack junior, he works for Mobil Oil in Saudi Arabia, and he came. Not Jack senior, though. He called me a week before, tried to talk me out of it, said I was robbing Lisa's youth, she deserved better—babies, a family, the whole nine yards."

"You didn't want children?"

"I wouldn't have minded, but Lisa didn't want them. I didn't tell him that, of course. But Lisa made that clear right from the outset. She was the least domesticated girl I've ever met, but Jack thought she should be some high-achieving housewife. He's a very domineering guy. Surgeon, used to giving orders. He was tough on Lisa when she was growing up."

"Tough in what way?"

"Perfectionistic—high standards. Lisa had to get straight A's, go out for every extracurricular activity, excel in everything. She told me when she was twelve, Jack bought her a horse, so she had to learn jumping, dressage, compete whether or not she wanted to. Not the pageants, though. Those were Vivian's idea."

"Sounds like a lot of pressure."

"On all sides. Lisa said it was hell. That's probably why she married me."

"What do you mean?"

"When we were together, Lisa could do whatever she wanted. Sometimes . . ." He waved a hand.

"Sometimes what, sir?"

Ramsey sat straighter. "Sometimes I think I was too easy-going, and she thought I didn't care. I don't want to tell you how to do your job, but I can't say I see the point of all this . . . biography, Detective Connor. Lisa was murdered by some maniac, and we're sitting here talking about her childhood."

A topic you brought up. "Sometimes it's hard to know what's relevant, sir."

"Well," he said, "I just don't see the point."

Petra drew an oval on her pad and placed a horizontal line two-thirds of the way down. A few more pen strokes turned it into Ramsey's tailored mustache. She sketched in his blue eyes, tilted them downward a bit, made him look sad.

"Any other reason for Dr. Boehlinger to hate you other than your being too old for Lisa?"

"I don't know," he said. "Jack and I never had any hassles, so I honestly don't know."

"No problems at all?"

"None—why?"

"He mentioned something to me, Mr. Ramsey. The incident—"

"That," said Ramsey sharply, and now she saw something different in his eyes. Wary. Hardened. "I figured we'd get around to it. Do you know why Lisa went public? In addition to hurting me?"

"Why, sir?"

"Money."

"The show paid her?"

"Fifteen thousand. She called it adding insult to injury."

"She must have been pretty mad at you."

"Beyond mad—Lisa has Jack's temper."

Present tense, again. On some level, she was still there with him.

"Tell me about the incident, Mr. Ramsey."

"You don't watch TV?"

"I'd like to know what really happened."

His lower jaw slung forward and he clicked his teeth. "What can I say? It was sleazy, tawdry, inexcusable, it still makes me sick. We'd been out to dinner, came home, had words—I don't even remember about what."

Bet you do, thought Petra.

"It heated up, Lisa started shoving me, hitting me. With a closed hand. Not the first time. I put up with it because of the difference in our sizes. This time I didn't. There was no excuse. What can I say? I lost it."

He looked at his fist, as if unable to believe it had ever caused damage.

Petra remembered the news clip. Lisa's black eye and split lip.

"It only happened once?"

"Once," he said. "One single, solitary time, that's it." He shook his head. "One stupid moment you lose control, and it's forever."

As good a description as any of murder.

"I felt like crap, just like absolute filth, seeing her on the floor like that. I tried to help her up, but she screamed at me not to touch her. I tried to get her an ice pack—she wouldn't have anything to do with me. So I went out to the pond, and when I came back, her car was gone. She stayed away for four days. During that time she went to *Inside Story*. But she never told me about it, came back and acted as if everything was fine. Then, a few days later, we were eating dinner and she turned on the TV and smiled. And there we were in the hot tub, and she gives me this grin, says, 'Insult to injury, Cart. Don't ever lay a fucking hand on me again.'"

Ramsey studied the offending body part again, opened the palm. "I never did—I'm going to get something to drink. Sure you don't want?"

"Positive."

He was gone for several minutes, came back with a can of Diet Sprite. Popping the top, he sat back and drank.

Petra said, "You just mentioned going out to a pond. I don't remember seeing one out back."

"That's because it was our other house." *Our,* not *my.* Another indication he hadn't severed all the ties. Nor had he lapsed into distancing language, the way murderers sometimes do in the middle of their chronologies, starting with *we* and switching to *she* and *I.* Petra had read an FBI report claiming linguistic analysis could offer major clues. She wasn't convinced, but she was open-minded.

Ramsey drank more soda, looked genuinely miserable.

"Your other house?" said Petra.

"We have a weekend place up in Montecito. Actually, a bigger house than this. It's pretty nuts, maintenance-wise. There's a little pond there I used to find peaceful."

"Used to?"

"Don't go there much anymore. That's the way it is with second houses—I've heard the same thing from other people."

"They don't get utilized?"

He nodded. "You think you're getting yourself some refuge and it just becomes another set of obligations—the place was too damn big in the first place. God knows this one is, too."

"So you don't go up there much."

"Last time had to be . . ." He looked at the ceiling. ". . . months ago."

Suddenly his body jerked, an almost seizurelike movement that snapped his head down and brought his attention forward. His eyes met Petra's. Wet. He wiped them quickly.

"The last time Lisa and I were up there together," he said, "was *that* time. We never went back together. A few days after the show aired, she moved out again and I got served with papers. I thought everything was patched up."

Petra kept the poignancy at bay and thought: The DV episode had gone down in Montecito. She'd call Ron Banks and save him more searching.

Ramsey rested his chin in his hand again.

"Okay," she said. "This is helpful. Now, if you don't mind, let's talk about the night Lisa was murdered."

## CHAPTER 27

MILDRED BOARD WOULD HAVE LIKED TO SCRUB the kitchen floor.

Years ago, she'd accomplished the task every single day. A one-hour commitment, up to the elbows in soapy water from six A.M. to seven. Excellent thinking time, no distraction from the slosh or the circular movements of cotton rags on yellow linoleum.

Once the arthritis set in, all that stooping and rubbing became unbearable, and she was lucky if she was able to attend to the floor once a week.

The dining room parquet required attention as well. The wood was faded, buckling and cracked in spots, long past due for a refinish.

Every inch of wood visible; the dining room was empty, all the missus's furniture shipped off to those Sotheby's people in New York.

Mildred felt an uncomfortable tightening around her eyes. She breathed in and straightened her back and said, "One does one's best," in a firm voice.

Firm and loud. No one to hear her. The missus was upstairs. So many other rooms between them, all empty and closed off.

The kitchen with its old cherrywood cabinets, industrial refrigerators, and three ovens was big enough for a hotel. The pots and pans and cutlery remained, as did the missus's favorite bone china set and a few sentimental silver pieces in the butler's pantry. And the magnificent linen press the Sotheby's people said they couldn't hope to sell. But the lovely things—the treasures the missus and him had acquired in Europe—were all gone. Brought in fine prices, they had, even after the auctioneer's premium and the taxes. Mildred had seen the check, known everything was going to be all right. For a while.

She and the missus had never discussed the . . . financial situation. The missus continued to pay her, insisting upon full salary, though Lord knew Mildred didn't deserve it—what use was she in this state?

*Destructive thoughts. Banish, banish.*

She noticed a water spot on the cabinet below the sink, found a rag, wiped it clean.

Back in the old days, the kitchen had been a bustling place, the missus and him entertaining constantly, caterers milling about, waiters rushing, pots steaming, stainless steel counters blanketed with platters of savories and sweets. Not the least of the latter were Mildred's pies. No matter who the missus hired for catering, she'd always craved Mildred's pies, most notably the plum, the Dorset apple, and the mixed-berry. So had him. So had . . . everyone.

Mildred had cooked and cleaned in the big house for forty-one years, two years after the missus and him moved in. The lodge at Lake Arrowhead as well, but lakeside weekends had only been an occasional thing, even when him was alive, and often the missus called in a cleaning service to remove the tarpaulins and clear the taps.

The lodge hadn't been used for over a decade. Not since the terrible weekend.

Mildred sighed and tamped her hair. Forty-one years, shining the silver, shampooing the wall-to-walls, cleaning nearly a hundred windows, even the leaded glass panels him had acquired from a church in Italy. Oh, the missus always provided another girl to help, but none of them ever managed to keep up.

For the first decade, her workmate had been Anna Joslyn, that dim, skinny girl from Ireland. Not quite focused, mentally speaking, but a good worker and strong as a brood mare. Then the big loud one from Denmark with the vulgar bosoms, that one hadn't worked out at all—what a mistake!

After the Dane, all the agency sent were Mexicans. Good workers, most of them, and generally honest, though Mildred kept her eyes open. Some spoke English, some didn't. Either way, it was their problem. Mildred refused to learn Spanish—English and French were quite enough, thank you. Miss Hammock's class at the orphanage had emphasized only English and French, and eight decades of its graduates had worked in the finest homes of Britain and the Continent.

The Mexicans weren't a horrid lot, but they seldom lasted very long. Rushing to some family crisis in Mexico, children, husbands, paramours, saints' days, who could keep score of all those Catholic assignations. Mildred would have preferred young ladies properly churched and educated, straight-backed girls who knew the difference between Royal Crown Derby and Chinese Export. But one accepted.

The problem, she knew, was that there were no more orphanages—all those babies cut from the womb or allowed to remain with unfit welfare slatterns. One had only to read the paper.

No need anymore for Mexican girls. Or anyone else, for that matter.

Mildred was seventy-three, and she wondered if she'd live long enough to witness the final collapse of everything rational and right.

Not that she expected to keel over any day soon. Except for the arthritis, she felt quite fine. But one never knew. Look what had happened to the missus. Such a beautiful woman, the most graceful woman Mildred had ever seen on either side of the ocean. Nothing but kind words ever left her lips, such patience, and Lord knew living with *him* had often required patience.

Look at her now . . . thinking about it, Mildred's eyes felt weak.

The coffeepot hissed. Right on time. Mildred poured the missus's coffee into a Victorian pitcher. Clumsy-looking piece, probably a gift from some dinner guest. The lovely pitcher—the Hester Bateman—was gone. George III, a banner year, proper hallmarks and all. Him had brought it back from one of his London trips, a first-class shop on Mount Street. Someone else might have relegated it to a display case. The missus believed in using the fine things. It had been her breakfast pitcher.

Till four years ago.

Cartons of silver, paintings, even formal gowns, shipped off like . . . vegetables.

When she'd first been hired, Mildred had been afraid to touch any of the missus's treasures, fearful of marring something. Even back then she could recognize quality.

The missus, just a girl back then, but so wise, had put her at ease. *This is a home, dear, not a museum.*

And a fine home she'd made for him.

Light wound its way through the branches of the ancient twisted sycamore on the breakfast patio, filtering through the kitchen window and settling on Mildred's recalcitrant hands.

Gnarled as badly as the tree. But the sycamore sprouted green every year. If only people merited autumn renewal . . .

Mildred shook her head and stared at the floor, in need of mopping. Such an expanse. Such a big room . . . not that the last girl had been any use. What was her name—Rosa, Rosita. Three months on the job and fooling with one of the gardener's boys. Mildred had been forced to call the agency yet again.

*Hello, Mr. Sanchez.*

*Hello, Miss Board. And what can I do for you today?*

Cheerful, he was, and why not? Another commission.

Mildred set up three interviews with "ladies," then the missus told her.

*Do we really need someone else, Mildred? Just you and me, all we really use is the kitchen and our rooms.*

Fighting to sound gay, but biting back tears. Mildred understood. She'd packed the silver and the paintings and the evening gowns.

So this is what it had come to. All those years, the missus putting up with him and look how him had left her.

That temper of his. No doubt, it had hastened his death. High blood pressure, the stroke, and him only a young man. Leaving the missus alone like that, poor dove, though he had provided for her in a financial way—one couldn't fault him there.

Or so Mildred had thought. Then, four years ago, the change.

Rooms purged and locked.

No more Mexican girls.

The gardening crew cut from every day to twice a week, then once. Then one skinny youth attempting to cover two acres with rapidly diminishing success. Gardens were like children, requiring a hawk eye lest they go delinquent.

The missus's garden, once a glory, had become a sad, shaggy thing, lawns spotted and burnt and incompletely mowed, untrimmed hedges swelling uncouthly, trees burdened with dead branches, flower beds whiskered with weeds, the fishpond drained.

Mildred tried her best, but her hands defied her.

Did the missus realize? She rarely ventured out anymore. Perhaps that was why. Not wanting to see.

Or perhaps she just didn't care. Not because of the . . . financial issue.

Because Mildred was forced to admit that the missus had changed a long time ago.

The terrible weekend in Lake Arrowhead. Then him. Tragedy upon tragedy. Not that the missus had ever complained. Perhaps it would've been better if she had . . .

The German railway clock over the left-hand freezer chimed.

Something else those nasal-voiced Sotheby's people had rejected. Not that Mildred could blame them, hideous it was. And grossly inaccurate. Nine o'clock on its face meant eight fifty-three. In seven minutes, Mildred would be at the missus's bedroom door knocking gently. Hearing "Please come in, dear" from the other side of the molded mahogany. Entering, she'd set the tray on a bureau, prop the missus while chattering encouragingly, fluff the mountain of pillows, fetch the wicker bed table, set it carefully over the missus's comforter, and arrange the service precisely. Silver-plate toast rack filled with triangles of extra-thin wheat bread, browned lightly, the coffee, freshly ground African blend from that little shop on Huntington Boulevard—one needed *some* luxury for heaven's sake! Decaffeinated now, but accompanied by real cream, thick enough to clot for the scones; what a job it was finding *that*! The golden marmalade that Mildred still made by hand, using fine white cane sugar and the few sour oranges she managed to find out back in the orchard.

The sour orange tree was dying, but it managed to produce a bit of lovely fruit. One thing California was good for was fruit. Mildred still loved to stroll the orchard and pick, pretending the ground wasn't hardpacked and lumpy, pretending the herbs were green and fresh, not the tangle of straw thatching the borders.

Pretending she was a girl back in England, out in the Yorkshire country. Shutting out the fact that on certain days—most days—one could hear the Pasadena freeway.

Fruit and weather. Those were the only things to recommend California. Despite living most of her life in San Marino, Mildred considered the place barbaric.

Horrid things in the newspaper. When she deemed them too horrid, she didn't bring the paper up with the missus's breakfast.

The missus never asked about it. The missus never read much anymore, except for those romance paperbacks and art magazines.

The missus never did much at all.

Nothing wrong with her, the doctors claimed, but what did they know? The woman was sixty-six but had suffered centuries' worth of tragedy.

The railway clock said 8:56 and Mildred had only three

minutes to cross the kitchen to the creaky rear elevator that rose up to the missus's bedroom on the third floor.

She picked a fine yellow rose from the three without mildew on the thorny grandiflora bush out back. She'd snipped at dawn, trimmed the stems, and placed the flowers in sugar water. Now she laid the blossom next to the covered platter of shirred eggs. The missus rarely ate the eggs, but one tried.

Lifting the tray, she walked speedily, steadily.

The kitchen didn't look too awful, all things considered.

"Very good," Mildred said, to no one in particular.

## CHAPTER 28

I SNEAK OUT OF THE PARK AND GO DOWN LOS Feliz, staying as far from the light as I can. No one walking up here, just cars whizzing by. Los Feliz ends and Western starts and now the junkies and prosties take over. I turn right on Franklin because it's darker, all apartment buildings; I don't want to be on the Boulevard.

Not too many people out tonight, and the ones who are don't seem to notice me. Then I see a couple of Mexicans hanging around a corner, in the shadow of an old brick building. Probably doing a drug deal. I cross the street and they look at me, but they don't say anything. A block later, a skinny prostie with spiky white hair and bright blue T-shirt and shorts comes out of an apartment carrying a tiny purse. She spots me and her eyes get wild and she says, "Hey, boy," in a drunk voice and wiggles her finger. She's short, just a kid, doesn't look that much older than me. "Fuck and suck, thirty," she says, and when I keep walking, she says, "Fuck you, faggot."

For the next few blocks I don't see anyone, then another prostie, older, fatter, who pays no attention to me, just stands around smoking and watching cars. Then three tall black guys

wearing baseball caps and baggy pants come out of the shadows, see me, look at each other. I hear them say something
and I cross the street again, trying to seem relaxed. I hear
laughter and footsteps and I look back and see one of them
chasing me, almost reaching me. I speed up and run, and he
does too. His legs are long and he's got his hand up, like
to grab me. I run across the street and a car's coming and it
has to move to the side not to hit me. The driver honks and
yells, "Fucking idiot!" and I'm still running, but the black
guy isn't.

I think I hear someone laughing. Probably a game for him.
If I had a gun . . .

I walk for a long time. At Cahuenga, there's more light and
the entrance to the Hollywood Bowl, a long curvy road that
climbs up. I'm not going up there. Too much like the park; I
don't want anything to do with parks.

So guess what comes next: another park, Wattles Park, what
a weird name. I've never seen it, never been this far. Not a
friendly-looking place—high fences all around and gates with
big chain locks and a sign saying the city owns it and it's closed
at night, keep out. Through the fence all I can see is plants. It
looks messy. Probably full of perverts.

Now Franklin ends, here's Hollywood Boulevard again, I
can't avoid it; like it's chasing me, this big burst of noise and
light, gas stations, cars, buses, fast-food places, worst of all
people, and some of them look at me like I'm a meal. I cross La
Brea, it gets quiet again, all apartments, some of them pretty
nice-looking. I've never thought of the Boulevard as anything
but stores and theaters and weirdos, but look at this—people
live here in pretty nice places.

Maybe I should have traveled sooner.

The cut on my arm is dry and it doesn't hurt much. The ones
on my face itch.

I'm breathing okay, though my chest still hurts. I'm hungry,
but three dollars isn't going to buy me much and I look for
Dumpsters to dive. Nothing. Not even a garbage can.

I walk a little bit more and turn off on a real quiet street. All
houses, a nice dark street. But no cans here either, or alleys.
Cars are parked bumper to bumper and down a ways I see
more light and noise, another boulevard. I stop and look around.

Some of the houses look okay; others are messy, with cars parked on the lawn.

Then I come to one with no car in the driveway or on the lawn. *Totally* dark. Old-looking, made of some kind of dark wood, with a slanted roof that hangs over a really wide porch. No fence, not even across the driveway. But the grass is cut, so someone lives here, and maybe they keep their cans in the backyard.

The driveway is just cement with a strip of grass growing in the middle, and I can't see what's at the end of it. I look around to make sure no one's watching and walk back there very slowly. As I pass the front porch, I see a big pile of mail in front of the door. All the windows are totally black. Looks like the people have been gone for a while.

No BEWARE OF DOG sign, no barking from inside the house.

I keep going and finally make out what's at the end of the driveway. A garage with wooden doors. The yard is small for such a big house, just a little grass and a couple of trees, one of them gigantic but with no fruit.

The cans are out behind the garage, three of them—two metal, one plastic. Empty. Maybe the people don't live here anymore.

I turn around and am heading back to the street when I notice a dot of orange over the back door. A small bulb, so weak it only lights up the top half of the door. A screen door; behind the screen is glass. The screen's held in place by two loop-type things with hooks, and when you twist them it comes right off.

The glass behind the screen is really a bunch of windows— nine squares in a wooden frame. I touch one lightly and it shakes a little but nothing happens. I touch it harder, knock a few times. Still nothing. Same when I knock on the door.

Taking off my T-shirt, I wrap it around my hand and punch a lower square on the left side pretty hard. It just sits there, but the second time I hit it, it comes loose and falls into the house and breaks.

Lots of noise now.

Nothing happens.

I reach in and feel around and find the doorknob. In the middle is a button, and when I turn the knob, it pops out with a click and the door opens.

Back on goes my T-shirt and I'm inside. It takes a few seconds for my eyes to see in the darkness. The room's some kind of laundry place with a washer-dryer, a box of Tide on top of the washer, some washrags. Next comes a kitchen that smells of bug spray, with lots of plants in pots all over the counters. I open the refrigerator and a light goes on inside, and even though I see food, I shut it fast because the light makes me feel naked. As the door closes, I notice a peace-sign sticker and one that says SISTERHOOD IS ALL.

My heart is really beating fast. But a different kind of fear, not all bad.

I walk around, from dark room to dark room, nothing but a bunch of furniture. Then back to the kitchen. A closed door on the way turns out to be a bathroom, with more plants on the toilet tank. I turn the light on, then off. Clear my throat. Nothing happens.

This place is empty.

This is sort of fun.

I go back to the kitchen. The window over the sink is covered by curtains with flowers on them with little fuzzy balls hanging down. *Sisterhood.* Women live here; men wouldn't have all those plants.

Okay, let's try the refrigerator again. On the top shelf are two cans of Barq's root beer and a gallon plastic orange juice container with just a little juice left. Three gulps of juice. It tastes bitter. I put the root beer cans in my pocket. Next is a tub of Mazola margarine and a stick of Philadelphia cream cheese. I open the cream cheese and it's covered with blue-green mold. The margarine looks okay, but I don't know what to do with it.

Below that is a container of strawberry yogurt and three slices of American cheese, stiff and curly around the edges. No mold. I eat all three.

These people have definitely been gone for a long time.

On the bottom shelf is a package of Oscar Mayer low-fat bologna that's never been opened—I put it in my pocket, along with the root beer—and a whole pineapple, with the green thing still attached on top and soft in a few places.

Leaving the refrigerator door open for light, I bring the pineapple to a counter and open drawers until I find forks and knives. In there with them are bobby pins and hair bands.

I take out the biggest knife and slice the pineapple in half. The soft spots turn out to be brown spots, and they're spreading all over the pineapple like a disease. I cut around them—this is really a good knife—and manage to get some really nice, ripe pieces of delicious, supersweet pineapple.

That makes me hungrier, and I taste the bologna and end up eating every slice, standing at the counter. Then more pineapple. The juice runs all over my chin and my shirt and I feel it burn my face where the cuts are.

Then one of the root beers.

Now my stomach's killing me because it's full.

I go back to the bathroom right off the kitchen, take a leak, wash my hands and face. Then I notice the shower. On a shelf are soap and shampoo and cream rinse and something called detangler.

Plenty of hot water. I add some cold, make it perfect, run it as hard as it goes. Locking the door, I pull off my clothes and step in. The water's like needles, hurting me, but in a good way.

I take the longest shower I've ever had—no Mom waiting to get in and spend half the day there getting ready for Moron; no Moron wanting to sit on the toilet for an hour.

I just keep soaping and washing off, soaping and washing off. Making sure every part of me gets attention: my hair and under my nails, inside my nostrils, deep up my butt. I want to get every bit of crud out of me.

Then around front, under my balls.

I've got a hard-on.

That feels good.

※

I'm sitting there drying off, loving being clean and safe, thinking about far places, imaginary places, huge mountains—purple majesty, like the song, a silver ocean, surfer dudes, Jet Skis, girls in bikinis dancing the hula, dolphins, Jacques Cousteau, blue tangs, yellow tangs, moray eels, nautiluses.

Then I hear sound and for a minute I think I've really spaced out, created a whole tropical island movie with a soundtrack, then the voices get louder.

Women's voices. Then a bang—someone putting something down.

Light under the door. From the kitchen.
A scream.
A real scream.

## CHAPTER 29

RAMSEY SAID, "I NEED A BITE, DO YOU MIND IF
we go in the kitchen?"

Nerves making him hungry? Petra said, "Not at all, Mr.
Ramsey." Good chance to see more of the house.

She followed him as he switched lights on, illuminating
terrible lithos, big furniture. Veering into exactly what Petra
expected: six hundred square feet of pseudo-adobe walls and
rustic-beamed ceilings, white Euro-cabinets, gray granite
counters, brushed-steel appliances, copper rack full of lethal
weapons hanging from the beams. On the counters sat an
array of food processors, toasters, microwaves. A green-
house window provided a view of stucco wall. The eastern
border of the house. A side door.

In the center of the kitchen was a long, narrow wooden
table, old heart pine, scarred and buffed to a satin finish, the
scars shiny dents. Probably a genuine antique, country French.
Petra saw it as a monastery piece. Nice. But the eight chairs
around it were chrome Breuer types with rawhide leather slings,
so discordant she wanted to scream. Whose idea of eclectic, his
or Lisa's?

Ramsey opened the fridge on the left. Fully stocked. A
bachelor who made himself at home. He took out another Diet
Sprite and a carton of cottage cheese with chives.

"Gotta watch the tush," he said, locating a spoon. "Sure I
can't get you anything? A drink, at least?"

"No thanks."

He sat down at the head of the pine table and she took a side chair.

"This must look weird," he said, lowering the spoon to the cheese. "Eating. But I haven't eaten all day, could feel my blood sugar drop."

"Hypoglycemic?"

"There's diabetes in my family, so I'm careful." He began eating cottage cheese, wiping white flecks from his mustache. Not caring what he looked like in front of her. Maybe she'd been wrong about the Don Juan thing. Or maybe he turned it on and off. She watched him take a swallow of soda, two more spoonfuls of cottage cheese, got his attention by taking out her pad.

"Okay, that night," he said. "I told you I was in Tahoe, didn't I? The first time you were here."

Petra nodded.

"Scouting locations for next season," he went on. "We've got a double script with some casino episodes, trying to figure out where we want to do it. We'll be shooting in a month or so."

"Who was with you on the scouting trip?"

"Greg and our locations supervisor, Scott Merkin. We looked at some properties by the lake, visited a few of the casinos, had dinner at Harrah's, and flew home."

"Commercial flight?"

He put the spoon down, drank some more. "All these details. So I'm a suspect?"

No surprise in his voice. The unspoken final word to the sentence: *finally*.

"It's just routine, Mr. Ramsey."

He smiled. "Sure it is. I've said the exact same thing tons of times to suspects—on the show. 'Just routine' means Dack Price is gonna go after the guy."

Petra smiled. "In real life, routine means routine, Mr. Ramsey. But if this isn't a good time to talk—"

"No, this is fine." The pale eyes locked in on Petra's. Ramsey ate more cottage cheese, raised the soda can to his lips, realized it was empty, and fetched another.

"I guess it makes sense, my being a suspect. Because of the . . . incident. That was the slant the news put on it."

Staring at her.

Rope. She could visualize it uncoiling, like a cobra.

"This whole thing," said Ramsey. "The way people are thinking about me after those news broadcasts. No, it wasn't a commercial flight, we went by private charter, we always do. Westward Charter, we use them all the time. Our usual pilot, too. Ed Marionfeldt. I like him 'cause he was a navy fighter pilot—real *Top Gun*. We flew out of Burbank, everything's recorded in Westward's log. Out around eight A.M., back by eight-thirty P.M. Scott drove home, and Greg brought me back here. He usually drives when it gets late, because my night vision isn't all that great."

"Eye problems?"

Though his mustache was clean, Ramsey wiped it again. "Early stages of cataracts. My ophthalmologist wants to laser me, but I keep putting it off."

Telling her he couldn't have driven Lisa to the park at night?

"So you don't go out much at night?"

"I do, it's not that bad, lights just bother me." He smiled. "Don't give me a ticket, okay?"

Petra smiled back. "Promise."

He dug the spoon into the cottage cheese again, looked at it, put it down. Petra noticed looseness around his mouth. Mottling behind the ears and several fine lines that had to be tuck remnants. Gray hair sprouted from an ear. In the bright light of the kitchen, every wrinkle and vein was advertised.

His body starting to fail him. Blood sugar. The eyes.

The penis.

Appealing to her sense of sympathy? Hoping for female tenderness sarcastic Lisa hadn't offered?

"So Greg drove you home," she said.

"We got here around nine-fifteen, nine-thirty, did some paperwork, then I just crashed. Next morning, Greg was up before me, working out by the time I got to the gym—I've got a home gym. I did a little treadmill, showered, we had some breakfast here, decided to practice some putting, then head over to the Agoura Oaks Country Club for eighteen holes. Then you showed up."

Sorry to spoil your day, Herbert.

"Okay," said Petra. "Anything else?"

"That's it," said Ramsey. "Who knew."

She closed the pad and they hiked back to the front door.

"How're the cars?" she said, passing the glass wall.

"Haven't thought about them much."

Petra stopped and peered through the black glass. Was the Mercedes parked in its allotted space? Without light, visibility was zero.

Ramsey flicked a switch. And there it was. A big sedan, gunmetal gray.

"Toys," said Ramsey, turning off the light.

He walked her to the Ford, and when she got behind the wheel, he said, "Give my regards to Greg."

Petra's turn to stare. He gave her a small, sad smile. An old man's smile.

"I know you'll be verifying the alibi," he said. "Just routine."

## CHAPTER 30

FEELING GUILTY AND USELESS BUT MAKING SURE to look calm and sharp, Stu tightened his tie and put on his suit jacket. Five hours of phone calls; no cases resembling Lisa Ramsey's. Or Ilse Eggermann's.

He didn't know what to make of the German girl's murder; wasn't getting any help from the Austrian police or Interpol or the airlines. Tomorrow he'd try U.S. customs and passport control. Asking them what? To keep an eye out for Lauch? Good luck. He stared at the Viennese mug shot. A conspicuous-looking guy, but it was beyond needle-in-the-haystack.

Maybe Petra was having some luck with Ramsey.

Maybe not. It was hard to care . . . he cleared his desk and locked it, walked across the squad room. Wilson Fournier was on the phone, but just as Stu passed, the black detective hung up scowling and reached for his own jacket. Fournier's partner, Cal Baumlitz, was out, recuperating from knee surgery, and

Fournier had been working alone for days and showing the strain.

"New call?" said Stu, forcing himself to be social.

"Poor excuse for one." Fournier was average-size and slim, had a shaved head and a bushy mustache that reminded Stu of one of the actors he'd seen on *Sesame Street* back when he'd worked nights, had mornings to spend with his kids.

Fournier hitched his holster and collected his gear, and the two walked out together. "Life sucks, Ken. You and Barbie get Lisa Ramsey, celebrities up the ying, and I get an end-of-shift, maybe-prowler/rapist/burglar gig with stupid overtones."

"You want Ramsey?"

Fournier laughed. "Yeah, yeah, I know fame has its price."

"What kind of a maybe-prowler/rapist?"

Fournier shook his head. "The rapist thing is crap—'scuse me, deacon, manure. We're supposed to be working homicide, for God's sake, and on this one, no one got hurt, let alone dead, so why's it my business? Meanwhile, I've got four open 187's and pressure from the boss. Goddamn brain-dead chief and his community policing manure."

A few steps later, just to be polite, Stu said, "What exactly happened, Wil?"

"House on North Gardner, two lesbians come home from a week in Big Sur, find someone's been in their kitchen, scarfed food, used the shower. They walk in on it—the shower's still going—freak, run screaming out the front door, and the perp rabbits out the back."

"What was burgled?"

"Food. Part of a pineapple, bologna, some soda. Big bad burglary, huh?"

"So where's the rape?"

"Exactly." Fournier gave a disgusted look. "Lesbians. A big pile of mail at the front door. Gone an entire week, do they think of putting a stop on it? Or leaving some lights on? Or getting an alarm or a Rottweiler or a poison snake or an AK-47? Man, Ken, what kind of folks still think they can count on us to do a damn thing about crime?"

# CHAPTER 31

█

*ROUTINE. AM I A SUSPECT?*

Was he playing with her?

She called Stu at the station. He'd checked out an hour ago, and when she tried his house, she got no answer. Out with Kathy and the kids? Must be nice to have a life.

Back in L.A., she bought some salads at a mom-and-pop grocery on Fairfax, ate them at home while watching the news—no Ramsey info. She tried Stu again. Still no answer.

Time to simulate a life for herself.

Changing into acrylic-spattered sweats, she put on Mozart and squeezed paint onto her palette. Hunched on a stool, she worked till midnight. First the landscape, which was responding a bit, she felt in the groove, that hypnotic time contraction. Then another canvas, larger, blank and inviting. She laid on two coats of white primer, followed by a luxuriant layer of Mars black, and, when that dried, began a series of hastily brushed-in gray ovals that became faces.

No composition, just faces, scores of them, some overlapping, like fruit dangling from an invisible tree. Some with mouths parted innocently, all with pupilless black eyes that could have been empty sockets, ghostly discs, each one portraying a variant of confusion.

Each face younger than the last, a reverse aging, until she was painting nothing but children.

Perplexed children, growing on an invisible child tree . . . her hand cramped and she dropped the brush. Rather than get psychological about that, she laughed out loud, switched off the music, snatched the canvas off the easel, and placed it on the floor, face to the wall. Stripping naked and tossing her clothes on the floor, she took a long shower and got into bed.

The moment the lights were off, she was playing back the interview with Ramsey.

Almost positive the guy was manipulating.

Not knowing what to do about it.

※

She woke up Wednesday morning still thinking about it. The way he'd flicked on the garage light, showing her the Mercedes, as if daring her to probe further. All those sympathy ploys—blood sugar, cataracts. Not much night driving.

Poor old guy, falling apart. But there was one health problem he'd never bring up.

One that could motivate some serious rage.

And still no lawyer, at least not out in the open. Some kind of double bluff? Ask the wrong question and in come the mouthpieces?

Or was he just feeling confident, because he had the perfect alibi?

Don't get sucked into it, no frontal assault. Go for the flanks. The underlings. Find Estrella Flores, have a chat with the charter pilot, though that wouldn't prove anything—there'd been plenty of time to get home, leave, pick up Lisa, kill her. Last but not least, Greg Balch, faithful lackey and likely perjurer. Petra was certain Ramsey had phoned the business manager the minute she drove off, but sometimes underlings harbored deep resentment—Petra remembered the way Ramsey had turned on Balch during the notification call. Balch standing there and taking it. Used to being a whipping boy? Put a little pressure on, ignite some long-buried anger, and sometimes the little people turned.

She reached her desk at 8 A.M., found a note from Stu saying he'd be in late, probably the afternoon.

No reason given.

She felt her face go hot; crumpled the note and tossed it.

The flight manager at Westward Charter confirmed Ramsey and Balch's Tahoe trip and the 8:30 P.M. Burbank arrival. Ed Marionfeldt, the pilot, happened to be in and she spoke to him. Pleasant, mellow, he'd done tons of trips with *The Adjustor*, no problems, nothing different this time. Petra didn't want to ask too many questions for fear of making Ramsey the prime suspect. Even though he was. She could imagine some defense attorney using Marionfeldt's testimony to illustrate Ramsey's normal mood that day. If it ever got to a trial—dream on.

A phone call to Social Security verified that Estrella Flores was indeed legal, her only registered address Ramsey's Calabasas house.

"So any checks would go there?" she asked a put-upon SSA worker.

"She hasn't filed for benefits, so there are no checks going out."

"If you get a change of address, would you please let me know, Mr. . . ."

"Vicks. If it comes to my attention I'll try, but we don't work with individual petitions unless there's a specific problem—"

"I've got a specific problem, Mr. Vicks."

"I'm sure you do—all right, let me tag this, but I have to tell you things get lost, so you're best off checking in with us from time to time."

She called Player's Management. No one answered; no machine. Maybe Balch was on his way up the coast to Montecito. Taking some downtime to obliterate evidence at the boss's request.

Next came the Merrill Lynch broker. Morad Ghadoomian had a pleasant, unaccented voice, sounded prepared for the call.

"Poor Ms. Boehlinger. I suppose you want to know if she had any financial entanglements. Unfortunately, she didn't."

"Unfortunately?"

"No entanglements," he said, "because there was nothing to tangle."

"No money in the account?"

"Nothing substantial."

"Could you be a little more specific, sir?"

"I wish I could—suffice it to say I was led to expect things that never materialized."

"She told you she'd be investing large sums of money but didn't?"

"Well . . . I'm really not sure what the rules are here in terms of disclosure. Neither is my boss—we've never dealt with a murder before. We do get deceased clients all the time, estate lawyers, IRS reporting, but this . . . suffice it to say Ms. Boehlinger only came by my office once, and that was to fill out forms and seed the account."

"How much seed did she sow?" said Petra.

"Well . . . I don't want to step out of line here . . . suffice it to say it was minimal."

Petra waited.

"A thousand dollars," said Ghadoomian. "Just to get things going."

"In stock?"

The broker chuckled. "Ms. Boehlinger's plans were to build up a sizable securities account. Her timing couldn't have been better—I'm sure you know how well the market's been doing. But she never followed through with instructions, and the thousand remained in a money market fund, earning four percent."

"How much did she say she was going to invest?"

"She never said, she just implied. My impression was that it would be substantial."

"Six figures?"

"She talked about achieving financial independence."

"Who referred her to you?"

"Hmm . . . I believe she just called on her own. Yes, I'm sure of it. A reverse cold call." He chuckled again.

"But she never followed through."

"Never. I did try to reach her. Suffice it to say, I was disappointed."

※

Financial independence—Lisa expecting a windfall? Or just deciding to get serious as she approached thirty by banking Ramsey's monthly support check and living off her editor's salary? A surplus of eighty grand a year could add up.

A reduction in the eighty would have upset Lisa's investment plans.

Had Ramsey balked after Lisa got a job, threatened to take her back to court, and was that why she hadn't followed through?

Or was it something simple—she'd chosen another broker?

Not likely. Why would she have left the thousand sitting there with Ghadoomian?

Was money another issue between the Ramseys?

Money and thwarted passion—no better setup for murder.

She spent an hour on the phone talking to civil servants at the Hall of Records, finally located the original Ramsey divorce papers. The final decree had been granted a little over five months ago. No obvious complications, no petitions to alter support, so if Ramsey had balked, he hadn't made it official.

Then a message came through to call ID Division at Parker Center, no name.

The civilian clerk there said, "I'll put you through to Officer Portwine."

She knew the name but not the face. Portwine was one of the prints specialists; she'd seen his signature on reports.

He had a reedy voice and a humorless, rapid delivery. "Thanks for calling back. This could be either a major-league screwup or something interesting, hope you can tell me which."

"What's wrong?" said Petra.

"You sent us some material from the Lisa Boehlinger-Ramsey crime scene—food wrapper and a book. We obtained numerous prints, most likely female from the size, but no match in any of our files. I was just about to write you a report to that effect when I got another batch, supposedly from another case—burglary on North Gardner, latents from a kitchen knife and some food containers. I had a spare minute, so I looked at them, and they matched yours. So what I need to know is was there some kind of mix-up in the batch numbers, the forms getting screwed up? Because it's bizarre, two batches coming from Hollywood, one after the other, and we get the exact same prints. We caught hell about our cataloging last year. Even though we're careful, you know how much stuff we process. We've been bending over backwards, meaning if there is a problem on this one, it's on your end, not ours."

How could a guy talk so fast? Enduring the speech, Petra had dug her nails into her palm.

"When was the burglary?" she said.

"Last night. A Six car handled it and referred it to one of your D's—W. B. Fournier."

Petra looked over at Wil's desk. Gone and checked out.

"What kind of food containers were printed?"

"Plastic orange juice jug, the prints were on the paper label. And a pineapple—that was interesting, never printed a pineapple before. There're some other samples supposedly coming, says here a Krazy Glue tape from stainless steel plumbing fixtures, and a bottle of shampoo, also tape from . . . looks like a refrigerator, yes, a refrigerator. Sounds like a kitchen burglary. So what's the story?"

"I don't know a thing about the burglary. All we sent you from Ramsey were the food wrapper and the book and the victim's clothing."

"You're telling me this other material isn't yours?"

"That is exactly what I'm telling you," said Petra.

Portwine whistled. "Two sets of prints from the same person, two different crime scenes."

"Looks that way," said Petra. Her heart was racing. "Do you still have the Ramsey batch—specifically, the book?"

"Nope, sent it down to evidence yesterday at seventeen hundred hours, but I did keep a copy of the prints. Some pretty distinctive ridges, that's how I noticed the match."

"Okay, thanks."

"Welcome," said Portwine, grudgingly. "At least we don't have a problem."

※

She left Wil Fournier a note to get in touch. Still no message from Stu, and he didn't pick up his cell phone.

After driving downtown to Parker Center, she smiled her way into the employee parking lot and went up to the third-floor evidence room, where she filled out a requisition for the library book. The evidence warden was a dyed-blond black woman named Sipes who was unimpressed by the fact that the victim was L. Boehlinger-Ramsey and pointed out to Petra that she hadn't written in the case number clearly. Petra erased and rewrote and Sipes disappeared behind endless rows of beige metal shelving, returning ten minutes later, shaking her head. "That lot number hasn't been checked in."

"I'm sure it has," said Petra. "Last night. Officer Portwine from ID sent it over yesterday at five P.M."

"Yesterday? Why didn't you say so? That would be in a different place."

Another fifteen minutes passed before Petra had the evidence envelope in hand and Sipes's permission to take it.

Back in the Ford, she removed the book. *Our Presidents: The March of American History.*

Bag lady with an interest in government and burglary. Breaking into homes stealing food? Most likely schizo. She flipped pages, looking for notes in the margin, some overlooked bit of scrap. Nothing. Remarkably, the checkout card was still in the circulation packet.

The Hillhurst branch. She remembered that. No activity for nine months.

No activity since Bag Lady had lifted it?

Petra tried to imagine her living on the street, thieving, reading. Stealing food and knowledge. There was a certain crazy romanticism to that.

Squatting to pee on a rock. Schizo Girl–Thoreau.

She drove back to Hollywood, found the Hillhurst branch in a strip mall a few blocks south of Los Feliz. Strange setup, not what Petra thought of as a library. Windowless slab, pure government gray-think, right next to a supermarket. Loose shopping carts nearly blocked the front door. A sign said it was a temporary location.

She went in carrying the evidence packet and her business card. The place was one big room, a gray-haired female librarian at a desk in the corner talking on the phone, a younger woman at the checkout desk, one patron—a very old guy in a cloth cap reading the morning paper, a furled umbrella on the table near his elbow, though the June sky was baby blue and rain hadn't fallen in months.

Natural-birch bookshelves on rollers, reading tables of the same pale wood. Travel posters trying to take the place of windows—what a pathetic bit of pretense.

The older librarian was engrossed in her phone chat, and Petra headed for checkout. The young woman was Hispanic, tall, well dressed in a budget gray rayon suit that looked better than it deserved to, draped over her slinky form. She had a pleasant face, warm eyes, decent skin, but what caught Petra's attention was her hair—black, thick, straight, hanging below the hem of her miniskirt. Like that country singer—Crystal Gayle.

"May I help you?"

Petra introduced herself and showed the card.

"Magda Solis," said the woman, clearly thrown by the Homicide designation.

Petra slipped the red book out and placed it on the counter. Magda Solis's right hand flew to her left bosom. "Oh no, has something happened to him?"

"Him?"

"The little boy who . . ." Solis looked over at the gray-haired librarian.

"The boy who stole it?" said Petra. Small body impression, small hands, not a woman, a kid—why hadn't she thought of it? Suddenly, she thought of the painting she'd begun last night, the tree full of lost children, and fought the shudder that began at her shoulders and snaked its way down to her navel.

Solis scratched her chin. "Can we talk outside?"

"Sure."

Solis hurried over to the older woman in a slightly flat-footed gait that managed to be graceful, arms bent tensely, glorious hair flapping. She said something that made the boss librarian frown, and returned, gnawing her lip.

"Okay, I'm on break."

Out in the strip mall, near Petra's Ford, she said, "I'm a trainee, didn't want my supervisor to hear. Did something happen to him?"

"Why don't you tell me what you know, Ms. Solis?"

"I—he's just a little boy, maybe ten or eleven, at first I wasn't even sure it was him. Taking the books, I mean. But he was the only one who ever read the ones that were missing— this one especially he kept coming to, over and over, and then it was gone."

"So he took other books, too."

Solis fidgeted. "But he always brought them back—such a serious little boy. Pretending to be doing homework. I guess he didn't want to attract attention. I finally saw him do it—sneak something back. One that I'd marked missing. Something about oceanography, I think."

"Pretending to do homework?"

"That's what it looked like to me. Always the same few

pages of math problems—he always did math. Algebra. So maybe he's older. Or just gifted—from the things he read, I'll bet he was gifted." Solis shook her head. "He'd do a little math and then head back to the stacks, find something, read for a couple of hours. It was obvious he just loved to read, and that's so rare—we're always trying to attract kids, and it's a struggle. Even when they do come in, they goof around and make noise. He wasn't like that. So well behaved, a little gentleman."

"Except for stealing books."

Solis worried her lip again. "Yes. Well, I know I should have said something, but he returned them, no harm done."

"Why didn't you suggest he get a library card?"

"For that he'd need ID and an adult's signature, and he was obviously a street kid. I could tell from his clothes—he tried to look nice, damped down his hair and combed it, but his clothes were old and wrinkled, had holes in them; so did his shoes. And he wore the same couple of things over and over again. His hair was long, hanging over his forehead; looked like it hadn't been cut in a long time." Reaching back, she touched her own locks and smiled. "I guess we were kindred spirits—please tell me, Detective, has something *happened* to him?"

"He may have been a witness to something. What else can you tell me about him?"

"Small, skinny, Anglo, kind of a pointy chin. Pale complexion, like he's anemic or something. His hair is light brown. Straight. I'm not sure about his eyes—blue, I think. Sometimes he walks with good posture, but other times he hunches over. Like a little old man—he has an old look to him. I'm sure you've seen that on street kids."

"Did you ever speak to him?"

"One time, in the beginning, I came over to him and asked if there was anything I could help him with. He shook his head and looked down at the table. Got a scared look in his eyes. I left him alone."

"A street kid."

"Last year in college I did some volunteer work at a shelter, and he reminded me of the kids I saw there—not that they were into books. The things he read! Biographies, natural history, government—the presidents, this one, was his favorite. I mean, here was a kid society had obviously failed and he still believed in the system. Don't you think that's remarkable? He *must* be gifted. I couldn't turn him in—does my supervisor need to know?"

Petra smiled and shook her head.

Magda Solis said, "I figured the best way I could help him was let him use the library the way he wanted. He returned everything. Except the presidents book—where did you find it?"

"Nearby," said Petra, and Solis didn't press her.

"How long has he been coming to the library?"

"Two, three months."

"Every week?"

"Two to three times a week. Always in the afternoon. He'd arrive around two P.M., stay till four or five. I wondered if he chose afternoons because most kids are off from school then and he'd be less conspicuous."

"Good thinking," said Petra.

The librarian blushed. "I could be all wrong about him. Maybe he's a rich kid from Los Feliz, just likes to act weird."

"When's the last time you saw him, Ms. Solis?"

"Let's see . . . a few days ago—last week. Must have been last Friday. Yes, Friday. He read a big pile of *National Geographic*s and *Smithsonian*s—didn't take anything."

Last weekday before Lisa's murder. He hadn't returned since.

A kid. Living in the park. Reading in the dark—how? By penlight? Part of a street kid's survival stash?

From the Griffith Park lot to the North Gardner burglary was a good four, five miles. Traveling west—why? This was a kid who'd settled down, set up a routine, not a wanderer.

Scared? Because he'd seen something?

"I don't want to put him in danger," said the librarian.

"On the contrary, Ms. Solis. If I find him, I can make sure he's kept *out* of danger." Solis nodded, wanting to believe. The woman had bruised eyes. *Kindred spirit*—had she meant something beyond untrimmed hair?

"Thanks for your help," said Petra.

"You're sure he's not . . . hurt?"

He was okay last night. Breaking into a house and cutting

pineapple. "He's fine, but I do need to locate him. Maybe you can help me with that."

"I've told you everything I know."

Petra took out her pad and a number 3 pencil. "I draw a little. Let's see if we can come up with something."

# CHAPTER 32

▨

"*RAPIST!  POLICE!*"

Why are they screaming that? I throw on my clothes. The screams get far away, I crack open the door, look out, see nothing, and run out the back.

It sounds like they're out in front, still screaming "Rapist!" which is crazy. I'd never rape anyone; I know what it feels like to be hunted.

I run behind the garage, climb over the wooden fence into the next yard. Lights on in that house—colors, a TV behind the curtains; I hear someone laughing.

I run through the yard to the next street, then back up to Hollywood Boulevard, where I turn down another street, then up again, moving back and forth so no one will see me, walking, not running, blend in, blend in . . . no sirens. The cops haven't come yet.

If those women keep lying about rape, they might send up helicopters with those big white beams. That could turn me into a bug on paper . . . then I realize they never saw me; why should anyone think I'm the one?

I slow down even more, pretend everything's great. I'm on another quiet street. People locked inside thinking they're safe.

Or maybe worried they're not.

I'll keep going west, away from the park and Hollywood. Stupid women with plants all over the place who leave food to rot.

✖

The next busy street is Sunset. Weirdos, lots more kids than Hollywood, even more cars. Lots of restaurants, clubs. Across the street a place called *Body Body Body!* with a plastic sign of a naked lady. Then something called the Snake. Club with a big line out in front and two big fat guys not letting anyone in.

Is that guy in that red car looking at me weird?

I turn off to the next quiet street, back and forth again. Now my feet are hurting; I've been walking all day. West, maybe the beach. The beach is clean, isn't it?

I have no money. No way to protect myself.

Should have taken the pineapple knife.

## CHAPTER 33

✖

STU STUDIED THE DRAWING OF THE BOY.

He'd blown in just before 4 P.M., no explanation. Petra burned to have it out with him, but this new development, a potential witness, meant they had to stay on task.

"Good work," he said. "Don't show Harold."

Harold Beatty was a sixty-year-old Rampart narc who sometimes doubled as a sketch artist. All the faces he drew looked exactly the same. The Beatty Family, other D's called them behind his back.

Stu played with his suspenders and the casual gesture angered Petra further. She wanted acknowledgment that this could be something.

Because she wasn't confident it would lead anywhere.

At least the drawing was good. Guiding Magda Solis through every feature, Petra had produced a highly detailed, carefully shaded rendering. The librarian stared at the finished product and whispered, "Amazing."

A nice-looking boy with big, wide-set eyes—Petra left them medium-shaded to accommodate either brown or blue—a narrow nose with pinched nostrils, thin mouth, pointy chin with a dimple. Solis wasn't sure of the boy's eye color, but she was sure of the dimple.

Straight hair, light brown, thick, brushed to the right, sheathing the forehead to the eyebrows, hanging over the ears, fringing wildly at the shoulders. A skinny neck sprouted from a T-shirt. Solis said he was small, well under five feet, eighty pounds tops, wore T-shirts, jeans, tennis shoes with holes in them, sometimes an old ratty sweater.

Oh yeah, and a watch, one of those cheap digital things.

That interested Petra. Was the timepiece an old Christmas present? Something he'd boosted? Where was his home? How long ago had he run away?

A kid. When she applied for detective, she'd been offered the choice of Juvey or Auto Theft, had chosen hot cars. No one asking why . . .

Stu said, "He looks grim," and that was true. The boy's expression was beyond hurt; he looked burdened. Solis's phrase was "crushed by life."

"He takes food from the fridge, showers," said Stu. "Print match to ours. Unbelievable."

"Maybe it's providence," said Petra. "Maybe God's rewarding you for all that piety and church time."

"Sure," said Stu. His voice rasped. She'd never heard him this angry.

What was the big deal? She always kidded him about religion. Before she could say a thing, he stood up and buttoned his jacket. "Okay, let's go tell Schoelkopf."

Turning his back on her, yet again. Since he'd waltzed into the squad room, they hadn't shared a second of eye contact.

"Let's do it later," said Petra. "I've got paperwork—"

He wheeled suddenly. "What's your problem with doing it by the book, Petra? He made it clear he wanted to be informed, and now there's something to inform him about."

He'd made it to the door when Petra caught up with him and stage-whispered. "What the hell's going on?"

"Nothing's going on. We're going to inform Schoelkopf."

"Not that. What's with *you*?"

He kept going, didn't answer.

"Goddamn you, Bishop, you're acting like a complete god-damn jerk!"

He stopped, worked his jaws. His hands were fisted. Never had she cursed at him. She prepared herself for an explosion. This would be interesting.

Instead, his face slackened. "God*damn* me? You could be right."

❋

In Schoelkopf's office, they both clung to frozen calm.

The captain glanced at the drawing and put it down. "You did this, Barbie? Hidden talent . . . maybe we should retire Harold."

He sat back and put his feet on his desk. New shoes, Italian, the soles still black. "It ain't fish and loaves, but maybe it's half of something." He ripped the drawing out of Petra's pad. "Talk to Juvey officers, see if anyone knows this kid. Also shelters, church groups, welfare workers, whoever's dealing with run-aways nowadays. I'll make copies for P.I."

"Public Information? You're going to the press with it?" said Petra.

"You've got a better way of publicizing it?"

"Are we sure we want to publicize it right away?"

"Why the hell not?"

"When we first found the book, you thought it was weak—pointed out the unlikelihood of anyone reading in the dark. So what's the chance the boy actually saw anything? But if we let the world know what he looks like and he's a Hollywood street kid, we could set off a hunting frenzy. Also, if the killer knows Hollywood, he could get to him first—"

"I don't believe this," said Schoelkopf. "Maternal instincts." The feet returned to the floor. He looked ready to spit. "You want to solve a crime or mother some runaway?"

A sickle of rage cut through Petra. A serene voice that couldn't possibly be hers said, "I want to be cautious, sir. All the more so if he is a witness—"

Schoelkopf waved her silent. "You talk about the killer like it's an abstraction. We're dealing with Ram-fucking-sey. You're telling me *he's* gonna find a runaway before we do? Gimme a break—tell you what, Barb, if you're worried about child welfare, keep an eye on Ramsey. That might even work out to our benefit—he goes after the kid, we nab him, just like on TV." Schoelkopf's laugh was metallic. "Yeah, that's definitely part of your assignment. Surveil Ramsey. Who knows, you could be a hero."

Petra's lungs felt wooden. She tried to breathe, tried not to show the effort.

"So we're using the boy as bait," said Stu, and now Petra heard the father of six speaking.

"You too?" said Schoelkopf. "We're tracking down a potential witness to a homicide—Jesus, I can't believe I'm having this discussion. What the fuck have we talked about since the beginning of this case? Being careful. What the fuck do you think will happen if the kid *is* righteous and we make no effort to find him? Don't waste any more of my time. You two produced the lead, now develop it!"

"Fine," said Stu, "but if Petra spends her time on surveillance, our manpower on the rest of the case—"

"Doesn't sound like too much else is going on with the case—"

"Actually, there is something—those similars you told us to look for." Stu told him about Ilse Eggermann, the search for Karlheinz Lauch.

Schoelkopf hid his surprise with a satisfied smile. "So . . . there you go. Okay, you need more manpower—'scuse me, *person* power. Tell Fournier he's on it too. The kid's already his anyway, big bad burglar. The three of you do some real work. At the very least we'll keep the streets safe from refrigerator bandits."

※

Fournier said, "What do I do with my other 187's?"

"Ask *him*," said Stu. "You were the one complaining about no glory. Here's your chance."

"Yeah, I'm the Pineapple Protector—okay, how do we divide it?"

Petra said, "I'm supposed to keep an eye on Ramsey. I've already interviewed him, so recontacts are reasonable. But hell if I'm going to sit outside the gates at RanchHaven all day."

Fournier said, "Don't blame you." He palmed his shaven head.

She knew him casually, had nothing against him. Stu said he was bright. Hope so; she needed to educate him quickly.

She began. Fournier took notes. Stu was looking distracted again.

The final arrangement was Petra would follow up on Estrella Flores and Greg Balch, maybe take another shot at Ramsey, Stu would stay with the Eggermann case, and Fournier would contact Hollywood Juvey, local shelters and crash pads, try to find the boy.

Before the last word was out of Petra's mouth, Stu got up and walked away.

Fournier said, "He all right?"

"Just a little tired," said Petra. "Too much fun."

※

Back at her desk, she called Missing Persons at every LAPD substation, found several Floreses but no Estrella. She copied down the two who were similar in age—Imelda, sixty-three, from East L.A. and Doris, fifty-nine, from Mar Vista, phoned their families, came up negative.

Same for the sheriffs' bureaus. What now? Had Flores bolted back to the old country? Where was that? Mexico? El Salvador? Then she remembered something Ramsey had told her. Greg Balch had hired the new maid, so maybe he'd found Flores, too.

Another reason to chat with ol' Greg.

But first she owed a call to Ron Banks, to let him know the Ramsey DV had gone down out of L.A. County.

He was at his desk, said, "Oh, hi! Haven't gotten back to you because I haven't found any complaints yet."

"You won't," she said. "I just found out Ramsey has a second home in Montecito, Ron. The beating happened there." Something else she hadn't done yet, follow up on that . . .

"Oh, okay," said Banks. "That's Carpinteria Sheriff's." He cleared his throat. "Listen, about last time. Asking you out. I didn't mean to put you on the spot. The last thing you need is distraction—"

"It's okay, Ron."

"That's nice of you to say, but—"

"It's fine, Ron. Really."

"It was unprofessional. My excuse is I've only been divorced a year, not really good at this kind of thing, and—"

"Let's get together," she said, scarcely believing it.

Silence. "You're sure—I mean . . . great, I appreciate it—you name it."

"How about tonight—where do you live?"

"Granada Hills, but I'll be coming from downtown, so it doesn't matter."

"Do you like deli food?"

"I like anything."

"How about Katz's on Fairfax? Say eight."

"Fantastic." He almost sang the word.

She could do that to someone!

# CHAPTER 34

A SKY FULL OF STARS. THE OCEAN ROARS LOUDER than the zoo animals.

I'm at the beach, under the pier, smelling tar and salt, cold, even wrapped in the black plastic sheet.

Wet sand all around, but I found a dry patch near these big thick poles that hold up the pier. I can't sleep, watching and listening to the waves come in and out, but I don't feel tired. The ocean is black as the sheet, little dots of moonlight drawing a slanted line across the water. It's cold, much colder than in the park. If I stay here I'll need to get a real blanket.

A while ago some bent-over guy walked by on the sand, near the edge of the water. Just one guy on the empty beach, and the way he walked, clapping his hands together, jumping up and down every few seconds, I knew he was crazy.

When the sun comes out I'll have to leave.

Two nights ago I saw PLYR kill that woman and now I'm here. Weird. And I didn't even try; it just happened.

I was weaving between Sunset and side streets, passing so many restaurants my nose was stuffed with food smells, guys in red jackets parking cars, people laughing. My stomach was still full, but my mouth started watering.

I had no idea where I was going to end up, just knew I couldn't stand still. I came to a part of Sunset that looked fancier—shinier people, huge billboards advertising movies and clothes and liquor. Then more clubs, more big fat guys standing in front of the door, arms folded over their chests.

The club where it happened was called A-Void, on a dark corner next to a liquor store, painted black with all these black rocks glued to the front. The fat guy there smoked and looked bored. No one was trying to get in. A plastic sign over the door advertised the bands who were playing: Meat Members, Elvis Orgasm, the Stick Figures.

The liquor store was open and a guy in a turban was sitting behind the register. I thought about buying some gum, taking other stuff, but he looked suspicious at me when I stepped through the door so I left. Just then, this tall skinny guy with really long fuzzy black hair and pimples came out of A-Void carrying some drums, ran over to a black van parked around the corner, opened the back door, and put the drums in. The van was full of dents and scrapes, stickers all over the side. He didn't lock it.

He made two more trips and then he went back inside and stayed there.

He never locked it.

The fat guy had gone inside, too.

I slid around the corner, looked in the van's passenger window. It had only front seats; the rest was storage.

I opened the door. No alarm rang.

All I found on the seat was junk—candy wrappers, empty cans and bottles, pieces of paper. Maybe the radio, if I could sell it—how do you take one out?

Then I heard voices and saw the skinny guy standing on the corner, his back to the van. Talking to a short girl with yellow hair with a pink streak through the middle of it. She might've seen the van if she looked at it, but she was paying attention to him. It looked like they were arguing. He turned.

Too late to jump out.

I jumped in, closed the door, threw myself in back, and hid

behind the drums. They were half covered by this thick sheet of black plastic and I got under it, knocking my bones against metal. It really hurt; I had to bite my lip not to cry out.

The plastic was cold and smelled like bleach.

The back door opened again and the van shook as something landed near me.

Slam. Another slam.

I heard the girl's voice from up front: "You guys were hot."

"Bullshit."

"No really, I mean it, Wim."

"We sucked and everyone knows we sucked, so don't bullshit me—did you bring my jacket?"

"Uh . . . sorry, I'll go back and get it."

"Shit! Get in there fast!"

Another open and slam.

Cough. "Fucking witch . . ." The motor went on and the metal floor beneath me started to vibrate and I tried to hold on to something so I wouldn't roll, but the drums were round and I didn't want to make noise so I pressed against the floor like a spider.

The radio went on. He tried a bunch of different channels, said "Fuck this shit!," turned it off.

A rubbing sound, then a click, and I smelled something familiar.

Weed. Back in the trailer I went to sleep with my nose full of it, wondering if it would give me brain damage.

Slam. "Here you go, honey."

"Do you know what that is? Lambskin from fucking Mongolia or Tibet or some place. And those nailheads are, like, hammered by hand and put in by blind peasants who say special prayers or something—I gave my fucking blood for that, and you leave it in there! Shit!"

"I'm sorry, Wim!"

They both smoked. No one talked. The motor was running, and I was just pressing my fingers to the floor, trying not to move or breathe, wondering where this was going to take me. No way out, because the drums blocked the back door.

At least it was warm.

She said, "Gimme another taste—ah, that's good shit."

"Hey, don't give it a blow job—give it back."

"Where you wanna go, Wim?"

"Where? Europe—where the fuck do you think? Home, I need to crash."

"You don't wanna go over to the Whiskey?"

"Fuck no, why would I wanna do that?"

"You said—remember?"

"Huh?"

"Before we left we were talking, you know, maybe like afterwards we'd check out the Whiskey, someone you know might be there, maybe you'd jam—"

"That was then, this is now . . . someone I know. Right. Knowing is fucking bullshit. *Doing* is the name of the game and tonight we did fucking *nothing*—man, I can't believe how bad we sucked. Skootch was, like, brain-dead and that guy in the second row I'm pretty sure was maybe from Geffen and he left early—fuck, I'm gonna die without being famous!"

"You will be fam—"

"Shut the fuck *up*!"

The van started moving, going awhile—south—then turning right, which meant west again. Wim drove angry, speeding, making sharp turns, fast stops.

It took a while for the girl to talk again. "Hey, Wim?"

Grunt.

"Wim? What you said before?"

"Whuh?"

"About not giving head to the joint? But there are other joints, right?" Giggle.

"Yeah, right, I had a triumphant night and now I'm ready to be romantic—just shut up and let me get us home—I can't believe how bad we sucked!"

After that no one talked at all.

I tried to follow each turn, drawing a map in my head, but with all those turns I lost track.

Finally, he stopped and I thought, I'm cooked. He's going to get his drums, find me, take his anger out on me.

I felt around under the plastic, wanting something to swing with, touched cold metal, but it wouldn't come free. Totally cooked.

Open. Slam. Footsteps. That got softer. Disappeared.

I got out from under the plastic. The van smelled like one big joint.

It was parked on a quiet street full of apartments.

I climbed into the front seat, unrolled the window. This could be anywhere. Maybe he'd even taken me back to Hollywood. The air outside was cold, so I crawled in back again, managed to pull the black plastic sheet loose, folded it, tucked it under my arm, returned to the front, and got out.

A new smell.

Salt. A fishy salt.

Once when I was little, Mom took me to the beach, a long bus ride from Watson. I don't know exactly what beach it was and we never went back there, but the sand was smooth and warm and she bought snow-cones for both of us. It was hot and dry and crowded and we stayed there all day, me digging holes in the sand, Mom just sitting there in her bikini listening to the radio. She didn't bring any sunscreen and we both got burned. I'm lighter than her and got it worse, turning blistery, feeling like my whole body was on fire. All the way back on the bus I screamed, Mom telling me to be quiet, but not like she meant it—she was pink as bubble gum, knew the pain was real.

Back in the trailer, she tried to give me wine, but I wouldn't take it, the smell bothered me, and even though I must have been only four or five, I'd seen her drunk, was afraid of alcohol. She tried to force me, pushing the bottle up against my lips and holding one of my hands down, but I just kept twisting my head, pretending my mouth was glued shut, till finally she left me alone and I just lay there, every inch of my body roasting while she finished the wine herself.

Smelling the salt, I remembered all that.

And more: Mom sitting on a towel; her bikini was black. Maybe she was hoping some guy would notice her, but no one did, probably 'cause of me.

So here I was. The beach.

Nowhere to go after that.

# CHAPTER 35

STILL NO ANSWER AT GREG BALCH'S OFFICE. Petra decided to eyeball the place.

At 6 P.M., she drove out of the station lot, picking up Cahuenga at Franklin and taking it over the hill.

Studio City was the Valley, but to her it had always seemed un-Valley-like. North of Ventura Boulevard, the neighborhood was the usual grid of anonymous apartment tracts, but to the south were pretty hills up to Mulholland, winding trails, stilt houses that had survived the quake. The commercial mix along Ventura was a little shabby in spots, some strip-mall development, but also plenty of antique shops, recording studios, sushi bars, jazz clubs, a few gay bars—definitely funkier than the rest of the Valley.

Nothing avant-garde about Player's Management's home base, though. The company occupied a dreary two-story box the color of chocolate milk, set back from the street and fronted by a parking lot. Weeds whiskered through the asphalt, gutters sagged, stucco corners were chipped. H. Carter Ramsey wasn't much of a landlord.

Balch's black Lexus was the only vehicle in the lot. So he was in, not answering the phone—orders from the boss to discourage the media? She peeked inside the car. Empty.

Two tenants took up the ground floor of the chocolate cube, a travel agency sporting the green tree flag of Lebanon and advertising discount flights to the Middle East and a wholesale-to-the-public beauty-supply store. Both closed.

Rusting open steps on the right side climbed to a cement walkway, and three mustard-colored doors were in need of refinishing. Suite A housed Easy Construction, Inc.; B was something called La Darcy Hair Removal; and tucked in back was Player's Management. No windows on the west wall. Oppressive.

She knocked, got no answer, knocked again, and Balch opened.

He was wearing a black zip-up velvet sweat suit with white piping and looked genuinely surprised to see her. Odd. Ramsey had to have called him. Maybe he was an actor, too.

"Hi." He offered a soft hand. "C'mon in. Detective Conners, was it?"

"Connor."

He held the door for her. The suite consisted of two low-ceilinged rooms connected by a door, now open. The rear space looked bigger, messy. Piles of paper all over the cheap green carpet; take-out cartons. The front room was furnished with a gold couch and a scruffy oak desk piled with yet more paper. Flagrantly grained fake rosewood walls were covered with photographs, mostly black-and-whites, the kind you saw at every dry cleaner's in town—big airbrushed smiles of stars and has-beens, dubious autographs.

But only one celeb in these. Ramsey as cowboy, police officer, soldier, Roman centurion. An especially ludicrous shot of young H. Cart decked out like some kind of space alien—plastic body suit armored by exaggerated pecs, rubbery-looking antennae protruding from his puffy sixties mop-top. No mustache; wide, white, hire-me smile. A passing resemblance to Sean Connery. The guy had been a looker.

A color photo at the top showed Ramsey decades later dressed in a nifty sport jacket, turtleneck, looking flinty, striking an action pose with a 9mm. *Dack Price: The Adjustor.* She should probably watch the damn show.

She was about to enter the back office when she noticed something that confirmed her guess about Balch as performer. At the bottom of the wall, half hidden by the desk. Low man in the exhibit—not a coincidence, she was willing to bet.

Balch in his twenties. He'd been decent-looking, too. A good fifty pounds lighter, sun-blond, nicely defined muscles, like a hero in one of those beach movies she used to watch for laughs—Tab Hunter or Troy Donahue.

But even in his youth, the business manager had worn a dull, subservient smile that robbed him of star quality.

"Antiques," said Balch, sounding self-conscious. "You know you're old when you don't recognize yourself anymore."

"So you acted, too."

"Not really. I should take that stuff down." The sweats were tight around his paunch, baggy at the seat. New white sneakers. Now that she had a good look, she could see that his thin, waxy hair was a mixture of blond and white. Pink scalp peeked through.

"Can I get you some coffee?" He indicated the rear office, stood by the door, waiting for her to enter.

"No thanks." She stepped in. Finally a couple of windows, but they were covered by chenille drapes the color of old newspaper. No natural lighting, and the single desk lamp Balch had on didn't do much to pierce the gloom.

The clutter was monumental—papers on the floor, chairs crowding another cheap desk, bigger, L-shaped. Ledgers, tax manuals, corporate prospectuses, government forms. On the shorter arm of the desk was a white plastic coffeemaker spotted with brown. Kentucky Fried Chicken box in a corner, grease stains on the underside of the open lid. A glimpse of breaded fowl.

Total slob. Maybe that's why Ramsey maintained him in low-rent circumstances. Or maybe that was the essence of their relationship.

All those years playing lackey. Could she wedge the guy? He did live in Rolling Hills Estates, very pricey. So Ramsey paid well for loyalty.

Balch cleared an armchair for her, tossing papers into a corner, and sat behind the desk, hands laced on his belly. "So how's it going? The investigation."

"It's going." Petra smiled. "Do you have any information that might help me, Mr. Balch?"

"Me? Wish I did, I still can't get over it." His lower jaw shifted from side to side. "Lisa was . . . a nice girl. Little hot-tempered, but basically a great person."

"Hot-tempered?"

"Listen, I know you've heard about Cart hitting her, all that stuff on TV, but it only happened once. Not that I'm excusing it—it was wrong. But Lisa had a temper. She went off on him all the time."

Trying to blame the victim to excuse the boss? Did he realize he was offering a motive for the boss's rage?

"So she had a tendency to criticize Mr. Ramsey?"

Balch touched his mouth. His eyes had gotten small. "I'm not saying they didn't get along. They loved each other. All I'm saying is Lisa could be . . . that I can see her—forget it, what do I know, I'm just talking."

"You can see her getting someone pretty angry."

"Anyone can get anyone angry. That has nothing to do with what happened. This is obviously some kind of maniac."

"Why do you say that, Mr. Balch?"

"The way it—it was done. Totally insane." Balch's hand rose to his forehead, rubbing, as if trying to erase a headache. "Cart's devastated."

"How long have you and Cart known each other?"

"We grew up together, upstate New York, went to high school and college together at Syracuse, played football—he was the quarterback, damn good one. Scouted by the pros, but he tore his hamstring at the end of the senior season."

"And you?"

"Offensive lineman."

Protecting the quarterback.

"So you go back a long ways."

Balch smiled. "Centuries. Before your time."

"Did you come out to Hollywood together?"

"Yup. After graduation, one of those last-fling things before we settled down. Also to cheer Cart up—he was pretty upset about losing out on the NFL. His dad owned a hardware store and wanted Cart to take it over and he thought he'd probably do that."

"And you?"

"Me?" Surprised that she cared. "I had a business degree, some offers from accounting firms, figured eventually I'd get a CPA."

Petra gazed around at the sty he called an office. Weren't bean counters supposed to be organized?

"So what led you to acting?"

Balch stroked the top of his pale head. "It was one of those weird things. Not exactly Lana Turner at Schwab's—are you old enough to know about that?"

"Sure," said Petra. Knowing it from her father. The honeymoon he and his bride had taken to California. Kenneth Connor had loved L.A.; saw it as an anthropologist's dream. Look at me now, Dad. Hobnobbing with the never-greats. Working the *industry*.

"You and Cart were both discovered?" she said.

Balch smiled again. "No. Cart was. It was right out of a script. We were a few days from going back to Syracuse, having a couple of beers at Trader Vic's—over at the Beverly Hilton, this was before Merv owned it. Anyway, some guy comes over and says, 'I've been watching you two fine-looking young men; would you like parts in a movie?' And gives us his card. We're thinking it's got to be a scam, or maybe he's a que— Some gay guy hustling. But the next morning, Cart pulls out the card and says, Hey, let's call, for the hell of it. 'Cause we were gonna go home and get jobs, why not be adventurous. Turns out it was for real, a casting agency. We went down and auditioned, both got parts—not that it was any big deal. Not even a B movie, more like D. A western. Straight to the Dixie drive-in circuit."

Balch moved papers around atop his desk, making no impact on the clutter. "Anyway, one thing led to another and we decided to stay in L.A., got a few more jobs over the next year, nonunion stuff, barely enough to make the rent. Then I didn't get any more calls, but Cart started getting lots, better ones, then an agent, and he was making some decent money, mostly in westerns. I decided to go home. It was winter, almost Christmas, I remember thinking my folks were already mad at me for taking the year off, what would Christmas dinner be like."

"So you lost faith in Hollywood?"

Balch smiled. "It wasn't a matter of faith. I wasn't qualified, didn't have the talent to make it—never got speaking parts, just crowd fillers, walk-throughs, that kind of thing. Couldn't find any accounting jobs and I'd blown all my job offers back East, but I figured something would turn up. Then Cart asked me to stay, said it would be fun, we could continue to hang out, he'd find me something. And he did. Bookkeeping gig at Warner Brothers."

He spread his arms, smiled again. "And that's the whole glamorous story."

"When did you start managing Cart's business?"

"Soon as he began making serious bucks. He'd seen what unscrupulous managers could do, wanted someone he could trust. By then I was working in business affairs at ABC, knew something about the industry."

"Do you manage anyone else?"

Balch shifted his weight, smoothed out a black velvet fold of sweatshirt. "I do a few favors for people, facilitate a deal now and then, but Cart's investments keep me busy."

"So he's done pretty well."

"He's earned it."

Spoken like a true lineman.

"So you handle his contracts?"

"He's got an entertainment lawyer, but yeah, I vet things."

"What else do you do for him?"

"Prepare his taxes, keep track of things. We're diversified—real estate, securities, the usual. There's some property management. It keeps me busy—anything else I can do for you?"

"Just what you're doing," said Petra. "Filling in personal details."

"About Cart?"

"Cart, Lisa, anything."

As if the matter required great contemplation, Balch closed his eyes. Opened them. The hands were back on his middle. Blond Buddha.

"Cart and Lisa," he said very softly, "is a very sad story. He really flipped for her, felt embarrassed about it. The age difference. I told him it didn't matter, he was in better shape than guys half his age. And Lisa was crazy about him. I thought they were the best thing ever happened to each other." A pained expression crossed his puffy face. "I really don't know what happened. Marriage is tough." The eyes opened. "Been there twice. Who's to say what makes people tick?"

Petra produced her pad and Balch moved back a bit, as if repulsed by that bit of procedure. "If you could please give me the timetable for Sunday—the trip to Tahoe and after you got back. As precisely as possible."

"Timetable . . . sure." His story matched Ramsey's and that of the pilot, Marionfeldt, detail for detail. The Tahoe trip, nonstop business, uneventful flight back, both men asleep before 10 P.M., waking up, exercising, showering, eating breakfast, putting golf balls.

Pleasant dreams during the time Lisa had been murdered.

Petra said, "Okay, thanks . . . by the way, I was just curious why you call your company Player's Management."

"Oh, that." Balch let out a snort-laugh. "Football days. We were amateurs, looking for something catchy. And anonymous—no mention of Cart's name. I came up with it."

Petra wondered if that was all of it. In the industry, players were those with power. Had he dreamed of that once?

"So your job," she said, "is protecting Cart's interest. What did you do after Lisa went public with the domestic violence incident?"

"What was there to do? The damage was already done."

"You didn't ask her not to go public again?"

"I wanted to, but Cart said no, it was personal, not business. I disagreed."

"Why's that?"

"This town, personal and business sometimes can't be separated. But that's what Cart wanted, so I listened."

Flipping pages, Petra said, "So you pay all of Cart's bills."

"They go through me, yes."

"Including Lisa's spousal support."

"Yup—there's an example of the kind of guy Cart is. Lisa's lawyer made an outrageous request. They'd only been married for a little over a year. I'd been through it twice, had a pretty good idea what she'd settle for, but Cart said no negotiation, give it to her."

Frowning now. Resentful? Jealous?

"So he's pretty generous," said Petra.

"Exactly." He stood up. "Now, if you don't mind, it's a little late—"

"Sure," said Petra, smiling and rising, too. He waited by the door again, and as she passed close she smelled him. Heavy fruity cologne and sweat.

Out in the front room, she said, "Oh, one more thing. Cart's maid Estrella Flores. Any idea where she went?"

"Cart told me she quit without notice. How's that for loyalty? I got him a new girl."

"Through the same agency?"

"Yup."

"Remember the name?"

"Of the agency? Some place in Beverly Hills—the Nancy Downey Agency." He shot a cuff and looked at his watch.

"I appreciate your time, Mr. Balch."

Before she left the office, she glanced at the wall of photos. Two young guys striking poses. Players. Next to the pictures, Balch did look old.

## CHAPTER 36

SHE DROVE TO A GAS STATION PAY PHONE, GOT the number of the Nancy Downey Agency, and called it, though it was well past business hours. No machine. Something to wake up for tomorrow.

Taking Laurel Canyon back to the city, she reviewed the interview with Balch.

Nothing dramatic, but he had provided a possible lead to Estrella Flores, and had offered evidence of friction between Lisa and Ramsey.

*She went off on him all the time.*

Consistent with what Kelly Sposito had said about Lisa's sarcasm.

Impotent ex-hubby; sharp-tongued wife. Ramsey said she had a habit of shoving him. Had she finally pushed him too far?

How much did Balch know? Had he heard Ramsey leave the house during the early-morning hours? Go into the car museum and pull out the Mercedes? Or the Jeep?

How far would the lineman go to protect the quarterback?

Players. Actors. What was real, what was scripted?

Time to talk to the night guard who'd been on shift Sunday. Then she thought of something. RanchHaven. A place that big, smack in the fire zone, there'd have to be a second way out for safety. If so, was it guarded too? Or was there some way for residents to exit without tipping off the security staff?

Too many question marks. Not quizzing the guard right away had been amateurish; she felt like a blind painter.

Was it worth a ride out to Calabasas right now? She'd been going all day, and if she didn't let go of it, she wouldn't sleep and wouldn't that be pretty—one groggy, impaired D mucking things up further.

Tomorrow morning her artwork would appear all over the news and leads about the boy in the park would start pouring in, most of them useless. The whole thing was a distraction. And something about the boy's eyes bothered her—he'd already seen plenty. She didn't even want to think about an eleven-year-old witnessing something like that.

She thought about him. Eating dinner alone in Griffith Park. Reading. Stealing books. Pathetic but charming—enough! Go home, E.T. Soak in tub, eat sandwich—oh, Jesus, she couldn't go home. The eight o'clock appointment with Ron Banks! What had possessed her to *do that*?

She zipped across Sunset and checked her watch. Seven forty-six. Barely enough time to get to Katz's, let alone freshen up and change.

The guy would be forced to stare across the table at a hag.

Big deal; this was no real date.

What was it, then?

She made it at three minutes to, paid for parking in a nearby lot, and walked into Katz's corned-beef air. Greeted with a wide, false smile by a dyspeptic waitress who remembered her cop tips, she took a booth toward the back, ordered a Coke, headed for the ladies' room to wash up.

In front of a soap-specked mirror, she fluffed her hair and disapproved of her face. Definitely haggard, every bone showing. Paler than usual, too, and something seemed to be tugging her mouth down—some cruel god sketching in the wrinkles that would soon be engraved there? At least the black pantsuit of the day was holding up okay—let's hear it for viscose.

When she returned, the drink was there and Banks was walking through the front door. She waved him over.

He smiled and sat down. "Good to see you again." His hands settled on the table, fingers drumming. Unfolding the paper napkin, he placed it on his lap. His hands kept moving.

"Hit much traffic coming over?" she said.

"Not bad." He looked different. A stranger.

As opposed to? She was sitting across from a stranger—an uncomfortable stranger; look at those hands. Straining for conversation when a hot bath would have proved celestial.

The waitress brought a bowl of sour-pickle slices and Petra took one. Defining the ground rules right from the start: garlic on the breath; don't think of getting close. That seemed to relax Banks and he reached for one, too.

"These are great," he said. "Never been here."

"Good place."

"Sometimes I go to Langer's, on Alvarado. People are getting shot over at MacArthur Park and they're still lining up for pastrami at Langer's."

"Been there," said Petra. "I'm kind of a deli freak."

"No cholesterol worries?"

"Good genetics," she said. "Cholesterol-wise, anyway."

He laughed. Why did he look so different? Younger, even more boyish than at Ramsey's house. Despite being dressed more formally—navy double-breasted suit, pale blue shirt, maroon tie. Nice. Had *he* somehow found time to spruce up?

Then she realized what the difference was. The mustache was gone. She remembered it as a smallish, blond-gray thing, no big soup-strainer like his partner's. But its absence made a difference. No gray in his head hair; losing the 'stache took off years. He had a pleasant face—a little narrow, the nose a little off-center, but the eyes were well placed. Hazel. Long lashes. The now exposed mouth yielding, but not in a weak way. Hairless hands. Young skin. She saw him as someone who'd gone through puberty late, would preserve well.

The mouth turned up slightly at the corners—a perpetual smile that might have gotten him into trouble as a schoolboy: *Banks, stop smirking.*

She realized she was staring; touched her upper lip and arched an eyebrow.

"Got rid of it last night," he said, almost apologetic. "It was an experiment. My daughters didn't like it, said it tickled. I shaved it off right in front of them. They thought it was hilarious."

"How many daughters do you have?"

"Two. They're five and six."

Knowing he'd carry pictures, she asked if he had any.

"As a matter of fact . . ." he said, pulling several from his wallet.

Two pretty little things, both dark-haired but with fair skin, somewhat Latina-looking. Big brown eyes, long hair styled into ringlets, identical pink, frothy dresses. No obvious resemblance to Banks, though she thought she saw something in the younger one's smile.

"Totally adorable. What are their names?"

"The older one's Alicia and the baby's Beatrix. We call her Bee, or Honeybee."

A and B. Someone liked order. She handed the photos back to him, and he took a peek before slipping them behind his credit cards.

The waitress stomped over and asked if they were ready.

Petra knew what she wanted, but she picked up her menu to give him time.

The waitress's foot tapped. "I can come back—"

"No, I think we're okay. I'll take the pastrami-coleslaw combo. With fries."

"And you?"

Banks said, "Smoked turkey on a kaiser roll. Potato salad."

"Something to drink?"

"Coffee."

Alone again, she said, "How often do you get to be with them?"

"They live with me."

"Oh."

"Their mom's Spanish—from Spain. She trains horses, teaches riding. She went back to work at a resort in Majorca and gave me custody. She visits every few months, is still trying to figure out where she's going to live."

"Must be tough," said Petra.

"It is. I'm trying to tell them Mommy loves them, cares about them, but what they know is she isn't there. It's been really tough. I just got them into therapy; hopefully it'll help."

Most cops ran from anything psychiatric unless they were filing for disability. Banks's easy admission interested her.

She watched him eat another pickle. Narrow hands; the free one continued to drum. The fingers long but sturdy. Impeccable nails.

He chewed slowly. Everything about him seemed slow and

deliberate. Except the hands. All his tension filtered down to his fingertips. "She was always after me to grow a mustache. My ex. Said it was *muy macho*." He laughed. "So after she's gone, I do it. Guess a therapist would have something to say about *that*. Anyway, she's still trying to find herself. Hopefully, she will soon."

"How long's it been?"

"Final decree was just over a year ago. I'm able to feel sorry for her now, see her as someone with serious problems, but— Oh, by the way, I talked to the Carpinteria sheriff and he said Lisa Ramsey never filed any DV complaint on Ramsey there, either. They've got no calls to the house, period."

Whiplash change of subject. He knew it and blushed, and Petra groped for a way to rescue him.

The waitress solved that problem, setting down his coffee hard enough to slosh the saucer and barking, "Your food's coming up."

She hurried off, and Petra said, "Thanks for checking, Ron."

"Least I could do."

The two of them worked on their drinks. The restaurant was almost full, the usual mixture of soup-sipping old folk and Gen-X depressives showing they didn't care about dietary fat. Behind the stocked case, countermen sliced and wrapped and cracked jokes, the briny aromas of herring and cured meat and stuffed derma yielding to sweetness as fresh rye loaves came out of the kitchen on steel trays.

Suddenly, Petra felt hungry, a little more relaxed.

"How about you?" said Banks. "Been married?"

"Divorced two and a half years ago, no kids." Getting that out of the way before he could ask. "So you've got them full-time. Must be challenging."

"My mom helps out—picks them up from school and baby-sits when I have to work late. They're great girls, sweet, smart, into sports—Alicia does soccer, gives the boys a run. Bee's not sure if she likes soccer or T-ball, but she's pretty coordinated."

Sports dad. Her father had gone that route with all five kids. Football for the boys, softball for Petra. Every Sunday, into a hideous uniform. She hated the entire experience, faked enthusiasm to please him, stuck with it for three summers. Years later he told her she'd done him a big favor quitting; he'd yearned for some free time on weekends.

Single father—was that why she'd gotten together with Banks?

He seemed so unguarded. What was he doing as a cop? She asked him how he got into law enforcement.

"My dad was a fireman—it was either that or police work," he said. "Always wanted one of the two."

"I don't want to sound chauvinistic, but why the sheriff's and not LAPD?"

He grinned. "Wanted to do real police work—seriously, back then Lulu—my ex—was talking about opening up her own equestrian school one day, we figured we'd be living somewhere unincorporated, so I applied to the sheriff. How about you?"

She gave him a very spare version of the artist-to-detective transition.

He said, "You paint? Beatrix is kind of artistic. Or at least she seems that way to me. Her mom tried to do pottery. I've still got the wheel at home—just sitting there, as a matter of fact. Want it?"

"No thanks, Ron."

"You're sure? It seems a waste."

"I appreciate the offer, but I just paint."

"Oh, okay. What kinds of things do you paint?"

"Anything."

"And you actually did it professionally."

"I wasn't exactly Rembrandt."

"Still, you must be good."

She gave him a rundown of her ad agency days, her mouth running while her brain thought: How cute, each of us shifting the focus to the other. In her case, defensiveness, but Banks seemed really interested in her. Polar opposite of Nick. All the other men she'd dated since Nick—artists, then cops. Even when they talked about you, it was really just a ploy to get it back to me me me.

This one seemed different. Or was she just flattering herself?

She ended her recitation: "Like I said, no big deal."

"Still," he said, "it's tough making any kind of living creatively. I had an uncle did some sculpture, could never make a dime—ah, here comes the food, whoa, look at those portions!"

He ate slowly, and that prevented Petra from wolfing. Good influence, Detective Banks.

In between bites, they chatted about work. Dry stuff: benefits, insurance, the usual gripes, comparing blue and tan bureaucracies, good-natured kidding about intramural sports competitions. Finding more common ground than differences. She noticed he wasn't wearing his gun.

When their sandwiches were gone, they each ordered apple pie à la mode. Petra finished hers first, tried idly to pick up crumbs with the tines of her fork.

"You like to eat," said Banks. "Thank God."

The fork paused midair. She put it down.

He blushed again. "I—no offense—what I mean is, I think that's great. Seriously. It sure doesn't show—at least as far as I can—" He shook his head. "Oh, Lord, I am *not* good at this."

She found herself laughing. "It's okay, Ron. Yes, I do have a healthy appetite when I remember to sit down for a meal."

He continued to shake his head, wiped his mouth with his napkin, folded it neatly, and placed it next to his plate. "Whatever I just gargled out, please take it as a compliment."

"So taken," said Petra. "You're saying love of food's a healthy thing."

"Exactly. Too many girls these days get crazy about food. I think about that because I have daughters. My ex always bugged them, obsessed with being skinny—" He stopped himself again. "Not too cool, bringing her up every minute."

"Hey, she was a big part of your life. It's normal." Implying that she'd done the same with Nick. But she hadn't. She'd never talked about him to anyone.

"Was," he said. "Past tense." He raised one hand and sliced air vertically. "So . . . how's the case coming?"

"Not too brilliantly." She talked about it without giving him details. Liking him but not forgetting that he was non–LAPD.

He said, "Situations like that, publicity, no way you can do your job properly."

"Ever have one like that?"

"Once in a while." Touching his napkin, he looked away. Wary, too?

"Once in a while?" she echoed.

"You know us country bumpkin lawmen, runnin' down rustlers, protectin' the pony express."

"Ah," said Petra. "Anything I'd have heard about?"

"Well," he said, "Hector and I did do some work on the County Gen slasher."

Mega-case, three years ago. Wacko killer cutting up nurses on the grounds of the county hospital, four victims in three months. The bad guy turned out to be an orderly who'd served time for rape and assault. He'd faked his way through personnel screening—worked the surgical floors, of all things. Before he was caught, the nurses had threatened to strike.

"That was yours?"

"Hector's and mine."

"Now *I'm* impressed."

"Believe me, it was no big sherlock," he said. "Everything pointed to an insider. It was just a matter of flipping paper, checking time cards, eliminating negatives till we found the positive."

Petra remembered the feminist frustration, media noise—hadn't there been an initial task force? "Were you on it from the beginning?"

He blushed again. "No, they called us in after a few months."

"So you two are rescuers."

"Sometimes," he said. "And sometimes we get rescued. You know how it is."

What she knew was that the County Gen slasher was a major case and that he was a rescuer, top dog. And that's who the sheriff had sent for the notification call to Ramsey?

Why was he being so cagey about it? Modest? Or sent by the tans to pump her for details?

"Any ideas on Ramsey?" she said.

"Like I said at his house, the guy rang my bell, but I'm not a big one for bells." He smiled. "Give me time cards anytime."

She smiled back. He drummed the table. Rubbed the spot where his mustache had been. The waitress gave him the check and, over Petra's protests, he insisted on paying for it. "Hey, you put up with me, you deserve a sandwich."

"Nothing to put up with," she heard herself say.

They left the deli and he walked her to her car. A warm night; still a bit of foot traffic on Fairfax and the newsstand across the street was crowded with browsers. The food smells from Katz's followed them. He didn't walk close to her, seemed to be consciously avoiding it.

"So," he said, when they got to the Ford. "This was great. I—is there some place you'd like to go? If you're not too tired, I mean—maybe some music. Are you into music?"

"I'm a little bushed, Ron."

The crushed look on his face said the evening was personal, nothing to do with the case, and she felt bad for suspecting him.

"Sure," he said. "You'd have to be."

He held out his hand and they shook briefly. "Thanks a lot, Petra, I really appreciate it."

Had a man ever thanked her before just for spending time? "Thank *you*, Ron."

He tilted forward, as if ready to kiss her, then rocked back, gave a small, salutelike wave, and turned, hands in pockets.

"What kind of music do you like?" she said. Figuring country; it had to be traditional country.

He stopped, faced her again, shrugged. "Mostly rock. Old stuff—blues, Steve Miller, Doobie Brothers. Used to play that kind of stuff in a band."

"Really?" She fought a giggle. "Did you have long hair?"

"Long enough," he said, walking back to her. "Don't get me wrong—we weren't professionals. I mean, we did a few club dates, played the Whiskey way back when. That's where I met my—" Clamping a hand over his mouth.

"Sure," said Petra, laughing, "and not just her, right? You met tons of babes. That's why you joined a band in the first place. Don't tell me—drums." Those active hands.

"You got it."

"Drummers always get the girls, right?"

"Don't ask *me*," said Banks. "I was always too busy trying to keep the beat."

"Still play?"

"Not for years. My old kit's rusting in the garage."

Along with the potter's wheel, bikes, probably piles of old toys, kid stuff, heaven knew what else. Petra pictured a small house full of Levitz furniture. Far cry from the horse ranch that had never materialized.

"So where do you go to listen to music?" she said.

"Used to go to the Country Club, in Reseda. It's not a country place, it's rock—"

"I know where it is."

"Oh. Sorry."

"What about this side of the hill?" she said.

"Don't know," he said. "Don't go out much." The admission embarrassed him, and he looked at his watch.

"Need to get back?" she said.

"No, they're asleep by now. I called them before I left. My mom's staying over. I just want to phone, make sure everything's okay—"

"Call from my place," she said. "It's not far from here."

Thinking: He'd told his mother he'd be late. Big plans or blind optimism?

For some reason, she didn't care.

※

While he talked to his mother, she fixed her makeup. Thankfully, the apartment was in decent shape. She'd barely lived in it since the case broke. She invited him to take off his jacket and hung it up. Standing in the kitchen, they each had a glass of red wine. He complimented her decor. At his insistence, she showed him her art. Not the works in progress, her old portfolio, color blowups of pictures she'd sold through the co-op gallery.

He was impressed; didn't try to touch her.

They moved to the living room and went through her small CD collection, trying to find something they both owned, coming up only with Eric Clapton's *Derek and the Dominos*.

Sitting two feet apart on Petra's couch, they listened to half the album, then his hand shifted six inches closer to hers and remained there. She covered her half of the distance and their fingers touched, then entwined.

Sweaty hands, but neither of them dared wipe. She found herself gripping his knuckles too hard and reduced the pressure.

He breathed faster but didn't move.

During "Bell Bottom Blues" he tilted his head toward her and they kissed.

Closed-mouthed, mutual garlic, for what seemed like a long time, then a wide, open exploration full of clicking teeth and swirling tongues, hands on back of neck, soft lips—he had very soft lips; she was glad the mustache was gone. When they broke, they were both robbed of air.

He was ready for more, but the hunger in his eyes shook Petra and she pulled away. They listened to the rest of the song sitting still, holding hands again. She was wet, her nipples ached, her body demanded loving, but she didn't want it, not with him, not now. One more song and she got up to use the bathroom. When she returned he was standing, jacket on.

She sat down again, an invitation, but he remained on his feet, in front of her, reaching down to touch her hair, her cheek, her chin. She looked up, saw his bottom teeth pinching his upper lip.

She was trembling now, and had he tried again, who knew what would have happened.

He just stood there.

She got up, put her arm in his, and walked him to the door.

He said, "I'd really like to see you again."

More confidence in his voice, but still unsure.

"I'd like that, too."

A half hour later, alone in her bed, naked, having touched her-self and bathed, someone's late-night TV squeaking through the darkness, she thought of everything she needed to do in the morning.

# CHAPTER 37

THE SUN COMES UP BEHIND ME, ORANGE. BRIGHTER than in the park, no trees to cover it. The ocean is roaring, gray. The black plastic's too thin; I'm cold.

No one's out on the beach yet, so I just lie there watching the sun and the few cars up on the coast highway going back and forth. The thick poles that hold up the pier are black with tar and crusted with barnacles. I see one that's open, reach over and poke it, and it closes.

The Jacques Cousteau book had a chapter about barnacles. They stay where they are, eat whatever floats by. They make their own glue and it's as good as Krazy Glue. Sometimes they're impossible to move.

Okay, now it's warming up a little; I better move. I get up and shake the sand out of my hair, fold the plastic and tuck it behind one of the poles, using a rock to weigh it down.

Time to get some new stuff. Food, money. A hat. I remember that sunburn. Maybe some sunscreen, too.

Where should I go? Should I leave L.A.? Not up north, 'cause that's closer to Watson. Down south, like to San Diego? But what if that doesn't work out? The next stop would be Mexico and there's no way I'm going to any foreign country.

If I stay in L.A., where will I hide?

I think about it for a long time and get really scared. Same feeling like when I watched PLYR—I need to stop thinking about that . . .

It's stupid to even be thinking of a plan. I have no future. Even if I survive for a few months a year, two years, so what? I'd still be a kid, no schooling, no money, no control over anything.

Still no one out on the beach. It looks so tan and peaceful. The ocean, too, gray as steel except where the tide comes rolling in, throwing up spray, like spitting at the sky.

Spitting at God . . .

Wouldn't it be nice to just walk into the water, let yourself be carried away? Maybe you'd drown. Or maybe there'd be a miracle and you'd wash up like one of those bottles with a message in it on some island with palm trees. Girls wearing just grass skirts, long black hair down to their butts, and you'd come out of the ocean like some god and they'd be all thrilled to see you, fight with each other to be your girlfriend, take care of you, feed you some barbecued pig with an apple in its mouth and fruit that they just pick from the trees, no one has to work.

Either way, no worries.

I get up, walk across the beach to the tide line, roll my pants up and stand there, let the waves trickle over my toes.

*Cold.* My feet get numb and they look like white wax.

How long would it take before you stopped feeling cold? Before your body stopped feeling anything?

I read in a nature book that gazelles and wildebeest chased by lions stop feeling pain, so their death becomes easier.

That didn't happen to me with the pervs, so maybe it's just animals.

Or maybe I just didn't get . . . close enough.

If you didn't feel or worry, you could just give yourself up like some sacrifice—like Jesus did.

I must have walked, because now I'm in the water up to my knees and my pants are getting wet and kind of ballooning and swirling around. Not so cold anymore. It feels clean. I keep going. The water's sloshing against my belt and I stand there and look across the ocean; maybe I'll see a boat or a whale spouting.

A few birds are out there, flying around, diving. I take another step. Just one, but it makes a big difference, the ground drops out from under me and all of a sudden *I'm up to my neck, trying to step back, but I can't get a hold on to anything and now I feel the water moving under me and I'm in over my head, swallowing water, choking—up again, I can see the top of the water, the beach is getting smaller. I start to swim, but it doesn't help. Something's pushing me forward, I have no control, start kicking, waving my arms around, knowing this is stupid, you have to stay calm stay calm, but I'm being pushed out, forced, I don't want this! I'm tiny, weaker than a barnacle, because I have no glue. Why am I thinking about Mom now, how bad she'll feel, so cold, my eyes burn, my throat burns, my eyes got to keep them open but ohnocan'tkeepmyheadabov*

Up in the air again, coughing spitting, eyes burning, throat hurts like a knife scraping it and I'm still being carried out by the—no, the beach is getting closer—

The ocean tosses me up, the sand gets even closer. Releasing me, like Jonah? No, no, here I go under again, swallowing so much water I think I'll explode, then up, coughing, vomiting, rocks in the water, hitting me, stinging.

The ocean playing with me. Which way will it throw me now?

Stones scraping the bottom of my body. The ground. Sand. Back on shore.

Sand sticks to my soaked clothes. Salt in the scratches makes them burn. I roll away from the water.

Safe.

Another chance.

God?

Or did even the ocean think I was trash, spit me back like bad food?

❖

I hurry back toward the pier, still coughing and spitting up salt water, collapse, stay there trying to get a little sun, dry out. A few people are out on the beach now. I just mind my own business. After an hour I'm drier, but still wet, my chest hurts and I'm scratched up by the sand but . . . I'm here.

I need to concentrate. Money and a hat. Some food. Sunscreen.

Mostly dry, I take a walk up to the pier. There's a Ferris wheel, some bumper cars, and a merry-go-round, but they're all shut and locked and there's nothing to take there. A few restaurants, but they're closed, too, and the only food around is dry bits of popcorn stuck to the floor.

All the way at the end of the pier is a bait shack that's open, some dirty-looking guy behind a counter and big white bathtub-type tanks full of anchovies, some of them already dead and floating to the top. A few people are fishing, mostly old Chinese guys and a few black guys. No one's catching anything; everyone looks bored.

The two garbage cans I find are full of fish guts and they stink so bad I almost puke. I leave the pier.

Up above the beach is a street full of fancy-looking restaurants and hotels; nothing there for me. North is a small park with some old people and homeless guys, and if you keep looking, the street just seems to disappear. All those trees—too much like you-know-where.

So I walk south and things start to look a little more familiar—motels and apartment buildings, weirdos who could be from the Boulevard. I find half a doughnut on the street and it looks okay so I eat it. Next block, I see part of a Twix bar left on the sidewalk, but it's too melted and gross-looking and I only eat a small bit of it.

A while later, a sign says I'm in Venice. Small houses,

people, lots of Mexicans. I walk down a street. At the end is the ocean again, and soon I'm on this big wide path called Ocean Front Walk, like a giant sidewalk, the ocean on one side, stores on the other, all sorts of people—punks, blacks, beautiful bikini-girls on roller skates, their butt cheeks hanging out, guys looking at them. Young guys—like college students—old people sitting on benches, bikers with tattoos, lots of big, mean-looking dogs. Some Arnold Schwarzenegger–type guys are exercising in these fenced-off areas, their bodies all greased up so the muscles look like grapefruit trying to burst through the skin. Lifting weights, rubbing chalk on their hands, being huge and cool, showing off.

The stores here are mostly small and cheap-looking. Fast food, stands selling ice cream, cold drinks, sunglasses, souvenirs, postcards, T-shirts, bathing suits.

Hats that say CALIFORNIA! or MALIBU! or VENICE! I'd love some dry clothing, but there are too many people around to take something.

Still, this might be a good place to hang out, see what happens later.

I decide to walk from one end of Ocean Front to the other, see what turns up.

Halfway down, I see a little gray building with a six-pointed star over the door. A Jewish star—I know that from my history book, the chapter "The Middle East: Birth of Civilization."

A Jewish church—what do they call them, synagons? I go over. Jewish letters next to the door, then English ones. Over the door it says CONGREGATION BETH TORAH.

This might be good. The Jews always have money. At least that's what Moron used to say—he'd go off on how they were all fucking bankers, sucking the blood out of the country, killing Jesus, and now they wanted to take our money, too.

Like he ever had money.

Then I think: Why would he be right? He was wrong about everything else. But still . . . what's a church doing in the middle of all these businesses unless they're out to make money?

It wasn't just Moron; Mom used to agree with him, say, Cowboy, they really got a talent for making money, must be in the blood.

"You stupid bitch." He laughed. "It ain't talent, it's 'cause they cheat us. Fucking ZOG—know what that is? Zionist Occupation Government, they want to take us over, not even human—come from the devil fucking a snake, didja know that? The Aryan race is the bona fide chosen people."

That night I was sitting at the kitchen table trying to study the Civil War. But then Mom started telling a story and I listened. About some rich Jewish family who owned a big strawberry farm down near Oxnard; her parents and her used to pick there when she was a kid. How the Jews had a big white two-story house and a Cadillac.

"Fucking bloodsuckers," Moron said.

"Actually, they was okay, kinda nice—" she started. But he looked at her and she said, "Except they sure loved their money. The wife always dressed like she was going out to dinner, and she was just a farm wife. And here was this big house, maybe it was even three stories, buncha TV antennas all over the roof, but we slept in these little migrant shacks, kerosene heaters."

"Fucking A."

Even if it's mostly lies, sometimes lies have some truth. And I don't need thousands of Jewish dollars, just some spare change.

A sign next to the synagon door says prayers will be held on Friday night and that the time for lighting candles is 7:34 P.M., whatever that means.

No one's looking. I try the door. Locked. The next place over is called Cafe Eats, and it's closed too.

There's a space between the church and Cafe Eats. I slip around to the back, where there's an alley, parked cars, but none driving. Two spaces behind the synagon but no cars. They're praying Friday night. That's tomorrow.

I check out the back door. Plain wood, with some little wooden thing nailed to the frame on the right side, also with a Jewish star. Probably some kind of good-luck charm, maybe asking God for money.

The back door's locked, too. Right next to it is a window, a small one, too small for a man to fit through, but not for me. A screen over it, just like at the pineapple house. Also like that one, it comes right off.

I don't have to break this window; it's loose. When I push up on it, it jiggles. So I shove harder and feel it give some more, then something pops and it slams open and I look up and down the alley.

Still no one. I'm in.

I'm getting good at this.

※

The room I land in is a bathroom, small but clean—a toilet, a sink, and a mirror. No shower. The mirror tells me I don't look as bad as I thought, just the scratches on my face and some white crust around my ears and my lips. I wash it off, use the toilet.

Considering I almost drowned, I look pretty good.

I thank God, in case it *was* Him; wash my hands.

Now, let's find some Jewish money.

## CHAPTER 38

※

PETRA AWOKE CONFUSED, AT 6:30, HER HEAD crowded with Ron Banks, Estrella Flores, Ramsey, the boy with the presidents book—she wrapped herself in a robe and collected the morning paper.

There it was, page 3, the drawing smack in the center of the article, no credit given to the artist.

The gist of the article was no progress; the implication, those bumbling police. Salmagundi, the department spokesman, careful not to make too big a deal about the witness angle. The boy was "just one of several leads we're looking into."

The last paragraph made her inhale sharply.

Twenty-five-thousand-dollar reward to anyone providing information about the boy or anything else that led to the arrest of a suspect. Money put up by Dr. and Mrs. John Everett Boehlinger, all calls to be directed to Hollywood Detectives.

*Her* extension. Blindsided. They must have gone through Schoelkopf, goddamn him. She couldn't work this way.

All day fielding crank calls—had Stu seen it yet?

Normally, she'd call him. Nothing was normal anymore.

She got dressed in the first thing she pulled out of the closet, took the paper with her, and drove much too fast to the station.

There were already ten messages on her desk: nine sightings of the boy, and a psychic from Fontana claiming to know who'd murdered Lisa. What would the afternoon bring?

Stu hadn't come in yet. To hell with him. Fournier was checked out, too.

She stormed into Schoelkopf's office waving the article. He was sitting at his desk; jumped up and jabbed a finger at her.

"Don't get all pissy with me. The parents blew into town yesterday, went straight to Deputy Chief Lazara—he calls me at ten P.M. I have to come down here to deal with them. The father's an obvious asshole, used to having his way. Who knows what he'll try to do next."

I tried to warn you, idiot, and you brushed me off.

"You could've called me," said Petra.

"I could've bought Microsoft at ten bucks—what's the point, Barbie?"

The nickname had never bothered her. Now it was a razor scraping raw nerve fiber. "The point is—"

"The point is I've been running interference on this for you from day one and you've produced squat. I get yanked out of bed, get dirty looks from Lazara because *he's* working late, he cuts out, leaves me with Mommy boo-hooing, Daddy delivering these fucking speeches: After Menendez and O.J., everyone knows LAPD can't find a felon in the penitentiary. So I give him what I've got, which is this artwork of yours, figuring maybe it'll calm him down. He says okay, what are you doing about it, and I say we're looking for him, Mr. Boehlinger. And he says *Doctor* Boehlinger, then he tells me it's not enough, he wants some incentives here—post a reward. I try to explain that rewards bring in mostly nuts, and even if we wanted to do that, it would take time. He picks up my phone, calls some lawyer named Hack, and says, Talk to your buddy at the *Times* and your other buddies at the TV stations. Showing me this Hack's connected. Which he obviously is—it was already eleven and he got the picture in. So sue me, I didn't wake you up at midnight. You think you've got a grievance, file a complaint. Meanwhile, go do your job."

He waved her out.

A TV cop would have handed in the badge and gun.

A real cop kept her mouth shut. She liked the job and the department was paramilitary, would always be, meaning lockstep rhythm, death of the individual, hierarchies. You pissed down, not up.

Look at Milo Sturgis—she'd worked with the gay detective on one case, had seen him as the ace he was. But before that she'd heard only curses affixed to his name. The highest solve rate in West L.A.; to the department, that didn't make up for sleeping with a man.

She returned to her desk, put aside the ten message slips, and phoned the Nancy Downey Agency in Beverly Hills. A woman with a Latin accent said, "You should talk to Mr. Sanchez. He's at our other office in San Marino."

San Marino and B.H. Covering the high-priced spreads, east and west.

A man answered there, similar accent.

"Mr. Sanchez?"

"Yes."

She identified herself, told him she was looking for Estrella Flores.

"I am, too."

"Pardon?"

"I just got a call from her son in El Salvador. He's worried, hasn't heard from her since Sunday. Is this about Mrs. Ramsey's murder?"

"We'd just like to talk to her, sir. Why's the son worried?"

"Usually she calls him two, three times a week. He said he phoned the Ramsey house but got only a machine. I tried; the same thing happened to me. I left a message, but no one's called me back."

"Mrs. Flores quit working for Mr. Ramsey, sir."

"When?"

"The day after the murder."

"Oh."

"So she didn't call you about another placement?"

"No." Sanchez sounded concerned.

"Any ideas where she might be, sir?"

"No, I'm sorry. She worked for the Ramseys for . . . hold on, let me look . . . here it is. Two years. Never complained."

"Where did she work before that?"

"Before that . . . I couldn't tell you." Wariness had crept into his voice.

"She wasn't legal?"

"When she came to us, she was legal. At least she presented papers. We do our best to—"

"Mr. Sanchez, I have no interest in immigration issues—"

"Even if you did, Detective, we have nothing to hide. Our women are all legal. We place them in the finest homes, and there must never be a hint of—"

"Of course," said Petra. "Please give me Mrs. Flores's son's name and number."

"Javier," he said, reciting an address on Santa Cristina in San Salvador and a number. "He's a lawyer."

"You don't know of any other places she worked?"

"She told us she worked for a family in Brentwood, but only for three months. No name—she didn't want to use them as references because they were 'immoral.' "

"Immoral in what way, sir?"

"I think it was something to do with drinking. Mrs. Flores is a very . . . moral woman."

Petra hung up, thought about the maid's disappearance. If Flores had left of her own accord, why hadn't she contacted her son? It didn't take much morality to be repulsed by murder. Had she seen something? Or been seen?

Where to go with it . . . more calls to substations, to see if Flores had turned up somewhere as a victim? Unlikely. If she'd been eliminated by Ramsey because she could blow his alibi, he'd have made sure to conceal the body.

Better to scope out RanchHaven, talk to the guard service, ask long-overdue questions. While she was there, she could drop in on Ramsey again, slip in some hints about Flores, see how he reacted.

Wil Fournier appeared in the squad room door, beckoning her with a wiggling finger. He looked angry. Something to do with the boy? She hurried over.

"What's up?"

"Got some people can't wait to meet you." He angled his

head down the hall. Petra looked out and saw a couple in their fifties standing at the far end. Well dressed, backs to each other.

"The parents?"

"None other," said Fournier. "Schoelkopf snagged me as I came in, said they wanted a firsthand report from all three of us. Where's Ken?"

"Don't know." Her tone made him stare. "What exactly do they want?"

"Info. Got any?"

"Nope, how about you?"

"Talked to a few shelters, churches, some of our Juvey people. No one knows the kid; a couple of social workers thought they might've seen him around, but he hasn't checked in anywhere."

"Outdoor kid," said Petra. Thinking what guts it took for an eleven-year-old to go it alone in the park.

"Let's go do some hand-holding," said Fournier. "Female D and a coal-colored one. These people look like the type who still think lawn jockeys are funny."

※

Mrs. Boehlinger was everything Petra expected—petite, perfectly groomed, handsome; long-suffering Pat Nixon handsomeness. A puff of cold-waved hair the color of dry champagne crowned a roundish face. Contoured eyebrows. Trim figure in a conservatively cut black St. John's Knits suit. Black suede pumps and purse. Red eyes.

Her husband defeated expectation. Petra had pictured a big man, hearty, someone like Ramsey. Dr. John Everett Boehlinger was five-five, 140 pounds tops, with narrow shoulders and a homely face full of homely features: fat nose, small dark eyes, rubber-mask looseness around the jowls. Bald on top, thin fringe of gray at the sides. A clipped stainless steel goatee—he could have played Freud in the country club Halloween bash.

He wore a black vested suit, white shirt, gray tie printed with tiny black dots. White silk hankie in the breast pocket. Onyx cuff links. Cap-tip shoes were polished shiny as motor oil.

Two small people in funeral garb. Mrs. Boehlinger remained

focused on the wall in front of her, clenching and unclenching one hand. The other gripped her purse. Her french nails were glossy but chipped. She still had her back to her husband, didn't look up as Petra and Fournier approached.

Dr. Boehlinger had focused on them immediately, body canted forward, as if ready to spar. When they were ten feet away, he said to Petra, "You're the one I spoke to on the phone."

"Yes, sir. Detective Connor." She extended her hand, and he submitted to a half second of skin contact before withdrawing. Wiping his hand on his suit—oh, for God's sake.

The she reminded herself: The poor man's lost his child. Nothing worse than that.

*Nothing.*

He said, "Vivian?" and his wife turned slowly. Ravaged eyes, the corneas a scramble of ruptured capillaries. The irises bright blue—like Lisa's. There was more than a suggestion of Lisa in the fine facial structure. Would Lisa have ended up like this—a fashionable matron, buttoned to the neck, all propriety?

"Detective Connor, Vivian," the doctor singsonged scoldingly.

Vivian Boehlinger's expression said, *So what the hell am I supposed to do about it?*

She said, "Pleased to meet you," and proffered an icy hand.

Petra smiled. "And this is Detective Fournier—"

"We've already met Detective Fournier," said Dr. Boehlinger. "Where's the third one—Bishop?"

"Out in the field," said Petra.

"Out in the field—sounds like he's planting vegetables."

"Actually, sir," said Fournier, "it's kind of like that. We cultivate leads—"

"Wonderful," said Boehlinger. "You know what a metaphor is. Now eliminate the chatter and tell us what you've cultivated about Ramsey."

Mrs. Boehlinger stared, turned, showed him her back once more. He didn't notice. "Well?"

A detective named Bernstein stepped into the hall, coffee cup in hand, started forward, returned to the squad room.

"Let's talk somewhere private," said Petra.

All three interrogation rooms were horrible—smaller than jail cells, no windows, the obvious wall of one-way mirror that most of the idiots brought in for questioning took early note of, then promptly forgot.

Bad smell in all three: sweat, pomade, cheap perfume, tobacco, hormones.

She chose Interrogation One because it had three chairs instead of two. Fournier fetched a fourth and they crowded around a tiny metal table. Forced intimacy. Mrs. Boehlinger kept looking at her nails, her knees, her shoes, anywhere but at another human being. The surgeon looked ready to slice flesh.

Petra shut the door and let in some claustrophobia. Mrs. B. was picking at her knit skirt. Boehlinger was trying to stare down Fournier.

Trying to dominate. To what end? Force of habit?

She remembered what Ramsey had told her about both parents trying to run Lisa's life. "Let me start by saying how sorry we are for your loss. We're doing everything in our power to find Lisa's killer—"

Mention of her daughter made Mrs. B. weep. The doctor made no effort to comfort her. "We know who the *killer* is."

"If there's anything you can tell us to substantiate that, sir—"

"He beat her up, she left him. What more do you need?"

"Unfortunately—"

"This boy, the potential witness," said Boehlinger. "I'm sure there've been responses to our reward."

"A few calls have come in," said Petra.

"And?"

"We haven't gotten to them yet, sir. Been following up other leads."

"For Christ's sake!" Boehlinger's hand slammed the table. His wife jumped, but she didn't look at him. "I dip into my own damn pocket, do your job for you, and you don't have the decency to follow up—"

"We will, sir," said Petra. "Soon as we're free to do so."

"Why aren't you free?"

"We're here, sir," said Fournier.

Boehlinger's hand rose again, and for a second Petra thought he'd try to strike Wil. But the fist froze in midair. Slight tremor. Surgeon past his prime, or the stress?

"*We're* delaying you? *We're* the problem—"

"No, sir," said Fournier. "We appreciate all your—"

The hand slammed again. "You," he said very softly, "are a very rude man. You're both rude."

"John!"

"Typical," said Boehlinger, glaring at Petra and Fournier in turn. "Civil servants. So you know nothing about this boy. Price-less, just priceless. Affirmative action at its finest—I believe we're going to have to take this one step further, Vivian. Hire our own—"

"Stop it, John. *Please*."

Boehlinger laughed derisively. "We will most definitely hire our own investigator, because these two obviously aren't—"

"*Shut up, John!*"

The shriek filled the room. Boehlinger turned white and clawed the tabletop. His fingers failed to find purchase and his hands flattened. Without facing his wife, he said, "Vivian, I'd appreciate it if you—"

"Just shut *up*, John! *Shutup shutup shut up!*"

Now it was her turn to raise a hand. It sailed through the air like a flesh airplane, landed on her bosom, over her heart. She ran out of the room, swinging the door open, not bothering to close it.

Fournier's eyes begged for Petra to follow. Even Dr. Bile was preferable to a grieving mother.

❖

Petra caught up with her at the end of the hall, in the stairwell, sitting on the top step, forehead to the wall, the champagne puff bobbing with each sob.

"Ma'am—"

"I'm sorry!"

"No need to apologize, ma'am."

"I'm very sorry, very very very *sorry*!"

Petra sat down next to the woman and chanced putting her arm around the heaving shoulders. Beneath the knit fabric were small bones. Petra smelled makeup, breath mints, Chanel No. 5. "Let's find somewhere to go."

Vivian Boehlinger straightened and pointed at the interrogation rooms. "Not with him!"

"No," said Petra. "By ourselves."

No one was in the vending machine room, so she guided the woman in and closed the door. No lock. She placed a chair against it, sat down, motioning for Vivian Boehlinger to choose one near the folding table that served as the D's snack center.

"Coffee?"

"No thank you." Subdued voice now, that post-tantrum shame/fatigue. Small hands folded in a black-knit lap. Under the fluorescence, Petra could see hints of deep facial lines, muted expertly by makeup. The eyes were tormented, devoid of hope. So disturbing in contrast—everything else about the woman was so well put together.

"I'm sorry," she repeated.

"It's really okay, ma'am. Situations like this—"

"When all this is over, I'm going to leave him."

Petra didn't speak.

Vivian Boehlinger said, "I was going to do it this year. Now I'll have to wait. Thirty-six years of marriage, what a joke." She shook her head, made a terrible sound, more parrot squawk than laugh.

"He has affairs with sluts," she went on. "Thinks I'm stupid and don't know." Another bird sound. It made Petra's flesh crawl. "Cheap, slutty affairs. And now Lisa's gone."

Odd juxtaposition, but maybe not. Tabulating her miseries. Petra waited for her to take it further, but all she said was "My Lisa, my pretty Lisa."

Several more minutes of silence, then: "Ma'am, do you think Cart Ramsey did it?"

"I don't know." Quick answer. She'd thought about it. She gave a pitiful shrug and sniffed. Petra fetched a paper napkin. Dab, dab.

"Thank you. You're very sweet. I don't know what to think." She sat up straighter, higher. "John thinks he can buy everything. He offered Lisa money not to marry Carter and, when that didn't work, even more money to divorce him. So idiotic—Lisa was going to divorce Carter anyway. She told me. If John had ever communicated with her, he could have saved himself the offer. Which is all it was. Lisa divorced Carter, but did John keep his end of the bargain?"

A scary smile spread across the thin lips. Lipstick and liner had been used to extend the coral borders and radically change the mouth's contours. Without her morning routine, this woman would be unrecognizable.

"He didn't pay up?" said Petra.

"Of course not. He didn't give Lisa one dime. Said he hadn't been serious, it was for Lisa's own good anyway, she had nothing to complain about. Lisa didn't care, she knew who she was dealing with. But still. Don't you think that's terrible?"

"How much did he offer Lisa?"

"Fifty thousand dollars. So now he comes up with half?" She shook her head. "Don't expect him to pay any reward, Detective. I feel sorry for anyone who thinks they're going to get paid by John—do I think Carter did it? I don't know. To me, he always seemed civil. Then Lisa told me he hit her, so I don't know."

"How many times did she say he hit her, ma'am?"

"Just the once. They had a tiff, Carter lost control and hit her. More than a slap—her eye was blackened and her lip was split."

"Just once," said Petra.

"Once was too much for Lisa." That sounded boastful. Daughter asserting herself in a way mother never could? "She told me she wouldn't tolerate it. And I agreed with her. For all the things her father did over thirty-six years, he never laid a hand on me. If he had, who knows what I'd have done." She lifted her purse, hefted it like a weapon. "Of course, I didn't know Lisa was going to go on television. If she'd told me about that, I probably would have advised against it."

"Too public?"

"Tasteless. But I'd have been wrong. Why keep it all inside? What's the point of being quiet and pretty and tasteful?"

She cried some more, dabbed. "Do I think Carter did it? Why not? He's a man. They're responsible for all the violence in the world, aren't they? Am I as sure as John? No. Because no one's ever as sure as *John*."

She got up. "I know you're trying your best, Detective. John wants blood, but I only want . . . something I'll never get—my little girl back. Now, if you'd be so kind as to call me a cab."

"Certainly, ma'am." Petra stayed with her, holding the door. "Here's my card. If you think of something, anything, please let me know."

The two of them returned to the hallway. The door to Interrogation One was still closed.

"Your poor black friend," said Vivian Boehlinger. "John's prejudiced—I really despise him."

"I'll call that cab," said Petra. "Where to?"

"The Beverly Wilshire. *He's* staying at the Biltmore."

※

Barely after 9 A.M. and she was exhausted; the time spent with the Boehlingers had sapped her energies. Poor Wil was still in there.

What a pair, even allowing for tragedy. No marital role model for Lisa. How much free will did any of us have?

The message stack had grown; four more tips on the boy. She dreaded Dr. B.'s follow-up calls.

In some cases, you bonded with the victim's family. Here she was, wanting to punch Dr. B.'s lights out, creeped out by Mrs. B.'s avian laugh. Not good at all. And Stu still hadn't arrived. Obviously, he didn't give a damn anymore. Which didn't fit a career opportunity thing. So maybe it *was* marital.

She did some fruitless follow-up with Missing Persons on Flores, was putting down the phone when Stu said, "Good morning."

Freshly shaved, every hair in place. He wore a beautiful slate-gray gabardine suit, pearl-gray shirt, smoke-and-red paisley tie. So perfectly composed.

It pissed her off.

"Is it?" she said.

He turned around and left the squad room.

# CHAPTER 39

▪

SAM GANZER DIDN'T PARK THE LINCOLN CARE-
fully. The twenty-year-old land yacht was too wide for each of
the spaces behind the shul, so he used both of them.

Who was there to complain? The synagogue, once a social
center for Venice's Jews, had been reduced to a weekend
facility, Sam's maintenance calls the only thing that opened its
doors before Friday night.

Even on the weekend it was sometimes hard to get ten men
together for a minyan. Beth Torah wasn't Orthodox enough for
the yarmulke-clad yuppies who'd gentrified Venice, so they
started their own congregation a few blocks away, brought a
bearded fanatic rabbi from New York, installed a partition
between the men and the women. The old, mostly left-wing
crowd who patronized the shul wouldn't hear of it.

That had been five years ago. Now most of the regulars had
died off. Eventually, Sam knew, Beth Torah would close
down, the property sold. Maybe the yuppies would reclaim it,
which would be better than yet another cheap business added
to the dozens that lined Ocean Front Walk. Sam didn't mind
the yuppies as much as some of the old socialists did. He had a
deep-rooted distrust of authority but was, at heart, a businessman. Meanwhile, he'd park any damn way he pleased.

He felt he'd live forever. For seventy-one, his body was
working okay. His brother Emil, living down in Irvine, not
religious at all, was seventy-six. Good stock: generations of
thickset, robust metalsmiths and carpenters honed by bone-
numbing Ukrainian winters.

It had taken pure evil to cut down most of the Ganzer tree.

Mother, father, three younger brothers, two sisters shipped
off to Sobibor, never seen again. Avram, Mottel, Baruch,
Malkah, Sheindel. Had they made it to America, what would

245

their names have been? Sam's best guess was Abe, Mort, Bernie, Marilyn, Shirley. Last week, he'd raised the question with Emil, who didn't want to talk about it.

All in all, forty-five Ganzers and Leibovics had been rounded up by the Ukrainian police and handed over to the occupying nazi scum. Sam and Emil, muscular young men—Emil a lightweight boxing champ at the Kovol gymnasium—were spared and enslaved as forced laborers. Eighteen-hour workdays on thin soup and sawdust bread. Midnight escape through the snow, living in the forest on leaves and nuts, nearly starving till they'd been taken in by a saintly Catholic woman. When her son came back from the war, he wanted to turn them over; the Ganzer brothers ran again, walking till the brink of death, finally making it to Shanghai. The Chinese had been decent. Sam sometimes wondered what it would have been like to stay, marry one of those gorgeous porcelain girls. Instead, liberation, Canada, Detroit, L.A.

For years he hadn't thought about any of that crap. Lately, the memories had been returning, uninvited. Probably some kind of brain damage. His body was strong, but names, places were fading, he'd walk into a room, forget why. The ancient stuff, though, was as clear as day. All that anger—he could feel it pounding in his ears, bad for the blood pressure.

He turned off the Lincoln's engine, got out. On Friday night and Saturday, he assumed sexton's duties, had since Mr. Ginzburg died. With the unpaid position came maintenance obligations. Why not? What else did he have to do besides play the mandolin and sit outside his house getting too much sun—he'd already had four precancerous lesions cut off his face and one on his bald spot. Had to wear a stupid cap, like an old guy.

He took the hat off, tossed it into the Lincoln, locked up, enjoyed another look at how he'd parked. Better than leaving room for some drug addict to slump in a stolen car and inject himself. That had happened more than once. This neighborhood, always a little nuts, had become a crazy mix of gawking tourists on weekends, lowlifes crawling out of the woodwork at night.

Most of Ocean Front was one big gyp-joint now. Fly-by-nights selling cheap junk, weekends so jammed you couldn't take two steps without bumping into some yutz.

For forty years Sam and Emil sold hardware and plumbing fixtures from their store on Lincoln Boulevard, things you could use. Both of them knowing how to install as well as sell, pipe a house from scratch. You got to be handy, living on your own, never depending on anyone else. Leaving Shanghai, he'd vowed never to depend on anyone else. Maybe that's why he'd never married. Though the ladies loved him. He'd had his good times. Even now he once in a while got between the covers with soft-skinned grandmothers ashamed of what age had done to their bodies. Sam knew how to make them feel young and gorgeous.

He felt for the shul key in his pocket, found it, opened the back door. Not noticing the screen from the bathroom window lying on the ground, because it was partially blocked by his right front tire.

❋

Moments after he got inside, he knew someone had broken in.

The silver-plated *pushke* was sitting atop the platform where the Torah was read, shiny against the blue velvet coverlet, right out in the open. The charity box hadn't been used since Friday night, when it was passed around before services. Sam had put it away, personally, in a cabinet beneath the bookcases. Just a cheap combination lock, no reason to make a big deal—all it contained was a few dollars in coins.

But someone had tried anyway. And, look—food had been taken out of the same cabinet. Snack stuff for the handful of Saturday-morning regulars. Tam Tam crackers and a pink box from a bakery on Fairfax—sugarcoated *kichlen* shaped like bow ties. Sam had bought them last week. No preservatives, had to be stale; he'd forgotten to get rid of them.

Crumbs on blue velvet. A quarter and a dime had fallen out of the *pushke*. Hungry thief. What else had he taken?

The only things of value to a junkie were the silver finials and breastplates that graced the three Torahs in the ark. Sam started toward the carved walnut case, ready to draw back the blue velvet curtain, afraid of what he'd find.

Then he stopped himself, raised his heavy arms instinctively. Maybe the crook was still here. All he needed was some junkie jumping out at him.

No one did. Silence; no movement at all.

He stood there and looked around.

The shul was four rooms—small entry hall in front, gents' and ladies' lavs at the back; in between, the main sanctuary—rows of walnut pews, seating for 150.

A double-sided dead bolt protected the front door—you couldn't get in or out without a key. Same for the back. So how . . .

He waited a few more minutes, convinced himself he was alone, but made sure by inspecting. Then out to the front room. Still locked; no damage to the door.

In back was where he found it, the window in the ladies' lav. Closed, but the screen was off—there it was, down near his tire. Some white chips on the sill where dry paint had flaked off.

Closing the window after he'd left? Considerate thief?

He returned to the sanctuary, opened the ark, examined the Torahs. All the silver in place. The bottle-shaped *pushke* hadn't been emptied either, and the lock didn't show a scratch. Only Sam and Mr. Kravitz knew the combination, and they took turns emptying the weekly take and delivering it to the Hadassah thrift shop on Broadway. Once upon a time Congregation Beth Torah had proudly contributed fifty dollars a week to the poor; now it was down to ten, twelve. Embarrassing, so Sam augmented it with twenty of his own. What Kravitz did, he had no idea; the guy was a bit of a cheapskate.

He inspected the *pushke*, rattled it. Still full. Except for the quarter and the dime. Strange.

Several *kichlen* were gone and, from what Sam could see, quite a few crackers.

Hungry *gonif*. Probably some bum, too doped up to know what he was doing, one of those nuts who lurched up and down the walkway. Sometimes Sam gave them money, other times he wanted nothing to do with them.

A skinny nut, because the lav window was small. Junkies got skinny. And weren't they always hungry for sweets? Okay, no big loss. He dropped the coins back in the *pushke*, brushed crumbs from the velvet, closed the cracker box and the bakery box and carried them over to the bookcase. Opening the lower cabinet where the food went, he saw something else the *gonif* hadn't touched: booze.

Schnapps for the regulars. A nearly full bottle of Crown Royal, and a half-empty Smirnoff's vodka.

A junkie with one vice only, no taste for booze?

Next to the bottles were some folded prayer shawls. A bunch of small silk ones, striped blue, but also the big black-striped woolen *tallis* worn by the prayer leader. That one belonged in the compartment under the platform—how had it gotten there?

Had he put it there? Had Kravitz? He strained to remember, damn his memory . . . last *shabbos* . . . yeah, yeah, Mrs. Rosen hadn't felt good and Sam had left early to take her home, he'd left Kravitz in charge. The guy had no eye for details.

Removing the woolen shawl, he saw that Kravitz hadn't folded it properly, either. A klutz. He'd clerked for the Water Department all his life, what could you expect from a desk jockey.

Refolding the shawl, caressing the thick wool, Sam carried it to the platform, bent down and opened the compartment door.

Inside was a boy.

A small, skinny kid, curled up into a corner, looking scared as hell.

Breathing hard. Sam could see his chest moving, and now he could hear it, fast, raspy, like he had asthma or something.

Such a look on the face.

Sam knew that look. His siblings; faces through train windows.

Laborers in the camp who didn't make it.

Even tough Emil's face the time he got pneumonia; thought this was it.

Sam's own face when, in the dead of winter, he found a piece of broken glass in the snow, used it for a mirror, saw what he'd become.

This boy looked exactly like that.

"It's okay," he said.

The boy shivered. Hugging himself like he was cold, and even though this was June, Venice, California, a beautiful sunny day, Sam felt a Ukrainian freeze pass over his own body.

"It's okay," he repeated. "Come on out, I don't bite."

The boy didn't budge.

"Come on, you can't stay in there all day—still hungry? Crackers aren't enough, let's get you some real food."

※

It took a long time to coax the boy out, standing far back so the kid could crawl free. When he was finally out, he looked like he wanted to run.

Sam held him by the arm—skin and bones. More memories.

The boy struggled, tried to kick. Sam, knowing what it felt like to be restrained, let go and the boy dashed toward the front of the shul.

Rattling the door, but locked in.

Returning to the sanctuary, he gave Sam a wide berth. Wild-eyed, looking from side to side, trying to figure out how to escape.

Sam was sitting in a front pew holding a box of doughnuts the boy had missed. Real *chazerei*. Entenmann's chocolate-covered cake doughnuts, still unopened, hidden behind some old prayer books. Kravitz's secret lode—who did he think he was kidding? Next to the doughnuts was also a sealed jar of gefilte-fish balls in jelly. Sam couldn't imagine the boy going for it.

"Here," he said, holding up the doughnuts. "Take it with you."

The boy stood there and stared. Despite being dirty and ragged and skinny, with a scratched-up face, he was a nice-looking kid. Maybe eleven, twelve. What was he doing out here so young? There were plenty of runaways in Venice, but they were mostly teenagers, bigshot rebels, with needles and rings stuck into their bodies all over, crazy haircuts, tattoos, a bad attitude. This one just looked like a kid, undernourished and scared.

Definitely *goyische*—look at that upturned nose, that dirty-blond hair. Sometimes the goyim beat their kids, abused them, God knows what else. Maybe this one had run away. Jews, too, he supposed, though he'd never encountered that personally.

What did he know about kids, anyway?

Emil had one son, a lawyer, lived in Encino—drove a German car!—never talked to his parents or Sam.

"Here," he said, shaking the doughnut box. "Take it."

No response. The kid, distrustful, thinking Sam was up to something. Dirt stains all over his jeans and that T-shirt was full of holes. He was making fists, a tough little *pisher*.

Sam put the doughnuts on the floor, got up, said, "Fine, I'll open the door for you, you don't have to crawl out the window. But if you ask me, you should get some clean clothes, eat some real food with vitamins."

Dipping into his trouser pocket, he took some bills out of his wallet. Two twenties—way too generous for someone he didn't know, but what the hell.

He placed the money on the floor next to the doughnuts, walked to the back of the shul, and unlocked the rear door. Then he went into the gents' lav, to give the kid a chance to make a graceful exit, and because his bladder was killing him.

# CHAPTER 40

■

PETRA STARED AT THE DOORWAY THROUGH which Stu had just passed, then she went after him.

He reappeared in the doorway before she got there. Cocking his head.

*C'mere.*

Oh yeah, faithful little junior partner will jump up on cue.

They locked eyes. His face was stone; no apologies. Deciding to maintain her dignity, she followed him down the stairs and out of the building to the rear lot, where his Suburban was parked. The truck, usually spotless, had dirty windows. Crusted bird droppings freckled the white hood.

She said, "What the hell's going on, Stu?"

He unlocked the passenger door, motioned for her to get in, came around and sat behind the wheel.

"We're not going anywhere," she said, remaining outside. "Some of us have work to do."

He stared through the windshield. Sun from the east traced the contours of his profile in orange. A paperback-book model couldn't have posed for greater effect. Everyone a goddamn actor.

Petra got in and slammed the door so hard the truck shook.

Stu said, "I owe you an explanation."

"Okay."

"Kathy has cancer."

Petra's throat seized and closed, and for a moment she couldn't breathe. "Oh, Stu—"

He held up a finger. "She's going in for surgery tomorrow. She's been having tests done; we weren't sure. Now we are."

"I'm so sorry, Stu." Why didn't he tell me? Obviously, not close enough. Eight months of chasing bad guys doth not a deep relationship make.

"One breast," he said. "Her doctor found it on routine checkup. They think it's just a single tumor."

"What can I do to help?"

"Nothing, thanks, we're covered. Mother's taking the kids and Father's dealing with the hospital."

His right arm rested on the center console. Petra put her hand on his sleeve. "Go home, Stu. Wil and I will handle everything."

"No, that's the thing, I was going to take a leave of absence, but Kathy insisted I shouldn't. She wants me home tonight to take her to the hospital, told me I can stay until she falls asleep. And tomorrow, when she comes out of surgery, I'll be there. But in between she insists I keep working. Even when she gets radiation . . . maybe they can do just a lumpectomy, they're not sure."

"You're planning to stay on the job?" said Petra.

"Kathy wants it. You know Kathy."

Petra knew very little about Kathy. Gracious, pretty, efficient, supermom, never without makeup. High school prom queen, with a teaching credential she'd never used. During the family outings, Petra had observed a superorganizer.

A bit reserved—let's be honest, more than reserved. Despite superficial friendliness, the woman had always maintained distance, and Petra had thought of her as an ice queen.

Thirty-six years old. Six kids.

Petra thought of her own father, raising five children by himself. And all the while, Stu'd been fighting to maintain.

"She's so strong," Stu said. "I've never slept with anyone else."

Saying it with wonderment. Petra patted his arm.

"Most guys get tired of being with the same woman. All I ever wanted was Kathy. I really love her, Petra."

"I know you do."

"You try to do the right thing, live a certain way—I know there are no deals with God, He's got His own plan, but still . . ."

"She'll be fine," said Petra. "It'll work out, you'll see."

"Look at Ramsey," he went on. "Has a healthy wife, does that to her. The Eggermann woman. All the things we see."

He put his head down on the steering wheel, broke into startling, phlegmy sobs.

Vivian Boehlinger, now this.

This was different. This was part of her.

Petra reached over and held him.

# CHAPTER 41

AS SHE APPROACHED THE ELEVATOR, MILDRED Board heard footsteps from above. Then a toilet flush, the bathwater running. The big house was built beautifully, but if you stood in certain places, sound traveled freely through the rafters.

Missus drawing the bath herself. There was something new.

Perhaps it would be a good day.

She returned to the kitchen, ate the shirred eggs and drank the coffee at the old yew-wood table, dumped the coffee, made a fresh pot and waited, allowing the missus a nice long time to soak. By 8:45 she was riding up with the second batch of breakfast.

No newspaper on the tray. But not because she'd screened it for nastiness. The delivery service had skipped the house this morning. Again. Such a slipshod world.

She'd take care of it after serving, get right on the phone with the newspaper subscription office, give them what for.

Sometimes she wished the missus would allow the subscription to lapse. There was no need to read the kinds of things they printed.

The lift let her out on the carpeted top landing. She walked past the space where the upstairs Steinway grand had stood, past the ghosts of the Regency chest with its intricate tortoiseshell front, the pair of monumental Kang Xi vases, blue as the sky, white as milk, sitting high on Carrara-marble pedestals. A patch of dust in an alcove made her stop and wipe with the hem of her apron.

The walk to the missus's suite took her past the echoes of Chinese porcelain, the gilded cases, one filled with animalier bronzes, the other teeming with Japanese inro, jade, ivory, mixed-metal vases.

All irreplaceable. Like the boulle chest. It was illegal to kill tortoises now. Unborn babies, yes, but not reptiles.

She knocked on the missus's door, received the expected faint reply, and went in.

The missus was in bed, wearing the cream satin bed jacket with the covered buttons—what a quest it had been finding a proper dry cleaner for that—hair wrapped in a white French towel, no makeup but still beautiful. Rosewater scent sweetened the enormous room. The only items on the nightstand were a Limoges tissue-box holder and a black satin eye mask. The bed covers were barely mused; even in sleep the woman was genteel.

But the missus was acting strange—staring straight ahead, not smiling at Mildred.

Bad dreams again?

The room was still dark, both sets of drapes drawn. Mildred stood there, not wanting to intrude, and a second later the missus turned to her. "Good morning, dear."

"Morning, ma'am."

Her face so thin, so white. Tired, very tired. So it probably wouldn't be a good day.

Mildred resolved to try to get her out of the house a bit—a drive to Huntington Gardens? Last month the two of them had spent a glorious hour strolling at the missus's snail's pace. A week later Mildred had suggested they repeat it, perhaps the art gallery, but the missus demurred. *Maybe another time, dear.*

Once upon a time, a driver had wheeled the Cadillac and the Lincoln. The Cadillac was gone; Mildred wrestled with the Lincoln . . . how much petrol was in the tank?

If not a drive, at least a stroll out in back, some fresh air. Maybe after lunch.

"Here's some breakfast for you, ma'am."

"Thank you, Mildred." Saying it automatically, so politely that Mildred knew the missus wasn't hungry, probably wouldn't touch a thing.

The body needed sustenance. That was simple logic. Yet, despite all her education, the college degree from Wellesley— the finest women's school in America—the missus sometimes seemed unaware of the basics. During those moments, Mildred felt she was the older sister, caring for a child.

"You do need to eat, ma'am."

"Thank you, Mildred. I'll do my best."

Mildred put the food down, drew the drapes, fetched the bed tray, and set it up. She noticed a kink in the drapery pleats, straightened it, and looked out the window. The blue-tiled pool that him had modeled after Mr. Hearst's at San Simeon was empty and streaked with brown. The boxwood knot garden— too painful to see. Mildred looked away but not before being assaulted by a distant view of downtown Los Angeles. All that steel and glass, hideous from up close, but this far perhaps it did have a certain . . . stature.

When she turned fully, the missus was wiping her eyes. Crying? Mildred hadn't heard a sniffle.

The missus pulled a tissue out of the porcelain box and blew her nose inaudibly. Another cold? Or *had* she been crying?

"Here you go, ma'am, toast just the way you like it."

"Forgive me, Mildred, it's a beautiful breakfast but . . . maybe in a bit, please leave it."

"Some coffee to stimulate the appetite, ma'am?"

The missus started to refuse, then said, "Yes, please."

Mildred took hold of the cozy-wrapped pitcher and directed an ebony stream into the Royal Worcester cup. The missus lifted the coffee. Her hands were shaking so, she needed both to keep it steady.

"What's the matter, ma'am?"

"Nothing. Everything's fine, Mildred—what a beautiful rose."

"Giant blossoms this year, ma'am. It's going to be a good year for roses."

"Yes, I'm sure it will ... thank you for going to the trouble."

"No trouble at all, ma'am."

The same dialogue they exchanged every morning. Hundreds of mornings. A ritual but not a formality, because the missus's gratitude was genuine, she was gracious as royalty— more gracious. Look what royalty had become! It was hard to think of her as an American. More of an ... international.

The missus reached for another tissue and patted her eyes. Mildred picked up the first tissue, dropping it in the Venetian wastebasket beneath the end table, noticed something in there.

A newspaper. Today's!

"I got up very early and brought it up, Mildred—don't be cross."

"Early, ma'am?" Mildred had been up at six, taking her own bath, ten minutes of secret bubbles, ten minutes later. She hadn't heard a thing—the missus's escape concealed by running water!

"I went outside to check the trees. All those winds—the Santa Anas we had last night."

"I see, ma'am."

"Oh, Mildred, it's fine." The soft eyes blinked.

Mildred crossed her arms over her apron. "How early is early, ma'am?"

"I don't really know, dear—six, six-thirty. I suppose I went to sleep too early and my rhythm was off."

"Very well," said Mildred. "Would you be wanting anything else, ma'am?"

"No thank you, dear." Now the missus's hands were shaking again. Holding tight to the covers. Smiling, but it looked forced. Mildred prayed it wasn't another downturn. She looked down at the newspaper.

"You can take it," said the missus. "If you want to read it."

Mildred folded the horrid thing under her arm. Read it, indeed! She'd throw it out with the kitchen trash.

# CHAPTER 42

WHEN THE LOCK CLICKED ON THE BACK DOOR to the Jewish church, my brain froze and I couldn't move.

What would the Jews do to me? Now I was finished.

As the back door opened, I jumped under the big table, crawled into the cabinet, and closed the door quietly. I could hear footsteps from inside.

Just one person walking—yes, just one.

The cabinet was empty and smelled of wood and old clothes. My mouth tasted of crackers and fear. I pushed myself into a corner and didn't move. Praying whoever was in here wouldn't open the doors.

The sign said no prayers till tomorrow; did the Jews have secret prayers?

Whoever it was out there walked around, stopped, walked some more.

Now he was close to me. If he did open the cabinet, I'd jump out, I'd scream like a maniac, surprise him and escape.

Escape, how? Not through the back door, unless he'd left it unlocked.

The front—could you open it from inside? The bathroom window again—that would take time. My stomach started to hurt really bad. I felt like I was being suffocated.

I didn't even do anything really wrong—just ate some of their food, and it wasn't that good. Crackers with an onion taste, some butterfly-shaped cookies that were stale.

I didn't even mess with the silver bottle with the Jewish star on it, just shook it to see what would fall out. Even though the lock looked dinky. I thought about breaking it, but the bottle looked nice and I didn't want to damage it.

This was a Jewish place, but it was still a church, so maybe God was here, too.

I'd tell him all that if he caught me.

No I wouldn't, I'd yell and scream and run to the bathroom, lock myself in, get that window up.

I remembered what Moron said about Jews being out to kill Christians . . . that's got to be crazy, but what if . . .

Now he's farther away. Back and forth, back and forth— what's he doing?

Uh-oh, he's coming closer again. I hear rattling—he's shaking the silver bottle. Now it sounds like he's scraping the top of the table—probably cleaning up the cracker crumbs . . . now he walks away. Maybe he'll see no one stole anything and just leave—

Now he's walking back—

The door opens.

I don't jump out and yell.

I just push myself harder into the corner.

A face stares at me. An old face, kind of fat. Glasses with thick black frames, a big nose, red, kind of big ears.

A funny-looking old guy. He steps back. He's wearing old guy's clothes: a white shirt and baggy light blue pants and one of those zippered tan jackets. His fingers are really thick and his hands look too big for the rest of him.

He doesn't look mad. More surprised. I keep pushing myself into the corner. The wood is hard against my back and my butt, but I can't stop pushing.

He steps back some more, says, "It's okay," in a deep grumbly voice.

I just sit there.

"It's okay. Come on out, I don't bite."

Then he peeks in closer, smiling, showing me his teeth, like trying to prove they're not for biting kids. The pervert grandpa smiled that way, too.

He's giving me room to get out, but I can't move, I just can't move.

He starts saying it's okay, if I'm hungry I should eat right, not junk.

I figure if he gives me troubles I can just push him down. Even with those big, thick hands, he's an old guy.

Finally, my body relaxes and I crawl out. He grabs my arm and he's pretty strong and I try to kick him and he lets go and I run to the front of the synagon, but the door's locked with one of those locks you need a key for so now I'm stuck.

I go back. He's sitting down on a church bench. He laughs, holds out a box of chocolate doughnuts, tries to give it to me, but no way will I get close enough to him to take it.

Not just because he's Jewish, because he's a person and you can't trust anyone.

He starts talking again, telling me he'll unlock the back door for me, I don't have to crawl through the window.

Then he pulls out money! Two twenty-dollar bills—forty dollars!

What's he trying to buy?

I don't take it, and he puts it down on the floor along with the doughnuts and gets up and unlocks the door and goes to the bathroom.

I grab up everything and race out of there.

※

Outside, I breathe again. Inside my pocket, the money weighs a ton and the first doughnut I eat, walking through the alley, tastes fantastic. I eat another one. Then my stomach starts to hurt, and I decide to save the rest for later.

Stores are opening and more people are walking and skating, and the first thing I do is buy a hat, a Dodgers hat with an adjustable band in back. I fit it to my head and bend the brim over my face so it'll keep the sun off, and also to hide it.

Because buying it is a strange experience. The place I find it is this little shack a ways up from the synagon. The guy who sells it to me is ugly, with bad skin, mirrored sunglasses, and long greasy blond-and-gray hair. He looks at me funny. Like he knows me.

I guess he could be from Hollywood, but I never saw him before. He's got a weird accent, like a bad guy from a spy movie—Russian, he sounds like a Russian spy.

So why's he looking at me like that? I mean, I can't be sure he really is, because of the mirrored sunglasses. But it seems like he is—the way he turns his head toward me and just keeps it there. Taking a long time to give me my change.

As I turn away, he says, "Hey, you, kid," but I leave, pushing the hat down over my face. When I turn around a few moments later, he's in front of the shack, still looking in my direction, so I duck between some buildings and walk through the alley a little, then back to Ocean Front, too far for him to see me.

The ocean has turned pure blue, and my bones finally feel warm. I smell corn dogs and popcorn, know I have money to buy them, but I'm still full from the crackers and the doughnuts. All these people, and I'm walking along with them, like it's a moving sidewalk and we're all together doing some dance; no one's bothering anyone.

The corn-dog smell makes me feel I'm at a carnival. I was at a school carnival once. Had no money to buy corn dogs or anything. This feels like a warm bright dream.

I reach the end of the walkway and there's no place to go but sand.

The whole beach is like the end of the world.

I figure I'll try the other end, turn around, walk for a while, until I spot the ugly Russian guy coming my way. He's in the crowd, but he's not part of it. Everyone else seems to be having a good time. He looks angry. And his eyes are all over the place. Looking for something—me?

Another perv?

I don't want to find out. Slipping back over to the alley, I walk back in the direction I came from, checking over my shoulder a few times. I see a couple of people, but not him. Then the alley's empty again and here's the synagon. There's a huge old white Lincoln Continental with a brown top parked there. Must be the old guy's.

Jew canoes, Moron called them. Cadillacs and Lincoln Continentals.

Soft cars, he used to say, for soft people.

But the old guy had a strong grip.

The way he just gave me all that money—forty dollars, like it was nothing. So the Jews are rich. But he didn't want anything from me.

Maybe I can get some more money from him.

I'm still out in the alley thinking about it when he comes out, sees me, and gives a surprised smile. He's really short. This time I notice that his teeth are too white; they have to be false.

Mom had some false teeth made up for the back of her mouth where the rotten ones fell out, but she never put them in and her face started to get saggy.

He holds out his hands, like he's confused.

"What?" he says. "You already spent it all?"

# CHAPTER 43

STU LET HER COMFORT HIM, THEN, ABRUPT AS a power failure, he broke the embrace. It was the first time they'd ever touched.

"Back to work," he said.

Back at their desks, he told her, "I heard from one of my studio sources."

Scott Wembley had called last night. He gave her the basics, leaving out the whining in the A.D.'s voice: "It's no big deal, Detective, but you said call for anything."

"What do you have, Scott?"

"A few of us were sitting around schmoozing and Ramsey came up and someone said they thought his show sometimes shot in Griffith Park. Mountain areas, the horse trails—it's just across the freeway from Burbank."

"Recent shoot?"

"I don't know. That's all I know."

"Who brought it up?"

"Another A.D., and don't ask me where she heard it from, 'cause I didn't pump her—you said be subtle, right?"

"Did she know this for a fact, or was she guessing?"

"She said she thought so. Thought she'd heard it some-where. It was like . . . casual talk. People giving their opinions."

"What kinds of opinions?"

"One, really: Ramsey's the white man's answer to O.J."

"Okay, Scott. Thanks."

"Thank me by leaving me alone."

❖

Petra said, "So maybe Ramsey knows Griffith."

"But then why wouldn't he pick a more secluded area of the park?"

"Because then he'd have to drag Lisa along on foot. Using the parking lot meant he could drive in, get out of the car, ostensibly to talk, then stab her by surprise."

"You think he planned it."

"I think at some time during their time together he planned it. Also, the car may have had some significance—psychologically. Ramsey collects cars, Lisa liked to have sex in them. Where better to end their relationship than in a park-ing lot?"

"The perfect L.A. couple . . . good point. I like that." He put his hands on the steering wheel. He'd shaved carelessly, missing a tiny waffle of blond hair below his right ear. "Be in-teresting to know if any *Adjustor* episodes match the murder."

"Life imitating bad TV?" said Petra.

"These people have no imagination. Getting the actual scripts would take time, but I can scan a few years' worth of *TV Guide*s, see what comes up in the plot summaries."

"Fine," said Petra. More busywork. He looked grateful to do it.

Fournier entered the squad room, picked up a stack of mes-sage slips, and came over. "Hey," he said.

"Hey," said Stu. Nothing on his face to indicate this wasn't just another day.

Fournier waved the stack. "Took the liberty of burglarizing your desktop, Barbie."

"I'll pay you later," she said. "Anything new?"

"Still nothing on the kid from shelters, do-gooders, or Juvey, but he didn't just blow into town. I've got one nice lead—Korean guy runs the Oki-Rama on Western, says the kid bought food from him once in a while over a three-, four-month period. Always at night, he noticed, because the kid looked young to be alone at that hour, never talked except to order, never made eye contact, real careful about counting his change, every penny. 'A little banker,' the Korean guy called him. Said the kid also came by and swiped ketchup, mustard, mayo, thought he never noticed. And guess what: Last time the kid came in was Sunday night around nine. Bought a chili-burger."

"There you go," said Petra, thinking about the boy on his own for three months. Managing his finances. Where'd he get the money? Where did he come from? "Let's check the national runaway lines."

"Already faxed the picture," said Fournier. "They've got tons of files, it'll take time. Meanwhile, the Korean wants the reward." He laughed. "Along with everyone else. Along with the greedy types are a few just plain wackos. I got an alleged clair*voyant* from Chula Vista claiming some satanic cult murdered Lisa for her thymus gland. Seems there's a new rage for thymus glands among the horned crowd."

"Lisa's thymus was intact at the time of autopsy," said Petra.

"I told the lady she hadn't won the jackpot. Didn't know clairvoyants could cuss like that. One last thing: Schoelkopf blew in. They're leaning on him from the top, and we are instructed to inform him immediately about anything remotely resembling a lead. Do we have one?"

Stu told him the rumor about Ramsey's show filming in Griffith.

Fournier thought. "Nah, he can't take that to the press."

"He actually made it to the squad room?" said Petra. "Among the great unwashed?"

"For a whole five minutes, Barb. Turn up the heat and the grease spatters."

# CHAPTER 44

■

A WITNESS.

How was it possible?

He'd awoken this morning feeling pretty good about things. Stretched, yawned, made coffee, poured some juice. Opened the paper.

And there it was.

His bowels started churning.

*A kid?*

The article said *maybe* he'd been there; the police were developing other leads.

Meaning the police didn't know a damn thing or they were double bluffing, trying to draw him out.

He didn't do well with uncertainty.

*A kid?* In the park at that hour?

Maybe it was a bogus clue, a plant to flush someone out.

No, not with a reward. If a false clue got some innocent kid picked up by some money-hungry idiot and the parents sued, there'd be big-time legal problems.

So probably a real lead . . . but how would anyone know about the kid if he hadn't come forward?

Unless . . . some sort of physical evidence . . . had he left something behind?

Funny thing was, after doing Lisa, he'd thought he heard something. Up behind those rocks. A rustle, a scraping, above the sound of his pumping arm.

He allowed himself a moment of bliss: the look on Lisa's face. Even in the darkness, he'd seen it. Or maybe he'd just imagined it.

He'd convinced himself that he'd imagined the scraping. Had stopped, stood still, heard nothing, returned his attention to Lisa.

So nice and inert.

He had blood on his shirt but was careful to keep his shoes clean, because shoe prints could cause problems. Asphalt was good for that, too. Stay off the dirt. Before returning to the car, he took the shoes off.

So careful, and yet . . . a kid up there that late . . . it made no sense. He stared at the picture again. White, looked to be eleven or twelve. Could be any of a thousand kids. If he existed.

Even if they found him, what could he have seen in the darkness?

No way his face had been visible in the darkness.

Right?

What about the car? A flash of license plate . . . there were some lights on the edge of the lot. Had he passed under them?

He hadn't worried about it, had assumed no one was there.

If the kid did exist, why hadn't he come forward? So maybe it was bogus . . .

On the other hand, this could be a problem. Not a huge one—certainly nothing compared to Estrella, the evil-eyed bitch.

Throwaway people; L.A. was full of them.

A kid . . . consciously, he didn't feel worried, but, Christ, his heart was hammering away like a bastard!

He ripped the page out of the paper, squeezed it into a tight sweaty ball. Thought better of it and unfolded the picture. Tried to drink coffee, but it wouldn't go down.

Tried to cheer himself up by thinking of Lisa on the ground.

True love never dies, but she had.

So easily.

The best part had been her surprise.

Bygones be bygones, let's hug. Then wham!

Something quite different from a hug.

"Quite different," he said aloud, in a cultured British accent. David Niven voice—one of a thousand parts he'd never gotten to play.

No one appreciated his talent.

Lisa had, though, during the last second of her life. The look on her face: finally seeing him in a new light.

*You're capable of this?*

He'd made sure to look in her eyes as he jammed the knife in and yanked up.

One of those beautiful moments when everything came together. Best role he'd ever played. Just the two of them, dancing in the dark.

The two of them and a *kid*?

What could he have done to avoid it? Gone traipsing up in those hills, scattering blood and who knew what other kinds of forensic evidence all over the place? Even the LAPD nitwits might have found something.

They'd found out about the kid. *How?*

And now the reward. The old man throwing his weight around.

Maybe the kid *had* been there earlier but left before he and Lisa showed up.

*Maybe, maybe, maybe*—an old song, one of the doo-wop ones he loved. Some girl group, the Chantelles or the Shirelles.

All that money would probably bring in nutcases. Bottom line was, LAPD didn't have a clue.

"Not a bloody clue," he said in his David Niven voice.

Not the sheriff's clowns who'd showed up the first day or that pair from the police department. Bishop, strong and silent, yielding center stage to Connor.

Ms. Detective. Those long legs. No chest, but still, that was some piece of poon. What was she, twenty-six, -seven? That dark hair and pale skin. The kind of long, lean body that might look too bony naked but was okay with clothes on. He imagined her, white and smooth, not a scrap of fat on her, stretched out on a poolside lounge as she yielded to his hands, his mouth, his . . .

Another time, another place . . .

He laughed, stretched big arms.

Not a clue, any of them.

Except for this alleged *kid*?

Who wasn't coming forward.

Because he didn't exist?

Out there that late, he had to be a street punk, a runaway—maybe his mind was blown from drugs or AIDS.

Probably nothing to worry about.

He sat there for a long time, trying to convince himself.

Finally reaching the ugly conclusion: It needed to be taken seriously.

He'd research it. Unlike the cops, he wasn't bound by rules. Life had taught him to make his own rules.

After all these years, it all boiled down to one: Take what you want.

Like that night in Redondo, the German stewardess, sitting in that restaurant, arguing with that plug-ugly boyfriend.

He studied them from the bar across the room, nursing a Heineken, wiping suds from his false beard, wondering what a girl like that saw in someone that repulsive.

Noticing the girl because of her resemblance to Lisa. That boyfriend, a face like pigshit.

He watched them, conjuring up beauty-and-the-beast sexual fantasies that failed to arouse him. Because it was clear that they weren't getting along, glaring at each other, not eating much.

Finally the girl got up and stomped out of the restaurant. Looking so much like Lisa—a bit taller, bigger tits, the lush body in that short blue dress, those tight, muscular legs as she marched offscreen.

Pigshit tossed bills down and followed. Big guy, but soft, a sack of fertilizer.

He watched them leave, paid for the Heineken, made sure no one was watching, and climbed down to the parking lot behind the restaurant, finding a vantage point behind his car. Pigshit was trying to get Blondie into his car, lots of hand gestures on both sides. Every time she moved, those tits bounced—from the way they responded, not an ounce of plastic. Chest like that on a skinny girl, you didn't see it very often.

They kept arguing, then Pigshit grabbed her, she pulled away, he grabbed again, she slapped him, he slapped her, she fell, got up.

This was fun.

Now Pigshit looked like he was apologizing—the big idiot actually got down on his knees.

And what did Blondie do?

Spit on him.

Watching from behind his car, he almost laughed out loud. Uh-oh, here comes payback: Pigshit sprang up, swung at her, a giant roundhouse, but clumsy, too many drinks, he missed. Blondie ran across the lot, those wonderful tits heaving-ho, Pigshit shaking his fist but not following.

Blondie stopped at the edge of the lot, folded her hands across the wonder chest. Pigshit shook his head, got in a compact car, drove away.

Alone, she let her hands drop helplessly. Realizing it was dark, no one's around, the pier has emptied out, try finding a cab in Redondo Beach at this hour.

The smart thing would have been to return to the restaurant. Instead, she just stood there. Crying.

Well, Fräulein, stupidity has its rewards.

His turn.

Wonderful. His second time. First had been little Sally Tosk, back in Syracuse, tenth grade, well developed since eighth. He'd watched her chest grow, almost alarmingly. Not a true blonde, a strawberry blonde, still wearing braces on her top teeth. She'd come on to him all through football season; finally he'd graced her with a date. Secret date—she had a boyfriend but wanted to slut around with him, too.

He'd driven to her house in his father's new Buick, her parents out till late, some kind of Rotary dinner. The Tosks lived on a big piece of land beyond the city limits, used to be a farm. Sally was ready at the door, little nightie, nothing else. Gave him tongue in the living room, tit in the kitchen; they moved up to her bedroom, then she got all hysterical when he refused to say he loved her and tried to push him away, and he had to put a hand over her mouth to stop her from screaming.

Covering her mouth and her nose, and all of a sudden she was blue. He panicked. Then he started to see her in a different light and fooled with her body, just exploring. Careful not to leave anything behind, he drove home throbbing with terror and pleasure.

The Tosks came home two hours later. Big scare in town, rumors of a stalking sex maniac.

He lost sleep for weeks, because what if Sally had told someone she was meeting him? Lost weight and told his mother he had the flu.

But she hadn't told anyone; worried about the boyfriend.

The cops talked to the boyfriend.

No leads. He attended Sally's funeral, cried along with everyone else.

Nothing like young lust.

Sally. The German girl. Lisa.

Not that he was a serial killer. He had no compulsion.

But when the opportunity came up . . .

At Sally's funeral, he really lost it when the dirt hit the coffin. One of Sally's girlfriends, another cheerleader, took his hand and dried his eyes, told him later how sensitive he was.

"Dearly beloved," he intoned in a melodious voice. Not Niven—John Houseman, someone like that.

And the Oscar goes to . . .

# CHAPTER 45

I TELL THE OLD GUY, "NO, I'VE STILL GOT IT, but I wouldn't mind some more. Have any work I can do?"

He pushes his glasses up his nose. "So you *can* talk. Want to work, eh? How old are you?"

"Old enough."

He comes closer. "Listen, if you're in trouble, running away from something, maybe I can help you. Because a fellow your age shouldn't be out here all alone."

I back away. "I don't need help. Just work."

"Got a work permit?"

I don't answer. He says, "A work permit. It's the law. To protect kids. They used to force kids to work, not anymore. Not in the United States."

So he's not going to help me. I start to leave.

"Hold on—you want work? Fine."

I stop. "What do you have? How much do you pay?"

He smiles again. "A businessman. Okay, listen, the shul here—the synagogue"—he points over his shoulder—"is not used much during the week, but it would be good to have someone to clean the place up before Friday services. Keep an eye out on things, know what I mean?"

"A watchman?"

"Not a night watchman, a day watchman, because there's nowhere to sleep—you have someplace to sleep?"

"Sure."

"It's dangerous around here at night," he says, coming even closer. "You been on the streets awhile, haven't you?"

I don't answer.

"I'm not trying to be nosy, sonny, but maybe I can help. 'Cause I been there, believe me."

The way he says that, the change that comes over his face— like something I learned in science. Metamorphosis. I know he's telling the truth.

"That must have been a long time ago," I say.

He stares at me. Cracks up. "Yeah, a real long time. Back in the Stone Age."

His laugh is funny—deep, like it comes from way down in his belly. I can't help myself. My mouth turns up.

"Ah, he can smile, too. So maybe life's not so bad after all, eh?"

That wipes the smile from my face.

"It is?" he said. "Someone hurt you that bad?"

Inside the shul he shows me a little closet in the men's bathroom where the cleaning stuff is kept. A broom, a dustpan, a mop and pail, Windex for the glass, Lemon Pledge for the wood. Some silver polish, too, but he leaves that there. Sees me looking at it.

"C'mere, sonny—do you have a name, by the way? I'm Sam Ganzer."

"Sonny is fine."

He shrugs, holds out his hand, and we shake. His hand feels like a hunk of dried meat.

"Nice to meet you," he says.

"Same here."

He brings me into the main room of the shul. At the front is this big carved-wood cabinet that I never had a chance to open, reaching to the ceiling and covered by a blue velvet curtain. He pulls a cord and the curtain opens. Behind it are these doors with twelve little carved scenes—Bible scenes. I recognize Noah's Ark, Moses in the cradle. Some other stuff doesn't mean anything to me.

Nothing about Jesus. Of course. I think: This is weird; what am I doing here?

Behind the carved doors are three things also covered in blue velvet with Jewish writing with wooden poles sticking out on top and bottom and silver handles, just on top. The closest one says, *Dedicated by Saul and Isidore Levine in memory of their father, Hyman.* Hanging over the front are silver plates.

"Know what these are?" Sam asks.

"No."

"Torahs. The Jewish Bible—you believe in the Bible, don't you?"

I don't know what I believe in, but I nod.

"So you understand these are holy, right?"

"Don't worry, I won't steal the silver," I say.

He turns red as a tomato. "That's not what I was implying, sonny. I just want you to know that this is important stuff we're dealing with. So when I ask you to polish the silver, you'll be extra careful. Got it?"

"Got it." Even though I know what he was really saying.

※

We arrange it this way: I'll sweep and mop the entire shul, including the bathrooms, Windex the windows, and Lemon Pledge the wood. The last job will be polishing the silver, because he needs to bring me more rags.

"Also," he says, "the silver polish is pretty strong, so don't breathe it in too close, got it?"

"Got it."

"I'm serious," he says. "You don't sniff stuff, do you? Glue, paint—you don't do that, right? No drugs?"

"Never," I said. "Not once."

"I believe you," he said. "You seem like a nice kid. I'd like to know what you're doing out on the streets, living on crackers, but it's your business."

I say nothing.

He says, "I just don't want to come in here, find you knocked out by silver polish fumes. Believe me, I know about these things, owned a hardware store for forty years. At the end, junkies and lowlifes were coming in buying all the glue and fixative—it was pretty obvious none of them ever installed a commode."

Boy, he can really talk.

"I'll be careful," I say.

"Another thing. Today is Thursday, tomorrow night we have services. Saturday, too, so I can't use you at all on Saturday."

"Fine. After today, I don't think there'll be anything to do."

He puts his hands in his pockets. "So now the important part: How much do you want?"

"Whatever you think is fair."

"Whatever *I* think? Meaning if I say two pennies an hour, you'll be happy?"

"I think you'll be fair."

"Flattered, sonny, but if you're gonna be a businessman, learn to set a price."

I think for a while. How much do they pay kids to flip burgers at McDonald's? I don't know. I really don't know. "Two dollars an hour."

"Two dollars an hour? Minimum wage is over five. You don't think you're minimum wage?"

"Okay, six."

"Five-fifty."

"Fine!" I shout, and it surprises me.

"I'm not deaf," he says. "Five-fifty an hour, and I figure you've got, what, eight, nine hours—let's say fifty bucks total. Here's an advance."

Out comes his wallet and suddenly there're two ten-dollar bills in my hand and, not believing my good luck, I stick them in my pocket.

"The rest you'll get when you finish—I'll come by in a few hours to check."

He moves closer again, stops. "One more thing: This is a cash deal, no withholding for taxes, Social Security. So don't report me to the government, okay?"

# CHAPTER 46

THE WAY MOTOR MORAN FIGURED IT, IF HE'D had a good scoot, he'd nevera noticed it.

He was thirty years old and, except for those four months guarding that junkyard in Salinas, had never worked a real job. Arts-and-crafts prison shit didn't count—he'd never been in a real pen, anyway, just local shitholes, DUI, drunk and disorderly, a month here, a month there.

Life owed him something before he died. This could be it.

The kind of scoot his dick was quiverin' for cost. Like a '72 Shovelhead, Zenith carbs, nuclear displacement, polished cases—*everything* polished, *satin* chrome. Somethin' chopped, Paughco Fishtails, unleaded valve seats, powder-coated frame with a lot of flake in it. Give the whole thing a nice big stretch with some Kennedy long-forks, or just some wide-glides if you didn't want to hard-on that much. Skirted seat with a backrest, because his back hurt, specially in the mornin'.

A double seat. Chromed passenger pegs, 'cause you had to have a chick in back, holding on for dear life as you took her on a face-blasting putt.

Not Sharla, that stoned-out skank. One of those wenches you saw in *Easy Rider*. The putt would turn her on, and pulling over at some rest stop, he'd serve her some Motorized pork for lunch.

Oh, man, if he had the dough, he could have it all.

His current scoot was an Abomination Before the Lord, thrown together from corroded spare parts, fastened with Bondo and rewelds and prayer. He'd even snuck some Jap parts in places you couldn't see. H-D emblem on the frame, but for all the Harley parts in there, the fucking thing might've said Slant Special.

At least it made noise. The Jap stuff never made noise.

The day he took the bus into Bakersfield, the bucket o' bolts hadn't started for three days straight. He found the trouble quickly enough. *Troubles:* starter gear so rotted there was a fucking hole in it; spark coil stone-dead; plugs wasted. The worst thing, the voltage regulator had wires that were coming apart, rattier than Sharla's hair. A hundred bucks minimum, so far, and the belt assembly looked ready to go, another two C's.

All he had left of Sharla's FDIC was sixty bucks, and he took it, left her snoring, and began the painful walk to the Bolsa Chica bus station.

Knowing sixty wouldn't get him far with Spanky, but maybe he could haul trash outta the shop, do some construction work over at Spanky's house—his bitch was always remodeling.

Anything to be rollin' again.

Riding the fuckin' bus, all those greasers staring at him. Those drippy brown eyes askin' the question any retardo would ask: Where's your scoot, man?

'Cause he was a putter, you could tell by lookin' at him he didn't take no bus. If there was a roof on a ride, it sucked.

He *looked* like a putter, goddamnit. Independent jeans—so oil-soaked they stood by themselves—black XXXL T-shirt with the death's-head Angel insignia—when no Angels were around. Nailheads, steel boots, leather, leather, leather.

Nice bandanna-style ripper cap—fuck the helmet law!

The bus ate twelve of the sixty bucks, came late, made stops along the way to drop greasers off at orchards. Half the day to get to Bandit Cycles and when he arrived at the store it was crowded, weekend warriors glomming the new stuff Spanky had customized. Guys in suits drooling over outrageous '95 Rigids, coupla Softtails, a few antiques that tightened his ball sac. Lookit that Knuckle/Pan—black-cherry lacquer with a dancing chick in pink.

Rich pussies checking out the merchandise like they knew what it was. Spanky pointing out details, kissing ass.

And if a pussy bought one, what would he be? A pussy on a scoot.

Motor cruised around the showroom, examining parts, leafing through the latest *Rider*—the Fox of the Month was a greaser, but lookit them brown nipples!

Then back to the grease room behind the store, where two

mechanics were working on bikes. Bolting away, two assholes he'd never seen before.

*More Mexicans!* What got into the Spankster?

Finally, the pussies left with brochures and Spanky went back behind the counter, untied his ponytail, and shook out two feeta hair—shit, the guy had gotten gray. No meat on him, face like a skeleton, those rotten teeth, asshole looked like a death's-head. When did he start wearing glasses?

Motor walked up to the counter. Spanky had a bottlea Bud in one hand, his right arm was covered with tattoos from shoulder to fingertips. Not the left one, though, that just had Spanky's old lady's name, Tara, on the bicep. Once Motor had asked him about it and Spanky had said, "Use the left one to wipe my ass. Like the Hindus."

Weird.

"Hey, man," said Motor.

Spanky didn't look up. Draining half the Bud, he picked up a flyer about the Chillicothe meet, pretended to read. Motor read the back. Primo putt, Labor Day, all the way to Ohio. Lord, that was one he woulda loved to do, cruise in formation by the penitentiary, brothers behind the fence lifting their fists in solidarity.

Spanky kept reading, paying him no attention.

"Chillicothe," said Motor. "Only thing better would be Sturgis, right? Or maybe Memorial Day at Laconia, hey?"

Spanky continued to ignore him.

Motor coughed and finally the skinny bastard looked up.

"Hey, man," he said. "What's happening?"

Spanky waited a while before he muttered, "Buell."

Using the name Motor hated.

"Hey, Spank." Motor raised his hand for a high five. Spanky didn't move. Then he slipped a ring through his beard, turned it into a gray horsetail. Finishing the rest of the beer, he tossed the bottle over his shoulder onto a pile of trash.

"No credit, Buell. You're still into me for those switchblade wheels."

"I paid you, man."

"Yeah, right—took you two years. Wheels like that, coulda moved 'em in two days. You take two years."

Which was bullshit—the wheels were used, pulled off a

wreck and reshaped, onea them totally skanked where kick-back gravel had knocked out a chunka rim.

"Spank—"

"Forget it, Buell."

"Listen, it's only a few small ones. And I got dough."

"How much dough?"

Motor peeled off a twenty and a ten. Spanky looked at the money like it was dogshit.

"C'mon, man, you know I'm good for it."

Spanky sighed and his chest sucked in like a ho's cheeks givin' head. No hair on his chest or his arms, but that gray beard growing up to his eyes was thickern Santa's.

"It's a down payment," said Motor.

"Yeah, sure—tell you one thing, you ain't gettin' no virgin pieces. If I let you have anything, it'll be off the spares pile."

"Fine," said Motor. "Lemme scrounge."

"Scrounge? You think for thirty bucks you can scrounge?"

"Thirty down, man. Old lady's got a check comin' in next week." Total lie; Sharla had no income till the enda the month. "First thing the check comes in, you get it—I'll bring it in person."

"In person?" Spanky smiled and the ringed beard moved around like ten pounds of lint. "Why don't you FedEx it to me, Buell? Everything comes FedEx now—ever use FedEx, Buell?"

"Yeah, sure." Total lie.

"Got your own FedEx account, do you? We got one. Got a computer, too." Spanky slapped the register. "Everything's computerized, Buell. Got another computer in back for ordering parts. Got E-mail, too. Know what E-mail is, Buell?"

Motor didn't answer. What an asshole. It dawned on him that Spanky looked . . . Jewish. Like onea them rabbis with that beard—put a hat on him, send him back to fucking Israel.

"E-mail, Buell. You send messages through the computer, phone calls, doesn't cost. You can get dirty pictures on the computer too, Buell. Amateurs, anals, facials, anything. Or just use your E-mail to write 'fuck you' to some asshole—anything you want. What I'm saying, Buell, is it's a new world out there, dude's gotta change with the times. Once upon a time a dude could sit on his ass, scrounge himself a scoot, live free. Now you got to have more than gas money."

Spanky looked at him with a mixture of pity and contempt. What was the asshole getting at?

"Nowadays you gotta produce something, Buell. Goods and services—like making a scoot or tuning it. I get doctors, lawyers, already have the Mercedes, but they're heavy into the putt. People *producing* something."

"Lawyers," said Motor, "produce more shit than a bear with the runs."

Spanky didn't laugh. Not even a smile. "Right, Buell. That's why they can pay for their parts and you're trying to give me thirty bucks."

"Hey, man—"

"Yeah, yeah, you wanna scrounge the parts pile, awright, but this is the last time, man. And first you gotta go over to the Bell and get me some grub." Spanky scratched the interior of his left nostril. "Three tacos—get me the soft ones and a beef burrito, extra guac, extra sauce. And a cheese enchilada. And a jumbo Coke. You pay for my dinner, maybe I'll let you scrounge. At least you're producing something— no goods, but at least it's a service. It's all about *economics*, Buell."

⬛

The Taco Bell was three blocks away and Motor's heels hurt with each step, all that weight pounding down, the worn-down boots not helping. His thighs chafed through filthy denim. When he got there, he was sweating from exertion. He ordered Spanky's food, scowling at the beaner kid, who said, "Yes, sir?" and stopped smiling when he saw Motor's face.

He was about to leave when he saw it, on one of the tables.

L.A. newspaper. He didn't read newspapers—who gave a shit. But this one, the picture, made him notice.

Fuck if it didn't look like Sharla's rug rat.

He picked it up. It took him a long time to finish the article, and he had to go over it twice to be sure. He'd always had trouble reading, words not making sense, some letters upside down. His old man called him a retard, look who's talkin', fucking unemployed janitor, dead at forty-five from a fucked-up liver. Mom not much better in the booze-slave department, but at least she didn't bug him. She couldn't read good, either.

Finally, he got through it. Was this for real? Witness to a murder? Hollywood?

He studied the picture some more. Looked *exactly* like the little rat.

*Had* to be the rat—he'd split, what, four months ago?

And kids always split to Hollywood. Motor had ended up there himself, Old Brain Fry kicking his ass after he flunked tenth grade for the third time, finally telling himself, Fuck it, I'm gone.

He took the Greyhound that time, too, stealing bucks out of Brain Fry's jeans. Scared when he got there, the place was huge, but walking tall, letting people know he wouldn't take shit.

Full grown, he looked older than his age, had few problems on the streets of Hollywood, where he strong-armed money from smaller kids, mugged old farts, ripped off a Jap bike from the Roosevelt Hotel parking lot, stripped it, sold the parts, got himself an old hybrid H-D Shovelnose from one of the bikers who drank at the Cave.

Best scoot he'd ever owned. Someone had stolen it from right under him.

He bunked in an abandoned building on—where was it?—Argyle. Yeah, Argyle, big empty apartment fulla junkies, place smelled of puke and shit and he never slept good, always looking out in case someone was out to get him. His size helped; so did beatin' the shit out of anyone smaller who crossed his path. And the nigger he knifed for looking at him the wrong way—that got around, he got himself a street rep.

The black leather jacket he bought at a Van Nuys swap meet got him tight with the bikers at the Cave. Onea them sold him fake ID so he could go inside and drink. Gettin' nice and thick with them, thinking he'd be able to join some club, then they just stopped actin' friendly—he never really understood why.

So kids split to Hollywood for sure.

The rat, too? Why not? The little shit was too small to fight for himself, so he was probably whorin' that skinny little bod, catchin' it backdoor, probably had AIDS.

Gone four months. Sharla still cried once in a while and he had to yell at her to shut the fuck up. Cryin' but not doin' a damn thing to find the rat. Pretendin' to give a shit—what a stupid whore. Once she sat up in bed, middle of the night, shoutin' about sick-eydas, sick-eydas, over and over, him shaking her, saying what the hell is a sick-eydas. Her looking at him, saying, Nuthin', cowboy. I had a bad dream.

It was time to move on, get a real chick.

Twenty-five grand; *this* could be the way.

He was already ahead of the pack: knew Hollywood, knew the rat.

If he had to fill his scoot with blood, he'd get down there.

It was well after dark by the time he made it back to the trailer.

Sharla was in the kitchen, popping a beer. "Hey, cowboy, whereya been?"

Ignoring her, he found a flashlight, went outside, taped the light to his handlebars, and began installing the scrounged parts. The plugs were brand-new; he'd lifted them when Spanky wasn't watching. Latest *Rider*, too; the Fox of the Month was Jody from El Paso, Texas; those black nipples. She said she liked to putt without any panties on.

He was doin' good when the trailer door opened. Sharla stood there, T-shirt and shorts, no shoes. Hands on hips, onea those kiss-me smiles.

He said, "Go inside, make me somethin' to eat."

"How 'bout a kiss?"

"Get me somethin' to eat. Move it."

She gave that hurt little baby look. "What do ya wannna eat?"

"What I want I can't get, so cook me up twoa those TV dinners. Macaroni and cheese, Salisbury steak—go on, move!"

She obeyed. At least one thing the bitch did good.

※

By 11 P.M., he'd gotten the scoot humming, filled his gut, had three beers.

*Twenty-five g's!* Like onea them bounty hunters.

Sharla waited for him to finish, then tried to get romantic. He pushed her head into his lap and finished quickly.

Hoovered, zipped, ready to roll!

She was in the bathroom washing her mouth out when he pawed through her purse, found five more bucks in change.

He was at the door when she came after him, said, "Hey."

He ignored her, checked his pocket for his keys.

"Where ya goin', cowboy?"

"Out."

"Again?" That tone of voice he hated—like a trannie about to fail.

She took hold of his arm. "C'mon, cowboy, you just got here."

"And now I'm splittin'. "

"C'mon, I don't wanna be *alone*."

"Watch TV."

"I don't *wanna* watch TV, I want *company*. And hey." Battin' her lashes, puttin' his hand on her tit. "I made *you* happy, how 'bout me?"

The feel of her—the way she looked and sounded—made him wanna puke. It was always that way. He'd get horny for her, then he'd finish with her and he'd think she was maggoty meat.

He shook her hand off. She grabbed him again, got into that whining thing.

"You want it so bad," he said, "go fuck onea them sick-eydas."

"Huh?" she said. "What're you talkin' about? Bugs?"

That confused Motor, and when he was confused he got mad. He backhanded her across the face, and she fell back against the kitchen counter and lay there—didn't move, didn't argue anymore.

He opened the door—the night was warm—kicked it closed.

Seconds later, he was cruising along the access road to the trailer park. When he got to the highway, he remembered to switch on his headlights.

# CHAPTER 47

■

THURSDAY, AT 6:30 P.M., AFTER SPENDING
more fruitless time on the Eggermann murder, Stu got ready to
leave. Petra was in the ladies' room; he supposed he should
wait to say good-bye to her.

Tomorrow, he'd go through *TV Guide*s. Any decent-size
library would have them. He'd find one near the hospital.

He locked his desk, tried to free his mind of the Worry. Bad
margins on the tumor. Lymph nodes full of cancer.

When he was with her, he was Mr. Positive. She'd let him
know right away that's the way she wanted it.

*We've got to keep everything normal for their sake,
honey.*

The children came first. He agreed with that—family
was everything, but what kind of family would there be
tomorrow?

*Mommy's going to the hospital for a little checkup, guys.
Just a couple days, everything's fine.*

She hadn't shed a tear, spent every day since the problem
began the exact same way: car-pooling, cooking, church auxiliary. Even lovemaking. Stu'd been reluctant, but she'd insisted and he hadn't wanted her to feel damaged.

Nineteen years ago, she'd been homecoming queen at Hoover
High, Miss Glendale the following year, then a sorority sweetheart at Occidental, a 4.0 history major.

Just one tumor, Drizak assured him, relatively small. The
family history wasn't terrible: Kathy's mom was healthy, but
an aunt had died of breast cancer.

All in all, a decent prognosis, Drizak claimed. But Stu was
a doctor's son, knew how imprecise medicine could be.

Bad surprises, Father had told him more than once, are

part of a surgeon's life. That's why we all have to trust in the Lord.

Stu *ached* to trust, and for the past few days he'd been praying with the conspicuous fervor of a missionary. Inside, he was hollow as an atheist.

All those Please, Gods; Dear Jesuses. What right did he have to petition?

For the sake of the children. Always the children.

A hand on his shoulder made him jump.

"Sorry," said Petra.

"Thought I'd shove off."

Her hand remained there. "Look, if there's anything I can do . . ."

"Thanks, but we're fine, Petra. I'm sure it'll all go smoothly."

"What time's the surgery?"

"Six A.M."

"Don't rush back," she said. "Wil and I will handle everything."

"Okay," he said, wondering if she'd try to hug him again. He hoped not. Not here, in front of all the others.

"What are your plans?" he asked.

"Thought I'd mosey over to Ramsey's place, talk to security, see if there's any other way out of RanchHaven."

"Good idea," he said. Petra had pointed out that they'd neglected to question the night guard immediately, and he'd been appalled . . . *What would he do without Kathy?*

He told Petra she was doing a great job and left.

Walk steady; one foot in front of the other. But his knees were weak, and it felt as if someone were shoving him.

# CHAPTER 48

EL SALVADOR TIME WAS AN HOUR LATER THAN
L.A., and Petra doubted Estrella Flores's son would still be in
his law office. She tried anyway, got no answer, connected
with an international operator, found three more listings for
Javier Floreses, and lucked out on number two.

"I'm worried about my mother," said the attorney in heavily
accented but sound English. "Your city is dangerous. My mother
doesn't drive. Where would she go? I phoned Ramsey, but he
didn't call back. My mother told me he lives out in the country.
How could she just walk out of there? She didn't drive. Where
would she go? This isn't right!"

Flores talked like an interrogator. Articulate, educated. So
what was his mother doing cleaning houses?

As if he was used to the question, he said, "I've been after
her to come back and live with us, but she's very independent.
But still, she didn't drive. Where would she go? It can't be related to Mrs. Ramsey—is it?"

"Your mother told you about Mrs. Ramsey?"

"No, the last time I spoke to her was Sunday, the day before
it happened. I read about it in the papers, I read American
papers. What are you doing to find her, Detective?"

"I've contacted every missing persons bureau, sir. I called
you to make sure there was no place your mother could have
gone. A relative, a—"

"No, no one," said Flores. "She knows no one. So you don't
think it had anything to do with Mrs. Ramsey?"

"We have no evidence of that, sir—"

"Please!" Flores exploded. "I'm not stupid! Could she have
learned something that put her in danger?"

"I honestly don't know, Mr. Flores. So far, there's no

283

evidence of that. Did your mother ever say anything about the Ramseys that could be relevant? Especially last Sunday?"

"No, they didn't come up. She asked how her bank account was doing, that's all. She wires me her money, I deposit it. She's saving up for her own house."

"All her money goes to El Salvador?"

"Except what's taken out for American taxes."

"What about past conversations?" said Petra. "What was her opinion of the Ramseys?"

"She said the wife was young, nice, not too picky."

"Was Mr. Ramsey picky?"

"A little—he had these cars he wanted polished all the time. But it was a good job, better than the one she worked before. Very picky people, they always criticized."

"Do you remember their names?"

"People in another part of town—Bel-Air. Hooper. Mr. and Mrs. Hooper. The man always ran his finger along the furniture, looking for dust. The woman drank too much, and they didn't pay her well."

"First names?"

"I don't—wait, the address is here in my book, unless I threw it out when she . . . no, here it is, Hooper—here's the number."

Petra copied it down. "I'll call them, Mr. Flores."

"I'll call them too," he said. "But I don't think my mother would have returned to them."

"Anything more you can tell me about the Ramseys?"

"The one she didn't like was the business manager—he was in charge of paying her, was always late with the check. Finally she complained to Mrs. Ramsey, and that helped."

"Mr. Balch?"

"She never mentioned his name, said he was a . . . snob. Out to show he was important. Him, she didn't like."

"What about Mr. Ramsey?"

"She didn't talk about him much. Do you think he killed the wife?"

"Mr. Flores, at this point, I—"

"Okay, okay, all I care about is my mother."

"I'll do everything I can to find her, sir. So as far as you know, there were no conflicts with Mr. Ramsey? No reason for your mother to suddenly quit?"

"He wasn't home that often. It was a big house, she didn't like being alone so much." His voice broke. "I know there's something wrong."

The moment Petra hung up the phone, it rang. The civilian clerk on duty said, "A Dr. Boehlinger called."

"Did he leave a message?"

"Just to call him back. Telling, not asking."

Just what she needed. Clenching her jaw, she dialed Boehlinger's hotel. He was out. Thank God for small victories.

She phoned the Hoopers in Bel-Air. Busy. Maybe Javier Flores was already on the line.

She tried again, connected to a husky-voiced woman. "Oh, Jesus, I just spoke to her son. No, I haven't seen her." Snorting laugh. "So now the police are trying to bring illegals *back*?"

"Thank you, Mrs. Hooper." You're the one who hired her when she was illegal, Mrs. Hooper. Click.

Wil Fournier came over and showed her a piece of paper. Forty or so names, all but three checked off. "Tipsters. Our little burglar's been spotted all up and down the state, but it's mostly garbage—who unlocked the asylum?" He loosened his tie. The tan pad of his hand was ink-stained. "One sweetheart from Frisco claims he's the son she gave up at birth, she was just about to call *Unsolved Mysteries*, the money would sure come in handy because she wants to become a psychologist. One guy claims the kid's not a kid, he's some kind of mystic guru—an apparition, appears in times of crisis and 'renders deliverance.' The world may be coming to an end."

"He might have something there," said Petra.

"Long as I get my pension," said Fournier. He tapped each of the three unchecked names. "These are possibles. Two come from the same place—some farm town called Watson, between Bakersfield and Fresno. Neither of the callers know the kid by name, but they both think they've seen him around. They didn't sound wacko or greedy, and two tips from a small place like that is interesting. I put in a call to the local law. Must be a real hick place, because it's a two-man sheriff outfit and both guys were out. I talked to some woman at the desk who sounded about a hundred years old. This last one probably is greed, Russian accent, but at least the guy sounded sane. Insisted he'd seen the kid in Venice this morning, described his clothes—T-shirt, jeans—said the kid looked like he'd been sleeping on the street, had crusted salt on his face, like he'd washed with ocean water. Scratched up, too."

"Good eye for detail."

"That's why I'm not dismissing him. He runs a souvenir stand down on Ocean Front in Venice, claims he sold the kid a hat this morning. Then the kid took off north. The guy thought it was weird, a kid being out by himself, middle of the day. And buying a hat—he never sells hats to kids."

"Trying to hide his face?" said Petra.

Fournier shrugged. "Could be. If the kid read today's paper, and we know he's a reader. On the other hand, you're homeless, broke, a runaway, someone's offering twenty-five g's for your presence, wouldn't you turn yourself in, try to collect?"

"He's a child, Wil. Probably an abused child. Why should he trust anyone? Feel enough in control to scheme? And if he saw the murder, he could be too scared to think about profit."

"Guess so. Or maybe the kid was there but not during the murder, figures why bother. Anyway, this Russian is definitely after the money."

Petra read the man's name out loud. "Vladimir Zhukanov."

"That's another thing," said Fournier. "His being Russian. I don't want to be prejudiced, but you know the scams those guys have been pulling off." He folded and pocketed the list. "I'll stop by to see him—have a date in Santa Monica tonight, dinner at Loew's. Ever been there?"

Petra shook her head.

"Zhukanov said he'd stay late to talk to me. One last thing: Schoelkopf called me into the office again, pumping for details. I may have to give him something, Barb. And then, boom, right in to the media and we run around like little windup toys."

"If you have to, you have to," said Petra. "It's already out of our hands."

※

She was ready to leave at seven when the phone blared again.

A young woman said, "Hold please for Lawrence Schick." Ten seconds of bad music, then a sleepy male voice said, "To which detective do I have the pleasure of speaking?"

"Detective Connor."

"Evening, Detective Connor, this is Larry Schick."

Meaningful pause. She was supposed to know who he was. And she did. Six-hundred-bucks-an-hour lawyer, criminal defense, mostly celebrity drunk drivers, actors' kids playing with guns, other delicate felonies. She'd seen him doing sound bites but had never met him. Her typical perp couldn't even afford a Western Avenue hack.

"Evening, Mr. Schick."

"How're things on the Ramsey case?"

Finally, the wall goes up. "Are you asking as a concerned citizen, sir?"

Schick laughed. "I'm always concerned, but, no, Detective Connor, I've been retained by Mr. Ramsey to represent him in this matter. So please channel all future communications through my offices."

Offices, plural. *Look, Ma, I'm important!*

"Communications," said Petra.

"Anything pertaining to the case," said Schick.

"Are you saying we can't talk to Mr. Ramsey without clearing it with you first, Mr. Schick?"

"At this point in time," said the lawyer, "that would be advisable, Detective. Good night."

"Same to you," Petra said to a dead phone. Yesterday, she'd chatted with Ramsey in the kitchen. Now this. From Ramsey's point of view, two things had transpired: the reinterview and the talk with Balch. Had she raised something with either of them that worried him?

Grabbing her notepad, she reviewed her notes. The talk with Ramsey had covered nothing earth-shattering . . . he had mentioned being a suspect—scratch that. One new topic: Estrella Flores.

She flipped to the Balch interview. His and Ramsey's Hollywood "discovery," Lisa's temperament, the DV episode. Estrella Flores.

Was the maid the hot button?

What had Flores seen that night?

Or did it have something to do with the boy in the paper? Ramsey thinking he'd pulled off the perfect crime, only to encounter every bad guy's worst nightmare—a mystery witness.

She would have loved to stare into those baby blues right now, probing for fear.

So, of course, she couldn't.

But no one, not even an overpaid B.H. lawyer, could stop her from just happening to be in Ramsey's neighborhood and dropping in.

❖

Stopping for a roast beef sandwich at an Arby's on Sunset, she ate in the car, chewing on meat and suspicion, watching night creatures emerge from the dark, knowing years ago she'd have been scared to get this close. At 7:40 she set out for Calabasas. Post–rush hour, she sailed, arriving at the RanchHaven guardhouse by 8:33.

The guard on duty was a young man, weak-chinned, with discouraged posture. Thin everywhere except around his middle, where the uniform shirt strained. When she drove up, he folded his arms across his chest. Grim watchfulness—ludicrous in the absence of threat—faded when he saw her up close. A crooked smile split his bland pie of a face. Flirtatious. Great. The guy's eyebrows were very faint, nearly invisible. His badge said D. Simkins.

He came out, looked at her, opened the gate. She drove up to him.

"How's it going?" No *ma'am*. Easy tone coming into play because she was driving a Honda, not a Porsche, not one of the locals.

Petra showed him her badge.

"Oh," he said, stepping back and hitching his trousers. "It's about time, Detective."

"For what?"

"I was on shift the night Lisa Ramsey was killed. Kept wondering when you were gonna come by." Wagging a finger in mock disapproval.

Petra's turn to smile. "Well, here I am, Officer Simkins."

She parked, got out, entered the guardhouse without asking permission. He followed. The booth was a glass closet, barely enough room for both of them. Simkins leaned against a counter, looking her up and down, no shame.

Not much inside: small cabinet for supplies, a single wheeled chair that Simkins offered her. She stayed on her feet.

She extricated her pad while checking out the security hardware. Multiline telephone, two-way radio setup, handheld walkie-talkie. Two closed-circuit TV screens suspended above the counter, one highlighting the mouth of the main road, the other so dark she could barely tell it was switched on. Next to the phone, a greasy paper bag and a copy of *Rolling Stone*. Some rock star instant-emperor on the cover, pierced eyebrows, a silver stud through the tongue.

Simkins said, "So what can I do for a fellow officer?"

Petra dredged up another smile. "So you were on all that night, Officer Simkins?"

"Doug. Yes, I was. It was real quiet, but I don't know, I had a feeling, like it was too quiet. Like something could happen."

"Did anything happen?"

Simkins shook his head. "But you know, I just felt it was a weird night. Then the next morning when I heard what happened I said, Oh man. Like one of them psychic things."

Lord, deliver me from dunderheads. "This place seems like it must be pretty quiet in general."

"You'd be surprised," he said, suddenly defensive. "You get stuff. Like fires. With fires, we call a first-stage alert."

"Which is?"

"Letting people know we might have to evacuate."

"Scary," said Petra.

"That's why we're here." Touching his own badge. Stainless replica of LAPD's—could the department sue?

"So, Doug, what time were you on duty that night?"

"Seven to three's my regular shift, then the morning guy called in sick, so I did double duty."

"Till when?"

"Eleven, when day watch starts."

"Day watch being Officer . . . Dilbeck." Retrieving the old guard's name from her memory banks.

"Yeah, Oliver," said Simkins, frowning. Probably miffed that Dilbeck had already been interviewed.

Petra said, "Did anyone from the Ramsey house come in or out during that time?"

"He did. Mr. Ramsey. He and his friend, a blond guy I always see him with. They came in that night."

"What time?"

"Nine or so."

*Or so.* They didn't log entries and exits?

"Do you have a written record of that?"

"No, we don't hassle with that." Defensive again.

"Who drove, Doug?"

"The friend."

"Did either Mr. Ramsey or his friend go out again that night?"

"Nope," said Simkins decisively, smugly. Delivering the punch line: "No one from the entire development left after that, though a few more people came home. Like I said, it was a quiet night."

"What about Mr. Ramsey's maid?"

"Nope. Never left. It's real quiet around here. Too quiet. I like action."

Petra suppressed laughter. "Know what you mean, Doug. Anything else you can tell me about the Ramseys?"

"Well," Simkins said, pondering, "I've only been working here three weeks, just see him going in and out. Same for that friend of his. You think he did it?"

"Don't think much of anything yet, Doug." Three weeks on duty. He'd never known Lisa. Even with a brain, the guy would've been useless to her. "Is Mr. Ramsey home right now?"

"Hasn't come in or out on my shift."

"Are there any other ways in and out of RanchHaven?"

"Nope."

"What about that second screen there?"

Simkins's eyes flashed to the console. "Oh, that. That's just a fire road, way back at the rear of the property, but no one uses it. Even when we were on evac alert, the plan was to get everyone out through the front."

"The screen looks pretty dark."

"It's dark back there."

Petra bent close to the monitor. "No officer there?"

"Nope, just one of them card-key doohickeys. The residents get issued cards. But no one uses it, no reason to."

"I'd like to go over there myself, Doug. Just to take a look."

"I dunno . . ."

"You can come with me if you want." She stepped closer to Simkins. Their chests nearly touched. The guard was perspiring heavily.

"Well . . ."

"Just a quick look, Doug. I promise not to steal any dirt." She winked. It made Simkins flinch.

"Yeah, okay, just don't disturb any of the residents, okay? Because that would be my butt. They like their peace and quiet. That's what they pay me for."

"How do I get there?"

"Up the main road, to the top." He gestured, managed to move closer, their shoulders touching. "On the way to Ramsey's house, matter of fact. But instead of turning right, you bear left, and after a while you'll see this big empty lot that was supposed to be a nine-hole golf course but it never got built, probably 'cause the residents all play at clubs anyway. Keep bearing left, all the way around it, and the road'll curve up, suddenly switch directions. Just keep going till you can't go any more."

She thanked him, patted his shoulder. He flinched again.

※

She drove very slowly, pausing when Ramsey's house came into view. The outdoor lighting was on full blast. Weaker illumination leaked from inside. No cars in front. Damn that museum—impossible to know if the guy was home.

She stared at the house. Static. So were the nearby structures. The more expensive neighborhoods got, the deader they looked.

Simkins's directions led her on a ten-minute loop past the would-be golf course, now just a flat gray table planted with young junipers and surrounded by wrought-iron fencing. The road compressed to barely one lane and the brush along both sides thickened to high dark walls. Above them, she could see the kinked and coiled branches of oak trees, dwarfed by a black dome of sky. A few stars struggled through haze. The moon was oversized, gray-white, streaked with fog.

The smell of horse manure and dry dirt.

Her headlights created an amber tunnel through the gloom. She switched her high beams on, continued at ten miles per. Suddenly the fire exit was there. A single gate, twelve feet high, electric, same iron motif as the main portals. Stout brick posts, warning signs. The card slot topped a steel post.

She stopped ten yards in, pulled her flashlight from the glove compartment, let the car idle, and got out.

The horse aroma was stronger up here. Quiet, not even a bird. But she could hear the freeway baritone, insistent, remote.

She swept her flashlight across the road. Poorly maintained, dusted with soil. Simkins claimed no one used the back exit, but she could see the faint corrugation of tire tracks. A few horse prints, smaller ones that could be dog or coyote—she was no gung-ho tracker.

Dad could have helped her with prints.

Keeping to the side of the road, she walked to the gate, then back. Repeated it. The dirt was so compacted it didn't granulate under her feet. Some rust around the card slot. Another slot on the other side of the fence.

Easy entry and exit.

And Ramsey's house was at the upper edge of the development, meaning he wouldn't have to pass many neighbors to sneak out.

She thought about how he'd do it.

Wait till Balch was asleep—or put something in Balch's drink to help sleep along. Then roll the Mercedes out of the mega-garage. Or the Jeep, if it had been brought back from Montecito. Headlights off, cruising slowly. With houses so far from the road, all those fences, gates, high foliage, there'd be no reason for anyone to notice. People with pools and Jacuzzis and home theaters and putting greens didn't sit by their front windows.

People who craved that level of privacy often pretended nothing existed beyond their four walls.

She took a closer look at the tire tracks. Degraded, no tread marks; she doubted they'd be of much use. But, still, she'd have loved to get a cast. No way to do it without a warrant, and no grounds for a warrant. And now Larry Schick, Esq., was on the scene—forget approaching Ramsey about anything.

Even if they pulled a match to one of Ramsey's cars, it had been four days since the murder. Ramsey could admit being up there, claim he'd taken a cruise in the hills, trying to mellow out, deal with his grief.

The hills . . . great place to get rid of a body.

Was Estrella Flores buried somewhere out there?

Did the fire road lead anywhere other than out to the Santa Susannas?

She backed down till the nearest shoulder, turned around,

and returned to the guardhouse. Simkins saw her coming, put down his *Rolling Stone*, and opened the exit gate. His window was closed; no desire to talk. Petra stopped alongside the booth. He screwed up his mouth and came over. His big moment over, feeling down, he wanted her gone.

"Find anything?"

"Nope—just like you said, Doug. Tell me, where does the fire road go?"

"Out into the mountains."

"And then?"

"It connects to a bunch of little side roads."

"Doesn't it merge with the 101?"

"It kinda hooks back toward it, but doesn't actually merge." He managed to make the last word sound dirty.

"But if I wanted to reach the freeway through the back roads, I could."

"Yeah, sure. Everything reaches the freeway. I grew up in West Hills. We used to come out here, hunt rabbits, before they built this place. Sometimes they'd run onto the freeway, get turned to freeway butter."

"The good old days," said Petra.

Simkins's weak face firmed with recollection, and a resentful frown captured his features. Rich folk moving in on his childhood memories?

"It can get beautiful out there," he said. Real emotion. Longing. At that moment, she liked him a little better. But not much.

## CHAPTER 49

SAM SAYS, "HEY, NOT BAD."

I've been working all day, going over and over the windows until there are no streaks, mopping the wood floors, using the Pledge to shine them up. I've done only half the seats, but what

I finished looks pretty good, and the room has a nice lemon smell.

Sam tries to give me the rest of the money.

"I'm not finished yet."

"I trust you, sonny—by the way, now that you work for me, are you ready to give me your name?"

That catches me by surprise, and Bill pops out.

"Nice to meet you, Bill."

It's been so long since anyone's called me by my name. Since I've *talked* to anyone.

Sam shows me a paper bag. "I got you some dinner—Noah's Bagel, just a plain one, 'cause I didn't know if you liked onions or one of those fancy bagels. Also, cream cheese—do you like cream cheese?"

"Sure. Thanks."

"Hey, you're a working man now, need your nutrition." He hands me the bag and walks around the shul. "You like the Pledge, huh? Running out of the stuff?"

"Almost."

"I'll buy some more tomorrow—that is if you want to work tomorrow."

"Sure."

"Go ahead, take the money."

I do. He looks at his watch. "Time to quit, Bill. We don't want to be accused of exploiting the working man."

We walk outside and he locks the shul. The alley is empty, but I can hear the ocean through the space on the side of the building, people talking on the walkway. That big Lincoln of his is parked crazy, the front bumper almost touching the building. He opens the driver's door. "So."

" 'Bye," I say.

"See you tomorrow, Bill." He gets in the car and I start to walk away—south, away from that Russian perv. I'm liking the feel of all that money in my pocket but wondering where to go. Back to the pier? But it was so cold. And now I have money . . .

I hear a loud squeak, turn, and see Sam backing the Lincoln out of the alley. He has plenty of room, but he keeps backing up and stopping, jerking the car; the brakes are squeaking.

Uh-oh, he's gonna hit the fence—no, he misses it. I figure I should direct him before he hurts himself, but he makes it, turning the steering wheel with both hands, his head kind of pushed forward, like he's struggling to see through the windshield.

Instead of driving forward, he backs up, stops next to me. "Hey, Bill. You really got somewhere to go for the night?"

"Sure."

"Where? The street?"

"I'll be fine." I start walking. He stays next to me, driving really slowly.

"I'd give you money for a hotel, but no one's gonna rent to a kid, and if you show all that cash, someone's gonna take it from you."

"I'm fine," I repeat.

"Sure, sure . . . I can't let you sleep in the shul because what if you slip and fall, we got a liability problem—you might sue us."

"I wouldn't do that."

He laughs. "No, you probably wouldn't, but I still can't—listen, I got a house, not far from here. Plenty of room; I live alone. You wanna stay for a day or two, fine. Till you figure out what to do."

"No thanks." That comes out kind of cold, and I don't turn to see his face, because I know he's going to look insulted.

"Suit yourself, Bill. Don't blame you. Someone probably hurt you. You don't trust no one—for all you know, I could be some crazy person."

"I'm sure you're not crazy." Why did I say that?

"How can you be sure, Bill? How can you ever be sure? Listen, when I was your age—a little older—people came and took away my family. Killed all of them, except me and my brother. Nazis. Ever hear of them? Only, when I knew them, they weren't nazis, they were my neighbors, people I lived with. My family lived in their country for five hundred years and they did that to me—I'm talking the Second World War. Goddamn nazis. Ever hear about any of that?"

"Sure," I said. "Learned about it in history."

"History." He laughs, but not a funny laugh. "So who am I to tell you to trust people—you're right, plenty of schmucks out there." He stops driving and I stop walking. More money lands in my hand. Two tens.

"You don't have to, Mr. Ganzer."

"I don't have to, but I want to—oh hell, sleep in the shul tonight. Only, don't fall and break your neck. And if you do, don't sue us."

Then he jams his car into reverse and backs up all the way to the shul. It's scary, the way he weaves and swerves all over the place. It's a miracle he doesn't smash into anything.

# CHAPTER 50

PETRA OPENED HER FRONT DOOR EXHAUSTED, not feeling like a night owl anymore. Thought of Kathy Bishop's ordeal tomorrow. Real problems. No self-pity allowed for you, kid.

She popped a can of Coke, checked the phone machine. A long-distance phone service promised to be her slave if she signed up, Ron Banks had called at seven, leaving an 818 number, probably home, please get back to him. Adele, one of the civilian clerks at the station, requesting the same thing at eight-fifteen.

She would have loved to talk to Ron first. To be with him, the two of them talking, making out on the couch, wherever that led. Business first: She called Adele.

"Hi, Detective Connor. Got a message for you from Pacific Division, a Detective Grauberg. Here's his number."

Pacific was Ilse Eggermann territory. Had something new come up? Grauberg was out, but a D named Salant came on. "Already spoke to you guys."

"To who?"

"Hold on—says here Captain Schoelkopf. Guess Grauberg couldn't reach to notify, got kicked upward."

"Notify what?"

"Got an auto carcass you were interested in. Black Porsche, registered to Lisa Boehlinger Ramsey."

"A carcass? Gutted?"

"Gutted and left for the vultures. Probably a Tijuana taxi by now. Got a witness says it was parked there for at least four days."

"Where?"

"Behind the bus lot near Pacific Avenue. The witness is one of the drivers."

"Gutted right from the beginning?"

"Progressively gutted. Someone set fire to it last night. That's how we got called in."

Four days and not a single report.

"You can't see it from the street," Salant added. "Blocked by storage buildings. We get hot cars stashed there all the time."

"Where is it now?" said Petra.

"Downtown. Have fun."

She talked to several criminalists before locating a female named Wilkerson who was working on the Porsche. The car was a charred shell, no wheels, seats, engine, front windshield.

"Like locusts swept in," said Wilkerson.

"What about prints?"

"Nothing so far. I'll let you know."

She drank Coke and tried to put together Lisa's journey from Doheny Drive to Griffith Park. Where did Venice fit in? Just a dumping ground for the Porsche, or had Lisa driven it behind the bus yard? Meeting up with her date on a deserted street in a high-crime neighborhood?

Was the last-date scenario totally wrong? Had Lisa indeed been carjacked and abducted, forced to drive to Venice by a stranger?

Or by someone she knew? Setting out from Doheny for a date with someone else. The murderer watching, stalking, following, pulling off the snatch.

Ramsey would fit that picture.

Venice . . . Kelly Sposito, Darrell Breshear's current flame, lived on Fourth Street, walking distance from the bus yard.

Where was Breshear's home base? She looked him up in her pad. The DMV data had him on Ashland, Ocean Park, the border between Santa Monica and Venice. Very close.

Everything gravitating toward the beach. Including the boy, if Wil's Russian tipster could be believed.

Breshear. Another former actor. Everyone performing . . . news of the recovered car would be in the paper tomorrow. She had to get to Breshear before he had time to construct a story.

It was nearly 10 P.M. Was he with his wife or with Kelly? Betting on the former, she got dressed again and drove west.

❖

Ashland was a pretty, sloping street in the best part of Ocean Park, houses of all sizes, every conceivable architectural style. Breshear's place was at the top, a small, well-maintained craftsman cottage with lots of cactus in the front, thatches of sword plant instead of lawn. White BMW ragtop in the driveway, behind an iron gate. Bright lights over the gate hinted at a fantastic backyard view. She rang the bell, and Breshear answered, wearing a black T-shirt and baggy green shorts, holding a bottle of Heineken. When he saw her, his eyes bulged.

"This is a bad time," he said. "My wife . . ."

"It could get worse," she said. "I think you lied to me. We found Lisa's car today. Right here in Venice. Did you have a date with her Sunday night? If you did, we'll find out."

He looked over his shoulder. Closed the door and came out and said, "Can we move out to the sidewalk?"

"Won't your wife get curious?"

"She's in the bath."

Petra accompanied him to the sidewalk.

"It wasn't really a date," he said. "She just said she wanted to talk."

"About what?"

"I don't know—oh hell, yeah, she wanted to get it on."

"So you'd continued your relationship past those glorious seven days."

"Not really," he said. "Just once in a while, maybe once a month."

"Your idea?"

"Definitely not. Lisa's, one hundred percent."

"My, my," said Petra. "Lisa, Kelly, your wife—what's her name, by the way?"

"Marcia." Breshear looked back at the house. "Look—"

"Busy guy," said Petra.

"It's no crime."

"Obstructing justice is."

"I didn't obstruct anything. It—I had nothing to say that would help you, because by the time I got there, she was gone. What would it look like, saying I went to meet up with her that night." Staring at Petra. "A black man, we know what that's all about."

"Cut the racial crap," said Petra. "The only civil rights that were violated were Lisa's. What time were you supposed to meet her?"

"Ten-thirty."

"When did you set it up?"

"She set it up. That day. She called me at work around seven."

"You were working Sunday?"

"Doing a final cut. Check with the lot guard—I signed in."

"I will," said Petra. "So Lisa called you to get together."

"She said she was lonely, down, had been sleeping all day, took some coke, now she was wired, couldn't sit still, how about a cruise."

*The car; always in the car.*

"A cruise," said Petra.

"She wanted to get together at nine, but I told her I'd be working till then, had a date at Kelly's place right afterward, but I'd see if I could slip out around ten-thirty, meet her behind the bus yard."

"Why there?"

"We'd met there before. It's . . ."

"Clandestine?"

"I didn't like it, too much crime around there, but Lisa did. The risk turned her on." He shrugged.

Petra said, "Go on."

"I had trouble getting out. Kelly . . . kept me busy till after eleven. Finally, I told her I needed to get some air, was going to take a little drive. I made it by eleven-ten or so and Lisa's car was there but she wasn't. I waited around till eleven-twenty, figured she'd showed up and left."

"The car was there, but she wasn't," said Petra. "That didn't worry you?"

"Like I said, Lisa liked to take risks. Doing it at traffic lights, a cop car right next to us. Coldwater Canyon, that kind of thing. I figured maybe she'd met up with someone else, was having a good time. Which was okay with me. I really didn't want to see her that night. Didn't want to see her at all, but . . ."

"But what?"

"You know how it is. I have trouble telling women no."

"When did you get back to Kelly's?"

"Had to be eleven twenty-five, eleven-thirty."

"And you spent the night there."

"That's the absolute truth."

"The perfect alibi Kelly gave you wasn't."

"Come on," he said. "I was only out for half an hour max. No way could I have made it to Griffith—"

"You and Kelly are both liable for perjury and obstruction," said Petra.

"Come on. Please! You're making a big deal out of nothing!"

Petra walked up close to him, pointed at his chest, but didn't touch it. "At the very least, you cost me a lot of hours, Mr. Breshear. If there's anything else you know, spill it now."

"I don't, that's it."

She stared him down.

He repeated, "I don't."

"Listen to me," she said, pointing again. "I'm not arresting you. Yet. But don't even come close to thinking about going anywhere. There'll be police officers watching your house and the studio. Surveillance on Kelly, too. You guys make the wrong move, it all hits the fan. Including a nice long chat with Marcia."

Breshear blinked convulsively.

This feels good, Petra admitted to herself. Finally, someone she could intimidate on this damn case.

As she walked away, the front door opened and a woman's voice said, "Darrell honey? Who was that?"

※

She drove back to her apartment, head suddenly clear, the basic structure of Lisa's last night alive taking form—if Breshear was finally being straight.

A meet at 10:30, abducted between then and 11:20, taken to Griffith Park, at least a half-hour ride, probably longer. Murdered between midnight and 4.

The car. Which one? PLYR 1? PLYR 0? Some other set of

wheels? Ramsey, with his multiple vehicles, multiple houses, fences, gates, Larry Schick, was a nightmare suspect. Crime paid if you started out rich.

It was nearly eleven when she walked through the door. Too late to call him? She did anyway. Four rings, then a little girl's munchkin voice said, "When you hear the beep, leave a message. Beep. And beep and beep and—"

Ron broke in. "Banks."

"Hi, it's Petra."

"Petra." Saying her name with pleasure. She could use some adulation. "How's it going?"

She told him about the Porsche, Breshear's revised story, the new time frame.

"Think he's dirty?"

"Unless his girlfriend's lying big-time about his alibi, he didn't have the time, but who knows? What's up?"

"I phoned Carpinteria Sheriff's again, asked if they could keep an eye on Ramsey's house. They said they'd upped patrols already, and today at six forty-five, I got a callback, tried to reach you at your office but they said you'd already left. Turns out Ramsey hasn't been spotted there for a while, but Greg Balch showed up this morning, left his Lexus, and drove back in a Jeep that belongs to Ramsey, license plate—"

"PLYR ZERO," said Petra.

"So you know already."

"I knew Ramsey owned the Jeep, didn't know Balch picked it up."

"Didn't want to step on your toes—calling Carpinteria— but I'd already made contact with them, figured it would be efficient. A deputy stopped Balch driving off the property around noon. Balch showed him ID, a business card, snapshot of him and Ramsey, keys to the house. Said he was there to pick up the car, bring it down for service. Which seems odd— there are plenty of mechanics in Santa Barbara."

"An extra-careful cleaning?" said Petra. Or Ramsey wanted a four-wheeler because he was planning to do some heavy-terrain driving? Those hills . . .

"Maybe Ramsey's spooked now that you've got a potential witness."

"Maybe." She told him about Larry Schick's call.

"There you go," he said. "Anyway . . ."

"Thanks again, Ron. Your daughter has a cute voice."

"Wha— Oh, that's Bee, she loves to perform. They're both asleep now. Finally."

"Have your hands full?"

"It takes a while to get them tucked in. My mom says they run rings around me. Tomorrow, though, I get to sleep in. Day off. Mom's driving them to school."

"Good for you," said Petra. "I may just drive up to Montecito tomorrow. Care to join me?"

"Sure," he said quickly. "It's a pretty drive."

❋

Lying in bed, in darkness so total she felt suspended, she thought about Lisa being abducted and butchered, Balch's picking up the Jeep.

Ramsey edgy because of a little boy who stole books . . . wherever he was.

The fact that no one on the street knew him intrigued her. He hadn't taken up with other runaways, hadn't sought help from any agency. A loner. Made sense. A kid who loved to read wouldn't fit in. He'd probably been an outcast back home, too. So why hadn't he been reported missing? Where were the parents?

Had to be abuse. An eleven-year-old intellectual . . . running from God knew what. A kid like that witnessing a murder. No reason for him to trust anyone.

A survivor. And now the police had turned him into quarry. *She* had.

❋

She'd just fallen asleep when the phone rang. It was well after midnight, and her heart pounded as for one horrible, irrational moment she panicked about her father's condition, then realized he was beyond worry. One of her brothers in trouble—Kathy?

A nervous-sounding woman said, "Detective Connor? This is Adele again, from the station. I'm really sorry to bother you this late, but a call came in for Detective Bishop, long-distance, international, and no one answers at his house. You're his partner, and seeing as it's international, I—"

"International from where?"

"Vienna. A police inspector named Tauber. I guess he didn't figure out the time difference."

"Thanks, put him on."

A scratchy voice said, "Detective Bishop?"

"This is his partner, Detective Connor."

"Ah. Yes, yes, this is Inspector Ottemar Tauber from Vienna." Clear connection; the scratchiness was the Austrian's vocal quality. He coughed, cleared his throat a couple of times.

"Hello, Inspector. Is this about Karlheinz Lauch?"

"Two days ago Detective Bishop submitted an inquiry concerning Herr Lauch," said Tauber. "We have located Herr Lauch for you. Unfortunately, he is unavailable to you for questioning as he is deceased."

"When did he die?"

"It appears to have occurred fifteen months ago."

"What was the cause of death, Inspector?"

"It appears to have been cirrhosis of the liver."

"A young man like that," said Petra.

Tauber clucked his tongue. "These things happen."

Lauch eliminated as a suspect for Lisa. Meaning the similarities between Lisa and Ilse Eggermann weren't worth a damn.

Or were they?

*Ramsey* a multiple killer? No, too weird.

Tauber's call had burned away any drowsiness. She was wired. Going into the kitchen, she drank ice water, paced, sat down at the table, got up, and put on the stereo. *Derek and the Dominos*. There'd been no music in the apartment since Ron's visit.

Think, think . . . Lauch eliminated for Lisa meant concentrate on Ramsey. Stalking Lisa, following her. DV offenders were often obsessive; it made sense.

Did his dispatching Balch to get the Jeep mean the four-wheeler was the murder vehicle? The Mercedes a distraction, just as she'd wondered? She recalled the way Ramsey had flicked on the lights in the car museum. Showing her the gray sedan—probably hoping she'd ask for a look, because he knew she'd learn nothing.

Balch doing the dirty work.

All at once—maybe it was the dark room, her fried nerves— her mind took a hairpin turn.

*What if Balch was an active part of it?*

*Or working for himself?*

She sat there, tight as a fiddle string, viewing the case through a whole new prism.

*Just a slight shift of angle and everything changed.*

*Balch as bad guy.* Flashing back to all her hypotheses, she inserted Balch's name in Ramsey's slot.

Everything fit.

Lisa and Balch . . . yet another older man. Something romantic—*and* financial?

Because Balch wrote the checks, managed Ramsey's finances, probably understood them better than the boss. You heard about that all the time—business managers soaking celebrities.

Balch colluding with *Lisa* to soak Ramsey? Ex-wife and long-suffering lackey finding common ground in their resentment of the man with the dough.

Lisa had talked to Ghadoomian the broker about setting up investments, being financially independent, soon. But she'd never followed through.

Daddy reneging on the fifty thou? Or other plans laid to waste?

Had Lisa gotten greedy, leaned on Balch, caused their partnership to disintegrate?

Petra thought about it for a long time. Balch was no prize, but Lisa was no conventional girl. Balch's motivation was no big puzzle: Bedding the quarterback's ex—the woman Ramsey had failed to satisfy—would be the ultimate thrill for an underachiever like him.

All those years protecting Ramsey on the football field and in real life, watching his own screen dreams fade as Ramsey earned millions. For all of Balch's adoration of his buddy, the payback had been limited: Ramsey hadn't helped Balch progress past those first few grade-D flicks. Balch said he had no talent, but the same was true for plenty of small-time players. Surely Ramsey could have gotten him something in the industry. Instead, he'd stuck Balch in that dingy office, shuffling papers, while he himself lived a star's life. Why not a better office, at least?

Ramsey telling Balch: You don't deserve better.

What if Balch finally decided he did?

With Lisa's help. *She* liked taking risks. Had she stepped too far over the edge?

Then something else hit her: Balch lived in Rolling Hills Estates, near Palos Verdes. Ilse Eggermann's body had been dumped near Marina del Rey, but her date with Lauch had taken place in Redondo Beach, just a few freeway stops away from the peninsula.

She pictured Balch stopping off at the Redondo pier for dinner or drinks. Watching Ilse and Lauch quarrel, Ilse walking out on Lauch. Allowing Balch to move in.

Noticing Ilse because she reminded him of Lisa?

Picking her up wouldn't have been that tough. Kindly older guy, chivalrous. Ilse would have been vulnerable, alone at night, a foreigner.

After a pig like Lauch, Balch might have even seemed suave.

The resemblance between Lisa and Ilse not a coincidence! Because Balch had been lusting for Lisa for years.

The underling, always the underling . . . Balch rescues Ilse, tries for sexual payback, gets shut down.

In a rage, he butchers her. Gets away with it.

Years later, blackmailed, up against the wall, why not do it again?

She ran it through again. Balch managing to get out of the house while Ramsey sleeps. Using the fire road, driving one of Ramsey's cars. But Estrella Flores spots him. She'd never liked Balch in the first place, might have viewed anything he did with suspicion.

He eliminates her.

One more time: It still fit.

Maybe in the morning it would seem ludicrous. Right now, she liked it.

# CHAPTER 51

WIL FOURNIER HAD CHANGED INTO HIS BEST suit for the date with Leanna the Macy's model from Ethiopia. He didn't want to get close to the Russian; the guy oozed sleaze.

Selling T-shirts, tourist crap, the outward trappings of a legit business; but those eyes, that demeanor. Wil had worked Wilshire Bunco and Fraud for two years, collaborated with West Hollywood Sheriff's on lots of Russian scams. The weirdest case was five years ago, an immigration racket, strong-arming new arrivals. Wil and a sheriff's D making a call to the apartment of one of the suspects, the guy opening the door, covered with blood, holding a carving knife. He'd just dismembered another Russian. What had he been thinking, answering the door like that?

Sharing the bust, Wil found out he liked Homicide, transferred.

He was sure the souvenir vendor had run angles.

The way Zhukanov had leaned over his counter giving him the eye, all that junk hanging from every inch of the stall. Trying to stay cool, like the whole thing didn't matter to him, he was just a citizen trying to do his civic duty. But Wil's mention of the twenty-five grand raised sweat on the Russian's pitted nose.

Absolutely certain he'd seen the kid. It sounded to Wil like he'd practiced all day convincing himself. Because how could he be that sure? Petra's drawing was good, but to Wil the kid didn't look *that* distinctive.

He smiled to himself. All white kids looked the same, right?

He was noncommittal with the Russian, took notes as Zhukanov pointed north, up Ocean Front, where the kid had supposedly disappeared. But when Wil traipsed there, showing the picture to café owners, none of them knew a thing. Most of the other businesses were closed for the evening, so he supposed a revisit was called for. But he doubted it would produce anything. This whole case had a futile smell to it.

He retraced his steps and the Russian was still there, way past closing time, waving as Wil passed him and headed toward his car. Leanna was due at Loew's in twenty minutes—five-course dinner, wine. He'd met her at a club, those huge brown eyes—

"Sir!" Zhukanov called out.

"Yes, Mr. Zhukanov?"

"I will keep my eyes open for you. I call you when I see him again."

Just what Wil needed, some Moscow mafioso playing junior detective.

※

Now here it was, the next morning, and all he could think about was the sun on Leanna's shoulders. Beautiful morning.

He'd arrived at seven on the dot, energized. A bunch more crank tipster messages on his desk, but the Russian hadn't called, so maybe the kid was gone from Venice or, more likely, he'd never been there.

Those two tips from Watson interested him a lot more. Two righteous-sounding old women both thought they might have seen the boy in town. He was still waiting for a callback from the Watson sheriff.

His phone rang. A new day dawns.

"Hey, Dubba-yew, it's Vee."

"Vee, long time."

Val Vronek was a D-II Wil had worked Narcotics with at Wilshire, now handling hush-hush major crime stuff from downtown. Vronek loved undercover—his favorite thing, posing as a biker meth dealer. Big and heavy, he'd grown his hair shoulder-length, raised a beard that looked like a health hazard.

"Guess what, Wil, I'm in your neighborhood."

"Oh?"

"Can't discuss details, but if you guessed outlaw biker crank empire I wouldn't contradict you. Just happened to be spending time in some shithole called the Cave."

"Right up your alley, Vee, white-trash roots and all that."

"You bet. Daddy rode high, Mama ate bugs," sang Vronek. "That's an old country tune. Blue-eyed soul."

"Blue-eyed soul is the Righteous Brothers."

Vronek laughed. "The reason I'm calling is, in the course of said assignment to said shithole, something happened I thought you should know about. Late last night, some guy came in showing around the picture of that kid you've been looking for, implying anyone who could help him would get a cut of the reward."

"Why would anyone do that?" said Fournier. "Least of all, leather-scum. If they knew where the kid was, they'd turn him in themselves, take the whole twenty-five."

"Didn't say the guy was smart, Wil. Just there. And none of the assembled patrons jumped on the offer. It was like, 'All those who give a shit step forward.' No big boot ballet. I pretended to be one-quarter fascinated, tried to get a feel for the guy. He came across big-time stupid."

"Got a name?"

"Nope, the situation didn't call for that level of intimacy. Here're the vitals: white male, twenty-eight to thirty-five, brown and blue, wavy hair, reddish muttonchop sideburns, my height, add at least fifty pounds."

"A big boy," said Fournier.

"He came on like some heavy-duty Angel, but no one knew him. I told him I'd look out for the kid, where could I reach him? He said he'd be stopping by again tonight, around eight. You want me to, I'll come out to the sidewalk when he shows and let you know."

"Deal, Vee. Thanks."

"Anytime. Too bad I won't be able to buy you a drink. They don't like colored folk."

Just as Fournier hung up, Schoelkopf called. "You're there. At least someone on Ramsey is."

"What can I do for you, sir?"

"You don't read the paper?"

"Not yet—"

"You should, this is a public case. They found the girl's car. Burned out in Venice, I had to learn it from the damn paper. Read it, then get in here."

# CHAPTER 52

NIGGER.

Not taking him seriously. Vladimir Zhukanov pulled a troll doll down from the rack and squeezed its belly. Blond-haired troll, SURF DUDE! printed on the shirt. He hated the way the damn thing smiled. Some Swede or Dane had invented the original one. This one was made in Korea, pirated. Zhukanov had bought ten gross from an old Moscow friend of his who worked the docks down in Long Beach, a hundred bucks, no questions asked.

A Georgian named Makoshvilli—they'd busted heads together while in the army, breaking up protests near the Kremlin, braining Yids, assorted cosmopolitan dirt.

He brought the trolls in a few at a time, pocketed the cash, fuck the boss.

Vladimir Zhukanov, sergeant in the Moscow police, reduced to trafficking in toys!

America, land of dreams. He'd claimed to be a Yid to get over here, paid a fortune to some immigration lawyer to lie for him, bunked down in some West Hollywood hovel full of Yids while he tried to find a niche for himself in L.A. A few months later, Yeltsin opened the gates to anyone, the bastard.

The city was all niggers and brownies. He had yet to find his niche. He'd driven a cab, tried unsuccessfully to sell his head-busting services to a Van Nuys forgery ring, managed to get into a West Hollywood car-theft ring but couldn't hot-wire fast enough so they fired him. He worked nights for a while, bouncing at a Russian club on Third Street till some punks broke his nose—five against one, stupid club owners insisting no weapons, how could they claim it was his fault?

Now this. Five bucks an hour from the Yid who owned the souvenir stand. Zhukanov skimmed at least 5 percent regularly, the Yid knew it, didn't care—he was raking it in from twenty other stands all around the city, living in Hancock Park, buying that hook-nosed wife of his diamonds.

One day, Zhukanov figured, he'd break into the house, get those diamonds.

Meanwhile, he sold toys. Till now: salvation in the form of the kid.

Had to be him. Zhukanov had done his share of hunting, knew what prey smelled like.

Handing it to the nigger cop, but the black bastard wasn't taking him seriously. No wonder this multicultural shithole had so much crime—nigger cops. Like having foxes guard chickens.

No way would he let that screw up his plans. Twenty-five grand meant out of here, maybe a quick grab for the boss's diamonds, fly to New York, Brighton Beach, Coney Island— no shortage of outfits there who'd welcome his talents; but with that kind of money he'd start his own business.

He was already self-employed: personal hunter of the kid.

How far could the little bastard have gone? He was sure to turn up again, and Sergeant Zhukanov would grab him.

A flash of optimism lightened his mood. A little vodka, maybe stop off somewhere for a nice meal.

Starting tomorrow, he'd be on full alert.

## CHAPTER 53

FRIDAY MORNING, PETRA WOKE THINKING ABOUT Balch as suspect. It still made sense, but so did Ramsey.

Which one of them? Both of them? Neither of them—a horrible thought.

The report of Lisa's burned-out car was on page 5, along with a smaller reprint of her drawing, but nothing about the

Venice tip or those from Watson. So Wil hadn't been forced to report yet.

As she showered and soaped her body, she realized Kathy Bishop's body was under the knife right now. She'd call Stu later. When things had settled. Meanwhile, there were some details to take care of before she set out for Montecito.

Dr. Boehlinger's hotel room didn't answer—out already, doing who knew what. A recheck of Missing Persons brought no clue to Estrella Flores's whereabouts, and by 9 A.M. she was on her way to Granada Hills to pick up Ron.

When she drove up, he was standing at the curb, holding a cell phone.

His house was a tiny Tudor on a sun-splashed side street, one story, the sharply pitched shake roof and half timbers and pseudo-gables silly but somehow touching: Someone had cared enough to lay in details. The grass was mown and edged but pale; two rosebushes flanking the stone walkway were knobby with deadheads, and half the oranges on a fifteen-foot Valencia had browned.

He was at the car door before she shifted into park. His hair was shower-moist, cowlicks sprouting like new wheat. A blue V-neck sweater, yellow button-down shirt, and off-white Dockers made him look younger—grad student, business administration. Oxblood penny loafers. Somewhere along the trajectory from rock drummer to cop he'd touched upon preppy. Dressed casually, he looked *much* younger, maybe younger than she did.

"Hi," she said.

He got in. "Hi." Lime-scented aftershave. He hadn't worn that the first time. That seemed like years ago. He made no move toward her now; locked the door and put the phone in his lap, explaining, "Just in case my mom needs to call."

"I should move into the twentieth century, finally get one of those."

"Get one of those hands-off deals," he said. "Talk in the car, make everyone think you're psychotic, and they'll leave you alone."

Laughing, she pulled away from the curb, wondering if she should mention the theory jolt about Balch. No, too speculative at this point. He had years on her. He was a rescuer. She wanted to look smart in front of him.

As she drove, they chatted. Small talk, but intelligent. He gave off an air of stability. Too boring for the Spanish equestrienne? Or would he reveal some grub-under-the-rock dark side if she waited long enough?

You are one untrusting broad. Thank you, Nick.

"Beautiful day," she heard him say. His hands were quiet now. No gripping of the door handle or other signs of anxiety about her driving. The loafers looked freshly polished. Sharp crease in the Dockers—wasn't that sort of an anti-Dockers thing? Petra smiled at the thought of *him* wanting to impress *her*.

By the time they reached the 101 on-ramp, they were really talking.

※

She sped through the west Valley—past RanchHaven—into Thousand Oaks, Newbury Park, Camarillo, the produce fields and fertilizer stink of Oxnard. At Ventura, Ron pointed out a Golf N' Stuff on the east side of the freeway, telling her he sometimes took his girls there—they also had U-bump cars and miniboats, the latter a lot of fun if you don't mind getting wet. Getting all enthusiastic, but the bounce went out of his voice when Petra, thinking about Balch again, said, "Sounds cute."

"If you're into that kind of thing," he added, embarrassed.

"I am," she said, hastening to salvage the conversation. "Grew up in Arizona, didn't see too many boats, mini or otherwise. After we solve the case, let's stop off on the way back and get wet."

He didn't answer. She turned her head far enough to catch the blush on his neck.

Oh, jeez. How could a size-9 shoe fit completely in a mouth?

"Or," she said, "we could golf. But only after we solve Lisa. We're gonna wrap the whole thing up today, right?"

"Sure," he said, grinning. "Arizona. Didn't they move London Bridge there?"

※

She exited at Santa Ynez, asking him, "Do you know Montecito?"

"Only by reputation."

"Which is?"

"Rich."

Pulling to the side of the grove-bordered road, she consulted her *Thomas Guide*, located Ramsey's street two miles in, a pair of right turns and a left, and resumed driving. Montecito was ten degrees cooler than L.A., a perfect sixty-eight. Private groves bordered Santa Ynez Road. Rich indeed.

Petra had been up to Santa Barbara a few times with Nick— Sunday outings, eating seafood on the pier, scorning the sidewalk art. They'd passed Montecito on the freeway, Nick rhapsodizing about the estates, great Spanish architecture, old money, real class—it made Beverly Hills look like crap. Getting into one of his blind-ambition grooves, going on about how one day they'd have enough money to get a place there. But he'd never pulled off to show her.

She picked up speed. No town in sight yet, just the clean stretch of asphalt cutting through the umber fudge and chlorophyll of old trees, coral bursts of bougainvillea, oranges and lemons sparkling like gems. The sky was blue, the clouds were white, a clean yellow sun rose from behind the mountains, diecut sharp, black, dabbed with lavender. What a place.

Ramsey had all this *and* the place in Calabasas, the cars, the real estate. Money wasn't everything, but it sure made things nice. What led rich people to screw things up so badly? She looked over at Ron, and from his expression she guessed he was asking himself the same thing.

Montecito's business district was four corners of earthtone low-rise upscale shops. Then more road. Ramsey's street was skinny, darkened by shaggy eucalyptus, his property at a dead end, announced by blue-gray stone posts and a high black scrollwork gate, wide open. A Carpinteria Sheriff's car blocked the entrance, one deputy standing near the driver's door, hand on holster, another facing the vehicle, hands on hips.

"Welcoming party?" Petra said to Ron. "Did you tell them we were coming?"

"No."

As they got closer, the deputy at the front of the squad car walked into the center of the road and halted them with his palm. Petra stopped. By the time the deputy reached them, she had her badge out.

He studied it. A kid. Tall, husky, red crew cut, two weeks of rusty mustache, swollen biceps. He looked over at Ron.

"Banks, L.A. Sheriff's. I spoke to Captain Sepulveda."

"Yeah, he told us. Since the murder, we've been upping our patrols anyway. Good thing. Just caught a trespasser." He hooked a thumb.

"Right now?" said Petra.

"He made it easy, left the gates open. Looks like a nutcase, verbally abusive. Claims he's Ramsey's father-in-law."

Petra squinted at the cruiser. Through the rear window Dr. Boehlinger's goateed face seethed. She watched Boehlinger butt the glass with his shoulder, then retract, clearly in pain. A surgeon. Brilliant. The deputy watching him must have said something, because Boehlinger started screaming. Too far away to hear, but his mouth was wide open. The window glass gave him a preserved look. Rage in a jar.

She said, "He *is* Ramsey's father-in-law."

"Come on," said the red-haired cop. His name was Forbes. "Dr. John Everett Boehlinger. Didn't he have ID?"

"Yeah, that's what his ID said, but that didn't mean anything to us." Forbes grimaced. "He sure doesn't act like a doctor—got a toilet mouth."

"What'd you catch him doing?"

"Coming out of a toolshed out back. The door was smashed—he obviously kicked it in, was carrying a shovel. Looked to us like he was planning to break a window in the house, do an unlawful entry. So he's really her father? Come on."

Petra nodded.

"Shit." Forbes cracked massive knuckles. "His demeanor, we figured a loony for sure. And he was *talking* crazy, bodies buried out here, he was gonna dig them up. We had to restrain him. Hands *and* feet. Kind of tough, hog-tying an old guy like that, but he tried to bite us." Forbes looked at his hand, smooth and tan at the end of the buffed arm. The thought of bodily injury was a narcissistic insult. Working in a rich, quiet town, he'd actually managed to keep himself smooth.

"Small guy," he added, "but incredibly feisty. Finally we

got him quiet enough to untie his feet. Didn't want a heart attack or anything." He shook his head. "Her father—*shit!*"

"Where does he say bodies are buried?" said Petra.

"We didn't ask. We figured him for a loony-tunes starfucker—we get them from time to time, all the Hollywood types with second homes up here. Tabloid reporters, too. We've been preparing ourselves for problems with Ramsey."

"Had any?"

"Not till now. Maybe no one knows he's got a weekend place here yet."

"Does Ramsey come up here much?"

"I've never seen him, but maybe he comes up at night. Lots of the Hollywood types do. Flying up at night to Santa B in copters or private planes, or they just limo straight up from L.A. The whole thing with them is *not* to be spotted. It's like a game, you know? I'm famous, but you can't see me. They never come into town to shop, have people doing things for them. And with the size of these properties, it's not like they've got real neighbors."

Petra took in the surroundings. Long stretches of ten-foot wall on both sides. Through Ramsey's gate was a winding stone motor path flanked by palms. The guy loved palms.

"Who takes care of Ramsey's house when he's not here?" she said.

Forbes shrugged. "Probably a cleaning crew. There is a regular gardening crew, comes here Tuesday and, I think, Saturday." Forbes touched an eyelash, scratched the side of his nose. "Ramsey's also got a gofer, comes up to check out the house. I ran into him on patrol a couple of days ago."

"Greg Balch?" said Petra.

"Yeah, that's the one."

The other deputy had turned his back to the cruiser. Shorter, darker than Forbes, thick arms crossing a barrel chest. Another buff-boy. Department must have a good gym.

"Switching cars," said Petra.

"Yeah, a Lexus. Still parked behind the house. At first it looked funny, but he had the keys, a letter from Ramsey authorizing him to drive all his cars."

Thumping noises sounded from the patrol car. Dr. Boehlinger, kicking the window.

"Why don't you let him out?" said Petra.

"You wanna take custody of him?"

"I want to talk to him."

✻

It took a long time to calm Boehlinger down. He was wearing a gray Washington U. sweatshirt, baggy gray tweed wool trousers, probably from an old suit, and white sneakers. Flecks of spit whitened the corners of his mouth, wisps of hair flew at random angles, and his goatee looked grizzled.

Finally, thirty seconds of silence earned him unlocked cuffs. The moment his hands were free, he brandished fists at the deputies. "You stupid fucking imbeciles!"

Forbes and the shorter man—Beckel—ignored him. Before uncuffing him, they'd held the little man at arm's length as he shouted and kicked—a cartoon situation. Now they headed back to their cruiser, conferring with Ron, as Petra ushered Boehlinger to her car.

"Idiots!" Boehlinger shouted. He coughed, spit phlegm into the dirt, started to rant again. Petra tightened her grip on his shoulder. He was shaking like a lapdog, still frothing at the mouth. "Brain-damaged idio—"

"Please, Doctor!"

"Don't please *me*, young la—"

Propelling him faster, Petra talked into his ear. "Dr. Boehlinger, I know you've been through hell, but if you don't settle down, we'll be forced to let them arrest you."

Boehlinger said, "*You're* an idiot, too! That butcher walks free, bodies pile up, and you threaten me! Goddamn all of you, I'll have you all collecting welfare—"

"Bodies where?" said Petra.

"In there!" Boehlinger jabbed toward the gate. "Behind the pond—there must be a God! I came to get into the house, go through the butcher's papers, some evidence of what he did to Lisa, but I saw a helluva lot more than I bargained for—"

"What kind of evidence were you looking for, Doctor?"

"Anything," Boehlinger said quickly.

"What made you think Ramsey'd left any evidence behind?"

"I didn't *think*! I *hoped*! Lord knows *you* people haven't done a *damn* thing! I dip into my own pocket, and you don't have the brains and the decency to follow—"

"Dr. Boehlinger," Petra said firmly. "What evidence were you hoping to find here?"

Silence. Boehlinger's watery blue eyes lowered. "I didn't have a . . . clear concept. But what could it hurt? This is the place he beat my Lisa. What's to say he didn't write notes to himself—or something Lisa wrote— Stop interrupting my train of thought, young lady, the point is, I went to find something to break the window—"

"The shovel."

"No, no, no! I chose the shovel *after* I saw it! I was looking for a *chisel* to pry the lock. I'm good with tools."

The last sentence a pathetic boast. *Look, Mom, I'm useful.* Sulfurous breath blew out from between Boehlinger's lips. His eyes were frightened. Maybe he hadn't been the best father in the world, but Lisa's death had ripped him up. Such a small man.

Petra said, "You switched from the chisel to the shovel after . . ."

"After I saw the grave. Behind that pond of his."

"A grave? How can you be—"

"Put your money on it," said Boehlinger. "Fresh excavation, about six feet long. Far side of the pond. Plants trampled, plants missing. I've been here before. After the wedding, the bastard was trying to impress me. I have an eye for detail, saw the difference right away."

"Is the pond plumbed?" said Petra. "Maybe there'd been a repair—"

"And maybe Charles Manson's the pope-designate. Don't be *stupid*, young lady! I've assisted at autopsies, seen my share of crime-scene photos. I know what a *grave* looks like."

Ron came back, saying, "Looks like you're off the hook for now, Doctor." Boehlinger huffed.

Forbes waved from the cruiser and Petra went over.

"Okay, he's yours. Hope you're taking him straight back to L.A."

"We will eventually," said Petra.

"Eventually?"

"We're in a bit of a bind, Deputy. He claims he saw a fresh grave on the Ramsey property, but we have no jurisdiction, can't step onto the property to check."

"A grave? You're taking his bull *seriously*?"

"Given the details of our case, we can't afford to ignore it."

"Oh, come on. Burying someone right here?"

Petra shrugged.

"Oh, man." Forbes turned, and said "Gary?" to Beckel, who was sitting in the car writing an incident report. The shorter deputy had a broad, stoic face and a meaty chin. Forbes filled him in. Beckel said, "What, some kind of serial killer or something?"

"It'll probably turn out to be nothing," said Petra. "On the other hand, if something did occur, it's your jurisdiction."

"We can't just go in there," said Forbes. "No warrant."

"You've already *been* in there. Because of Dr. Boehlinger's trespassing—obvious criminal behavior gave you clear grounds for entry. Once on the premises you apprehended a suspect, then noticed something amiss. Fresh excavation."

"Oh, come on," said Forbes. "You're putting our nu— Putting us in a position."

"Okay," said Petra. "But I'll have to write this up for my boss, and you can bet the first thing Boehlinger's going to do when he gets back is contact the media. He's already played that game."

Forbes cursed under his breath.

Beckel said, "Let's call it in, Chick."

"Yeah," said Forbes. "I'm calling my boss."

When Petra returned to the car, Dr. Boehlinger was sitting in the backseat with Ron, talking animatedly. Dry-eyed, still tense, but conversing at normal volume. Ron listened intensely, nodding. Boehlinger smiled. Ron smiled back, said, "Interesting."

"Extremely interesting," said Boehlinger.

Petra got in the driver's seat.

"So?" said Boehlinger.

"I told them I thought they should take you seriously, Doctor. They're notifying their superiors."

"In their case," said Boehlinger, "that encompasses most of the world."

Petra couldn't help herself; she laughed.

Ron said, "Doctor?" in a prompting tone.

Boehlinger cleared his throat. "I apologize for everything I said before, Detective Connor."

"Not necessary, Doctor."

"Yes it is. I've been a rude lout . . . but you have no idea what it's like to lose everything."

"True," said Petra. Suddenly she pictured Kathy Bishop under the knife. It was almost noon—Kathy was probably out of surgery, chest stitched. How much had been taken from her? Petra resolved to call the hospital soon.

"So tell me, Doctor," said Ron. "Those autopsies you mentioned, were they part of your duties as ER chief, or special consultations?"

"That was years ago, Ron," said Boehlinger wistfully. *Ron?* "Back when I was chief resident. I actually deliberated going into pathology, spent some time with the St. Louis coroner's. Back in those days, the place was a regular—"

New man. Dr. Banks, master psychologist.

Shuffling sounds drew Petra's eyes to the side window. Forbes's big feet scraping asphalt. "Okay," he said, looking at Petra, avoiding Boehlinger. "The boss is coming. Then we'll have a look at this so-called grave."

❖

Captain Sepulveda was a blocky, silver-haired man around forty-five, with brown-suede skin and an impeccable uniform. He arrived in an unmarked with a third deputy, went onto Ramsey's property alone, and emerged moments later, ordering all three officers inside.

Petra and Ron and Boehlinger waited in the car as Boehlinger rambled on about medical school, graduating top of his class, multiple triumphs as an ER doctor.

Twenty minutes later, Sepulveda appeared, dirt streaks on his shirt, rubbing his palms together. A few athletic steps brought him to Petra's side. His eyes were slits, so compressed Petra wondered how he could see.

"Looks like we have a body. Female, buried four feet down. Maggots, some deterioration, but plenty of tissue still on it, so it's been days, not weeks."

"Maybe two days," said Petra, thinking: Had the car exchange been just a cover for Balch's trip? "Older Hispanic female? Approximately five-two, one-forty?"

The razor-cut eyes dipped at the outer corners. "You know her?"

"I believe I do. You might also want to have a look at that black Lexus."

"Look for what?"

"Blood."

# CHAPTER 54

SLEEPING INDOORS IS GREAT. AT FIRST I WOKE up every hour, but then I was okay.

The brown blankets Sam brought me are rough but warm. The sheets and pillows smell of old guy. Before I turned out the lights, I lay there looking up at the shul's ceiling, the red bulb in the silver holder hanging in front of that ark. Sam never said not to sleep in the shul, but I figured it wouldn't be respectful, so I set myself on the floor near the back door, next to the bathroom. Every so often I could hear a car drive through the alley, and once I heard someone's feet shuffling outside, probably someone Dumpster-diving, and it made me lose breath for a few seconds, but I was okay.

I think I fell asleep watching the red bulb. Sam told me it wouldn't go off, was something called an eternal light to remind the Jews of God. Then he laughed and said, "Wishful thinking, eh, Bill? The bulb dies every couple months, I get up on a ladder, take my life in my hands."

He tossed me a bagel, left, and locked the door.

It's 5:49 and I've been up ten minutes. I can see the colored glass windows in front of the shul get brighter. I want to go outside and have a look at the ocean, but I don't have the key to the front door. Shaking out and folding the blankets and sheets, I wash off in what Sam calls the gents' and finish the rest of last night's bagel. Then, opening the back door an inch, I look through.

The air's cool—cold, even—with tons of salt in it. The alley is empty. I step outside, make my way around the side of the shul to the front of the walkway. No one's out, just gulls and pigeons. The ocean's dark gray with spots of light in a few places, like orange-pink freckles. The tide's coming in very softly, then rolling back out like someone tilted the earth, back and forth, this whoosh-whoosh rhythm. I think of something I once saw on TV: panning for gold. God's tilting the whole planet, looking for something valuable.

I stand there, watching and listening. Then I think of that woman in the park and how she'll never see the ocean again.

I shut my eyes tight and blow out those thoughts.

Thinking of the ocean, the air, how salty it smells, how I like that smell. How this is the end of the earth, this is as far as you can run. There's some litter on the walkway—papers and beer bottles and soda cans—but everything still looks beautiful. Quiet and empty and beautiful. Not a single other person.

I will always love being alone.

Now the sky behind me starts to brighten up more and the skin of my arm turns gold and I spot the sun, rising, humongous and egg-yolk yellow. I can't feel any heat yet, but with a sun that big I know it will be coming.

Now I'm not alone anymore: From the south, maybe a block away, I see a guy coming toward me on roller skates, wearing nothing but a bathing suit, holding his hands out like he's trying to take off and fly.

The picture is ruined. I go back to the shul.

※

Sam's Lincoln is there, parked crazy as usual; and I find him in the shul, looking at a book.

"Good morning," I say.

He turns around fast, closing the book. He doesn't look happy. "Where were you?"

"Outside."

"Outside?"

"To see the ocean."

"The ocean." Why is he repeating everything I say? He puts the book down, walks toward me, and for a second I think he's going to hit me and I'm ready to defend myself, but he goes past me and checks the back door to make sure it's locked, stands with his back to the door, definitely unhappy.

"Do you want me to leave?" I say. "Did I do something wrong?"

He blows out air and rubs his neck. "We got a problem, Bill." He takes something out of his pocket. A piece of newspaper. "This is yesterday's edition," he says. "Dealing with you kept me busy; I didn't get to it until this morning."

He unfolds it and shows it to me. I see the word *murder*. Then a drawing of a kid.

*Me.*

I try to read the article, but the words are jumping up and down. So is my stomach. My heart starts pushing against my chest, I feel cold, and my mouth is dry.

I keep struggling to read, but nothing makes sense, it's like a foreign language. Blinking, I clear my eyes, but the words are still weird and jumping. I grab the paper from him and hold it close, finally start to understand.

The woman who got killed in the park has a name. Lisa. I have to think of her as Lisa now.

Lisa Boehlinger-Ramsey. Her ex-husband's an actor, Cart Ramsey. A show called *The Adjustor*. I've heard of it; I think Moron used to watch it.

Someone's offering twenty-five thousand dollars to find me.

I run for the back door. Sam doesn't try to stop me.

As I reach for the knob, my feet freeze.

Where can I go?

It's going to be a hot, bright day full of people out for that money; the sunlight will uncover me. Someone—maybe a bunch of them—will grab me and tie me up and turn me in.

Sam's still standing there. "You can stay here all day, but remember, tonight's Friday services, thirty, forty *alter kocker*—worshipers showing up a half hour before dark, nothing I can do about it."

I'm not breathing great and my chest feels tight; I open my mouth wide to capture some air, but not much comes in. My stomach hurts worse than it ever did and my heart's still bumping against my chest—*chuck chuck,* just like what happened to . . . Lisa.

"One thing you might consider, Bill: Twenty-five thousand's a lot of money. If you do know something about this, why not be a good citizen and help yourself in the bargain?"

"I don't know anything."

He shrugs. "Fine. I accept that. It's not you, just some kid who looks like you. But with the resemblance, how are you gonna traipse around?"

I slept so well last night, but now I'm tired, just want to lie down.

I sit down on a shul bench and close my eyes.

"To see something like that, Bill, of course you're scared. I know. I saw terrible things too."

I keep my eyes glued shut.

"You see things like that, you wish you didn't, because you know it'll change you. That's the big difference in this world, Bill. People who're forced to see terrible things, and everyone else, getting away with the easy life. I won't tell you it's good to see. It stinks—no one would choose it. The only good thing is, you can get strong from it—I don't have to tell you that, you already got strong. Being out there, taking care of yourself, you did a good job. Considering what you been through, you did great. It's true, Bill. You're handling things great."

He's saying nice things, trying to make me feel better. Why does it feel like a punch in the stomach?

"One part of my brain," he goes on, "is saying call the cops, protect him— No, no, don't worry, I'm not gonna do it, I'm just telling you what's going on in my brain. The other part—must be the strong part—is reminding me of what happened to me when I wasn't much older than you. Remember those nazis I told you about? Some of *them* were cops—devils in uniform. So it's not always simple, is it? A guy wants to do the right thing, not break the law, but it's just not that simple, is it?"

He reaches out and touches my shoulders. "Don't worry, you're safe with me."

He means it. It makes me feel good.

Why does it also make me bend over, so low my forehead's almost touching the floor and now my eyes hurt, too, and I can't stop myself from rocking back and forth and my body's shaking and I'm crying.

Like a damn baby, I just can't stop it!

With everything that's happened, why cry *now*?

# CHAPTER 55

WIL FOURNIER RETURNED FROM SCHOELKOPF'S office, thinking, Could have been worse.

The captain had been irritable but distracted, a meeting this afternoon with Deputy Chief Lazara. "Including your case, which I assume is stagnating." Schoelkopf's face started to redden.

Wil headed him off by volunteering the Russian's tip.

"When did this come in?"

"Late last night. The guy's a lowlife, I figured I'd do some checking on him first—"

"Check later, it's a solid tip and I want you back in Venice, searching for the kid. Where's Barbie?"

Wil wondered about that himself. "Don't know."

Schoelkopf glared at him. "Tight team you guys are running. How's Ken's wife?"

"I imagine she's being operated on right now, sir."

"She'll probably be okay, young woman like that—okay, back to the beach, Fournier. If the kid's there, I want him found." Schoelkopf picked up his phone.

Straight to the media. No one could see him, but he'd put on a media smile.

Before leaving for Venice, Fournier followed up on the two tips from Watson. Nothing new from one old woman, but the second, a Mrs. Kraft, said she was pretty sure the boy lived in a trailer park on the south end of town.

"Low-class place," she said. "They started it years ago for retired people, but trash moved in."

"The boy's family is trash?" said Wil.

"If he lives there, they probably are."

"But you don't know a name?"

"No, sir, I'm just saying I think he lived there because I

think I seen him around there. When I was out with my dog. My dog's a sweetie pie, but the boy didn't come near Jet, like he was afraid of animals. This happened twice. I'm not sure it's him, but I think so."

"Okay, thanks, Mrs. Kraft," said Fournier. "What's the name of the trailer park?"

"Sleepy Hollow," she said. "Like that book, the ghost story."

He called the Watson sheriff and got a busy signal. Could you believe that? Just as he tried again, Brian Olson, the D at the next desk, waved at him. "Someone for you on my line."

Fournier went over to Olson's desk and Olson used the break to get coffee.

"Fournier."

"Detective? This is Sheriff Albert McCauley from Watson, California. Woulda got back to you sooner, but I was attending a firearms conference up in Sacramento. Ever been to one of those? Very educational." Low, drawling voice. Plenty of free time.

"Not yet," said Wil.

"Educational," McCauley repeated. "So. What can I do for you?"

Fournier had left detailed messages. What was this, *Mayberry RFD*? He told McCauley about the boy and the trailer park.

"Runaway, huh?" said the sheriff. "Yeah, the Hollow's a scruffy place. Not much crime, though. Anywhere in Watson, for that matter. Quiet here. Only real problems we get is when the migrants blow in and hit the tequila."

The kid had run from something, thought Fournier. "If you could check, Sheriff—"

"Sure, no problem. Got some things to catch up on first, then I'll go over and talk to the Hollow manager, see if he can ID this boy. You say it was in the L.A. paper?"

"Two days ago."

"Don't usually read the L.A. papers. Not too friendly to law enforcement, are they?"

"Depends," said Wil, noncommittal. "I can fax you the drawing."

"Sure. Do that."

Wil thanked him again and hung up, resolving to call the Sleepy Hollow manager himself if he didn't hear back from McCauley by late afternoon.

He spent another two hours following up with shelters and social workers, and headed west, having lunch at an Italian place on the Third Street Mall in Santa Monica, then drove to Venice.

A beautiful afternoon at the beach was wasted talking to shopkeepers, restaurant managers, old folks, bodybuilders, Rollerbladers. Tourists who looked at him like he was crazy. Some people were scared of him, despite the suit and a flip of the badge. Black skin. Maybe one day he'd get used to the reaction, but probably not.

Sleazeball Zhukanov was back behind his souvenir counter, and the first time Wil passed the stand he ignored the Russian's hostile stare. On the way back, he stopped, asked Zhukanov if he'd seen anything.

The Russian shook his head and pushed stringy hair out of his face. Greasy face full of pits. Pus pimple in the fold of his left nostril. Zhukanov's beard was a poor excuse for facial hair, unevenly trimmed, a blemish, not an adornment. The guy didn't believe in deodorant, either. Who'd buy toys from him?

Zhukanov's eyelids drooped. "Not yet, but I keep eyes open."

"Do that." Wil started to walk away.

Zhukanov said, "How can I call you without number?"

Wil fished out a business card and placed it on the counter, ignoring Zhukanov's outstretched palm. Hatred filled the Russian's eyes. He picked a troll doll off the rack and put the tiny figure's neck between two fingers. Wil left, wondering if he'd decapitate the thing.

It was already 6:30 and he was due at the Cave by 8 for Val Vronek's signal about the fat biker's arrival. The value of that seemed less than iffy, probably just another fool out for the twenty-five thou, but digging dry wells was part of the job.

He called into the station. Nothing from Sheriff McCauley, so either the Watson lawman had checked out Sleepy Hollow and located the kid in question or hadn't bothered yet. Either way, Wil was annoyed.

The only message was from Petra, 818 area code. He returned it. *The mobile customer you are trying to reach is either away from the vehicle or . . .*

Obtaining a number for the Sleepy Hollow RV Park and

Recreational Facility, he phoned, got another taped message, another drawling voice.

Quiet place, McCauley had said. More like Zombie Town.

He called Leanna, asked her phone machine whether she was free for a late dinner tonight, let's say nine-thirty, ten. Another try at Petra's 818 cell phone, same outcome. It was nearly seven, and he was ready to kill the first machine he met. He walked along the beach, found a quiet bench, and sat down to enjoy the ocean for a while, watching the seagulls and the pelicans. He loved those pelicans, the way they just cut through the air, no effort, very cool birds. God, it was gorgeous here, if you concentrated on the water, forgot about the people.

Then he found himself turning around. Scanning the walkway. Just in case the kid happened by. Wouldn't *that* be something, a precious accident. Unable to relax now, he found another bench, one that put his back to the water and his eyes on business.

※

At 7:45 he was on Hollywood Boulevard, drinking an Orange Whip at a snack stand a few storefronts down from the Cave. The nightcrawlers were already out. Punks, dopers, he-shes, she-hes, all kinds of its, more dumb tourists, small groups of marines on leave—those kids always got into trouble. With their shaved heads, they looked just like skinners; maybe some of them were. As he sucked down the sweet, freezing drink, he saw something that really cracked him up: pudgy girl, around nineteen, shaved head except for one of those rooster-comb deals, leading a guy of the same age around on a leash. Saying, "Get going, get going." The guy was skinny, pale, mute, had a romantic smile on his face.

Fournier sipped a little more Whip, tossed the cup, and ambled by the Cave. Harleys were lined up in front of the bar. Even from here you could hear the music, some kind of country rock, way too much bass.

A half-open door offered a glimpse of dark room. Wil kept walking, made it to the corner, pretended to examine the cheesy clothes in a store window, turned around. When he reached the bar the second time, Val Vronek was coming out, all leathered and chained, looking almost as greasy as the Russian.

The undercover man paused just left of the doorway, lit up a cigarette, caught Wil's eye for a half second. His left cheek twitched, and he gave his head a very small shake.

No Fat Boy.

Wil took a stroll. Fifteen minutes later, Vee communicated the same thing, made sure no one was watching, flashed ten fingers three times. See you in thirty.

Half hour later, still no sign of the guy. Val lit up a cigarette, walked to one of the Harleys, checked the chain lock, loped down the street to the corner. A few minutes later, Wil followed. He found the undercover D in the darkened doorway of an apartment building just off the Boulevard. Black windows, city condemnation notice on the door.

"Sorry. Guy was probably full of shit," said Vee. "Or maybe he watches TV."

"What was on TV?"

"Your kid, didn't you see it?"

"Haven't been sitting in a bar all day."

Vee smiled. "Six o'clock news, Dubba. Some tipster put him in Venice. Maybe Fat Boy decided I wasn't worth dealing with and went there straight."

"Just came from Venice," said Wil. And the tipster. Had any of the bikers on the walkway matched Fat Boy's description? No, he would have noticed that. He hoped.

Vee said, "If he shows up, I'll call you. Gotta get back to scroteville." His face was glassy with sweat.

"Hot gig?" said Wil.

"Hell would be a vacation, Dubba. And the smell's something else. Not that you'll ever get a chance to know, being dusky."

Wil chuckled. "Hey, membership has its privileges."

Leaving Vronek his beeper number in case Fat Boy showed up, he drove home, wondering if Leanna had called back. Maybe she'd tried his apartment, thinking him back already. Logical, it was nearly nine-thirty—he'd sure given the citizens full service today.

The beep came just as he pulled into his driveway.

He read the number. Sheriff McCauley. Gee thanks, pard, finally moseyed on down to the ol' Holler, didja?

Collecting his mail, he entered his ground floor flat, checked the phone. No Leanna. Uncapping a bottle of Heineken, he called McCauley.

"Complications," said the sheriff. No more drawl; none of that country-bumpkin friendliness. "Got a tentative ID on your kid. The manager ID'd him. Name's Billy Straight. William Bradley Straight, twelve years old, approximately five feet, seventy-five, eighty pounds. No one's seen him for months. The mother was unemployed, living on welfare, always months behind on the rent. No father that anyone's ever seen. Not a good situation, but the boy never gave any trouble."

Gone for months, but no one in peaceful, quiet Zombieville had bothered to report it, thought Wil. Even country lanes could be mean streets.

"What did the mother say about his disappearance, Sheriff?"

"That's the complication. When I went over to talk to her, I found her dead in the trailer, looks like a couple days or so. Contusions to the occipital portion of the skull, some lividity, beginnings of rigor, some blowfly maggots. The trailer was hot, probably hastened the process, but neighbors saw her two mornings ago, so that helps fix the TOD."

Bye-bye, Andy Griffith; hello, Quincy.

". . . there was blood on the edge of a dresser, so it looks like she fell backwards and hit her head on the counter. Or was pushed—she's got some old bruises on her, too. There was a boyfriend living with her for a while, and all of a sudden he's gone. Biker type, loser with a petty record—we got an ID on him, too, from fellows at the local bar. Buell Erville Moran, white male, thirty years old, six-one, two-ninety—"

"Brown hair, blue eyes, reddish muttonchop sideburns," said Wil.

"You've got him?"

"No, but we want him."

# CHAPTER 56

THERE WAS ENOUGH SKIN ON ESTRELLA FLORES'S face for Petra to make the ID. The maid's throat had been slashed ear to ear, but no other wounds were evident. None of the overkill butchery visited upon Lisa.

Made sense, she supposed: Lisa was passion; this was snipping loose ends.

Balch or Ramsey? Or both? *Neither* was no longer a viable choice.

Dr. Boehlinger wanted to stay, but Sepulveda had Deputy Forbes drive him back to L.A., a match made in hell that caused Petra to grin inwardly despite the horror of the situation.

Poor Estrella. Talk about wrong place, wrong time. Still wearing her pink uniform. She'd probably been taken care of on Tuesday or Wednesday, driven up here on Wednesday.

Had to be late Wednesday or Thursday morning, the day Balch had been spotted leaving, because she'd interviewed him Wednesday evening and the Lexus had been parked in front of the Player's Management building. Empty. Clean. In contrast with the mess in the office. Had the deed already been done? *Had Estrella been lying in that trunk during the interview?*

She and Ron stood back as the local techs worked, hustling to finish up before darkness changed the game. Ramsey's Montecito spread was huge, the house old and stately, cream stucco and red tile, real Spanish, no bell tower, none of the crazy angles of the Calabasas castle. Giant oaks shaded the acre closest to the building. The landscaping took the shade into account: ferns, clivia, camellia, azalea. Lovely pathways of degraded granite had been laid out expertly.

The property dipped, leading the eye down to the pond, a hundred-foot disc of green water set out in full light. White and pink lilies claimed half the surface; flame-colored dragonflies zoomed past like tiny aircraft; a bronze heron stooped to drink. Cattails and more lilies in the background, yellow, white with amethyst centers. Petra could see the missing foliage that had tipped Dr. B. to the grave.

Precise eyes indeed.

The techs were concentrating on the black Lexus. The interior was onyx leather; black carpeting covered the trunk. Not the easiest surfaces for spotting bloodstains, but one of the criminalists thought he saw a patch the size of a dime on the inside of the trunk door, and Luminol confirmed it. Nothing on the car seats, but the test brought up Rorschach-like blots of blood all over the carpet.

"I'd say about a pint," said Captain Sepulveda. "If that. Meaning he killed her somewhere else, wrapped her in something, and it leaked out. Then he shampooed the trunk—I could smell it. Figured if it *looked* clean, it *was*."

Talking softly. Unhappy about being drawn in. Petra wondered if he'd ever been a homicide D.

He said, "We better get some warrants for the house and the grounds—who knows what else is out here." He turned to face Petra, and his slit eyes must have focused on her, though she couldn't see enough iris to tell. "I'm going to talk to a judge right now. What's next for you?"

"Balch drove the car up here, so he's obviously a suspect," she said. "I'm calling this in to my captain, asking to put out a warrant. Whether or not Balch was working for Ramsey remains to be seen, but I don't doubt this murder's related to ours. I need Balch and Ramsey located ASAP."

Telling, not asking.

"Fine," said Sepulveda. "I should be back within the hour. Any questions, talk to Sergeant Grafton." He indicated a slim, attractive, dark-haired woman in plainclothes taking notes by the side of the pond.

He left, and Ron handed Petra the cell phone. She phoned Wil Fournier first. Away from his desk. She left the number. Schoelkopf was out, too—meetings all afternoon—but she convinced a clerk to track him down. He called five minutes later.

"I was with Lazara, this better be good."

"Seems pretty good to me, sir." She told him.

"Shit—okay, we pick up both of them pronto."

"Ramsey's hiding behind Lawrence Schick."

"I know that, so we yank the bastard the hell out from behind Schick's skirts. Just to talk, not an arrest. You stay there, be an eagle eye, don't lose control of the situation. And keep the goddamn phone line open."

"Balch lives in Rolling Hills Estates," said Petra. "His office is in Studio City. I've got both addresses."

"Go."

She read off the numbers. Schoelkopf clicked off.

Ron said, "I should call in, too. Hector, and my mom. We're not getting out of here for a while."

She returned the phone. Nifty little Ericsson. "Is this private gear or department?"

"Private."

"I'll reimburse you."

He smiled and punched numbers. The Lexus was being winched to a tow truck; techs were setting up tape and post perimeters near the burial site; Sergeant Grafton paced off the area, pointing and instructing.

A Santa Barbara County coroner's station wagon drove up and two men in white got out with a folding stretcher. Estrella Flores's corpse was small. Those bowed legs, the gaping throat wound exposing a corrugated flash of trachea.

Ron couldn't find De la Torre, but he connected with his mother, and Petra walked away to give him privacy, thinking about the call she'd have to make to Javier Flores. Schoelkopf had ordered her to keep the line open. To hell with him. It was Ron's phone; let the department buy her one.

The tow truck backed out, manipulating the Lexus around oaks. Moments later, the coroner's guys carried the body to the wagon and followed. The garden looked trampled, fronds and leaves bent over, broken. Petra smelled a hint of ocean, Pacific currents managing to make it this far inland. Lilies swayed. The yellow tape danced.

Ron came back and gave her the phone.

"Well," she said, "it started out as a nice day."

"Still is." He moved closer to her and his fingers touched hers for a second. Taking hold of her index finger, he squeezed gently and let go. He was staring straight ahead. Drummer's hands tapped a beat on the side of his thighs, but his eyes seemed serene.

He loves this, she thought. He'll do homicide as long as they let him.

The phone beeped. "Connor."

Schoelkopf said, "Talked to Attorney Schick. He and Ramsey are on their way up there."

"What about Balch?"

"Ramsey said he was supposed to be in his office. We called there, got no answer."

"Same thing happened to me the time I interviewed him," said Petra. "He was in but didn't pick up the phone."

"Whatever. I've got officers headed there right now, and Rolling Hills has agreed to pay a house call."

"Why's Ramsey coming here?" she asked.

"It's his house, Barbie. He's very up*set.*"

## CHAPTER 57

MOTOR SLEPT LOUSY, AND NOW THE HEADACHE was a killer. No blanket, no pillow, just his leather jacket on the warped floor of an abandoned apartment on Edgemont.

Plywood over the windows and some sign about earthquakes on the door told him it was his place for the night. He used his Buck knife to pry the board up from the back door, rolled his scoot inside, and pushed it around from room to room. They were all the same: tiny; no furniture, light fixtures, or plumbing; graffiti all over the walls; linoleum pebbled with mouse shit, cockroach carcasses, oil stains, empty bottles. The room he finally chose was in the back. The whole building smelled of mold and wet dog, insect casts, burnt matches, and the worst thing: a chemical-like stink that made his eyes water.

But it was dark and he was wiped out from riding all day,

walking around Hollywood—the place seemed mostly the
same—then over to Griffith Park to scope out the rug rat's territory. But the park ended up being too big to get a handle on—
why the hell would a little fuck need such a goddamn big
place?

He bought three hot dogs with kraut, washed it down with a
chocolate malt, and cruised over to the Cave, parking his scoot
with all the others in front, hoping no one would look close.
Inside, he hoped for brotherhood, had to spend his last dough
on beer when no one offered to buy him one. Eating three
pickled eggs and stuffing some Slim Jims in his pocket before
the bartender evil-eyed him.

No one gave a shit about the picture of the rat. Everyone
was watching fuck films on big-screen TV. When some chick
did something especially nasty up on the screen, a low growl of
support rose up from the bar.

Forty, fifty crank-glazed eyes fixed on cum shots, no interest
in making twenty-five big ones, except for one dude who didn't
really seem that interested, either, but said he might know something. Motor arranged to meet with him at eight tomorrow—
maybe he'd bother; maybe he wouldn't.

So might as well bunk down. Not exactly the Holiday Inn,
but nothing he hadn't seen before. Even though the chemicals
gave him a headache, the aloneness turned him on, like the
time he was celling with a greaser in Perdido, a DUI rap,
three days of inhaling the motherfucker's stale farts, ready to
strangle him, and then the fourth day they took the guy away
because it turned out he had federal warrants.

Aloneness was like someone massaging your body, only
there was no one there, just the feeling.

Now it was Friday morning, ten o'clock, his eyes were
swollen, and all he wanted to do was cut off this fucking head
so he could replace it with one that didn't feel like it was about
to explode.

Pissing on the floor of an adjoining room, he spit out morning taste, rubbed his eyes till they focused, and wheeled his
scoot outside into the sun. *Strong* m-f sun—that didn't help
either. He was hungry, had no money; time to go to work.

It took him two hours to find a Mexican chick walking all
alone on a side street, no little gangbangers to protect her
honor. He drove past her, stopped, got off, walked toward her,

and she was scared right away. But he passed her by and she relaxed and that's when he turned around and grabbed her purse and shoved her to the ground.

Telling her, "Don't fucking move."

She didn't understand the words, but she got the tone of voice. He kicked her in the ribs just to make sure, walked as fast as his bulk would allow to his scoot, and drove a mile away.

Twenty-three bucks in the purse, along with a tin cross and pictures of little Mex kids in some kind of costumes. He took the money, threw the rest of it down a storm drain, drove back to the Boulevard, found the same stand where he'd bought the hot dogs, and got two more, along with a fried egg on a muffin with hot sauce on the side, extra-large coffee that he drained and refilled, an apple turnover, and one of those little containers of milk like he used to get in school and jail. Now he was ready for a day's labor.

He walked the picture up and down the Boulevard again, got nothing but dirty looks, was hungry again by three, forced himself to continue for another couple of hours, till he finally couldn't stand it anymore. Figuring he'd earned a real meal, he went over to Go-Ji's and used up most of the Mex chick's money on a corned beef sandwich, fries, onion rings, double banana split, more coffee. Telling the nigger waitress to keep filling his cup till she just left him a pitcher.

Someone had left parta the paper in his booth, but it was nothin' but words. The TV over the counter was going—news, sports, weather, dead stuff. Then he saw the rat's picture again; stopped eating bananas smothered with whipped cream and paid attention. His heart was zooming away—the coffee—and he was totally awake and ready to do something, anything.

Asshole on TV saying something about the beach—
" . . . reported to have been spotted near Ocean Front Walk in Venice."

So fuck the dude at the Cave.

Time to putt west—after dark. If the rat saw him, it wouldn't be good.

# CHAPTER 58

LARRY SCHICK WORE A CHEAP-LOOKING BROWN suit that probably cost three thousand dollars, all puckered around the lapels and sagging on his meager frame. Instead of a handkerchief in the breast pocket, he carried an ornately carved meerschaum pipe. The bowl hung out like a talisman. Woman's head. Creepy.

The attorney was younger than Petra expected, early to mid-forties, with a very tan pencil-point face, jet-black Prince Valiant 'do, and pink-plastic-framed eyeglasses. Snakeskin cowboy boots. Like one of those English rock stars trying to stretch the hip thing into middle age.

He and Ramsey arrived at the Montecito house just after six, Schick behind the wheel of a black Rolls-Royce Silver Spur. Malibu Colony sticker on the windshield, a bunch of club emblems fastened to the grille. Another car boy.

Ramsey got out first. He wore a faded denim shirt, black jeans, running shoes; looked even older than the last time she'd seen him. Taking in the scene, he shook his head. Schick came around from the driver's side and touched his elbow. Petra and Ron were with them before they could take another step. Ramsey kept staring at the crime tape.

The estate was quiet now; only a few techs still working. No word from Sepulveda on the warrants yet. Sergeant Grafton remained stationed near the pond. She'd introduced herself a while back. First name, Anna. Bright, art history degree from UCSB, which gave them something to talk about during the dead time. She was flying to Switzerland next week. "Major burglary, old masters. We recovered almost all of them. It'll never hit the papers." No interest in homicide, no attempt to take over the case.

Now she watched the arrival of the Rolls, met Petra's eye, studied Ramsey for a while, and turned the other way.

Petra said, "Evening, Mr. Ramsey."

"Larry Schick," said the lawyer, interposing his arm between them.

Ramsey stepped back. He looked at Ron, then zeroed in on Petra. "What the hell is going *on?*"

"Estrella Flo—"

"I know, I know, but what was she doing up *here?*"

"We were going to ask you that, sir."

Ramsey shook his head again and clicked his teeth together. "Unreal. The world's gone nuts."

Schick's facial muscles hadn't budged. He said, "What exactly happened to her, Detective?"

"Too early to give out details, Mr. Schick, but I can tell you she was murdered very brutally and buried over there." She pointed at the pond. The gravesite was marked by a stake.

"My God," said Ramsey, turning away.

Petra said, "Mr. Ramsey, did Mrs. Flores ever work at this house?"

"Sure."

"Recently?"

"No. Back when Lisa and I were together." By the end of the sentence, Ramsey's voice had thickened. He glanced at the stake again and winced.

Schick said, "Detective, why don't we do this a little later—"

"It's okay, Larry," said Ramsey. "Lisa and I used to spend weekends here. Sometimes Lisa brought Estrella with us to clean. I don't think Estrella had a key, though. And I can't see why she'd come up here."

"Who cleans the house now?"

"A cleaning company. Not regularly, maybe once a month. I never use the house anymore."

"What's the name of the company?"

"I don't know. Greg handles it."

"Does Mr. Balch come up personally to let them in?"

"Sure." Ramsey studied her.

"Where is Mr. Balch now?"

Ramsey looked at his watch. "Probably on his way home."

"He worked today?"

"I assume." Ramsey's voice had cleared.

"You haven't spoken to him recently?" said Petra.

"The last time I spoke to him was, let's see . . . two days ago. He called to ask if there was anything I needed. I said no. He tried to cheer me up. I've been mostly hanging around the house, trying to avoid the media . . . now *this* insanity."

Petra said, "We tried to call Mr. Balch at the office and he didn't answer."

"Maybe he stepped out—what's the big deal?"

"We're talking to everyone with access to this property."

"Access?" said Ramsey. "I suppose anyone could climb the gate. Never installed electric gates."

"No need?"

"Never got around to it. When Lisa and I came up, we used a padlock. The thing that bugs me is how did *Estrella* get up here? She didn't drive."

"Excellent question," said Petra.

Schick said, "Hopefully you people will come up with some answers." He removed the pipe, inspected the bowl, turned it upside down. Nothing fell out.

Petra said, "So you haven't asked Mrs. Flores to clean this house recently."

"Never. Listen, you have my permission to go over the whole place. House, grounds, anything. Don't bother with warrants—"

"Cart," said Schick. "Even in the spirit of helpfulness—"

Ramsey said, "Larry, I want to get to the bottom of this. No point slowing things down." To Petra: "Just do whatever the hell it is you do. Tear down the whole goddamn place for all I care."

He swiped at his eyes, turned his back, and walked several steps. Schick followed him and placed a hand on his shoulder. Balch had offered similar comfort that first day and Ramsey's response had been to turn on him. But he accepted the attorney's gesture, nodding as Schick told him something. Petra saw him pinch the top of his nose. He and Schick returned.

"Sorry, Detective Connor. Anything else?"

"Was there any reason for Mr. Balch to be up here recently?"

"Like I said, he comes up to fix things, let in workmen. If there was something to fix, he'd have a reason."

"But you're not aware of anything specific."

"I *wouldn't* know," said Ramsey. "Greg takes care of things."

"Both houses?"

"Absolutely."

"Does that include exchanging cars?"

"Pardon?"

"Bringing the Jeep to L.A. for maintenance," said Petra. "Leaving his own car here."

"What are you talking about?"

"Mr. Balch did that yesterday, sir. A local deputy saw him exit the property, and Mr. Balch told him you'd asked him to bring the Jeep down for maintenance. He left his Lexus here."

"Makes sense," said Ramsey. "The Jeep was for weekends here—Lisa liked it. I rarely use it, so maybe it seized up."

"But you don't know that."

"No, I'm guessing."

"Where do you take the Jeep for service?"

"Some Jeep dealer in Santa Barbara. I think."

"Any reason to bring it to L.A.?"

Ramsey shrugged and stroked his mustache. "Maybe Greg switched dealers. Maybe he had a problem with the one in Santa Barbara. Why all these—"

"I just need to get this straight," said Petra, feigning confusion. "You never asked him specifically to pick up the Jeep."

"Not specifically—what are you getting at?"

She pulled out her pad, scrawled. "Maybe nothing, sir." After writing, she snuck in a quick cartoon of Schick. The stupid haircut made it easy.

Ramsey was staring at her. "You think Greg—"

Petra didn't answer. Next to her, Ron was as still as a machine.

"Oh, c'mon," said Ramsey. "No way. No, that's absolutely crazy—"

"How did Mr. Balch and Estrella Flores get along?"

"They got along fine." Ramsey laughed. "This is totally nuts. If Greg says the Jeep needed maintenance, it did. What's going on here is probably some kind of psycho stalker. Someone with a grudge against *me,* so he goes after people . . . close to me."

"Mrs. Flores was close to you?"

"No—I don't know. All I'm saying is these nuts are all over. Look at John Lennon, all the crap people in the industry put up with. Have you checked out anything like that?"

"We're looking at all kinds of things," said Petra.

Schick said, "I know someone who can look into it, Cart."

Ron hadn't said a word. Petra glanced at him, letting him know it was okay. He said, "In terms of stalkers, do you have anyone in mind, Mr. Ramsey?"

"If I did, don't you think I'd tell you?" Harder tone with Ron. "Jesus."

Petra closed her pad. "Thanks for giving the okay to search, sir. It will save us time and paperwork. If you don't mind putting it in writing—"

Schick barked on cue: "Before we go that far, let's pin down the details."

"Let them do their job, Larry," said Ramsey. To Petra: "Whatever turns up, I guarantee you, it will have nothing to do with Greg."

Schick made his mouth very small and ran a finger under thick black bangs. Why would a grown man opt for a hairstyle like that? Something to catch jurors' attention? Maybe the meerschaum was a prop, too.

Reality, fantasy . . .

Petra said, "I'll get some paper for you to write on, sir."

Schick said, "Hold on please, Detective. Cart, you're upset, and you're going to get taken advantage of. I've seen the things that occur during searches. Breakage, pilferage. I strongly advise you—"

"Let them break stuff, Larry. I don't give a shit. Like I said, tear the whole place down." He faced Petra. "You're just theorizing, right? You can't be seriously thinking Greg had anything to do with this."

Schick said, "At the very least, I insist upon being present during any search."

"Fine," said Petra. To Ramsey: "One more thing: Greg Balch's behavior the night of Lisa's murder. When the two of you returned from Reno—"

"Detective," said Schick. "There has to be a better time for this."

Ramsey said, "What about his behavior?"

"Did he act differently in any way?"

"No. The same old Greg."

"The day we visited your house your Mercedes was gone. Where was it?"

"What does that have to do with Greg's behavior?" said Ramsey.

"Sir, if you'd just bear with me—"

"The Mercedes was being serviced," said Ramsey. He'd told her that, but if the redundant questioning bothered him, he didn't show it. "Too many toys—there's always something in need of fixing."

"Did Greg bring the Mercedes in?" said Petra. Ron had turned around, was studying the house.

"Or the dealer picked it up," said Ramsey.

"What needed to be done to the car?"

"I have no idea."

"So it was driving okay."

"Yes, it was fine. Maybe it needed a routine oil change, I don't know."

"What Mercedes dealer do you use?"

Ramsey put a finger over his mouth. "Some place nearby— in Agoura, I think." He laughed harshly. "As you can see, I'm very in touch with my life."

Petra smiled at him. "The second time I came to your house, the Mercedes was back in the garage. Who brought it over?"

"Same answer: Either someone from the dealer or Greg. I think it was Greg, but what's the diff—"

"How did Greg and Lisa get along?" Petra said, talking faster, a little louder. If Schick hadn't been there, she'd have stepped closer to Ramsey, invading his personal space, forcing eye contact. Even with the attorney hovering, it was a silver bullet of a question, and Ramsey's head moved back.

"Greg and Lisa? Fine—everyone got along fine."

"No problem between them?"

"No. I can't believe you're wasting time on— He's my closest friend, Detective Connor. We were kids together. He and Lisa got along fine. Hell, he *introduced* me to Lisa."

"At the pageant?" said Petra.

"At the pageant, but he knew her before. They—" Ramsey stopped.

"They what, sir?"

"They dated. Nothing serious, just a few times, so don't go

construing. It was over by the time Lisa and I started dating. Greg had no problem with it. If he had, would he have introduced us?"

Why, indeed. Suppositions drag-raced through Petra's head.

Beauty queen with sights set on the industry. Believing, at first, that Balch was a Hollywood heavyweight—maybe Balch had used that as a pickup line. They start dating, he pours on the b.s., but she sees through it, learns where the real clout is.

Throwing the small fish back, she goes for the whopper.

"Everyone got along," said Ramsey, but his voice had weakened and he was picking at his mustache.

Schick's stick face was all adrenaline, but he still wasn't moving. Same for Ron. It made Petra feel as if the two of them were fading out of view, bit players, spotlighting her and Ramsey.

She said, "Okay, sir, thanks for your help—do you have a key to the house?"

"Here," said Schick, taking out a ring and fingering a brass Schlage.

Someone else to answer for Ramsey, take care of him.

Being a star, even a minor one, was a return to childhood.

Drawing Ron fifty feet away, under the largest of the oaks, Petra kicked acorns and said, "Anything I missed?"

"Not that I see. Be interesting to know if the Mercedes *was* taken in for service. You're thinking it might have been Lisa's murder car?"

Petra nodded.

"Different cars for different kills," said Ron. "Keep us guessing."

"Balch is looking nice and dirty, isn't he?"

"Filthy."

"Want to try to call some Mercedes dealers?" said Petra. "Maybe some stay open past six."

"Will do." He removed the cell phone from his pocket.

She gazed over at Ramsey and Schick. They'd drifted back to the Rolls. Schick was leaning against the front fender, caressing the meerschaum, offering some kind of lawyerly counsel. Ramsey seemed uninterested.

"Cars," said Petra, "were also Lisa's preferred venue for sex. The case is pure L.A."

"The Jeep for Lisa would entail driving back and forth from

here," said Ron. "Balch and Ramsey got back from Reno just a couple of hours before Lisa was abducted. Not enough time, so I bet on the Mercedes or the Lexus or another of Ramsey's wheels—which would be good for Balch if he was trying to shift suspicion. We should also try Burbank airport, that charter company Ramsey uses. Balch has got to have access to the account."

"Rabbiting by charter?" said Petra.

"Just a possibility."

Images flashed: Two young bucks head for Hollywood, but only one ends up rich. With the girl, too. Balch had mentioned two failed marriages. Another reason for him to be bitter.

She remembered his remarks about Lisa's temper, her "going off on Cart." At the time, it had puzzled Petra. Why was good-buddy Greg giving the boss a motive? Now it made perfect sense.

Something else: Balch, a total slob, had been wearing brand-new white tennis shoes.

Because the old ones were soaked with blood?

She said, "I want to chat more with Mr. Adjustor. Thanks for making the calls."

"Remember the name of the charter company?"

"Westward Charter. The pilot they use is Ed Marionfeldt." Rattling off facts without consulting her pad. Everything coming together; a new rhythm. She walked back to Ramsey and Schick.

Still by the Rolls, but neither man was talking. Schick studying Ramsey; Ramsey staring at the ground. As Petra got closer, he looked up.

"Mr. Ramsey, when you returned from Tahoe, you were extremely tired, went to sleep earlier than usual. Correct?"

"I was bushed. We were going since early morning."

"Greg Balch drove the two of you from Burbank airport to your house."

"Yes." Mention of Balch's name seemed to weary Ramsey.

"Then you and Mr. Balch had dinner at your home and he had you sign some business papers—do you recall the nature of those papers, by the way?"

"Some kind of lease agreement. I own office buildings."

Petra copied that down. "All right, please bear with me: Who cooked dinner?"

Ramsey smiled. "We're talking sandwiches and beer."

"Who made the sandwiches?"

"Greg."

"Not Estrella Flores?"

"She went off duty at seven, was already in her room."

"Doing what, sir?"

"Whatever it is she did in there. I think I heard the TV."

"Where's the maid's room?"

"In the service wing. Off the kitchen."

"Okay," said Petra, adding some details to Schick's carica-
ture. Concentration lines on the forehead, pout creases. "So
Greg prepared the sandwiches and poured the beer."

"Yup. The beer was Grolsch, if it matters."

Imported lager with a barbiturate chaser? thought Petra.
Balch slipping Ramsey a mickey?

If so, had the underling stopped to deliberate? Wondered
about adding a little more powder?

Paying Ramsey back for all those years of friendship.

Some friendship. Not one single acting job, putting Balch
down in public, sticking him in that crappy office, a middle-
aged errand boy.

The unkindest cut of all: Lisa.

Because *he'd* met Lisa first. Gave her up to Cart. Always
Cart.

Petra could almost feel the rage, herself.

What had led Balch to stalk Lisa that night? Had she
reignited their old relationship, then cut it off? Or had Balch
just succumbed to his own fantasies?

Petra pictured the blond man waiting by Lisa's apartment.
Watching the Porsche drive out of the subterranean lot.
Following.

In one of Cart's cars. He had access to all the cars. All
the toys.

Tonight he'd play.

Taking what was his.

The same way he'd taken Ilse Eggermann?

Ilse. Lisa. The names were virtual anagrams.

Patterns. A crazy notion, but when it hit you in the face, you
said ouch.

How many other dead blond girls were there? Girls who
reminded Balch of Lisa.

Where the hell was Balch?

Or maybe she was all wrong and the lackey would show up, alibied, a perfect explanation, the case in tatters and some psycho *was* stalking Ramsey.

Or was Ramsey the *stalker*?

The boy in the park might know. Had Wil made any progress? She'd call him again as soon as she finished up with Ramsey.

"The beers," she said. "Did you drink them from bottles or cans?"

"From a glass," said Ramsey, as if she'd asked a rude question.

Cans you opened yourself; bottles you could open for someone else . . . "And right after you drank, did you feel even more tired?"

"No," he said. "I told you I was tired all day, I mean the alcohol might've been the topper, but—" The blue eyes widened. "Oh, c'mon—you've *got* to be kidding."

"About what, sir?"

"Something in the beer—no, no. No way in hell. I'd know if—no, it didn't feel that way. I was just bushed from overwork and travel. I conked out. We both did."

"How long did you sleep that night?"

Ramsey stroked his mustache, licked his lips.

Schick said, "Let's finish up here, Detective."

"Almost done," said Petra, smiling. The lawyer didn't smile back.

"I got up around eight, eight-thirty," said Ramsey. "So eleven hours."

"Is that your typical sleep pattern?"

"No, usually seven's enough, but—oh, come *on*. I would've felt something. Woozy, whatever. This is James Bond stuff, Detective Connor. I make movies. I know the difference between fantasy and reality."

His eyes told her a new, troubling logic had begun to worm its way into his brain.

True confusion or acting?

*The difference between fantasy and reality.* The phrase seemed to mock Petra.

"I'm sure you're right, Mr. Ramsey." She watched Ron pocket the phone as he returned. Schick was watching her.

She excused herself, and met Ron well out of Ramsey and Schick's earshot.

"Only one open Mercedes dealer," he said. "Sherman Oaks, never serviced Ramsey's cars. But bingo at Westward Charter. Balch tried to fly out last night. Called around eleven, wanting to book a solo trip to Vegas. Said it was a business trip. Westward doesn't take off past ten, and told him to check commercial flights. We'd better start calling airlines."

"Oh my," she said.

"Stupid move," said Ron, "trying to use the charter."

"Billing it to the boss," said Petra. Payback.

She noticed Ramsey staring at her. Had she given away something with her body language?

She ignored him. Nice to be able to do that.

## CHAPTER 59

I JUST GOT OUT OF THE BATHROOM. THAT'S where I ran after I stopped crying. When I came out, I almost hoped Sam wasn't there, but he was shining the silver charity bottle with a corner of his jacket. My eyes were dry. I felt I was walking through a bad dream.

"You got a few hours till they show up to pray tonight," he said, still polishing.

I sat down again and thought. No ideas came. The walkway, all those people, now it seemed like a haunted place.

I couldn't see any other way out, so I agreed to go to Sam's house. "But not during the day, I don't want anyone to see me."

"That's a little difficult, Bill. People start showing up before dark. And I have to be here to run things."

The way we finally work it out is: At six o'clock, he'll come back with some dinner and sneak me into his car. I'll hide there while the Jews are praying, in the backseat, covered by the blankets.

"How long do you pray?"

"An hour, give or take. I stay late to clean up. When the coast is clear, I'll let you know."

"Thanks."

"Don't mention it," he says. "Just take care of yourself." Then he laughs. "Who am I to tell you that? You been taking care of yourself fine."


# CHAPTER 60

NO ANSWER TO HER SECOND KNOCK, AND NOW Mildred Board was worried.

She'd heard the bath filling a half hour ago. Had the missus fallen? Suffered some kind of an attack? Maybe the doctors were wrong and she really was ill.

She turned the doorknob, called out "Ma'am?" as she entered the bedroom. Empty.

And the bed was made!

Not Mildred's tight-cornered creation but a decent tuck. First the bath, now the bed. Why on earth all this independence?

Yesterday, she'd been up extra early and ready. Hearing footsteps at 6 A.M., she went down to find the missus in the kitchen, folded newspaper in front of her, next to a cup of something that turned out to be instant tea.

"Are you all right, ma'am?" she'd said.

"Fine, Mildred. And you?" The missus was smiling but the look in her eyes was . . . distant.

"Ready to greet the day, ma'am."

"That's the spirit."

Fighting a frown, Mildred fixed a proper cup of English Breakfast while glancing at the paper.

The missus smiled. "I must be developing a belated interest in current events."

"Yes, ma'am. Up early, too."

"I seem to be doing that lately, don't I? Must be a change in my biorhythm."

Later that day, she'd found the missus out on the patio with her hand on a stone column, as if she needed support. Looking out at . . . what? The ruins of the garden? More like nothing. Her eyes had that blank look again, and when Mildred greeted her, they stayed that way for several seconds.

Strange things were happening.

Mildred walked through the bedroom into the first dressing room. No one. The bathroom was empty, too, the tub drained, towels folded.

A long corridor led to the walk-in closet. Standing in the doorway, Mildred repeated, "Ma'am?"

"In here, Mildred. You may come in."

Mildred hurried through the narrow passage. The rear closet was larger than most rooms, lined with mahogany shelves and racks, built-in drawers. Hand-printed hatboxes, scores of shoes arranged by color. All that was left of the missus's couture collection was a pair of wool coats, a rain slicker, five suits—black, brown, beige, two grays—and a few casual dresses and cashmere sweaters, all encased in plastic wardrobe bags. The missus was standing in front of the mirror applying makeup, fully dressed in one of the gray suits, a thirty-year-old Chanel. She wore pearl earrings, the small ones, lovely. Mildred remembered the diamonds him had showered on the missus. An annoying little man from San Gabriel had examined them with a loupe and a predatory smile.

The Chanel draped the missus's figure perfectly. But . . . her feet . . .

White lace-up tennis shoes over bulky white socks.

"I thought I'd go out for a walk, Mildred." The missus's thick, wavy hair was brushed and sprayed, chestnut embroidered with gray. Her makeup had been applied expertly except for one stray granule of lipstick near the corner of her beautiful mouth. Mildred restrained the impulse to flick it away, but she did give a pointed look and the missus caught the hint and dabbed.

"A walk. Lovely idea, ma'am . . ." Mildred's eyes lowered again. Those socks!

The missus laughed uneasily. "Not exactly the height of style, I know, but these are easy on the arches. My hamstrings are stiff, Mildred. I tried to stretch them out, but they're still bound up. It's been too long since I walked, Mildred."

Drawing back her shoulders and straightening her spine, she started down the corridor.

"Do be careful, ma'am. I watered the orchard just twenty minutes ago and drainage seems to be poor, especially in the rear area, the peach trees. Boggy and slippery, you'd think that gardener's boy would have the sense to—"

The missus stopped and placed a delicate hand on Mildred's shoulder. "I'm not walking on the property, dear," she said. "I'm going around the block."

"Oh," said Mildred. "I see." She didn't. "I'll be happy to come with you—"

"No thank you, dear. I need to think."

"With all due—"

"I'll be fine, Mildred." The missus's chin began to shake. She drew back her shoulders.

She took another step. Stopped. "I'm always fine, Mildred. Am I not?"

## CHAPTER 61

By 6:57 P.M., CAPTAIN SEPULVEDA STILL HADN'T returned and the techs had stopped working. The sun was low and the oaks blocked out straggling daylight. Sergeant Grafton had returned to her car. Petra was finished with Ramsey.

Lawrence Schick escorted his client back to the Rolls, remaining blank-faced as Petra tagged along. Ramsey got into the passenger seat and stared out the open window. He looked ancient.

Petra said, "If I need to reach you—"

"We're going for dinner," said the attorney. "The Biltmore, Santa Barbara."

"And after dinner?" said Petra.

Schick smoothed his bangs. "It's not exactly a night for brandy and cigars, is it, Detective, so I guess we'll return to L.A. Nice to meet you. Please continue to communicate through me." Tapping the meerschaum twice, he got into the driver's seat, turned a frail-looking wrist. The car woke up and sailed away, but for the merest spatter of gravel, silently.

A few minutes later, Sepulveda drove up with a handful of warrants, explaining, "Every judge was playing golf." He'd changed into sweats, Carpinteria Sheriff's insignia on the shirt.

Despite Ramsey's waiver, no search had begun because Sergeant Grafton had insisted on waiting for Sepulveda.

Petra called Schoelkopf to tell him about Balch's attempted flight to Vegas. No answer, and the clerk said he'd signed out for dinner; she didn't know where. No luck with Wil Fournier, either.

She was just about to call Stu when Sepulveda arrived. Ron was using the phone, talking to his kids.

"We'll concentrate on the house for now," said Sepulveda, waving the warrants. "Do the grounds tomorrow morning. I've got techs from our station and a fingerprint spec from Ventura used to work for us that I still think is the best. You planning to stick around?"

"For a while," said Petra.

"You know I can't let you participate in the search. Got to color within the lines."

"Can we observe?"

Sepulveda considered that. "Why don't you and your partner make yourself comfortable over there." He pointed to a wooden bench that curved around the trunk of the biggest oak. Drooping branches afforded semiprivacy.

"No way I can look, Captain?"

"Anything comes up, I'll give a holler."

Flashing him a smile, Petra walked to the bench. Rock-hard and cool. Ron came over, still talking. "I'm proud of you,

Bee. Thanks for listening so well to Grandma. 'Bye." He hung up, said, "We can't go in?"

"Banished to the sidelines," said Petra. "Another boss."

"Too many jurisdictions," he said. He sat down next to her, grazed her fingertips with his thumb. "But that's not always bad, is it? Never know who you'll meet."

She smiled, not minding his touch but unable to think about anything but work, all the things she had to do.

She borrowed the phone, tried Wil again. Still no answer, but Schoelkopf picked up.

"Ramsey was just here with Schick," she said.

"And?"

She summed up the interview, told him about Balch's call to Westward Charter.

"Well, that pretty much clinches it, doesn't it. Balch. Shit. And you guys were certain it was Ramsey. Can you imagine the field day the press would've had with that—near prosecution of an innocent man. Okay, no release of information till you hear from me, Barbie. Nothing. Understood?"

You're the one with a direct line to Public Information, jerk. "Of course, sir."

"I mean it. Tighter than a . . . whatever. I'll handle Vegas for you—I know people in Metro over there. They keep a pretty tight handle on hotels and motels. If he's there, we'll find him. Meanwhile, you call the airlines. Get Fournier on that too."

"Haven't been able to reach Fournier," said Petra.

"I saw him this afternoon. Try his home. What's going on over there now?"

"They just started to search the house."

"Keep an eye on those hicks. Flores is clearly the fruit of Lisa's tree, so it's our case."

"What about Flores's son in El Salvador?"

"What about him?"

"He's worried about her. I promised to let him know."

"I said keep it all under wraps for now. Another day or two isn't going to improve his quality of life. They find evidence in the house, let me know right away."

He clicked off.

Ron remained silent.

Petra said, "Don't say I never took you anywhere interesting. Your kids okay?"

"Fine."

"If you want to head back, I'll find a ride somehow."

"No, I'll stay. Anything to do besides wait?"

"Call the airlines." She looked at the phone. "Your bill is going to rival the national debt."

He laughed. "You'll get an invoice."

He'd stuck with her all day, remaining in the background. The guy was a veteran, it had to be hard, and all she did was keep borrowing the damn phone. "You're sure Alicia and Bee are okay?"

"Mom's taking them out for pizza; she'll sleep over."

"Nice mom."

"The best," he said. "After my dad died, I thought she'd fall apart. Her whole life seemed wrapped up in his. She was pretty depressed at first, but then she came out of it, took up paddle tennis, joined a library group, went on some tours. She misses him—they had a great marriage—but she's doing okay."

"When did your dad die?"

"Two years ago."

"Mine too."

He reached over, squeezed her hand, let go.

Petra said, "I have no mother. She died in childbirth."

Ron said nothing. Smart man. She didn't look at him; didn't want that level of contact right now.

※

The third try at Fournier's house paid off. He said, "Been trying that 818 number for a couple hours, where are you?"

She told him everything.

"Unreal," he said. "So Balch could be anywhere by now."

"He was stupid enough to call Westward Charter using his real name, so maybe we'll get lucky."

"How do you want to divide it?"

"Any way you want. Also, S. wants a total seal on it."

"We put a want out on Balch, but don't tell anybody?"

"Not till he hears from upstairs."

"Great," said Wil. "So where does this put the kid?"

"Lower priority."

He snorted. "Of course it is, now that I have a name for him. The Watson tips panned out: William Bradley Straight, twelve years old, lived in a low-life trailer park, missing a few months. If he did see Lisa get murdered, that's not his only problem. Someone killed his mama, push-and-shove case. Got a probable suspect, her boyfriend, some hairbasket named Buell Moran. And guess what: He's been spotted in Hollywood, showing the kid's picture."

"Oh no," said Petra. "Going after the twenty-five thou."

"It would motivate me, and I don't live in a trailer."

"Lord," said Petra. William Bradley Straight. A kid with a survival plan, thinking he had a chance. Pathetic. What had they done to him?

"Okay," said Wil. "Let's divide up those airlines."

When she hung up, Ron said, "What's wrong?"

"Another orphan."

## CHAPTER 62

Bound volumes of *TV Guide*, each with a no circulation tag.

An hour into the surgery, Stu found himself going crazy in the waiting room. Leaving the hospital, he drove to a branch in downtown Burbank, used his badge and good manners, finally convinced the librarian to let him check out a decade's worth.

Now here he was back at St. Joe's, waiting with other worried people.

Hundreds of *Adjustor* plot summaries.

*Dack Price comes to the aid of a woman harassed by street thugs.*

*Dack Price helps expose drug dealing at a local high school.*

*A woman claiming to be Dack's sister, abandoned at birth . . .*

*Dack Price saves a political reformer's reputation when blackmailers . . .*

The same old garbage, over and over.

No mention of any parks, let alone Griffith. Rarely was the setting ever mentioned, except when it was considered exotic: *Dack Price investigates several murders aboard a submarine.*

He kept turning pages, sitting by Kathy's bedside as she slept off the anesthesia.

Snoring. Kathy never snored. A padded dressing was taped to her chest like some bulletproof vest. The IV dripped, a catheter drained, machines graphed and beeped the saga of his wife's physiology. Stu had watched the blood pressure for a while until he was certain it was normal. At the last temperature check, Kathy'd registered a slight fever. Normal reaction, the nurse claimed.

The room was a private with a view, courtesy of Father's clout. Cheerful wallpaper, ten-dollar Tylenol. The nurses seemed smart and efficient.

Drizak had taken Kathy's left breast.

Stu knew the minute the surgeon came out in his greens. Droning on about lymphovascular invasion, nodal status, margins of excision, best efforts at breast conservation.

"So you did a mastectomy."

"The bottom line is we want to save your wife's life."

"Did you?"

"Pardon?"

"Did you save her life?"

The surgeon scratched his chin. "The prognosis is excellent, Mr. Bishop, given proper follow-up, radiotherapy. She went through it like a trouper."

Stu thanked him, pumped his hand, and grateful for the lack of outward anguish, the surgeon walked away with a bounce in his step.

The breast didn't matter to Stu—not as an object—but how would Kathy react to the loss?

What to tell the kids?

Mommy was sick, now she'd be getting better.

No good; when the side effects of radiation showed up, they'd think he lied.

Kathy stirred and moaned. Stu put the book down, leaned over the bed rails, and kissed her forehead lightly. She didn't react. He touched her hand. Cold and limp. Why wasn't the blood circulating to her extremities?

He checked the machines. Normal; everything normal.

Her padded chest proved it, rising and falling.

It was 8 P.M. Surgery had been delayed twice because of emergencies—Kathy wheeled up to the OR, then down, the entire process repeated again. Waiting in the hall on a gurney as the priority patients were rushed through.

A car crash and a shooting.

Stu watched Burbank officers come up to the surgical floor, accompanying the med techs as they wheeled in the shooting victim. Young Hispanic kid, sixteen, seventeen, bad color, vacant eyes. Stu knew DOA when he saw it. Another stupid drive-by.

The cops didn't notice him—just some guy in a sweater reading in the corner of the waiting room.

Young-blood cops, swaggering. Like they knew what they were doing.

Pathetic. No one had a clue. God was a comedian.

Look at Ramsey.

*Had a wife but couldn't keep her.*

No way was the actor going down for Lisa's murder. Not with what they had so far. No help from *TV Guide.*

He suppressed bitter laughter.

*Dack Price butchers a woman. Now a word from our sponsor.*

# CHAPTER 63

I'M TALKING TO MOM, TRYING TO EXPLAIN SOME-
thing important to her, but she's not getting it. She's not even
listening.

I get mad at her, start to yell; she just stands there, arms at
her side, this weird look in her eyes. Like I don't matter.

Then her face starts to melt and blood shoots out of her eyes
like from red faucets. She cups her hands to catch the blood,
splashes it all over her face, and then throws some at—

I wake up sweating. My head hurts, my arms hurt, my
stomach *kills* worse than ever, I can't breathe.

I'm in a dark box with cold, hard walls. Glass walls. Trapped,
like a bug in a jar—I *really* can't breathe—no air holes in the
box. No matter how hard I suck in the air, it won't feed my
lungs—then I see it. Crack at the top of one glass wall. A window left a little open.

Car window.

I'm in Sam's car. The backseat. Must have fallen asleep
under the blankets.

It's making me sick being cooped up here. I want to break
out, but the alley at night, who knows what's out there? At least
let me open the window a little wider—nope, electric, they
don't budge.

My Casio says 8:19. The Jews have been praying for a
while. When they finish, Sam will take me with him. He's a
stranger, and I don't know anything about his house, but
there's no other place to hide, not with that $25,000 reward.

Maybe I *should* try to get the money, like Sam suggested . . . no, the police would never give it to a kid. Even if
they did, Mom and Moron would find out and take it all and I'd
be back in the trailer and they'd have dope money.

I could call the police without telling them who I was, let